Jeanne Whitmee bega͟n _____
her marriage and a pe͟r_____
and drama, she achieve͟d_____
a professional writer. Sh͟_____
freelance writer for popul͟_____ ͟s, writing
short stories, serials and, ͟_____ a weekly column.
To date she has published ͟more than thirty novels under
various pseudonyms.

Jeanne Whitmee has two married daughters and four grand-
children and now lives with her husband in Cambridgeshire.

THE LOST DAUGHTERS

Jeanne Whitmee

WARNER BOOKS

A *Warner* Book

First published in Great Britain
by Judy Piatkus in 1996
This edition published by Warner Books in 1997

A CIP catalogue record for this book
is available from the British Library.

ISBN 0 7515 1829 8

Typeset by Hewer Text Composition Services, Edinburgh
Printed and bound in Great Britain by
Clays Ltd, St Ives plc

Warner Books
A Division of
Little, Brown and Company (UK)
Brettenham House
Lancaster Place
London WC2E 7EN

Chapter One

Edgware, London 1955

For as long as Cathy could remember she had lived in the house in Laburnum Close with Daddy and Johnny, which was her name for the motherly war widow who came in each day to look after them. Mary Johnson was the only maternal figure in Cathy's life. She had no memories of her real mother at all. There were photographs of her of course: a large one on the mantelpiece in the front room and another beside Daddy's bed. Cathy knew that her name had been Jenny and that she had curly auburn hair and green eyes just like her own. She knew too that her mother had loved her very much, but only because Daddy told her so. Sometimes when she was in bed at night she would close her eyes and try very hard to remember, but however hard she tried the memories refused to come.

Number thirteen Laburnum Close was the semi-detached Victorian villa where Daniel Oldham had taken his young bride when they married in 1943. It had been his parents' house then and Cathy had been born here while Daniel was still in the RAF. Soon after that Cathy's grandparents had both died, leaving number thirteen to the three of them. But their family life had been sadly curtailed when Jenny Oldham died too, leaving Daniel and his baby daughter alone. All this Cathy had learned from her father. All she remembered was being here with Daddy – and Johnny of course.

All the houses in Laburnum Close had been built in the nineteenth century. They had high corniced ceilings, panelled doors and a long narrow hall that led right through from front door to kitchen. It had a floor of blue, red and black mosaic tiles. Cathy had used this to devise complicated hopping games that she played on wet days when she couldn't go out to play. Upstairs there were three bedrooms and a bathroom and above them an attic reached by a steep staircase. The attic had sloping ceilings and one small dormer window. It was stiflingly hot in summer and icy cold in winter, so it was used mainly for storing junk and unwanted items of furniture. Cathy loved to play up there on rainy days, dressing up in the old discarded clothes packed away years before by her grandmother, and acting out the fantasies that fill the minds of all lonely children; fuelled by an over-developed imagination and derived from all the many stories she had read.

Downstairs there was a big living room and a cosy kitchen with a big cooking range. But the front room was Daniel's. His grand piano stood in the bay window – in almost solitary splendour because there was very little space in the room for anything else. It was where his pupils came in the daytime; an endless stream of people with musical aspirations. They came in all shapes and sizes, all ages and both sexes, and filled the house for hours each day with the sound of the scales and arpeggios which they pounded out with varying degrees of skill and proficiency.

In the evenings Daniel would put on what he called his 'penguin suit' and go off to work, playing with a dance band at various venues all over London, leaving his young daughter with Johnny or an obliging neighbour. Cathy was used to the arrangement. She would watch television and do her homework, then go to bed dutifully at the appointed time.

Through her early years when Cathy knew of no other way of life it had all seemed quite normal and acceptable. She loved her father, and although she often wished she could share more of his time, she was always happy enough to be with Johnny. It was only when she started school that she began to see other girls led quite different kinds of lives. They had mothers as well as fathers; fathers who went to work in the daytime in offices or factories and came back to spend their evenings and weekends at home with the family. Some, like Carla Maybridge, had brothers and sisters too.

Carla was the most popular girl in the class and Cathy could hardly believe her luck when the pretty, outgoing girl befriended her. The first time she was invited round to the Maybridges' house for tea she got a glimpse of what real family life could be; a glimpse so attractive and seductive that she longed to be part of a big, noisy family herself.

The Maybridges lived two streets away in a house very similar to her own home. But the similarity ended with the bricks and mortar. The moment you stepped inside it was all so different. Carla's family filled the house to bursting point. Every room, including the attic, was lived in with a delightful carefree abandon that would have had Johnny shaking her head in horror.

Carla had four elder brothers and a sister, and the six of them plus their parents filled the three-bedroomed house to bursting point. Toys, sports equipment and school books littered every available space. No one ever seemed to put their clothes away or hang up their coats or school bags. Cathy loved it, and when she returned to Laburnum Close after one of these visits, her own house seemed silent and empty by comparison.

Mrs Maybridge was a plump lady who always wore an apron and seemed to live permanently in the kitchen. She was totally unconcerned by the chaos all around her; never shouted or got cross. Mr Maybridge was a cashier at the local bank. He had thinning hair and horn-rimmed glasses and seemed to spend most of his spare time digging in the back garden which was full to bursting with every kind of vegetable and fruit.

On Sunday mornings the family went to Mass at the little

3

Catholic church near the park but once they were home the rest of the day was spent pursuing whatever activity they wished. They were all allowed to have friends round to the house – as many as they liked. The more the merrier, Carla said with a nonchalant wave of her hand.

Sitting in the large untidy living room Cathy would watch as Mrs Maybridge opened up the big round gate-leg table and began to set it for tea. Surreptitiously Cathy would count the cups to work out whether she was expected to stay. Usually she was. Mrs Maybridge didn't stand on ceremony. She didn't issue formal invitations. If there were ten children in the house she provided tea for them all. It just meant making one tin of salmon do the work of two.

When Cathy was eleven and the time came to move schools Carla announced that she was going to St Margaret's, which was a Catholic school. Cathy begged her father to let her go too.

'But you already have a scholarship to the high school,' Daniel argued. 'St Margaret's is private for non-Catholics. It would be very expensive. I don't think we can afford it.'

Cathy pouted. 'Carla says that if you're clever enough you can get in cheaper. You have to take an entrance exam.' She watched her father's face for signs of the vulnerable chink in his armour that she almost always managed to penetrate. 'Everyone says what a good school it is and all the people I like best are going there,' she said wistfully. 'If I have to go to Mitchell Street High I shan't know a soul. I'll be lonely and miserable.'

Daniel gave in in the end. Cathy was interviewed by the headmistress of St Margaret's. She sat and easily passed the entrance examination, and Johnny took her along to be kitted out with the smart blue and gold uniform.

Cathy loved her new school, but at St Margaret's the differences between her own home life and that of her friends soon became even more apparent. Now elder brothers and sisters were bringing home their teenage friends. There

4

were parties, and the passing down of trendy clothes and the latest records. Christmas that year was preceded by weeks of secret preparations, noise and surprises. A time charged with excited anticipation. At thirteen Laburnum Close, although Daniel did his usual best, life seemed tame and lonelier than ever before.

'Why haven't I got any brothers and sisters, Johnny?' asked Cathy one afternoon towards the end of term, as she sat watching the housekeeper preparing the evening meal.

Johnny turned to look at her and realised for the first time that the child was growing up. 'Your mother died before she had time to have any for you,' she said softly. 'I'm sure if she'd lived you would have had some, duckie.'

'But you've only got Matthew and you're not dead,' Cathy pointed out.

'Ah, but Matthew's father died in the war. It takes a mother *and* a daddy to make babies.' Johnny would have thought that Cathy would already know this and made a mental note to have a word with Daniel about telling his daughter the facts of life. It really was time someone prepared her for womanhood. Daniel Oldham was a good man and a conscientious father, but there were times when she wondered if he realised that Cathy wouldn't always be a little girl.

When his housekeeper tactfully pointed out to Daniel that he was neglecting his parental duty, he was dismayed. Somehow he hadn't given a thought to his daughter's growing up and all that it entailed. He shook his head.

'I don't think I know where to start, Johnny.' He looked hopefully at the housekeeper. 'I suppose you wouldn't . . .'

She frowned. 'Well – I will if you really want me to, but I must say that I think it would come better from you.'

Daniel raked a hand through his thinning fair hair. 'What did you do – about Matthew, I mean? It must have been difficult for you too, as a widow with a young son.'

'Luckily they have sex education classes at his school,' she said. 'And somehow it doesn't seem so important with boys. There aren't so many – well, physical complications.'

Daniel smiled and kept his opinions on that to himself.

'I have explained to him that girls and women should be treated with consideration and respect,' Johnny went on. 'But he's a sensible boy. Kind and sensitive too. I haven't any real worries about him.'

Daniel nodded. 'I must admit that I'd find it less awkward if Cathy were a boy,' he said. 'But I suppose I'll just have to do the best I can.'

On Saturday afternoons she always had her music lesson. It was a special time for both father and daughter, one of the rare times they spent together. Cathy played the piano well for her age and Daniel was proud of the way she always practised without being reminded, as soon as she came home from school each afternoon.

After her lesson they would have tea together and Daniel would hear what had been happening at school and try to sort out any problems that Cathy might have. So it seemed natural to choose this time to make his first fumbling attempt at acquainting his daughter with the facts of life.

'Cathy – you're twelve now. You're growing up,' he began awkwardly. 'Soon certain – things will be happening – changes in your life and your – body. Maybe you will have noticed that – er . . .' He slipped a finger inside his collar and it was only then that he noticed that Cathy was smiling. It was a wise, sympathetic, womanly little smile and all at once he had the odd feeling that their roles had been reversed; that he was now the child, Cathy the parent.

'It's all right, don't worry, Daddy, we've done all that growing up stuff at school,' she told him reassuringly. 'Carla told me some too. She's got an elder sister and lots of brothers too, you see.'

Daniel was taken aback. 'Oh – well, that's all right then. I just wanted you to know that if there's anything you don't

6

understand – anything that worries you – you can ask me. I'd rather you came to me than anyone else.'

She smiled at him. Thanks, Dad.'

He looked at her anxiously. He had the distinct feeling that he was getting away with this just a little bit too easily. Did she really know, or did she just *think* she did? And how did he find out for sure? 'So – is there anything you're not sure of? Anything you want to ask me now?'

Cathy considered for a moment, her head on one side. 'Well, there is one thing,' she said thoughtfully.

'Yes?'

'How old do I have to be before I can . . .?'

Daniel's mouth dried. 'Yes – before you can what?'

'Wear high heels? I've seen this lovely pair in Mason's in the High Street and I wondered . . .'

Daniel laughed, relief making him light-hearted. She was still his little girl after all. At least for a while yet. 'I should think you'd need to be at least sixteen for that kind of thing,' he said, ruffling her hair. 'But I'm no expert. We'll ask Johnny, shall we?' He took an envelope out of his pocket and placed it on the table. 'Now young lady, when you've finished your tea there's a surprise in there for you.'

Her eyes lit up. 'Tell me. Look I've almost finished anyway.'

He nodded towards the envelope. 'Open it for yourself.'

Shaking with excitement, she tore open the envelope and stared at the two slips of paper inside. 'Tickets for a concert. At the Royal Festival Hall. *Tonight*. Oh, Daddy!'

'Have you seen who the soloist is?'

She looked again at the tickets. Gerald Cavelle. *Uncle Gerald!*

Jumping up from the table, she threw her arms round Daniel's neck.

'Thank you, Daddy. Oh, I can't wait.'

*   *   *

Cathy cherished the Saturday afternoon music lessons. Daniel's life was so busy all week. When he wasn't teaching or playing with the band he was working away in the front room on what he called his 'composition'. Playing a few bars, making alterations and playing again, his glasses low on his nose and his brow furrowed in concentration as he filled in the notes on the manuscript paper. Cathy knew that composing meant writing music and she wasn't to disturb him when he was doing it. She resented it a little. There was so little time for them to share. Surely there was already enough music for people to play and listen to without him writing any more? But when she confided her resentment to Johnny the housekeeper explained patiently that it was his hobby and important to him.

'Leave him to it, Cathy, love,' she would say kindly. 'It helps him relax.'

Because of his preoccupation with his music, having him all to herself was a special treat, which was partly why Cathy took so much trouble over her practice. She was afraid that if she gave up the piano maybe they would have no time together at all.

There was nothing she liked better than to get him into a reminiscent mood. She never tired of hearing about his youthful days at music college and the things he and his best friend, Gerald Cavelle, used to get up to.

When the war broke out Daniel had to give up his studies and go into the RAF. And by the time it was over he had married Jenny and Cathy had been born, so that returning to his music studies had been out of the question.

His friend, Gerald, had been luckier. He was a year younger than Daniel and had gone into ENSA when he was called up, where he could continue with his music. After the war he had returned to college and now he was a well-known concert pianist.

In spite of the fact that he was her father's best friend and her own godfather, 'Uncle' Gerald Cavelle had been no more than an exalted name to Cathy for years. She listened to his records of course. Daniel had them all. And she had occasionally heard him on the radio, so the idea of seeing and hearing him in the flesh was so exciting she could hardly contain herself.

Cathy had seen the Festival Hall from the outside when Daniel had taken her to the South Bank Exhibition four years ago in 1951. She sat enthralled, stunned by the atmosphere of the beautiful concert hall and thrilled by the music she was hearing live for the first time in her life. When it was time for the piano concerto and the conductor led Gerald on to the platform to a storm of enthusiastic applause, she stared hard at the tall handsome man dressed immaculately in tails and white tie. Nudging her father she whispered: 'Is that really *him*, Dad? Is that Uncle Gerald?'

Daniel squeezed her hand. 'That's him,' he said proudly. 'How would you like to meet him after the concert?'

She looked at him, her eyes round. 'Oh – could I?'

'Of course. He knows we're here and has invited us to go round afterwards.' He squeezed her hand and lowered his voice. 'Shhh now, they're about to begin.'

When they tapped on the door and stood waiting in the corridor Cathy looked up at her father and reached for his hand. She was suddenly overcome with shyness and her heart was beating fast. Gerald Cavelle's playing had been magnificent, better than anything she had ever heard, and now she felt very much in awe of the famous godfather she had never met.

But the voice that called 'Come in' sounded normal enough. A pleasant deep voice that sounded much like anyone else's. Daniel smiled reassuringly at her as he turned the door handle.

Gerald sat at a dressing table, his back to them. He had taken off the black tail coat and white tie and now he wore a dressing gown over his shirt and trousers. Catching sight of Daniel in the mirror he jumped up, turning to greet them, his face beaming with pleasure.

'Daniel, you old so and so!' He grasped Daniel's hand and shook it vigorously. 'So glad you could make it. It's wonderful to see you. It must be years.' He stopped short at the sight of Cathy standing behind her father. 'And who is this little lady? Not my goddaughter surely?'

'Certainly is,' Daniel said proudly. 'Quite the young lady, isn't she?' He gently pushed his daughter forward. 'Say good evening, Cathy,' he prompted.

Tongue-tied and pink-cheeked, she mumbled a polite greeting. Gerald sat down and reached forward to take her hands and draw her towards him, looking intently into her face.

'The last time I saw you, you were about the size of sixpence and yelling your head off at the font,' he said. 'And now look at you.' He smiled. 'Now tell me, what did you think of my playing this evening?'

'It was – very nice.'

He laughed. 'Very nice? Is that all?'

She wanted to tell him that it was the most wonderful, magical music she had ever heard. That she had loved every minute of it and would remember it for ever. But she was far too shy. Acutely aware of the pressure of his cool hands and the dark eyes searching her face, she blushed crimson and stared at her feet. Daniel came to her rescue.

'Cathy enjoyed the concert very much,' he said. 'Especially your playing.'

Gerald smiled and gave her hands a final squeeze before releasing them. Turning back to the mirror again he said: 'I'm only teasing. I wouldn't expect a child of your age to enjoy anything that went on for so long.' He took up a silver-backed hairbrush and began to brush back his smooth dark hair. 'Poor baby, you must have thought it would never end.' His eyes smiled at her reflection in the mirror. 'I wouldn't blame you if you were bored stiff.'

10

'I *wasn't* bored,' Cathy said, stung out of her shyness. 'I listen to your records all the time at home. And the Grieg Concerto is one of my favourites. And anyway, I'm not a *baby*. I'm twelve.'

'Cathy!' Daniel stared at his daughter in dismay, but Gerald threw back his head and roared with laughter.

'I can see I've underestimated your daughter, Dan,' he said. 'Of course you're not a baby, Cathy. And to make up for insulting you I shall insist that you let me take you and your dad out to supper.'

Cathy was too excited to sleep that night. Long after she was in bed she was still thinking about the wonderful evening she and Daddy had spent with Gerald Cavelle. He was a very special, magical kind of person, like no one she had ever met before. Closing her eyes she pictured his tall, slim figure and the handsome face with its high forehead and dark eyes. Tanned skin was drawn tautly over high prominent cheekbones, and the faint shadow on his jaw gave him an exciting, slightly foreign look. Best of all she liked the smooth dark hair with its slight frosting of silver.

Over supper he had been very courteous to her, treating her as an adult in a way that she found quite intoxicating. The restaurant where he had taken them was sumptuous and plushy with crystal chandeliers and soft red carpets. The head waiter had greeted Gerald like royalty, ushering him and his little party to the best table and pulling out the chair for Cathy with a flourish that was fit for a queen. They had eaten exotic, delicious food and Gerald had insisted on pouring her a glass of wine.

'Only half a glass, Dan,' he said to Daddy with a twinkle in his eyes. 'It can't hurt her. After all, it is a special occasion.'

Afterwards, as they said goodnight, Gerald had insisted that they must certainly meet again.

11

'It's so sad to lose touch with old friends,' he said. 'We mustn't go for so long again without making contact. It's been marvellous seeing you both.' He shook Daniel's hand warmly.

'Thanks for the tickets,' he said. 'And for the supper. It's meant a lot to Cathy.' He lowered his voice. 'And so will the other. You'll never know how much.'

Gerald smiled. 'I'm glad I was able to help. Do let me know if there's anything else I can do for you, Dan. You and I go back a long way. Don't forget, I'm only a telephone call away.' He bent to tilt up Cathy's chin with one long finger. 'As for this little lady – well, she really is quite something. I shall certainly look forward to seeing more of her.'

Cathy cherished fond hopes of developing a regular relationship with Uncle Gerald. She boasted about him quite shamelessly at school after that special night. But although he had sounded utterly sincere at the time he made no attempt to get in touch again. Cathy talked about him incessantly in the weeks following the concert. She often asked Daniel why they didn't go again to see him play, or why they didn't telephone to invite him to come and see them. Daniel always shook his head, saying that Gerald was busy with an overseas tour or that he wouldn't be able to find time for them in his busy schedule.

'Maybe Uncle Gerald could help you get a better job,' she suggested. 'I heard him say he'd help you if you asked him. When I'm sixteen I could leave school,' she urged, her face serious. 'I could get a job and then you can get Uncle Gerald to fix up some concerts for you.' Her face lit up as she visualised a golden future. 'It would be lovely to have your picture on all those record sleeves like his and to go abroad, wouldn't it? I could come with you. We'd have a lovely time.'

Daniel shook his head. 'It's not as simple as that, love.'

'You work so hard though, Dad,' she added anxiously. 'And you get so tired. You know you do.'

But Daniel only smiled and gave her a hug. 'Concert pianists begin when they're very young. I used to dream about it when I was younger, but I'm too old a dog to learn new tricks now.' His expression was wistful. 'Maybe I never really had that kind of talent anyway. Perhaps I've only ever been good enough to be a useful jobbing pianist anyway.'

'You're not to say that,' she told him, vehemently. 'I bet you could have been as good as Uncle Gerald if you'd had the chances he's had – *better* even.'

Sometimes Cathy wondered if it was her fault that her father hadn't had the chances he deserved. If she hadn't been born, who knew what heights he might have reached? But she kept these thoughts to herself, a little too afraid that they might be true to voice them.

Cathy had just had her sixteenth birthday when Daniel knew for certain that he was seriously ill. For weeks he wondered what to do, who he could confide in. At last it was his housekeeper he turned to.

He chose a Monday morning after Cathy had left for school, an hour before the arrival of his first pupil. They sat at the kitchen table as they often did at this time of day, sharing a pot of coffee.

'Johnny, I've got something rather shocking to tell you,' he said suddenly.

Mary Johnson looked up. She had known Daniel Oldham for fourteen years and she liked and respected him. Although she was only a few years his senior she always felt that he was much younger. She mothered him much as she did her son, Matthew. He had never shocked her and she didn't believe him capable of doing so now. She smiled.

'Shock away. My mind is as broad as my back.'

He looked up into her eyes with a look she was never to forget. 'I'm afraid I'm going to die, Johnny.'

13

She put down her cup very carefully on its saucer and stared at him. 'Oh please don't say things like that.'

'I'm sorry if that was rather abrupt, Johnny. I'm afraid it's true though. I didn't know how else to tell you. I've got this wretched tumour thing, you see. Oh, I'm all right at the moment and apparently I will be for a while. But it will get worse.'

Swallowing hard at the lump in her throat, she asked: 'But surely – an operation . . .?'

He shook his head. 'No. Apparently not. Eventually I'll have to go into hospital of course and I'm worried sick about what will become of Cathy.'

'Well, you can stop worrying about her at once,' she said firmly. 'I've looked after her all these years. She's like my own child. I'll not see her without a home and someone to care for her.'

'But you've got your son to bring up on your own, and your mother living with you too. I couldn't expect you to take on my daughter. Especially as you'll be out of a job with me gone.'

'I'll get another job all right,' she told him. 'And my mother's a great help. Why shouldn't I take Cathy? She's a good girl and no trouble.'

'But she's growing up, Johnny. And, to be truthful, I haven't much money to leave, to provide for her. There's the house, of course, but it's her home. The only home she's ever known. I wanted her to stay on at school – maybe go on to university. I believe she's capable of it. She deserves the best I can give her. I might just have managed if I'd kept going.' He sighed and rubbed a hand across his jaw. 'Somehow I must find a way to provide the means.'

Johnny reached across the table to cover his hand with her own. 'You shouldn't be fretting like this,' she said. 'Cathy's got a good head on her. She'll make her own way in the world. She wouldn't want you to worry about her future.'

'But I do. What shall I do, Johnny?' He looked up at her with haunted, despairing eyes.

'What you should do is to make these last months with her as happy and memorable as you can,' she told him. 'You're not without friends. And you can be assured that I won't see Cathy alone in the world.'

'Do you think I should tell her – prepare her?' he asked.

Her heart went out to him. 'No. At least, not yet. She's too young to cope with news like that. Just enjoy the time you have together. Make these coming months ones she'll remember with happiness.'

'You're right, Johnny.' His face brightened. 'I know, I'll take her on holiday. We haven't had a proper holiday together for years. She's grown up so much these past couple of years – right under my nose without my noticing. It's time I got to know my daughter properly while there's still time.'

They went to Bournemouth during the Easter holidays. It was early April and quiet. The holiday season hadn't really started, but neither of them minded that. The weather was pleasantly warm and as they walked along the almost deserted sea-front they talked as they had never talked before. In the evenings they went to concerts or to the pictures, but one afternoon when it was raining Daniel took his daughter to a tea dance at The Pavilion.

She'd never been to a proper grown-up dance before and at first she was a little nervous. Daniel danced the first dance with her himself, but after that she didn't lack partners. As he watched her circle the floor in the arms of a series of young men he realised for the first time that his little girl really was a woman now. And so like her mother that at times it hurt him to look at her. For a moment he was angry that he wouldn't see her grown to full maturity, know the joy of giving her away in church to the man she loved on her wedding day; never hold her children in his arms. Surely to God he might have been granted that one small thing in return for the disappointments life had dealt him – all the years he had spent alone. Was it really so much to ask? But his anger soon faded. His main concern was for Cathy. Had he really done all he could to prepare her for life? It was at that moment, watching her enjoying herself, that he decided the time had come for him to tell her the secret he had kept from her since childhood. There might not be another chance.

When they emerged into the late-afternoon the rain had stopped and the air was fragrant with the earth-rich scents of spring. They walked back to their hotel through the pleasure gardens, enjoying the freshness of the air after the rain, the spring flowers and the tangy scent of the pines.

Cathy was in a happy mood. Her step was so light that her feet hardly touched the ground as she danced along at his side. She was humming one of the tunes the band had played: *All I Have To Do Is Dream*. Her sweet, light voice tore at his heart.

'Let's sit down a minute,' he said. 'There's something I want to tell you, Cathy.'

She stopped singing and looked at him. 'What is it, Dad?'

'Nothing to worry about. Just something I think you should know.'

They sat down together on one of the benches and Cathy looked at him anxiously. 'You look very serious. Is it something I've done?'

He shook his head. 'No, of course not. Look, Cathy, it's about your mother. There's something I really should have told you a long time ago.' He paused for a moment, looking apprehensively at her expectant, upturned face. He'd started now. There was no going back. He was no good at beating about the bush, there was only one way to say it. He cleared his throat. 'The truth is – she didn't die.'

16

Her eyes widened. 'You mean – she's still alive?'

'Oh, no. She was killed in a car accident about eight years ago. The fact is – she left us, Cathy. When you were a baby.'

'*Left us?* But why, Dad? Didn't she love us? Didn't we make her happy?'

'I thought we did. I *believed* we did. I'm still convinced that she was happy – until . . .'

'Until what?'

'Until she met someone else, Cathy. Someone who captivated – obsessed her, heart, body and soul. She had to be with him – said she couldn't help herself.'

Cathy was shaking her head. 'I don't understand. Didn't you try to stop her?'

He bent forward on the seat, elbows on his knees, hands clasped. How did you explain the heartbreak, the stark, gut-wrenching misery of rejection to a sixteen year old? 'You can't make people love you, Cathy,' he said sadly. 'Not once they've really stopped. Of course I tried. I pleaded with her to stay with us, if only for your sake. Looking back now, I suppose it was emotional blackmail. I wanted her to stay so much I didn't care what I did or said to make her. But in the end I could see that it was no use. It was tearing her apart not being with him. In the end I had to let her go.'

Cathy bit her lip. 'So she wouldn't even stay for her own child – not even for – me? And you've always said she loved me, Dad.'

'She did love you. Nothing surer than that. It broke her heart to leave you. I know it did.'

'But she left just the same.' She felt the hurt of betrayal bite deep into her heart, and when she looked at her father she saw her own pain reflected in his eyes. 'Why didn't you tell me this before?' she asked, her voice thick with tears.

He shrugged his shoulders. 'At first you were too young to understand. It was easier to let you believe she was dead.

After all, she wasn't coming back and you didn't remember her. Then, when she was killed . . . It didn't seem right somehow to betray her memory. I suppose if I'm honest I didn't want you to know I'd lied to you all those years.'

'Who was he, this man?' she asked angrily. 'Did you go and see him?'

'She never told me.'

'Didn't you ask her? Didn't you try to find out?'

'She said it was better I didn't know. And I suppose I was cowardly enough to prefer to remain ignorant.'

'Did they get married?'

'No.'

'How do you know?'

'They couldn't. We were never divorced. All I know is that she went abroad to live. I never saw or heard from her again – except through a solicitor of course, after the accident.'

They sat for a moment in silence, then Cathy said: 'So – so why are you telling me now, Dad?'

He looked into her eyes, saw the deep hurt his revelation had inflicted and decided that he couldn't tell her the real reason. 'You're a woman now,' he said. 'I saw you this afternoon how grown up you are. I thought it was time I levelled with you. Can you forgive me, Cathy?'

For a moment she searched his eyes, then she threw her arms around his neck and hugged him hard. 'Of course I can. Poor Dad. How unhappy you must have been. I'm so *glad* it was you who brought me up. You've done a terrific job – been both mother and father to me. I couldn't have had a better childhood.' She kissed his cheek. 'I love you so much, Dad. I'll always love you.'

'I love you too, sweetheart.' Daniel cleared his throat and made himself laugh as he disentangled her arms from his neck. 'Hey, come on, just look at the pair of us. We're getting all soppy.' He stood up and pulled her to her feet, tucking her hand through his arm. 'Come on now, time we were getting back to the hotel. I'm starving, aren't you? What are we going to do this evening? Shall we go to the Winter Gardens again? Or do you fancy that film at the Westover?'

It was late in October 1960 when the leaves from the sooty plane trees in Laburnum Close carpeted the ground, that Daniel died. He had kept his illness from Cathy almost to the end, hiding his pain and putting his weariness down to hard work until his final collapse. He had been in hospital only a few days when the end came. For Cathy it was a devastating blow. For days she went around in a daze, unable to take it in.

Johnny took her home to stay with her. At first the girl was stunned and disorientated, asking repeatedly why he hadn't told her and why no one had done anything to help him?

'There was no more they could do, love,' Johnny told her gently. 'He knew that. He just wanted to keep going till the end, for your sake. And the doctors were able to help him with that. It was all he asked.'

But to Cathy it made no sense. She felt angry and cheated, terribly alone and afraid. There was so much she wished she had done and said. Now she would never have the chance. Why hadn't he treated her as a grown up – trusted her?

When the solicitor wrote, asking her to see him at his office, Johnny decided that she must go along with her. No doubt the question of whether to sell the house would arise and goodness only knew what else there was to be sorted out. How could a girl of barely seventeen be expected to make such monumental decisions about her own future?

Sitting side by side on the other side of Mr MacAlister's enormous oak desk they looked at him expectantly. He was a tall man with sparse grey hair and heavy horn-rimmed spectacles which made his pale eyes look large and impersonal.

'Your legal guardian will be joining us shortly,' he said,

pulling out his watch impatiently and peering at it. 'I do hope he isn't going to be late. I really can't begin until he arrives.'

Cathy and Johnny exchanged a puzzled look. 'I'm sorry, but there must be some mistake,' Cathy ventured. 'I haven't got a legal guardian.'

Mr MacAlister looked at the copy of Daniel's will which lay on the desk before him. 'Oh, but you have. Did your father not acquaint you with the fact?'

'I didn't actually know he was dying,' Cathy said wryly. How much more was there that he hadn't told her? 'Do you think you could tell me who this guardian person is, please?'

The solicitor looked at her incredulously for a moment, then . . . 'The name I have here, the person I've been in contact with on behalf of your father's estate, is Mr Gerald Cavelle, of Albany Place, Mayfair. He is also your father's executor.' He cleared his throat and frowned at them over his spectacles. 'I'm told he's a – *ahem* – a musician. A concert pianist in fact.'

Cathy was staring at him. '*Uncle Gerald?*'

The solicitor looked relieved. 'Ah – so you do know who I'm talking about?'

'Of course. He's my godfather.'

Mr MacAlister nodded. 'I see. Very suitable. He would be the obvious choice.' At that moment the door opened and his secretary ushered Gerald in. Cathy sprang to her feet and went to meet him.

'Uncle Gerald!'

He took both her hands. 'My dear child. I'm so desperately sorry about your father. I was abroad at the time or I would have been at the funeral. I only got back two days ago.'

The solicitor cleared his throat pointedly. 'Hrrrmph. If we might get down to business? I have another appointment in twenty minutes.'

* * *

As soon as the details of Daniel's will had been gone through Gerald took charge. First he put Cathy and Johnny into a taxi and took them to tea at Fortnum's.

'Now – what's to be done with you, young lady?' he asked, smiling at Cathy across the teacups. 'How much longer do you have at school?'

'I can leave now,' Cathy told him eagerly. 'Right after I've taken my O levels.'

Johnny glanced at her and leaned forward. 'I know it's really none of my business, sir, but I do know that Mr Oldham wanted Cathy to take her A levels and go on to university.'

Cathy looked at her in dismay. 'I'd never get to university, Johnny,' she said. 'I'm not clever enough. I'll be lucky to get any O's. I don't even *want* to stay on. Besides, by the time I've done another two years at school all the money will have run out, won't it?'

Gerald leaned across the table. 'You needn't let that worry you, Cathy. If university is what you want, I'll see you through.'

She blushed. 'I couldn't let you. Dad wouldn't have wanted that,' she muttered. 'Besides, I really don't want to go – *honestly*.'

He glanced at Johnny. 'I'll arrange for the sale of the house. There will be a lot to do. Maybe Cathy and I could go along together some day soon and sort things out there. The place will have to be cleared before the sale. I'll invest the money for her. No need to worry about that. I have a very good financial adviser.' He looked at Cathy. 'Maybe you'll change your mind about university by the time you get your exam results. In the meantime, where are you to live? It would hardly be proper for you to move into my bachelor flat. Besides, I'm hardly ever there.'

'She can stay on with me indefinitely,' Johnny put in quickly. 'She's perfectly happy with Mother and Matthew and me, aren't you, love?' Cathy nodded reluctantly. 'And I don't live far away from Laburnum Close,' Johnny said conclusively. 'So it's handy for her school.'

Gerald nodded. 'That sounds like an ideal arrangement. I'll see that you're appropriately recompensed, Mrs Johnson. And I'll open a bank account for you, Cathy, and see that an allowance is paid in monthly.' He looked at Johnny. 'I haven't much of an idea about what young girls need, so perhaps you'd better work something out on a monthly basis and let me know the amount.'

Johnny blushed. 'Well – if you say so, sir, though I'd like you to know that she's as close to me as my own child and I'd gladly have looked after her without an allowance.'

'I'm sure you would, Mrs Johnson, and I'm very grateful to you for all you've done, but I'm sure you'll agree that it is better to have things on a proper businesslike footing. After all, I am Cathy's legal guardian.' Gerald smiled at Cathy. 'Meantime, young lady, maybe you and I should start getting to know one another better. I'll make sure we keep in touch.'

Cathy wondered if he would remember or just fade into obscurity again as he had before. But he was as good as his word, telephoning regularly every week to ask how she was and if there was anything she needed.

The house in Laburnum Close sold quickly. The price was right and the young couple who bought it saw potential in the spacious, elegantly proportioned rooms. Gerald rang Cathy as soon as the offer was accepted to let her know.

'You realise what this means, of course,' he said.

Cathy bit her lip. 'I'll have to go and sort Dad's things out, you mean?'

'No, *we* will. I told you I'd go with you. It's not the kind of thing you should have to tackle alone. When do you want to go? What about next weekend? I think the sooner the better, don't you?'

The following Sunday was decided upon. Gerald suggested they should make an early start, offering to take Cathy out to lunch afterwards. He called for her soon after breakfast in his smart little sports car. Creating quite a stir in Chestnut Grove as he unfolded his long legs from the driving seat and walked up to the front door. He wore casual clothes: jeans and a sweater. Cathy thought he looked terribly handsome and as she settled into the car beside him she felt very proud and grown-up.

The late-November day was grey and cloudy and the moment she opened the front door of number thirteen with her key, the sad loneliness of the abandoned house hit her. Standing in the hall, she was aware for the first time of how old and shabby everything was. Johnny's little semi-detached house in Chestnut Grove wasn't luxurious, but it had a woman's touch. There were flowers and pretty ornaments in the living room, scented soap and talcum in the bathroom, and sparkling white net curtains at all the windows. Standing in the hall she wished she could have made this house more homelike for Dad. If she'd been older maybe she would have learned how to do it – how to keep house and make him more comfortable. She looked up at Gerald apologetically.

'I wish you could have come here before,' she said. 'When Dad was alive it didn't feel so – so sad and empty.'

He slipped a comforting arm around her shoulders. 'Come on, let's make a start, shall we? I suggest we make a tour of the rooms first and pick out the things you want to keep. I've brought some labels with me. The sooner we begin the sooner we'll be finished.'

'I don't see how I can keep anything,' she told him wistfully. 'Not furniture anyway. I've nowhere to keep it.'

'Is there anything you particularly want?' he asked her.

'I would have liked to keep the piano, but . . .'

'If you want to keep it, then you shall,' he told her

23

firmly. 'It can stay at my flat. And you can come and play it whenever you want to.'

Her eyes lit up. 'Can I? Oh, Uncle Gerald, thank you!'

He winced. 'When I say you can have it, I'm making one condition.'

'What's that?'

'That you stop calling me *Uncle*, for God's sake. It makes me feel as though I ought to have a long white beard. Just plain Gerald will do, thanks very much.'

She laughed. 'I'll try to remember.'

They worked hard all morning. Gerald took charge, organising everything with brisk efficiency, and to Cathy's relief it turned out to be much easier than she had imagined. Together they packed the china and saucepans; sorted through Daniel's clothes, setting aside the best for the Salvation Army to collect. They labelled the furniture ready for the saleroom and made the decision to leave carpets and curtains in situ in the house. When the time came for the attic to be investigated Cathy asked if she might have a little time to herself there. She wanted to look through the boxes full of old letters and photographs she knew were there. Maybe there was something of her mother's she could keep as a souvenir. Gerald nodded understandingly.

'Take as long as you need. I'll go and root around in the garden shed,' he told her.

It was cold and dark in the attic. The one small window was festooned with cobwebs and dust lay thick on everything. Cathy found that many of the old boxes full of letters and photographs that she knew were there had gone. Johnny had told her that Dad had known he was ill for some time. He must have come up here and destroyed everything personal before he died. Disappointment overwhelmed her. She'd hoped to find some relics of happier days; some of her mother's clothes. Maybe even her parents' wedding photograph, which she didn't remember ever seeing. She searched through the boxes that remained. They contained nothing but rubbish. There were some of her old toys, most of them broken now and useless. The old clothes she used to dress up in, that had belonged to her grandmother, were moth-eaten and ragged now, fit only for the dustbin.

She sat on the floor and looked around her dejectedly. Was this really all there was to show of the life she and Dad had shared? It was as though her whole childhood lay here in the dark little room under the eaves, dusty and disintegrating. This time next week it would all have been carried away by the dustman – over and forgotten. Tears began to trickle down her cheeks. Suddenly the stark, final reality of her father's death hit her like a hammer blow.

'Oh, Daddy,' she choked back the tears. 'Daddy, *Daddy*, I miss you so much.'

She didn't hear the footsteps on the stairs and when the attic door creaked open she started violently, her head twisting round as she looked up at the dark figure blotting out the light.

'Cathy, I'm sorry I startled you.' Gerald crouched beside her. 'What is it, darling? What have you found?'

'Nothing. That's just it, *nothing*. I thought there might be some old letters – snapshots – but there's no trace of anything. It's as though we – Dad, my mother and I – never existed. I feel like – like a *ghost*.'

He put his arm round her shoulders and drew her close. 'Have a good cry. Don't bottle it all up. It's not good for you.' He tipped up her chin to look into her brimming eyes. 'I wouldn't mind betting you haven't had a proper cry since Dan died, have you? Go on, let it all out. There's no one to see but me.'

Totally overwhelmed by his gentleness, she gave vent to the emotion that welled up inside her. It was such sheer luxury to drop her head on to his shoulder and sob out her grief, gasping and hiccupping with the abandon of a five year old.

Gerald had been right about the tight rein she'd kept on her emotions since Daniel had died. She'd been afraid to weep in front of Johnny; afraid that the kindly meant sympathy and the fussing that would inevitably result would be interpreted by the other two members of the household as monopolising her. Cathy was acutely aware that they had first call on Johnny's time and attention. They were her family. She, Cathy, was the outsider. There was Matthew, Johnny's nineteen-year-old son, tall and serious seeming to show with his silent, unsmiling forbearance just how much he resented the presence of this female interloper. She would have died rather than weep in front of him. Then there was Johnny's mother, old Mrs Bains, whose sharp eyes seemed always to be watching her, waiting to seize on the first sign that she was taking advantage.

But Gerald was impartial. He quietly stroked the auburn head that rested on his shoulder and let her cry, saying nothing.

After a while the sobs ceased and she began to feel much better. Without a word, Gerald pulled out a large clean handkerchief and pressed it into her hand. She sat up, mopped her face and blew her nose, then she looked up at him.

'Sorry.'

'Don't apologise for doing what you should have let yourself do long ago.'

She managed a smile. 'Thanks, Gerald.' Suddenly to her surprise she saw him quite differently. Until now she had held him in awe, but now they had shared this small intimate moment she felt they were closer – almost equal.

He glanced around. 'Is there anything up here that you want?'

She shrugged helplessly. 'No. It can all go out for the dustman.'

'Right. Give me a hand to stack the boxes at the top of the stairs then. Oh, and Cathy . . .'

'Yes?' She paused in the act of lifting a box.

'Don't ever let me hear you say you feel like a ghost again.' He took the box from her and put it on the floor. Then he took both of her hands in his. 'You're young and full of vitality. One day quite soon you're going to be a beautiful young woman. Your whole life is in front of you and from now on you have to look forward, not back. That's how your father would have wanted it. And that's the way it's going to be.' He bent and brushed her forehead with his lips. 'That's a promise. Now, come on, let's get these boxes downstairs. I don't know about you but if I don't get something to eat soon I shall fade away.'

Cathy had dreaded Christmas that year; her first without Dad and in the house of people who, however hard they tried, were not her family. The little house was crowded with the four of them. There were only three bedrooms and Johnny had doubled up with her mother in order to accommodate Cathy. She was acutely aware of the sacrifices that were being made on her account, and so afraid she would feel like an intruder at Christmas. But as it happened it was better than she had thought.

Johnny loved Christmas. She was a wonderful cook and made sure that she involved Cathy in all the preparations. She set Cathy and Matthew the task of decorating the house whilst she and her mother went out to buy last-minute food and presents on the Saturday afternoon before the holiday.

It was the first time that Cathy had been alone with Matthew and she felt rather shy. She knew that he worked as a junior clerk in a solicitor's office, but they had never talked about it so she hadn't the slightest idea what his work involved. When he came home from work each evening he disappeared upstairs to his room as soon as he had eaten. She had always assumed it was because of her. But today, dressed in jeans and a sweater instead of the formal clothes

27

he wore to work, and whistling a popular tune as he worked, he seemed more human somehow – more approachable.

For the first ten minutes they worked together in silence, she handing up the brightly coloured paper chains and he pinning them.

'Do you like your job?' she asked at last, remembering Mr MacAlister's forbidding office and the baffling legal language used in all his correspondence. 'Isn't it boring, trying to work out what it's all supposed to be about?'

He looked down at her with a slightly surprised expression. 'Not really. Not when you get used to it. And going to court is really interesting. The law is a fascinating subject, you know.'

'I suppose it is, but you only work in the office, don't you?'

'At the moment, yes, but I don't intend to be a clerk for the rest of my life.'

'Oh? What are you going to do then?'

He came down the ladder and began to bunch some sprigs of holly together. 'Didn't Mum tell you? I'm studying for my law exams in my spare time. Some day I'm going to be a fully qualified solicitor.'

Cathy looked at him with a new respect. So that's what he did upstairs in his room all evening. He wasn't keeping out of her way at all.

'Won't that take ages?' she asked him. 'I thought you had to go to university for that.'

'You can do it this way too. It does take longer, but I don't care as long as I can be earning while I study,' he said stoically. 'Mum had a real struggle to bring me up. My dad was killed at Dunkirk, you know. She had to work hard to keep me on at grammar school. And now she's got Gran to look after too. I mean to pay her back one day.'

'I know what you mean.' Cathy was thoughtful. 'My father made sacrifices for me too,' she said, remembering how she'd selfishly insisted on going to St Margaret's without a thought of what it might mean to him. 'I'd have liked the chance to pay him back. Now I never will.'

He looked at her a little apprehensively, hoping she wasn't about to cry. The fact that she didn't sent her up in his estimation. He smiled at her for the first time ever. 'I'm sorry about your dad, Cathy,' he said awkwardly. 'It was rotten luck. I was only a baby when mine died so I don't remember him.' He touched her shoulder awkwardly. 'But I don't suppose your father would have wanted paying back anyhow. I expect he was happy to do it for you.' He gave the bunch of holly a final twist. 'Will you hold the step ladder for me while I fix this over the mirror?'

They smiled at each other and Cathy knew that any resentment, real or imaginary, that had been between them in the past had vanished once and for all.

On New Year's Eve Gerald rang to say he was taking her to a concert. Cathy wore her best dress, the one that Dad had bought her the time they went to Bournemouth, and sat proudly in the front row at the Wigmore Hall. She longed to tell the people on either side of her that the soloist was her guardian. He played Rachmaninov's Second Piano Concerto and as she listened wraptly Cathy was convinced that it had never been played with more style and brilliance. After the concert an attendant came to escort her round to Gerald's dressing room where he was waiting to take her out for dinner. They went to Quaglino's and Gerald encouraged her to order all the things she liked best.

It wasn't until they reached the coffee stage of the meal that she discovered why.

'I'm afraid this is by way of au revoir, Cathy,' he told her. 'I'm going on a concert tour in two days' time: the United States and Canada. I'll be away for about eight months. No need to worry about anything though. I've arranged for your allowance and Mrs Johnson's to be paid into the bank and if there are any problems just ring my agent. Here's his address and phone number.' He passed her a card across the table.

The news came as a blow. Although she had known of course that he spent much of his time out of the country, she hadn't been prepared for him to go away this soon – or for so long. She slipped the card into her handbag without looking at it, her cheeks pink and her eyes downcast. 'I see. Thanks, Gerald.'

He laughed gently at her crestfallen face. 'Don't look like that. I'm not deserting you. You've got a very busy few months ahead of you at school, haven't you? It'll go very quickly, and I'll be back in this country in time to hear your exam results. Then we can celebrate.'

She pulled a face. 'If there's anything *to* celebrate.'

'I'm sure there will be. And we'll need to talk about your future by then, won't we? Whatever happens.'

'I know all that. It's just – just . . .'

'Just what?'

'Just that you're – the only family I've got now and I'll – miss you.'

She felt foolish the moment she'd said it and to her dismay found her eyes filling with helpless tears. She fumbled miserably in her bag for a handkerchief, fighting off the embarrassing display of emotion. Now she'd ruined the whole evening. How *could* she be so stupid?

Gerald hurriedly asked for the bill and, when he had paid, took her arm firmly and escorted her out of the restaurant. When they were seated in the car she looked at him apprehensively.

'I'm sorry.'

'What for?'

'For being such an idiot – for embarrassing you.'

He smiled wryly. 'Don't give it another thought. I've been in much more embarrassing situations and lived to tell the tale,' he told her. 'Actually it's rather flattering. Most of the women in my life are glad to see the back of me.'

She wondered a little at this remark. So he saw her as a woman? *Most of the women*, he said. How many were there in his life? As far as she knew he had never been married, but a man as good-looking, as famous and talented as Gerald, was bound to have had dozens of glamorous girlfriends.

'Tell you what,' he was saying, 'when I come back we'll have a grand reunion celebration – anything you like. You can choose. And look – any time you want to visit the flat, just go along. I'll tell the caretaker to let you in. You can play the piano or just be by yourself if you feel the need. I know it's a bit of a squash at Mrs Johnson's. How does that appeal?'

She sniffed, nodding into the darkness. He was placating her. He didn't think of her as a woman after all. He still saw her as a child. But she *wasn't* a child any more. She was seventeen now. She hadn't felt like a child for ages; not since Dad died.

But in spite of everything Gerald had been right about the time flying. Once the holidays were over and she was back at school there was so much to do. She hadn't forgotten Matthew's words about paying his mother back for her sacrifices. Perhaps it was too late to pay Dad back, but he had wanted her to do well so she would do it for him anyway. Now Cathy too disappeared to her room with her books each evening. Johnny complained that she and Matthew were like lodgers.

'Ships that pass in the night,' she said, half joking, half serious. 'I'm sure all that bookwork can't be good for you. You'll ruin your eyesight, the pair of you.' But secretly she was proud of her hard-working son, and of Cathy too, for the industry she knew came hard to the girl. In spite of what she had said, it seemed that she meant to pass those exams and stay on at school after all. There had been a time soon after Daniel Oldham's death when Johnny had worried that the child didn't care any more. But it seemed her fears were unfounded.

With Cathy's new desire to succeed came other changes. In her friends for instance. Carla made no secret of the fact that she disapproved.

'I don't know what's got into you,' she complained. 'You're no fun any more. This is the fourth week you've refused to go dancing or to the pictures on Saturday. You have to have some time off. Don't you want to meet any boys?'

'I've got a lot of time to catch up,' Cathy said. 'I've let things slide.'

Carla sniffed disdainfully. 'You've changed,' she said. 'Ever since you've been living with the Johnsons you've turned into a swot. Don't tell me it's that awful Matthew? You don't fancy him, do you – spots and all?'

Cathy denied the accusation hotly. 'Of course I don't! Why does everything have to be because of some boy? If you must know, I want to repay Dad for all he did for me, that's all.'

'What for? He won't *know*, will he?' Carla said insensitively.

'Well, I'm doing it anyway. Gerald expects me to do well. I don't want to let him down.'

'Ah. Now we're getting to the truth.' Carla smiled triumphantly. 'Gorgeous Gerald the famous pianist. It's *him* you fancy, isn't it? I might have known. It's been nothing but Gerald this and Gerald that ever since last autumn.' She tossed her blonde curls disdainfully. 'You've turned into the most awful little name-dropping show-off since he came on the scene, and now you're a swot too – just like Rosalind Blair.'

'I'm not!'

Carla ignored her protest. 'It isn't as though you *have* to do it either. I mean, everyone knows that a girl as plain as Rosalind has to work hard. Can you imagine any man asking *her* to marry him?'

They were in the cloakroom and Rosalind was close

enough to overhear. Cathy blushed and whispered: 'Shut up, she'll hear you.'

Carla glanced round haughtily. 'I don't suppose I've said anything she doesn't already know,' she said, unabashed, and looked challengingly at Cathy. 'Right then, are you coming dancing with me on Saturday or do I ask someone else?'

'I think you'd better ask someone else,' Cathy said firmly.

'All right, I will. If you want to turn into a cabbage you'd better get on with it and the best of British luck!'

Cathy watched as Carla shook her head and walked away. She was beginning to see her friend for what she was: shallow and selfish. All the same, she missed their weekly outings and Sunday tea at the Maybridges' gloriously chaotic house. Working for her exams was hard going but she was determined to do the best she could so that Gerald would be proud of her. Whenever her spirits flagged she got out the postcards he had sent her from each of the places where he'd played: New York; Los Angeles; Boston. She imagined the hectic, glamorous life he must be having; the concerts and the parties; the beautiful women he must be meeting every day, all of them falling over each other to get close to him. And she wondered at the thought that he could actually find the time to write to her. He must be just a *little* bit fond of her. Then she would imagine the scene where she would tell him of her success, and picture the look on his face. It was all the incentive she needed.

She put on her coat and heaved the heavy satchel on to her back. She'd have to hurry or she'd miss the half-past four bus. She reached the door at the same time as Rosalind and when she saw the other girl blush and look away Cathy decided to try to apologise for Carla's cruel and thoughtless remarks.

'Look, Rosalind, I'm sorry about those things that Carla said. She can be very catty at times. Take no notice of her.

33

She was cross with me because I wouldn't go dancing with her on Saturday.'

Rosalind's colour deepened. 'It's all right,' she said, tugging at the strap of her satchel. 'There's no need for you to feel sorry for me. I'm used to being called plain.'

'She thinks I'm a bore because I'm working hard for my exams,' Cathy went on. 'She was getting at me really. She knows how embarrassed I get when she makes loud remarks about people.'

'She was accusing you of being like me. How awful for you!'

Cathy looked at the other girl's hurt expression. 'Oh, no. I take it as a compliment. If I can do as well as you always do in exams, I'll be very pleased.'

'I work hard because I have a plan. Besides, there's nothing much else to do.' Rosalind looked up with a smile and suddenly Cathy saw to her surprise that she wasn't plain at all. The brown eyes behind the spectacles were large and lustrous and she had small, regular features and nice teeth. If she had her straight dark hair cut differently . . . Someone had once said that Rosalind's mother had been an actress before she married, though Carla had scoffed at that rumour.

'No actress would let her daughter walk around dressed like that,' she said. And Cathy was reluctantly inclined to agree. Rosalind came to school in a sad assortment of shapeless skirts and blouses that Carla insisted were rejects from a jumble sale.

The two girls had fallen into step but suddenly Rosalind stopped.

'Don't feel you have to walk with me, Cathy,' she said. 'I told you, I'm used to catty remarks – and to being on my own. You don't need to apologise for Carla either. I know you're not like her.'

'I don't feel I've *got* to walk with you, I want to. After all, we catch the same bus so why shouldn't we walk together?'

Cathy glanced at the other girl, hoping she hadn't sounded patronising. 'That's if you don't mind?' she added.

Rosalind hesitated for a moment, then smiled again, blushing, this time with pleasure. 'No. I don't mind,' she said. 'I don't mind at all.'

Chapter Two

Rosalind had a longer journey home than Cathy. It took her half an hour to get to the street in Burnt Oak where she and her mother occupied a flat. After she got off the bus there was a lengthy walk and by the time she arrived at Courtney Avenue the strap of her satchel was biting into her shoulder and her back ached. As usual she let herself into the rundown Edwardian house with her own key and trudged up the uncarpeted stairs to the first-floor flat.

Rosalind didn't mind coming home to an empty flat each afternoon. She was used to it. It meant she would have an hour's peace and quiet to get on with her homework before her mother got home from work. That hour was essential. Once she had her O levels behind her she was determined to go on and take her A's. Her whole future depended on how well she could do.

In the cramped little kitchen with its window overlooking the dusty back garden she put the kettle on for coffee and took down the biscuit tin, then went through into the living room and began to unload her books on to the table. She had set her sights on passing at least two subjects with good grades. She'd been told that she wasn't university material but already knew what she wanted to do so it wasn't a problem. She was determined to go to a business college, the best one she could find, and take a diploma course in hotel management. The careers mistress at St Margaret's had tried to talk her out of it, feeling that the quiet, somewhat withdrawn girl had none of the right attributes for hotel work. But it was all Rosalind had wanted to do ever since she could remember and she refused to be discouraged from her goal.

As she waited for the kettle to boil she thought about her brief and unexpected talk with Cathy Oldham. Ever since her first year at St Margaret's she'd admired the tall, striking girl with her auburn hair and green eyes. It was strange – people often talked of green eyes when they really meant grey, or blue-green, but Cathy's were a true, clear green, like emeralds. When you looked into them it was hard to look away; they were quite mesmerising. Yet Cathy wasn't at all the type one associated with green eyes. Rosalind had always felt that, and today it had been confirmed. Cathy was thoughtful and kind, just as Rosalind had always known she would be. She felt a sense of satisfaction in having her instinct proved right. She'd never really understood why Cathy and Carla Maybridge were such friends. They were so different.

Rosalind took a biscuit from the tin and munched thoughtfully. She wished in some ways that she could be more like Carla, who seemed to attract people like a magnet. But she was only too aware of the power she had and used it in all the wrong ways. She was self-centred and thoughtless, often to the point of cruelty to those less fortunate than herself; though goodness only knew she had no need to be. Everything seemed to fall effortlessly into her lap. She was pretty and popular with both girls and teachers alike, and although she only ever managed to scrape by academically she was always at the centre of things. Cathy on the other hand seemed quite unaware of her own attractiveness. She was a more serious, introspective kind of girl. Rosalind had heard about her father dying. She knew Cathy had no mother and that she'd had to leave the home where she'd grown up. Watching her at school she'd recognised the suffering in the other girl's face and manner and, herself the only child of divorced parents, had longed to reach out to her; to sympathise. But she hadn't known how, or where to begin. In the end, afraid of receiving a snub, or some scathing remark from Carla, she hadn't even tried. Today as they'd walked to the bus stop together she had searched her mind for some words to express her understanding and regret, but to her frustration, they'd refused to come.

Rosalind had been almost eight when her parents had divorced. Until then her life had been divided between Aunt Flora who kept a boarding house in Cleethorpes and the hotels and 'digs' up and down the country where her parents, Una and Ben Blair, stayed as they toured with their singing act. Flora Mawson wasn't a real aunt. She was Una's late mother's oldest friend and the nearest she had to a blood relative now that her parents were dead.

Rosalind had been born while her parents were touring with ENSA during the war. Una, furious to discover that she was pregnant and forced to take time off, had deposited her new baby with Aunt Flora in Cleethorpes as soon as she could, and rejoined Ben who was touring at the time with a production of *The Desert Song*. She was soon to discover that during her absence he had become more than friendly with a dancer in the same company. It was the beginning of a long string of infidelities and eventually the end of the marriage.

By the time Rosalind had reached school age she was spending term time with Aunt Flora in Cleethorpes and the holidays with her parents wherever they happened to be working. Aunt Flora had pointed out to Una somewhat tersely that the boarding house was her bread and butter. Heaven only knew, the summer season was short enough and fond as she was of Rosalind, she really couldn't have the child taking up one of her rooms while her parents 'gadded about' all over the country. So as soon as school broke up for the long summer holidays Rosalind would pack her suitcase and join the mother and father who were little more than strangers to her.

Sometimes they would be booked for a resident summer

show at the seaside, which was nice. Ben did his best to act the role of father, taking her on the beach and playing with her when he wasn't rehearsing. Una, on the other hand, needed all her free time for having her hair done and making sure she looked good off-stage as well as on. Less enjoyable summers would be spent touring, which meant long dreary Sunday train journeys and a succession of dingy digs and lodging houses where Rosalind would be required to keep quiet and not play on the stairs. In the evenings while Una and Ben were at the theatre she would stay in her room with the radio or a book. Later, she would lie awake, rigid with misery and unnamed fears as the sound of quarrelling initiated by her mother's emotional tantrums reached her through the thin partition walls.

It had been around that time that her ambition had been born. When she grew up she was going to stay in one place all the time. She would have the kind of life where she would feel safe; one which would certainly have nothing to do with the theatre. She hated the musty, cheerless backstage environment; the faces made bewilderingly unfamiliar with orange make-up; and the tense, highly-charged atmosphere that seemed to exclude everyone not associated with it. Stage people weren't like anyone else, she decided. It was as though they were split into two: one person on the stage and another off it. They seemed to keep all the best bits of themselves jealously guarded and stored up for the audience, so that there was nothing left over for those, like herself, who stood on the fringe of it all. Standing in the wings or occasionally seated 'out front' she found it difficult to believe that the two glamorous people on the stage, smiling so adoringly into each other's eyes as they sang their romantic love songs, were the angry, morose parents who came home every evening to quarrel and shout at each other until the other occupants of the house banged on the walls in fury.

But quite apart from her dislike of the theatre, Rosalind

recognised that she had no aptitude or talent for the life. She had not inherited her mother's lustrous violet eyes and mane of raven hair. Her own hair was an indeterminate brown and poker straight, and from the age of four she had had to wear glasses. Neither had she Una's vivacious, mercurial personality. The years of being pushed into the background and passed around had set their seal on her character. She was much too shy and lacking in confidence to make a performer even if she had wanted to be one.

By the time she was seven she had decided that when she grew up she would have a hotel of her own; one where people – especially children – were made welcome. It wouldn't be like Aunt Flora's boarding house with its porch full of rusting buckets and spades and wet mackintoshes. And it certainly wouldn't be like the cabbage-smelling, brown-wallpapered digs and theatrical lodgings where she spent her summer holidays. During the long hours she spent alone she planned it all. *Her* hotel would be warm and comfortable with cosy fires and bright lights in all the rooms. There would be delicious food to eat, pretty curtains and warm, soft beds. The bathroom wouldn't be cold and draughty and there wouldn't be any of those horrid hissing gas heaters where the hot water was always running out. Best of all, there would be a garden where children could play and go where they pleased. It would feel like a *home*, she told herself. It would *be* a home.

Soon after her parents' traumatic split-up Aunt Flora decided to retire. Her announcement spiked Una's guns on the awful weekend when she and Rosalind had arrived in Cleethorpes to throw themselves on her mercy.

'I'm going to sell Sea View and go down to Devon to live with my sister Gladys now that she's widowed,' she told a tearful Una as they sat facing each other across the kitchen table. 'So it's no use you expecting me to take the child on permanent like.'

It was evening and Rosalind was upstairs in bed,

supposedly asleep. But the sound of voices floated up the stairs to reach her through the open bedroom door. The mention of her own name brought her instantly alert. Throwing back the bedclothes, she tiptoed out on to the landing. Creeping down to the bend in the staircase, she crouched by the banisters and listened to the voices of the two women as they discussed her future.

'She's a nice little thing and no trouble, I grant you,' Aunt Flora was saying. 'But she's getting older all the time and she's coming to the age when she needs a parent's guidance. I'm sorry, Una but I'll be frank with you. I feel it's high time you were a proper mother to the child.'

'And how do you think I'm going to do that with no job and nowhere to live?' Una's voice was shrill with resentment. 'She's Ben's kid too. But does he want to know about her? Does he *hell*! Shouldn't think he gives a damn whether he sees her again. Off with his fancy bit of stuff, he is, and no thought for anyone but himself.' She gave a bitter little laugh. 'Groping the chorus girls – that's all he's ever been good for!'

'Maybe you should have thought of that before you married him,' Aunt Flora said dryly. 'After all, if I remember rightly, you took him off someone else in the first place. Quite cocky about it, you were too, at the time. Stands to reason if you could turn his head, then there'd be others who could do the same.'

'That's not getting my problem solved though, is it?' Una snapped. 'What the hell do I do with a kid? How can I work with her round my neck?'

'Get a day job,' Aunt Flora suggested. 'In a shop or something. She's at school in the daytime.'

Una gave an indignant little squeal. '*Me?* A shop girl? I'm an artiste, Flora. A *soubrette*.'

'That's as may be, but whatever fancy name you like to call yourself, the fact remains, you're that child's mother, and beggars can't be choosers.'

41

'You've hit the nail on the head there. That's what I'll be all right. A *beggar*. I should never have had her. I never wanted a kid. It's all his fault, the careless swine. Not taking proper care. Now I'm lumbered and off he goes, scot-bloody free.'

Una was working herself up into one of her 'states'. Rosalind knew all the signs. She'd heard her enough times through the walls late at night. But this time it was all about her. This time she was the cause of Una's anger. Aunt Flora always said, *'Eavesdroppers never heard any good of themselves'* and now she knew that was true. The words: *I should never have had her, I never wanted a kid* and *I'm lumbered* brought a big lump to her throat and made her eyes sting with tears. Getting up from the stairs she scuttled back to bed and pulled the bedclothes up over her head, pushing a fist into her mouth so that they wouldn't hear her sobs. No one wanted her. Not even Aunt Flora. But why? What had she done? She'd tried hard to be good and keep out of the way. She didn't make a noise or ask for things. She missed her father too. Happy-go-lucky Ben with his sparkling brown eyes and his big laugh. She'd always thought he loved her and the shock of her mother's revelation that he didn't want to know about her any more hurt intolerably. Suddenly she felt very scared. Would they put her in an orphanage? That's what happened to children that nobody wanted, wasn't it? To seven-year-old Rosalind the future looked bleak and frightening.

It hadn't turned out like that, though there had been times when she had almost wished it had. It was 1951 and variety theatres in provincial towns up and down the country were closing for want of support. Television was what people were interested in now. All the top-name artistes right there in your own living room. When you could see them all without getting out of your armchair, why should anyone pay to see number four touring shows with tatty costumes at the local Hippodrome? Especially with the price of admission going up the way it had since the war.

All through the school holidays Una dragged Rosalind up and down Charing Cross Road, trying one agent after another. They climbed endless narrow dusty staircases, drawing one blank after another. Una had walked out on the agent who had represented her and Ben in a fit of pique when he told her with brutal frankness that her voice was thin and didn't stand up without the backing of Ben's strong tenor. That had been a bad day; one of the worst. Back home in the bed-sitting room they shared Una had raged and wept by turn, calling Ben by every bad name she could put her tongue to. But there were bigger fish in the sea, she told Rosalind, her cheeks pink and her eyes glittering. She would find a better agent. She would be a big star and show them all. The trouble was – she hadn't. *Soubrettes* weren't in demand any more, except at Christmas time for panto. Una was offered the role of Fairy Bluebell in *Jack and the Beanstalk* at a converted cinema in Peterborough, but she had heard that Ben and his new partner were playing Birmingham that year, with no less than three well-known television personalities topping the bill. If he heard – and he certainly would hear – that she was playing a number three date in a *cinema*, she'd die of shame and humiliation. There were more emotional tears and tantrums, which Rosalind had to soothe and placate. By now she was getting used to it.

The divorce finally came through and Una was awarded custody of Rosalind. Ben's maintenance cheques came regularly, which should have pleased her. It meant that they could afford the rent of a better flat, and eat properly. But it also meant that if Ben could afford the maintenance, he was working, while she was not. The thought that he was doing better than ever without her tore her apart. Snippets of news of him reached them via the grapevine and his name appeared in *The Stage*, the theatrical paper which

Una still bought and read avidly from cover to cover. His new singing partner was an outstanding success. 'Ben and the lovely Benita', they were billed as. Her real name was Freda Morton. She was blonde, and, at a mere nineteen, much younger than Una, a fact that wounded her deeply. They were booked for a world cruise on a new P & O luxury liner. After that there was television and radio work. When Rosalind spotted a photograph of them in the *Radio Times* one week she had to tear out the page and pretend it contained something she needed for school. To have let her mother see it would have been to trigger off at least a week of black depression.

For Una, things went from bad to worse. She had a handful of cabaret engagements; two disastrous club bookings where she was booed off the stage for being inaudible above the chatter of drinkers; then the jobs dried up altogether. She began to go to pieces alarmingly. Slowly the roles of mother and daughter were exchanged. It was ten-year-old Rosalind who wheedled Una out of her abysmal depressions; coaxed her to get up and put on her make-up – have something to eat. It was Rosalind who cleaned the flat, did the shopping and most of the cooking while Una lay in bed and sulked, mourning her lost career and her broken marriage; bitterly blaming her errant husband for it all. Her moods would swing from frenetic optimism to bleakest misery. It was nerve-racking, but to her resigned daughter it became no more than the normal daily routine.

The only good thing to come out of it all for Rosalind was that she was able to get a place at St Margaret's School. Una's deceased Irish parents had brought her up in the Catholic faith and when Rosalind came home from school distraught over failing her eleven-plus through the tension and overwork of her home life, Una's conscience jerked her sharply out of her apathy. In many ways it had been her saving grace. Dressing in her most sober outfit, she had taken Rosalind along to St Margaret's and demanded to see the headmistress. Una could be very persuasive when she put her mind to it. She claimed indignantly that her daughter's ability had been shamefully underestimated and that, as a Catholic, she was entitled to a place at St Margaret's.

The kettle boiled and Rosalind made her mug of coffee and carried it through to the living room where she had laid out her books. She had an English essay to write and she'd better get on with it, she told herself, looking at the clock. When her mother came home she would expect the evening meal to be ready.

The achievement of getting Rosalind into St Margaret's had been a turning point for Una. It had proved to her that she could get things moving if she made the effort. That autumn she had finally pulled herself together and taken charge of her life. Admitting to herself that her stage career was over, she took a job in the gown department of a West End department store. She hadn't found it easy. At first she had arrived home each evening tired and dispirited. Kicking off her shoes, she would declare herself exhausted and unable to do the job one day longer. But as the time went by and the lure of the footlights gradually faded she seemed to grow resigned to her new role as a single working mother. More than that, the job began to grow on her. She was promoted to second sales, then first, which meant a rise in salary and status. She had been in the job for five years now and she and Rosalind had settled down at last to something approaching a normal life.

Occasionally Una had been invited out by a man, but it never lasted very long. She had little interest in men who worked in shops or offices. They failed to excite her. She found them dull and boring. Sometimes, Rosalind wondered if she still loved Ben, but she never dared to ask. The mere mention of his name was enough to throw Una into a rage for the rest of the day.

It was almost an hour later when Rosalind looked up from her finished essay. She had worked longer than she'd intended. Hastily stuffing her books back into her satchel she laid the table for the evening meal and went into the kitchen. It was only then that she noticed the letter. It must have come after she had left for school. Una had thrown it on to the kitchen table along with the newspaper and a couple of circulars. It was addressed to Rosalind in her father's handwriting. Intrigued, she turned it over in her hand, wondering what he could be writing to her about. She had seen her father only a handful of times in the last nine years. Ben made contact with her only occasionally, usually by way of postcards from the more exotic places he played. Una always said that they were really meant to show *her* how well he was doing and not because he gave a tuppenny damn about his daughter. He sent her birthday cards too, and always a present at Christmas, but she saw him very rarely and this was the first time she had ever received a letter from him. Curious, she slipped her finger under the flap of the envelope and drew out the sheet of paper inside.

My dear Rosalind,
This is to invite you to come and stay with us for a few days in the Easter Holidays. Freda and I have bought a nice little place of our own in a village in Northamptonshire. Now that they've built the new M1 it's easy for us to get to at weekends. We've got a week out at Easter before we start rehearsing for a summer show in Brighton and we'd both love you to come and spend it with us. Now that you're older I want you and Freda to get to know each other as I'm sure you and she would get along well. Please try to come, Rosalind. Maybe you don't realise it, but you are the only blood relative I've got and in spite of what you might think, I've missed you all these years.
Give my best regards to your mother.
Hoping to see you soon,
Your loving father

Slowly and thoughtfully Rosalind folded the letter and pushed it into her skirt pocket. She was filled with mixed feelings. It was flattering to think that her father wanted to see her. Una had always been at great pains to point out that he cared less than nothing for her. Sometimes she could be so convincing that Rosalind had almost believed her, but by the sound of this letter he *did* still care about her. She found herself moved by what he had written and keen to accept the invitation. She had to admit that she was intrigued to meet Freda too, and to see this home they had bought for themselves. But the thought of her mother's reaction filled her with apprehension.

Una arrived home that evening in a good mood. She breezed into the kitchen where Rosalind was peeling potatoes and did not seem to notice that the meal was hardly started.

'Guess what?' she challenged as she took off her coat. 'I've been offered a new job. I was called into the general manager's office this afternoon. *Shaking* with nerves, I was. I thought I was going to get the sack. Then – right out of the blue – Mr Blake said he wanted me to organise a series of fashion shows the store is about to promote. He thought I'd do well because of my stage experience and – get this, Rossie – because of my *flair for fashion*. Can you believe that?' She threw herself into a chair and kicked off her shoes. 'He said he'd noticed how well turned out and attractive I always am!' She rolled her eyes and stretched out one shapely leg, hitching up her skirt to peer at it critically. 'Maybe your mum isn't over the hill yet, eh? Of course I'd noticed him giving me the once-over when he came up to the department, but I thought he was just – well, older men are like that. So you see, Rossie, – your mum isn't as useless as you thought she was.'

'I never thought you were,' Rosalind said.

Una leaned back in her chair and stretched her arms

luxuriously. 'Oh, I've got *so* many ideas. Bring a bit of life to the place, that's what I intend to do. Drag the department into the twentieth century.' Rummaging in her handbag for her cigarettes, she lit one and blew out a cloud of smoke. '*Just think*, I'm told I'll be attending the managers' meetings – having my say. Imagine, Rossie, your mum, *fashion show organiser*. Next thing you know we'll be moving to a better flat – nearer to the West End perhaps – or even a house. How'd you like that?'

Rosalind went on peeling potatoes, making no comment. Una always over-reacted to everything. She liked to dramatise what happened to her, good things as well as bad. There had been promises of better flats, ships coming in and dreams coming true many times before, alternating with dire prophecies of poverty and destitution. Still, it was good that she had something to be excited about this evening, Rosalind told herself. It would make it easier to break Ben's news.

The meal was easy, cold meat and chips, with tinned plums and custard to follow. When they had eaten Rosalind fingered the letter in her skirt pocket and wondered if it was the right time to tell her mother what was in it.

'I had a letter today,' she said tentatively

'Oh, yes, who from?'

'Dad, actually.'

Immediately she had her mother's attention. 'Ben! What did he want?'

Rosalind took out the letter and spread it out on the table for her mother to read, watching her face anxiously as she did so. Una scanned the few lines briefly, then frowned and read it through again. Finally she threw back her head with a derisive snort.

'A little place of our own, eh? How *sweet*! He must be feeling his age if he wants to settle down in some dump at the back of beyond, that's all I can say. Perhaps he's scared of losing *her*, so he's planning to bury her in the country out of harm's way.'

Rosalind bit her lip. 'He says he'd like me to go and stay in the Easter Holidays.'

'I can see that!' Una snapped. 'I suppose it suits him to admit he's got a daughter now that she's grown up. What about all those years you and me struggled on our own? Did he want his beloved *only blood relative* to go and visit him then? Like hell he did! Dead scared he might have to do something for you!'

'He never forgot to send us the money though, did he?'

'He did no more than he had to,' Una said bitterly. 'He could easily have afforded to send a bit more with what he was earning. Anyway, I'd have had him in court so fast his feet wouldn't have touched the ground if he'd stopped my maintenance. He knew that all right. That'd have looked bloody good in *The Stage*, wouldn't it?'

Rosalind's heart sank. Clearly Una would see her acceptance of her father's invitation as blatant betrayal. She got up and began to clear the table. Una lit a cigarette, watching her daughter through narrow eyes.

'You want to go, don't you?' she challenged.

'No.'

'Don't lie to me. You're disappointed because you think I don't want you to.'

Rosalind turned and looked at her. 'Well, you don't, do you?'

Una shrugged exaggeratedly. 'Why should I care? Go if you want to. Actually I was planning to take a week of my holiday at Easter. It was going to be a surprise. I thought we could go off somewhere and have a little holiday. But if you'd rather spend it with your father and his *tart* . . .'

'It's all right. I never intended to go anyway.'

'No? Then why did you show me the letter?'

'I thought you'd want to see it. I've never kept secrets from you, have I?'

Una looked away. 'No, you haven't. You've been a good girl; a better daughter than I deserve.' She ground out her cigarette and looked at Rosalind, her dark eyes brimming with the sudden tears that were so typical of her. 'It's just that I couldn't bear the thought of losing you, Rossie. That's really what upset me. Ben's all right. He's successful and he's got *her*. You're all I've got. I don't know what I'd do if I lost you now.' Reaching out for her daughter, she hugged her close.

Rosalind gently disentangled herself from her mother's suffocating embrace. 'Don't be silly, Mum. Even if I did go and visit Dad, you know I'd come back.'

'But you won't go, pet, will you? We'll book up somewhere nice for the holiday. I've got a bit of money saved. We'll go to Southend if you like, or Hastings. You've always liked the seaside. We can celebrate my new job. Just the two of us.'

'Yes, Mum,' Rosalind said resignedly. 'That'd be lovely.'

She didn't know what to do about her father's letter. For the two weeks that followed it burned a hole in her pocket and tortured her conscience. Again and again she got it out and read it, knowing she must reply and wondering what excuse she could make. Una's comments had made her curious. What lay behind the sudden invitation? Just why did he want her to visit when he had made so little attempt to keep up their relationship before? Finally, knowing that she could put off writing her letter of refusal no longer, she made up her mind to do it that very evening as soon as she had finished her homework. But before she had the chance to begin something happened to decide the matter once and for all.

Una was always unpredictable. Her reactions were never what one expected and Rosalind was used to her erratic changes of mood. But when she arrived home that evening and announced that she had decided that Rosalind should accept her father's invitation, she took her daughter completely off guard.

'But – I thought you didn't want me to go?'

Una turned to look into the mirror over the fireplace, unable to meet her daughter's candid brown eyes. 'I know, darling, and it's true, I didn't. Not at first.' She fiddled with her hair, lifting it away from her neck and viewing herself sideways. 'I know what I said, but I've been thinking. You're not a child any longer. You're a young woman now, and I know I can trust you. Maybe I'm being mean to both of you. After all, Ben is still your father, whatever he's done to me.'

A thought struck Rosalind. Suppose her father were ill, as Cathy Oldham's father had been ill? Perhaps there was some special reason for his wanting to see her; one that perhaps her mother knew about. Her manner certainly suggested that she wasn't being completely honest about this sudden change of heart.

'Well, if you really don't mind, I would quite like to go,' she said.

'Then you go, darling.' Una turned to her with a smile. 'Write him a nice letter straight away.'

'And you really don't mind – about our holiday and everything – about being alone for Easter?'

'Not a bit,' Una assured her brightly. 'I shall spring clean the flat or something. I'll find plenty to occupy me, don't you worry about me.'

Ben replied by return, saying how delighted he was to receive his daughter's acceptance and how much he was looking forward to seeing her. Arrangements were made that she should travel to Northampton by train on Good Friday where he would meet her with the car.

When she first stepped down from the train and looked around her she thought he wasn't there. Peering into the faces of the milling strangers on the platform she saw no one

51

whom she could recognise. Then she saw the man standing close to the ticket barrier looking anxiously around him and her heart contracted sharply. She had been expecting him to look the same as when she last saw him, but this man looked so much older. She reminded herself that it had been several years – six in fact – since they had last met. Her mother was now thirty-seven and she knew that Ben was six years older. That made him forty-three. He had put on weight. And his hair, once thick and wavy, was thinner and touched with grey. To Rosalind's dismay he looked old and she felt a lump gather in her throat.

As she stood watching he turned his head and saw her. For a moment he hesitated. He took a step towards her, then another. Then he was almost running. She put down her case and held out her arms.

'Dad.'

Unable to speak, he drew her to him and hugged her for a moment, then he held her at arm's length. As his eyes searched her face the familiar smile lit his eyes and to her relief he looked young again; more like the father she remembered.

'You're so grown up,' he said, shaking his head. 'I can hardly believe it. My little Rosalind. I'd begun to think you wouldn't come until I got your letter. Oh, it's so *good* to see you, baby.' He drew her arm through his and lifted her case. 'Come on, the car's waiting and Freda's got the tea on at home. She can't wait to meet you, but she wouldn't come to the station – said it was our private moment; yours and mine. She's very sensitive, Freda. I know you're going to like her.'

Sherwood Magna was enchanting. Rosalind had never seen a real village before. She thought they only existed in the pages of picture books, but this one was everything she had ever dreamed of. It had a village green with a duck pond, a thatched pub and an ancient church complete with tall elm trees. As well as an abundance of pretty cottages there was a manor house and a Georgian vicarage standing slightly aloof on the edge of the village. Rosalind turned to her father as they drove through.

'Where is your cottage?' she asked excitedly.

'Right here.' Ben turned in through an open white gate and along a short gravelled drive. As the cottage came into view Rosalind gasped with delight. Built of honey-coloured stone, it was small and square, had latticed windows and a thatched roof through which protruded a stout red brick chimney. Surrounding it was half an acre of garden consisting mainly of old apple trees, frothy with pink and white blossom. Under them, growing among the grass, was a wild profusion of bluebells and daffodils.

'Oh – it's *lovely*!' Rosalind breathed.

Ben brought the car to a halt and switched off the ignition. 'It's not so bad, is it?' he said proudly. 'When we first saw it it was almost derelict and there's still a lot to be done. We want to build a new kitchen on at the back, but we got a grant towards installing the bathroom and having the mains water and electricity laid on. When we found the cottage the only water came from a well out at the back.'

'A well? I didn't know there were any left. Can I see it? Is it still there?'

Ben laughed as he got out of the car. 'It certainly is. I wanted to have it filled in but Freda wouldn't hear of it. She's planning to make some kind of feature of it.' He opened the boot and swung her case out. 'Come on then. Come and see the inside of the place and meet Freda.'

The front door was painted white and Ben swung it open and stood back for Rosalind to enter. He had to bend his own head to pass under the low lintel as he followed her into the dim, stone-flagged hallway. To their left an open door gave on to a square living kitchen that ran from front to back of the cottage with a window at either end. Rosalind could see an Aga standing in a tiled recess and a dresser, its shelves edged with red and white gingham frills.

The floor was of red quarry tiles and in the centre of the room a table was already laid for tea with a gingham cloth and willow-patterned china. The back door was open and through it Rosalind glimpsed a paved yard and the well that her father had told her about.

Ben looked around. 'Well, this is it. Freda must be around somewhere . . .'

As he spoke a woman appeared in the open doorway. At once Rosalind was struck by her youth. Then she remembered that Freda was still only twenty-six, less than ten years her senior. Standing there framed in the doorway, the sunlight turned her fair hair to spun gold. She was slender, with the kind of figure Una had once had but now had to struggle to retain. She smiled and took a tentative step towards them.

'So this is Rosalind,' she said, holding out her hands. 'I've wanted to meet Ben's daughter for so long. This is a special occasion.'

Rosalind took the hands held out to her and felt her own squeezed warmly. 'How do you do?' she said shyly.

Freda smiled, her blue eyes sparkling. 'I'm fine. And I can't tell you how much your father and I have looked forward to having you to stay. I'll show you your room. I'm sure you must want to freshen up. Then we'll have tea, it's all ready.'

She slipped an arm around Rosalind's shoulders and guided her back into the hallway and up the narrow staircase. 'We've only got two bedrooms so it was easy to decide where to put you,' she joked. 'We had to turn the third into a bathroom. Before that there was just a loo out in the yard.' She giggled. 'Not very cosy in the middle of winter.'

The room was tiny. The walls were painted white and the ceiling sloped. On the bed was a rose-patterned bedspread that matched the curtains. Rosalind looked out of the tiny dormer window into the garden below with its tumble of apple blossom, daffodils and bluebells. Turning to Freda, she said: 'It's lovely. The whole place is lovely. Thank you for asking me.'

'Not at all. I only wish you could have come the other times we asked you.' She was busy turning down the bed to reveal frilled pillow slips. 'Ben was so disappointed. He's worried a lot about you, you know. He felt you were growing up without knowing him.' She turned with a smile. 'You're very like him. Well, I'll leave you to unpack. Come down when you're ready. I'll put the kettle on.'

When she'd gone Rosalind sat on the bed. What had Freda meant about the other times they had asked her? She knew nothing about them. Had her father written before – telephoned perhaps? Had Una turned down the invitations on her behalf without telling her? Slowly and thoughtfully she began to unpack and put away her things. Somehow, without betraying her mother, she must find out.

The week went by all too quickly. The village and the cottage were a delight to Rosalind. Freda and she got along well right from the start, and getting to know her father again was much easier than she had thought. The weather was fine, warmer than normal for the time of year. They had picnics and drives out into the beautiful undulating countryside, fresh and green with burgeoning spring.

One evening Ben and Freda treated Rosalind to a première of the songs they'd been rehearsing for their latest repertoire. She sat enthralled in the pretty drawing room of the cottage as Ben played the little upright piano and the two of them sang. From the first it was clear to her that Freda's lovely bell-like soprano voice was better than Una's had ever been. It blended beautifully with Ben's melodious tenor. One of their new songs was particularly moving. Rosalind hadn't heard it before. It was from the new musical version of *Oliver Twist* and was called, *As Long As He Needs Me*. Something in the way Freda looked – the depth of emotion she put into the song's lyrics – seemed to

Rosalind to encapsulate her feelings for her father. Later, that night as she lay in bed, she reflected that, unpalatable as the fact might be to Una, it was undoubtedly Freda who was responsible for Ben's leap to success.

It was on her last day but one that Ben had a telephone call from his agent and had to go up to London. After they'd waved him off together at the gate Freda turned to Rosalind.

'Well, we've got the day to ourselves. What shall we do with it?'

Rosalind shrugged. 'I don't mind. We don't have to do anything. I just like being here.'

'Do you? Do you really?' Freda blushed with pleasure as she looked at her. 'Ben worried so much about whether you'd like it here – whether you'd like *us*. He thought you might be bored.'

Rosalind laughed. 'Bored? In a place like this. After Burnt Oak it's like a little corner of heaven.'

Linking her arm through Rosalind's Freda began to walk back to the cottage. 'He felt he didn't really know you, you see – the grown-up you, I mean. He had all sorts of notions about how you might have changed. It was almost like inviting a stranger. He was so apprehensive; nervous as a kitten on the day you arrived.'

'Nervous – at meeting me?' Rosalind guessed that what he had been afraid of was that she might have allowed Una to poison her mind against him. She looked at Freda. 'On the day I first came you said something about the other times he'd invited me?'

'That's right. We only had the flat in town then, of course, but we'd both have liked you to come. Ben was so pleased that you'd been able to get a scholarship to St Margaret's at a reduced fee and he wanted so much to keep track of your progress.'

Rosalind frowned. 'No. You've got it wrong. I got into St Margaret's free – on a scholarship.'

56

'Of course. How silly of me.' Freda turned away quickly but not before Rosalind had seen her flushed cheeks. Clearly there was more to all this than she realised and she was determined to get to the bottom of it.

'Tell me,' she demanded. 'Tell me the truth. I didn't get in for nothing, did I? Dad pays.'

They were inside the cottage now and Freda sat down at the kitchen table, her face troubled. 'Oh, dear. I've put my foot in it. I shouldn't have said anything. Forget it. Ben would be so cross if he knew.'

'I won't say anything,' Rosalind promised. 'Just tell me. I have a right to know.'

Freda sighed unhappily. 'Your mother wrote. It seems you passed the entrance exam all right, but when they knew Una had lapsed – that you hadn't actually been brought up in the Catholic faith – they weren't so sure. In the end, when your mother persisted, they agreed to a compromise and offered you a place at a reduced fee.'

'And Mum wrote to Dad and asked him to pay?'

Freda nodded. 'Oh, he was happy to do it, believe me. More than happy. He felt it was the least he could do for you. And it was your mother who stuck to her guns and insisted on a place for you.' She paused. 'All the same, Ben would have liked to see you more.'

'And she wouldn't let me come?'

'She thought it would unsettle you. She pointed out that you'd suffered enough over the break-up. And of course we were never in the same place for more than a few days at a time.' She reached out to take Rosalind's hand. 'Look, I know how you feel, believe me, I do. My parents were divorced too. They never stopped arguing, even after they split up, and most of their rows were about me. I know how guilty and wretched it makes you feel, but you shouldn't. It's not your fault, Rossie. Please try to remember that.'

Rosalind swallowed hard. Freda was trying hard to be fair, to make excuses, but they both knew that keeping her from her father had been Una's way of paying him back for taking a new and younger partner, and for being a success. 'Yes, I suppose all they both want really is what is best for me,' she said. 'Thank you for telling me.'

'It's between ourselves, mind?' Freda said anxiously.

Rosalind frowned. 'Of course. I promise. After all, I asked you to tell me.' She longed to go away by herself, creep upstairs to the privacy of her room to think it all through; to try to justify her mother's cruel deception. But Freda was changing the subject, obviously anxious to lighten the mood.

'Right. Now, have you ever thought of trying your hair in a different style?' she said brightly. 'And what about wearing something a little more frivolous – maybe a bright colour? Red would suit you. Let's go upstairs and see what we can find for you.'

When Ben came back that evening he looked in through the kitchen window and saw the two of them busy preparing supper; laughing together over the stove as relaxed and friendly as sisters or school friends. He could see that Freda had been doing Rosalind's hair. She'd washed and set it so that it fell in soft curls, framing her small face. She wore a little make-up too, and a red blouse that he recognised as one of Freda's. It warmed his heart to see them getting along so well. He'd had so many fears and misgivings about this visit; been so afraid that his daughter might be lost to him for ever.

It had been a good day. He'd just signed a new recording contract and heard that there was a strong possibility of a spot for them on a television Christmas Special to begin filming in the autumn. He had stopped off on his way home to buy a bottle of champagne with which to celebrate. He couldn't wait to see Freda's face light up when he told her. What a wonderful week it had been. Golden spring days in their new home; the prospect of well-paid work; but perhaps best of all, having his daughter back after the long parting.

On the day that Rosalind travelled back to London the weather broke. Ben drove her to the station and stood with her on the dripping platform as they waited for the train.

'Thank you for giving me such a marvellous time,' Rosalind said. 'I've enjoyed it all so much.'

'I'm glad. It's been wonderful having you with us.' Ben smiled down at her. 'Now that you've been once, I hope you'll make regular visits to the cottage.'

'I'd love to.' She looked up at him. 'Dad – are you and Freda going to get married?'

He smiled. 'I was wondering when you were going to ask me that.' He cocked an eyebrow at her. 'Did you ask her?'

She shook her head. 'No, I didn't like to. But I can see how much she loves you.'

Ben sighed. 'I love her too. And I know it's what she'd like, but I feel it isn't fair. She's so much younger than me, Rossie. All of seventeen years. I'm old enough to be her father. It's too big a gap.' He laughed. 'Do you really think a lovely girl like Freda deserves to be tied to an old man? It wouldn't be fair.'

'But you're not an old man. And if you love each other, surely . . .?'

Ben bent to kiss his daughter's forehead. 'It's not quite as simple as that, baby, as you'll find out for yourself one day. Sometimes love can be a selfish thing. And it's hardly ever enough on its own. Ask your mother,' he added with a wry smile. 'Sometimes there are . . .' The end of his sentence was drowned by the crackling of the public address system as the station announcer began to speak.

Rosalind wondered fleetingly if her father still had a weakness for other women; if that was why he didn't want to marry again. But she was sure he was wrong about

Freda. She wouldn't care about the age difference. She loved him unreservedly; anyone could see that. Rosalind hated the thought of sweet, gentle Freda being hurt or feeling rejected. She hadn't turned out to be at all like Una had led her to believe. She wasn't a tart at all.

The London train pulled in alongside the platform and Ben handed her case up to her and slammed the door securely.

'Bye-bye, baby. Write to us if you have a minute off from all that studying.'

Rosalind leaned as far out of the window as she dared. 'Dad,' she said urgently as the train began to move. 'Dad . . .' She reached for his hand and he took it, walking down the platform with the train. 'Take care of Freda.'

He laughed. 'I will.'

'And, Dad – I never thanked you.'

'Of course you did.'

'No. I mean for the – for my . . .' The train was beginning to gather speed now and Ben was forced to let go of her hand. '*For my school fees,*' she called. 'It was good of you to pay them. It's a nice school. I – I love it there.' The distance between them was lengthening, but she could still see his face clearly. His eyes were slightly puzzled as he looked at her, his hand half raised.

'I'll do well, Dad,' she called, her throat thick with tears. 'I'll work hard and make you glad. I promise.'

When she arrived home the flat was empty. She looked for a note but there was none. Una must have slipped out to the shop for something. Looking round she saw that her mother hadn't fulfilled her promise to spring clean the flat. There was dust everywhere and unwashed dishes in the kitchen. She went to her room and began to unpack, putting her things carefully away in the wardrobe and drawers. She was still wearing the red blouse that Freda had given her. It fitted perfectly and the colour made her feel light-hearted. Freda had shown her how to put the rollers in to her hair too, to give its straightness a lift. And as she was helping her to pack she'd popped the coral lipstick Rosalind liked into a corner of her case.

'I've never used it. It isn't really my colour,' she said. 'But it suits you beautifully so you might as well have it.'

Rosalind found it at the bottom of the case and put some on, peering into the dressing-table mirror as she pressed her lips together. It did make a difference. So did the blouse and the hair. They made her feel quite a different person. Perhaps she wasn't quite so desperately plain after all. Freda had told her she had nice eyes and that maybe next time they needed testing she could ask the optician about trying the new contact lenses. It would be lovely not to have to wear the glasses any more. She heard the sound of a key in the door and went out to meet her mother.

Una stood with her back to her in the small hallway, taking her key out of the lock. She wore her best suit and her highest heels with sheer black stockings, and there was a suitcase on the floor beside her. When she turned and saw Rosalind she gave a small cry of alarm.

'*Oh!*' She clutched at her throat with one gloved hand. 'Oh, my God, you scared the living daylights out of me. I wasn't expecting you home till later this evening.'

Rosalind was looking at the case. 'You've been away after all then?'

Una was instantly defensive. 'Yes. Anything wrong with that?'

'No, of course not. I just thought you said . . .'

'What on earth have you done to yourself?' Una interrupted, peering at her with narrowed eyes. 'Where did you get that awful blouse and what *do* you think your hair looks like?'

Rosalind put a hand up to her hair uncertainly. 'I set it – put some rollers in. Freda showed me how, and she gave me the blouse. She said the colour suited me.'

Una gave a disapproving grunt as she lifted her suitcase and headed for her bedroom. 'Huh! I might have known *she'd* had a hand in it. You look an absolute fright. The woman obviously has no taste at all.' She dumped her case on the bed and turned to look at Rosalind standing in the doorway. 'Well, don't just stand there. Come and give me a hand to unpack. Or better still, go and put the kettle on, I'm gasping for a cup of tea.'

Ten minutes later Una appeared in the kitchen doorway in her dressing gown and slippers.

'Tea's made,' Rosalind said. 'There aren't any biscuits though.'

Una sat down at the table. 'I know. I haven't had time to go shopping.' She glanced at her watch. 'The shops will still be open. When you've had your tea you'd better pop down to the corner and get a few things.'

Rosalind's heart sank. 'All right.'

'Well, don't sound so enthusiastic about it! I expect you've been spoiled rotten down in Little Piddling or whatever it's called, but you're home now. Time to come down to earth again.' She looked at her daughter speculatively. 'I take it you had a good time?'

'Yes, thanks.'

Una sipped her tea. 'Well – aren't you going to ask me if I did then?'

'I – thought you'd tell me if you wanted me to know.'

Una looked at her sharply. 'What's that supposed to mean? Being sarky, are we?' Before Rosalind had time to reply she hurried on: 'Well, as it happens I *did* have a good time. I stayed in a hotel in the West End and saw the latest shows. I had some wonderful meals too. We ate at the Savoy Grill on Friday, and last night . . .'

'We?' Rosalind looked at her mother enquiringly. 'Who did you go with?'

'I was coming to that.' Una put down her cup. 'I've been seeing Don – Mr Blake – ever since I started my new job,' she said. 'I never said anything before because he's been in the throes of divorce, poor love. His wife is a vindictive bitch by all accounts, so we've had to be very discreet. It's all over now though and this week has been a real tonic for Don after what he's been through. And for me too, of course.'

'I see.'

Una looked at her daughter sharply. 'No, you don't! It wasn't a dirty weekend or anything like that. Don has asked me to marry him.' She sat back, smiling with satisfaction. 'And you might as well know that I've said yes.'

Rosalind was already wondering just how much her mother's forthcoming marriage would change their lives. 'Does he – does he know about me?' she asked.

'My God!' Una raised to the ceiling. 'If that isn't typical. No – *Congratulations, Mum.* No – *I hope you'll be happy.* Just, *What's going to happen to me?*' She lit a cigarette and blew the smoke explosively at the ceiling. 'You're your father's daughter all right.'

'Of course I'm glad for you if it's what you want,' Rosalind said painfully. 'But I do need to know where I stand too.'

'You *stand* wherever you want to. Of course Don knows about you. How could I keep you from him? He's quite looking forward to meeting you if you want to know. He's perfectly happy for you to live with us when we're married.' She tapped ash thoughtfully into her saucer. 'Or perhaps after this week you'd prefer to go and live with your father?'

Rosalind coloured. 'I haven't been asked,' she said quietly.

Una laughed. 'No? And it's my guess that you won't be, so you'd better make the best of what's on offer, hadn't you?' She stubbed out her half-smoked cigarette and reached across the table to give Rosalind's shoulder a push. 'Oh, for God's sake, stop looking like a wet weekend and cheer up! Don's got a good job and plenty of money. We'll be living like lords when he and I get hitched. You'll be quids in.'

Rosalind washed up the cups while her mother went off to have a bath. The flat was no palace, but she hated the thought of moving into a new home with a man she'd never met. What was he like, this Don Blake? And would he really take kindly to sharing a house with her? She thought fondly of the cottage and dreamed of living there. But it was only a weekend home – not even that during the summer when 'Ben and Benita' would be sharing top billing in Brighton. She couldn't see any way she could live with them while she was still at school, even if they wanted her to. She dried the cups and put them away carefully. It boiled down to the same old thing really. Everyone else had their own lives. She was in the way again. An embarrassing liability.

Chapter Three

As the last notes of the concerto died and the audience broke into enthusiastic applause, Gerald rose to his feet with relief. His palms were sticky and his head was buzzing with tension. As Carl Kramer led him forward to take his ovation Gerald thought he caught a fleeting look of concern in the conductor's eyes. Those mishandled phrases in the slow movement, the faltering fingering. He had recovered in seconds. It would have taken a seasoned musician to spot them. But Carl Kramer *was* a seasoned musician. One of the finest conductors in the world. They had worked together many times and they respected each other. Carl would certainly have noticed. But it was clear from the audience's reaction that for them Gerald's performance had been as brilliant and faultless as ever. He took a final bow and walked off the platform.

In his dressing room he removed his tail coat and white tie and slipped into his comfortable dressing gown, then he poured himself a large Scotch: the treat he always allowed himself after the performance – never before. Sitting down at the dressing table he regarded himself critically in the mirror. The signs of fatigue were there in the lines of tiredness and the dark smudges around the eyes, the slight hollowing beneath the cheekbones. But surely it was only natural? The tour had been the longest he had ever made, the schedule heavy and exhausting. He flexed his fingers, trying to ignore the painful stiffness in the joints. What was worse than the stiffness was their sudden and unpredictable refusal to obey his commands; those inexplicable memory lapses. Works he had performed a hundred times would

65

be momentarily wiped out as though he had never played them before, often frighteningly, like tonight, in the middle of a performance. But surely even that was understandable at the end of such a punishing schedule? He tried to assure himself. It could all be put down to tension – nervous exhaustion – though he was forced to admit that he had never experienced it before.

As he sipped his whisky and felt the warmth seeping through his veins and relaxing him, he heard the first bars of the Beethoven symphony through the dressing room intercom. The concert was continuing. Music and the show, like life, went on. However talented, however acclaimed and celebrated a concert artist might be, there was always a new someone, more talented, more brilliant than ever before, waiting to thrill and inspire the fickle and voracious fans. Had his time come already at the age of forty-one? Was his career tottering on the edge of oblivion just when he should be in his prime?

He swallowed the last of his whisky and hurriedly changed into his outdoor clothes. The fans wouldn't gather until after the concert was over. He would get back to his hotel and have an early night. He didn't feel like seeing anyone. If Carl wanted an explanation then he should have one. He was entitled to that. But he must first think it out – make it a good and a plausible one. It wouldn't do to have rumours starting. And at the moment he didn't feel up to it. His mind didn't seem to be functioning properly.

Leaving his hire car in the car park he took a taxi back to the hotel. He couldn't face the mad jostle of the New York streets tonight. Once in his room he rang down to room service for sandwiches and coffee. He ate, then undressed and showered. He was just about to get into bed when there was a soft knock on the door. With a sigh he drew on his dressing gown and went to open it. Kay Goolden stood on the threshold. She wore a pastel mink jacket over her black Givenchy evening gown and the expression on her exquisitely made-up face was a mixture of anxiety and annoyance.

'So *here* you are! I went round to your dressing room after the concert and you'd gone. I've been worried sick.'

His heart sank as he turned back into the room, leaving her to follow. 'I'm sorry. I wasn't feeling too good. I thought an early night would . . .'

'But you didn't even leave me a message,' she interrupted indignantly. 'Surely you hadn't forgotten that we were having dinner together?'

Gerald sat down on the bed. He had forgotten. The worry over the mess he had made of the slow movement had rattled and upset him. The last thing he wanted at this moment was Kay whining about a forgotten dinner date.

Kay Goolden worked in the PR department of his recording company. They'd met when she was doing the publicity for his last but one album and they'd been lovers for the past year. Kay was good at her job, but he'd wished more than once since the tour began that he had never suggested her accompanying him. She could be protective to the point of claustrophobia. Sometimes she treated him like a retarded five year old, leaping in to speak for him as though he was incapable of speaking or thinking for himself.

He rubbed a hand across his brow. 'I'm sorry, Kay. I told you, I wasn't feeling too good.'

'What is it?' She crossed the room and placed a hand on his forehead. 'A touch of flu maybe. Shall I get you some Paracetamol?'

'No, thanks.'

'It's no trouble. I've got some in my room. Maybe I'd better move in here with you tonight, then I can keep an eye on you.' She crossed the room to the telephone. 'I'll ring down to room service and get them to . . .'

'Leave it!' He felt the familiar irritation twang his nerves.

'For God's sake, Kay, I told you, I'm all right. Just tired, that's all.'

'All right, there's no need to snap my head off.' She slipped off her jacket and moved closer to him, slipping her arms around his waist and rubbing herself against him provocatively. 'I think I know what you need to relax you,' she said softly.

He pushed her away. 'No, you don't. Not this time.'

Kay stiffened, her seductive smile changing to a pout of resentment. 'What's the matter, Gerry? You can tell me. Didn't the concert go as well as you wanted it to?'

He looked at her intently. 'What do you mean by that? Who's been talking to you?'

'No one.' She backed away from him. 'For heaven's sake, Gerry, why are you so damned touchy? What on earth is the matter with you?'

'I told you, I'm tired. It's the tour. Thank God there's only one more week to go.'

'It's not just that. You haven't been yourself since we left London. Are you tired of me – is that it?'

He sighed. 'Look, Kay, I don't need this just now. Leave me to get a decent night's rest, will you? I'll be fine in the morning.'

Her face darkened. 'You've found someone else, haven't you? It's so obvious. There was a time when you couldn't get enough of me, but ever since we came on this tour you've showed a marked lack of interest to say the least.'

'There's no one else, Kay. Why must you always assume that what ever is wrong with me is down to you?'

'What else am I supposed to think? It's not very flattering, lying in bed next to someone who turns his back on you night after night. I'm not so thick that I can't take a hint, you know. I don't have to be hit over the head with a sledge hammer!'

Gerald winced. Her voice was like a steel saw, grinding into his already aching head. 'For Christ's sake, Kay, surely you of all people can understand that the tension of two concerts a day for weeks on end . . .'

She gave an explosive little snort. '*Tension!* There was a time when all that adrenalin made you as randy as hell. Now you're saying it just claps you out, are you? Well, I don't believe you, Gerry. I wouldn't put it past you to be two-timing me with one of those giggling little groupies who hang around after you. But then I suppose at your age flattery and reassurance are pretty important, especially when your playing is on the skids!'

'What the hell do you mean?' His head was pounding as he reached out to grab her wrist.

'Let go of me!' She shook him off angrily. 'Who the hell do you think you are?' Tears of humiliation stood in her eyes as she faced him. 'I've had about enough of your temper tantrums on this trip, Gerry. You've really shown yourself in your true colours. I've worked damned hard ever since we met to build a good image for you and to shield you from the public. If this is all the thanks I get I might as well let your precious fans find out what you're really like!' She flounced to the door. 'Tonight is the last straw as far as I'm concerned. I'll be taking the first plane home in the morning. If you want another publicist you'd better get on to Zenith and get them to send you someone!'

He groaned as the door slammed behind her. A scene with Kay was the last thing he needed tonight. But truth to tell, all he really felt about her leaving was relief. Women could be so demanding. They wanted all of you. At first it was enough just to be seen with a celebrity – to bask in the reflected glory. Then they wanted more of your time – or your money, or both. Finally they wanted to own you, body and soul. To eat you up and swallow you whole. He'd first discovered this fact when he'd married Sara at twenty. She was a fellow music student and together they planned to take Europe by storm with their talent. The marriage had lasted just eighteen months. When it failed Sara had

69

blamed him for wrecking her career; accusing him of doing it deliberately because she had more talent than he had. Was there, anywhere in the world, he asked himself, an undemanding woman capable of thinking of someone other than herself?

Remembering Sara's wild accusations reminded him of Kay's remark about letting the fans see him as he really was. Was it a veiled threat? Would she really be vindictive enough to rat on him to the press? He decided not. It would cost her her job with Zenith Records and she'd never let that happen. Then he recalled something else she'd said; something even more disturbing. *Especially when your playing is on the skids.* Kay was hardly a music buff. If she'd noticed . . . His heart sank. It was even worse than he'd thought.

Gerald woke feeling much better. He had been worrying for nothing, he told himself. Last night's little lapse was due to nothing worse than fatigue. As for Kay – she had lashed out wildly, knowing that any remark about his playing would hurt. All the same, he hoped she'd meant it when she said she was catching the first plane home. She'd been getting far too possessive for comfort lately.

He got up and showered, planning the day ahead. The sooner he talked to Carl, the better, he decided. He was dressed and looking up the conductor's number when the telephone rang. It was Reception. Mr Kramer was here to see him. Could they send him up?

Carl Kramer was a handsome man in his late-fifties. His Jewish parents had arrived in America from Poland at the turn of the century and proceeded to bring up their large family. Parents and children were all musical and Carl had been involved with music since childhood. Since the end of the war he had risen to the heights, first as a concert violinist, then as conductor. During his career Carl had seen many concert soloists come and go. He and Gerald Cavelle had worked together on many occasions and he liked and respected the pianist enough to be concerned about him.

Gerald went out to the lift to greet the maestro with a feeling of apprehension. For Carl to be coming to him was ominous to say the least. But as the lift doors opened he put on his brightest smile and held out his hands in welcome.

'Carl! This is an unexpected pleasure. I hope you'll join me for breakfast.'

'Thank you, but I've already breakfasted.'

Almost as tall as Gerald, the conductor had a shock of silver hair and piercing eyes that were so dark as to appear almost black. Gerald met their searching look now with some trepidation.

'Coffee then? You'll have some coffee?'

The conductor smiled and bowed his head. 'That would be very pleasant.'

In the suite Carl took the seat Gerald offered him at the breakfast table, which had been laid out on the covered balcony that overlooked Manhattan. He watched as Gerald poured coffee, noticing the slight tremor of his hand as he passed him the cup.

'You must be wondering why I am here,' he said. 'I went to your dressing room after the concert last night and found you'd left.'

Gerald shook his head. 'As a matter of fact I was about to ring you – to apologise for last night.'

'There is no need. You covered the mishap extremely well. I doubt whether the audience was even aware that anything was amiss. I am concerned however – for you, my friend. I think you are not yourself. Are you ill?'

'No!' Gerald took a deep draught of his coffee. 'At least I don't think so. I don't really know. I put it down to tiredness. I certainly feel much better this morning.'

'I'm glad, but – forgive me, Gerald – there have been other occasions during this tour.'

71

He looked at the conductor sharply. 'You've heard . . . someone has said . . .?'

Carl lifted his shoulders. 'These things soon get around. Bad news travels fast, as they say.' He put down his cup and leaned towards Gerald. 'I'm here this morning to give you some advice as a friend and fellow musician, Gerald. Cancel the rest of your tour. There can't be many more concerts to go. See a doctor. Treat yourself to a good rest.'

Gerald's heartbeat quickened. 'What are you saying, Carl? You think I'm – finished?'

'No, *no*! It could be nothing worse than tiredness, as you say. But I have to be frank with you; the way you are playing at the moment is doing nothing for your reputation.' He reached across the table to touch Gerald's sleeve. 'Check on your health, my friend. Eliminate the worst possibilities and deal with what is left. It could be that your concentration is suffering through overwork and that all you need is a prolonged holiday.'

Gerald swallowed hard. Inside he felt the cold hand of fear clutch at his guts. He'd been fooling himself into believing that it was all in his mind. Now he knew otherwise. Others had noticed. It was true. He had a problem. A real problem. One that he was going to have to meet and cope with – alone. He forced himself to smile.

'Maybe I'll do as you say, Carl. Though I don't know about cancelling the rest of the tour. There'd be one hell of a stink if I cried off now. We're due to fly to Boston the day after tomorrow and it's a heavy programme. Twelve concerts during next week.'

'Then see a doctor today,' Carl advised. 'Face it, Gerald. You're not up to one more concert. Let alone twelve. If you go ahead you'll risk damaging your career, perhaps permanently. Cancel. They can hardly argue with a doctor's opinion.' He pulled out one of his cards and began to write on the back. 'This is the name of my own physician. He's the best there is. Tell him I sent you and he'll fit you in this morning.'

Gerald tried to control the trembling of his fingers as he took the card. 'You make it sound – so serious,' he said with a shaky laugh.

'It is,' Carl said candidly. 'What could be more serious than your health, Gerald? Especially when it is threatening to affect your career? Please, take my advice and see him.'

On his way out of the hotel Gerald enquired about Kay at the desk and learned that she had checked out at nine-thirty that morning – booked herself on the eleven-thirty flight for London. He looked at his watch. She'd be boarding about now. He'd been glad when she'd said their affair was over, but now he wasn't so sure. It might have been comforting to have had someone along with him when he saw this Doctor Brewster. As he crossed the hall he took out his dark glasses and put them on, then he asked the doorman to call him a cab.

Gerald came out of the Curie Medical Building and stood for a moment on the pavement watching the people and traffic rush by. People – scores of them – all going their own way, their minds intent on their own worries. Odd, but he'd never given them a thought before. Until now people had been divided into two groups. Music lovers and others. If they didn't go to his concerts, if they weren't fans, they simply didn't exist. Now, in his stunned state, he suddenly saw that to some extent they all had something in common. They were all basically insecure when it came to their own mortality; all afraid, not only of death but of facing the future alone.

Doctor Brewster had been chillingly positive in his diagnosis, but he had advised Gerald to seek a second opinion for his own peace of mind.

'When you get back to London you should see your own

73

doctor,' he had advised. 'There are tests you could undergo and it would be wise to do so, so as to be perfectly sure, you understand?'

'And the treatment?' Gerald had asked. 'How long does it take to be cured? I'm a concert pianist. I need to be able to work.'

His heart was leaden as he remembered the look on the doctor's face and the way he had shaken his head.

'I have to be perfectly frank with you, Mr Cavelle. Parkinson's Disease is manageable. Nowadays, thanks to research it can be controlled. As for a cure, that is something that so far has eluded medical science.' He looked thoughtful. 'I have a colleague who is working on a research project at Edinburgh University. I'm sure he would be interested in your case. I'll write to him if you like.'

'Are you okay, sir? Can I get you a cab?' The doorman was used to seeing people come out of the Curie Building looking dazed and he prided himself on his sympathetic and helpful manner. He put a tentative hand under Gerald's elbow but he shrugged the man off impatiently.

'I'm quite all right, thank you. It's only a couple of blocks. I'll walk.'

I've got to get home, he thought. There has to be an answer. It couldn't be possible in 1961 that there was no known cure. Even this morning the papers were full of the latest space shot. The Russians had already put a man out there and now the Americans were planning to do it too. Why were they so bloody keen to get to other planets when there were people dying of incurable illnesses on this one? It was ridiculous. There must be a doctor somewhere with the answer. He'd pin all his hopes on this doctor in Edinburgh. Being a guinea pig was better than nothing! He'd ring his agent – tell him to call off the rest of the tour. Then he'd get the hotel receptionist to book him on the next flight to London.

Home. He pictured the flat, its spacious rooms echoing with emptiness. His piano standing silently in the window. Then the thought of that other piano, Dan Oldham's baby grand that he was storing for Cathy. He wondered whether she had been to play it during his absence and found himself hoping that she had. It was comforting to think of her there. Suddenly, and with startling clarity, he remembered her eyes, green as the springtime sea, and that extraordinary amber-gold hair. *Cathy*. He said the name to himself, remembering how sweetly she had clung to him that afternoon in the attic of that hideous little house in Edgware. 'I'm coming home, Cathy,' he said aloud, and somehow found solace in the thought that there was at least one person who would be happy to see him.

Chapter Four

The envelope was waiting beside Cathy's plate when she came down to breakfast. Three pairs of eyes watched her as she nervously slid her finger under the flap. She glanced at Johnny.

'I can't look,' she said, passing the envelope across the table. 'You open it.'

Johnny shook her head. 'Oh, no. I think you should see it first, love,' she said. 'Go on. Take a deep breath and look. We're all waiting.'

But still Cathy stared at the folded sheet of paper. 'Oh dear. I wish . . .' Suddenly the letter was snatched from her hand by Matthew whose long arm shot across the table without warning.

'Oh, for heaven's sake, give it here.' He unfolded the letter and scanned it quickly, then gave her a rueful look across the table. 'Oh, well,' he said with a sympathetic look. 'Better luck next time, eh?' He tossed the letter back to her and rose from the table to pull on his jacket. 'Time I was going, I suppose.'

Cathy snatched up the letter, her cheeks very pink, and read it hurriedly, then she too was on her feet, half crying, half laughing. 'Matthew Johnson – you absolute *pig*!' She punched him on the shoulder.

Old Mrs Bains clicked her tongue disapprovingly. 'Oh dear, oh dear. What a way to talk. Young people nowadays.' She wagged an admonishing finger at Cathy. 'You may have failed your exams, young lady, but there's no need to . . .'

'But I *haven't*,' Cathy said, swinging round, her eyes shining. 'Look.' She held out the letter. 'Two grade ones, three twos, a three and a four. And that was only RE so as I'm not planning to be a nun it isn't important.' She laughed delightedly. 'Oh, I can't wait to tell Gerald.'

Matthew grinned at her. 'Took a good shock to make you look though, didn't it, chicken?' He looked at his watch. 'Have to go or I'll miss the bus. I'll have my champagne and cake when I get home, okay?'

After he'd gone Cathy helped Johnny to clear the table and wash up, her head still spinning with euphoria.

'I want to leave school now that I've got my O's, Johnny,' she said. 'I don't think I could face another two years of slogging away.'

'Your father had his heart set on your going to university,' Johnny told her as she put away the dishes. 'I think he felt you were capable of it.'

'Fathers always think their daughters are cleverer than they really are,' Cathy said. 'I want to get a job and start earning my living. Then I can pay you for my keep out of my earnings. It isn't really right that Gerald should keep paying.'

'I don't think he is, yet. There must still be money left from the house,' Johnny reminded her. 'I don't think you need worry yet awhile.' She looked anxiously at the girl who was like a daughter to her. 'It's a mistake to rush into some dead end job just for the sake of leaving school, love,' she said kindly. 'I dare say everyone feels as you do at this stage. If you really don't want to go to university how about training for something at college?'

Cathy stood staring out of the kitchen window dreamily. 'I can't really think of anything I'd like to study,' she said. 'My music isn't good enough and I hate the thought of shorthand and typing, or anything else that means being stuck in some office all day. I had thought about nursing. I like looking after people.' She turned with a smile. 'And I really enjoy helping you in the house – cooking and sewing and making things nice.

You've taught me such a lot about that since I've been here.'

'What about domestic science then?' Johnny said triumphantly. 'You could take a course in that. And maybe when you're qualified you could teach it in some nice school. It'd certainly stand you in good stead for when you have a home of your own.'

Cathy took the letter out of her pocket and looked at it again. 'It says we have to go to school tomorrow afternoon,' she said. 'There's a meeting with the head and the careers mistress so that we can make up our minds what we're going to do next term.'

'Right, then you can get it all fixed up.' Johnny wiped her hands and took off her apron. 'I dare say they'll be able to give you a list of colleges. Would you like me to come along with you?'

Cathy shook her head. 'I'd better go alone. I'm going to have to get used to doing things for myself from now on, aren't I?'

Upstairs in her room she made her bed and then sat down to look at her letter again. The grades were better than she'd dared to hope for. But then she had worked hard. Now all she wanted was to have the pleasure of telling Gerald and seeing his face. He'd be home very soon now. The last postcard she'd had from him was of Times Square, New York. *Only one more week*, he'd written. And that was a fortnight ago. She would be hearing from him any day now.

Would he be surprised that she hadn't taken up his invitation to go to his flat? she wondered. There had been lots of times when she had wanted to. She still missed Dad. On some days it was so bad that she just wanted to be by herself. Johnny always knew when she felt like that and left her alone, but playing his piano – even just touching it – would have helped so much. One Saturday afternoon she had even taken the tube up to the West End and walked right up to the building. But it had looked so grand and so formidable that she had walked straight past. She hadn't had the nerve to go in and ask the caretaker for a key as Gerald had suggested.

She wondered how all her friends had fared in the exams. Carla had hardly done any revision at all. She'd been much keener on going to the pictures or dancing. Rosalind Blair would have done well though. She always did. She had known exactly what subjects to take because she had no doubts about her future career. It must be nice to have no doubts about what you really wanted to do, Cathy thought.

When she arrived at St Margaret's the following afternoon the hall was full of excited chatter as the girls exchanged news and exam results. To Cathy's surprise Carla had scraped through four of the five subjects she had taken and seemed not to mind at all having low grades.

'I've decided to go to teacher training college,' she announced.

Cathy stared at her incredulously. 'Is that really what you want?'

Carla pulled a face. 'Dad's idea. He reckons it's a safe, secure job. His alternative was the bank. Teaching's the lesser of two evils, I reckon, and you do get lovely long holidays.'

'But it means you'll have to stay on and take some A's.'

Carla shrugged. 'I suppose so. Still, who knows what might happen in the meantime?' she said. 'I might meet some handsome millionaire and get married.'

Miss Hanley, Cathy's form mistress, was doubtful about the domestic science idea. 'I think you should go away and give it some more thought, Catherine,' she said. 'I really feel that you're capable of something a little more academic. Domestic science is fine, but you have a good enquiring mind and I'm afraid DS wouldn't stretch you enough.'

79

'I did think about nursing,' Cathy said.

Miss Hanley smiled. 'Well, I think that might suit you better, but you couldn't begin training until you are eighteen. You don't want to hang around doing nothing for almost a year, do you? So why not stay on for your A levels?'

All the way home Cathy's mind was full of what Miss Hanley had said. So much so that she walked right past the car that stood at the gate without looking at it. It was only as she was letting herself in at the front door that she heard his voice and stopped dead in her tracks. *Gerald!* He was back – and *here*!

She stood in the hall uncertainly, suddenly overcome with shyness. It was eight whole months since she had seen him. Had she changed? she wondered. She peered into the hall mirror and saw two shining green eyes and the mass of fly-away auburn hair that would never stay in place. Why do I have to be so *ordinary*? she asked herself despairingly. Not only that but she had a spot coming on her chin. Carla wore make-up all the time now, even for school. Maybe Cathy should start using it more. Slipping silently up the stairs, she combed her hair and applied a dash of the pink lipstick Carla had persuaded her to buy when they were in Woolworth's last Saturday. Standing back she regarded herself. Better, she supposed. Hardly the height of sophistication, but better.

He stood up when she came into the room and her heart gave a dizzying little jerk when he smiled at her.

She affected surprise. 'Gerald! I didn't know you were back.'

'I got in some days ago, but I had a few things to clear up,' he told her. 'There's always such a lot to do when you've been away.' Bending towards her he said teasingly, 'Well – does your old guardian rate a kiss after his long absence?'

Cathy blushed crimson and pecked his cheek.

'Mrs Johnson has been telling me your good news,' he

said with a smile. 'Congratulations. I think you deserve that special dinner I promised you. In fact, I think I should take you all out.' He looked at Johnny who shook her head.

'No, we couldn't let you do that, Mr Cavelle. Besides, it's Cathy's success. I'm sure you'll have a lot to discuss with her too.'

Gerald looked doubtful. 'I'd love to take you all out to dinner, Mrs Johnson. I owe you a lot for looking after Cathy so well.'

Johnny blushed. 'You don't owe me anything, Mr Cavelle,' she said. 'Cathy is like one of my own. I'd have taken her in anyway after her father passed on. Even if I'd had to keep her myself.'

Gerald felt chastened. 'Of course. I only meant . . .'

Mrs Bains, who was sitting in her chair by the window, a shawl over her arthritic knees, broke into his sentence with a sound that was half cough, half grunt.

'Besides, I like to be in bed by nine,' she put in. 'My days for gadding about to restaurants are over and done with.'

'That's right,' Johnny said with an apologetic smile. 'I couldn't really leave Mother anyway.'

Johnny treated Cathy to a shampoo and set at *Fleur Coiffeur* in the High Street on the day designated for the dinner date with Gerald. When she got home she went up to her room and studied her appearance in the dressing-table mirror. The hairdresser had backcombed and teased her auburn hair into the new bouffant style that was becoming so popular. She wasn't altogether sure that it suited her finely drawn features, but it certainly had the effect of making her look more grown-up. She took out her newest dress, made of pale lilac voile, and sat on the bed to shorten the skirt. Everyone was wearing them much shorter now and she was determined to look fashionable. With her pocket money she'd bought a pair of tights in a matching shade and she planned to wear her little black patent shoes with the flared heels. As she stitched she wondered whether she'd pass for twenty. With some mascara and eye shadow she felt fairly sure that she would. This afternoon she'd have a trial run with it.

When Gerald called for her she'd been ready for more than half an hour. Standing just out of sight behind the front room curtains, she watched patiently for the car. When she saw the long sleek bonnet of his new silver E-type Jaguar turn into the road and draw up outside she ran through to the living room where the family sat at their evening meal.

'Gerald's here,' she said breathlessly. 'See you later.'

'All right, love. Have a nice time,' Johnny smiled.

As the door closed Mrs Bains looked up, chewing on her steak and kidney pie ruminatively. 'Mark my words, there'll be no good come out of that,' she muttered darkly. 'I don't like the looks of that chap. Too conceited for his own good if you ask me.'

Johnny shook her head reprovingly at her mother. 'Mr Cavelle is Cathy's legal guardian, Mother,' she said. 'He's a famous concert pianist and he was Mr Oldham's best friend. Besides,' she added for good measure, 'I think he's rather handsome.'

Mrs Bains gave her characteristic grunt. 'Huh! Handsome is as handsome does,' she said predictably.

Matthew grinned across the table at his mother. 'You walked right into that, didn't you, Mum?'

The restaurant Gerald had chosen was quiet. There was a small dance floor and a band that played quietly and discreetly as they dined. Cathy thought Gerald looked a little thinner; tired too, but that was understandable after the heavy schedule of his recent tour. She asked him to tell her about the places he'd visited.

'You won't believe me when I tell you that the little I saw of any of the cities I visited was seen through cab windows,' he said with a wry smile. 'All I really saw was concert halls, hotel rooms and airport departure lounges.'

'I always hoped Dad would go on tour sometime and take me with him,' Cathy confessed. 'But he said he wasn't good enough to be a concert pianist. I'm sure that wasn't true, was it?'

She looked at him so appealingly that he couldn't meet her eyes as he answered. 'Your father wasn't as lucky as me. I had a wealthy grandfather who paid for me to study and kept me going until I was established.'

'Did you? I didn't know that.' She stirred her coffee thoughtfully. 'Did you know that Dad used to compose?'

'No, did he?'

'Yes. I used to think he might be successful with that someday. When we cleared the house I was hoping to find some of his manuscripts up in the attic.' She shook her head. 'He must have destroyed them all when he knew he was ill. He never had any confidence in himself, you know.'

'You still miss him, don't you?'

She looked up at him. 'I always will,' she said. 'I don't think I'll ever want to stop missing him, however much it hurts. Because if I ever did it would mean I'd started to forget and that's the last thing I want.'

He looked at her for a long moment. 'It must feel very special to be loved as much as that,' he said wistfully. He took a deep breath and smiled at her. 'Now, I suppose this is where I should ask you what you're planning to do next. What's it to be? A levels . . . University . . .?'

'Neither. I want to leave school,' she told him. 'There were two things I fancied doing: one was nursing and the other was domestic science. But you can't start training to be a nurse till you're eighteen. That would mean hanging around for another four months. So it's going to be domestic science, or rather Home Economics. There's a technical college quite near where I can go so I'll be able to stay on at Johnny's.'

He was laughing. 'You're a young lady in a hurry, aren't you?'

She shrugged. 'I've made up my mind. That's all.'

'Why Home Economics? I'd have thought with all those academic subjects, good grades . . .'

She sighed. 'Why do people always think that domestic science is for idiots? There are a lot of good careers to be had with an HE diploma. And anyway, it's what I want. Why should I do something I don't like just because I got good grades?'

He held up his hands in mock surrender. 'All right. I bow to your superior knowledge of the subject.' He reached across the table to pat her cheek. 'You'll make some lucky man a wonderful and accomplished wife some day,' he said.

She blushed and looked away. Did he really mean that, or was he just patronising her?

Cathy began her Home Economics course at the local technical college at the end of September. She enjoyed it and made some new friends. Occasionally she ran into some of the girls from St Margaret's. Carla envied her. She admitted that she was finding her A level studies a bore and complained about the mass of homework she took home every evening.

'And to think I've let myself in for two years of it,' she wailed.

Rosalind, on the other hand, seemed to be enjoying herself. When they met one rainy November evening at the bus stop she told Cathy she was taking Geography, Sociology, English and Maths. Hotel management was still her aim, she explained. She was interested in Cathy's course.

'Maybe some time in the future we'll find ourselves working together,' she said. 'After all, your subject and mine aren't entirely unrelated, are they?'

84

Cathy told her about the Saturday job she had just taken at the restaurant of the Queen's Head.

'It's a small place and you have to be willing to do a bit of everything,' she said. 'I help in the kitchen and occasionally wait on tables when they are busy or short-staffed. I think they're looking for another weekend girl. If you're interested I could ask for you.' She smiled. 'We could be working together sooner than you think.'

During the autumn Gerald was away again. Cathy received postcards from Switzerland and Edinburgh, but he was back in England again at the beginning of November and one Sunday he took Cathy out to lunch. He asked her what she planned to do at Christmas.

'Nothing special, just spending it at home as usual,' she said. 'Johnny loves Christmas and we always have a nice time. Why, what are you going to do?'

'I thought I might go abroad somewhere,' he told her. 'I have this favourite little place in Switzerland. It's high in the mountains and quite breathtaking in winter. I wondered if you might like to come with me?'

For a moment she was speechless with surprise. 'Why me?' She blushed. 'I mean – it's nice of you to ask me, but there must be someone who's longing for you to ask them.'

He smiled at her. 'I rather thought that someone might be you.'

She laughed. 'You're teasing me. You must have a friend – a girlfriend?'

'Actually no. At least, not one who likes me enough to spend a whole Christmas with me.'

'Oh.' She bit her lip, wondering just what that might mean. 'It's not that I wouldn't like to go, Gerald,' she said. 'It's just that I think it's only fair to help Johnny. There's always such a lot to do.' She looked at him. 'I know. Why don't I ask if you can join us?'

He shook his head. 'I don't want to impose. Besides, I have the distinct feeling that old Mrs Bains disapproves of me. I find that baleful look of hers and those snide remarks rather off-putting.'

'You shouldn't take any notice of that. She's the same with all of us. It doesn't mean anything.'

He slipped an arm round her shoulders. 'Don't worry about me. It was just an idea. I'll be fine.'

She frowned. 'But what will you do? Where will you go?'

'Probably nowhere. I'll stay at the flat and watch all the old films and Christmas Specials on the box.'

'Oh, Gerald.' Cathy chewed her lip, then suddenly she brightened. 'I know, I'll come and cook your Christmas dinner for you.' She pulled a comic face at him. 'If you think you're brave enough to risk it.'

He laughed. 'That sounds wonderful. But what about Mrs Johnson?'

'All the hard work will be over by then and she won't mind if it's just for Christmas Day,' she said. 'She'll probably invite you back for Boxing Day. Well, what do you say?'

He smiled. 'If you really want to do it, I'd love it.'

Cathy shopped for all the ingredients of the Christmas dinner, leaving Gerald to buy the wine only.

'I haven't learned enough about that yet,' she confessed to him. 'I'd probably choose something awful and poison you.'

He collected her and all the bags laden with Christmas fare early on Christmas morning and drove back to the West End. She found the flat looking much as she remembered it; almost clinically tidy and unlived-in. To Cathy it seemed unnaturally so.

Gerald had been surprised when he learned that she hadn't taken him up on his offer to use the place in his absence. Seeing her gazing longingly at Daniel's piano, he invited her to play it.

'I had it tuned when I got back from the tour,' he said,

'along with my own. They get so neglected and the central heating is bad for them.' He saw her hesitating. 'What's the matter – out of practice?'

She nodded. 'Afraid so.'

'What does it matter? There's no one here but us.'

She went over to the piano and ran her fingers lightly over the keyboard. The familiar smooth feel of the ivory brought back nostalgic memories of those Saturday afternoons; the precious times she and her father spent together. Sliding on to the stool she flexed her fingers and began to play a little Chopin nocturne. When the last note had died away she felt Gerald's hand on her shoulder.

'You play very nicely,' he said.

She looked up at him with a wry smile. 'Exactly. That's why I didn't even try to take it up seriously.'

He looked dismayed. 'Oh, but I didn't mean . . .'

'It's okay, Gerald,' she said. 'You don't have to flatter me. The only reason I kept on with my lessons was that it was the one time I could count on getting Dad to myself for a while. I know I haven't inherited his talent.' She swivelled round on the stool. 'Now, I'd better get that turkey into the oven.' She looked up at him. 'Are you going to help?'

He laughed. 'You bet. That's half the fun, isn't it? You'll have to tell me what to do though.'

The kitchen at the flat was equipped with every modern convenience. There was even a dishwasher and an electric tin opener, which intrigued Cathy. Gerald submitted to having an apron tied around his waist and, under Cathy's supervision, set about preparing the vegetables. When everything was under control he opened a bottle of wine and poured her a glass.

'I think we've earned this,' he said. 'And I must say I'm impressed. You've learned a lot during your first term at college.'

She laughed. 'I learned most of this years ago,' she

told him. 'Dad and I had been on our own a long time, remember?'

'Of course.'

'And Johnny taught me how to cook.'

'It's as I said. Some day you're going to . . .'

She stopped him with a look. 'Don't laugh at me, Gerald!'

His face dropped. 'My dear girl, I wasn't.'

'That's all right then. You can't go around pretending that a girl's only ambition is to walk down the aisle in white satin nowadays, you know.'

He looked suitably chastened. 'I stand corrected.'

She grinned disarmingly. 'That's okay then. You can set the table if you want to be really useful.'

After her admonishing remark Gerald was careful about what he said. Therefore when he complimented her on her cooking his tone was guarded. Her gracious response to his compliment filled him with relief.

'Cooking can be as much of an art as music,' she told him gravely. 'And as creative.'

'So you've just proved,' he said diplomatically.

After they'd eaten he gave her his present: a beautiful pair of earrings in pearl and jade that he'd bought in New York. They'd originally been chosen for Kay, whose birthday was in October, but he hadn't seen or heard from her since she'd flounced out of the hotel on what had proved to be the last day of his tour. And the green of the jade went so well with Cathy's colouring that it was easy to pretend they'd been bought especially for her.

When she opened them she was overwhelmed. 'Oh, *Gerald*! I've never seen anything so lovely. I'll cherish them always.' She passed his neatly wrapped gift across the table to him. 'I'm afraid this makes mine look so cheap.'

'Nonsense. I'm sure I shall love it.' He unwrapped the tie she had chosen so carefully and exclaimed with pleasure.

'Exactly what I wanted. It will go perfectly with my new jacket.'

'You're just saying that.'

'No, really.' He got up and held out his hand. 'Let's have our coffee by the fire. I've got something to tell you.'

He poured a cup of the coffee he had insisted on making himself and handed it to her. 'My one culinary accomplishment,' he told her as he sat down opposite her.

She sniffed at her cup. 'It smells delicious.'

'I always bring a supply back from Switzerland when I go.'

She sipped appreciatively, looking at him over the rim of her cup. 'You said you had something to tell me.'

'Yes. I've made a rather momentous decision, Cathy. I'm retiring from the concert platform – giving up my playing.'

She stared at him, lost for words. 'Giving up? But surely . . .?'

'Perhaps it would be more accurate to say that playing is giving *me* up,' he went on. 'I've developed a slight – health problem.'

Putting down her cup, she stared at him, her eyes filled with concern. 'Gerald, what is it? Please tell me.'

He shook his head, smiling. 'Nothing for you to worry about. It's a – a kind of arthritis, I suppose you could call it; a stiffening of the joints. I had a lot of trouble with it on the tour.'

'But – but that's terrible. Your music – you're at the height of your career. Surely you can't just throw it all away?'

He smiled ruefully. 'I don't seem to have much choice in the matter. I've still got some time to run on my recording contract. I'll be able to fulfil that. Mistakes can always be edited out. But I'm afraid live concerts are out from now on.'

She moved across to him and took his hands in hers, looking down at them. They looked as strong and powerful as ever. It was hard to believe that they were not. She looked up into his eyes. 'Isn't there something they can do?'

'Nothing, I'm afraid.'

'But – don't you mind terribly?'

He sighed. 'Oh, I don't know. At first it was a blow, but I've had time to think since and I've got a few plans chasing round inside my head.'

'Like what?'

'Ah, that'd be telling.' He bent towards her and kissed her forehead. 'I promise you this though. As soon as one of them begins to take shape, you'll be the first to hear about it.'

They stacked the dishwasher together and sat down to watch the Christmas afternoon movie on television. But Cathy couldn't concentrate on it. All she could think of was the devastating sacrifice that Gerald was having to make. What could she do to make it up to him? Looking across the room in the fading winter afternoon light she watched his profile. The firelight accentuated the hollows under his cheekbones and deepened the eye sockets so that she couldn't see his eyes at all – couldn't even begin to guess what he was feeling. Her heart stirred and she got up quietly and went to sit on the floor at his feet, laying her head on his knee. She felt his hand stroking her hair and presently she raised her head to look up at him.

'Oh, Gerald. Are you dreadfully unhappy?'

He shook his head. 'No. And I'll tell you why. I've found that when you lose something in life there's always a compensation – something to take its place.'

'Or some*one*,' she said. 'Like you came along for me when Dad died.'

'That's a very sweet thing to say.'

'But it's true. You helped me so much. I hope I can help you now that you need someone, Gerald. You will let me, won't you?'

He didn't speak for a moment, then he said quietly,

'You learn who your friends are on occasions like this, you know.'

She turned, kneeling to look at him better. 'Are you saying that your friends have deserted you?'

'I have to confess that it does feel a bit like that.' He sighed. 'But there again, I'm a firm believer that you get what you deserve. Maybe I haven't been a very good friend to others in the past.'

'I can't believe that.'

'Oh, but you should. My kind of life leaves very little room for loyal friendships.'

'Well, you've got mine and you always will have,' she said firmly.

He leaned forward and took her face between his hands. 'Thank you, Cathy. I can't tell you how much I appreciate that. Will you do something for me?'

'Of course. Anything.'

'Will you please let what I've told you be between ourselves for the present? It isn't common knowledge and I'm not sure that I want it to be. There's a lot for me to sort out before I make it generally known that I'm retiring too, so keep that under your hat too, will you?'

'Of course. I won't say anything, I promise.'

Still cupping her face in his hands he drew her towards him and kissed her very gently on the lips. As she felt his mouth, warm and firm on hers, she caught her breath, closing her eyes as she felt the room spin around her. Reaching up, she wound her arms about his neck, but after a moment he took them away and kissed her hands, holding them close to his chest.

'Dear little Cathy,' he whispered. 'You've grown up, haven't you? You're very sweet, just as I always knew you'd be, and we've had a wonderful Christmas Day together. But I'm going to take you home now, before – well, before it's too late.'

91

'But you're coming tomorrow, aren't you – to spend the day with us?'

'No, darling.' He smiled at her gently. 'I'm planning to go away for a few weeks.'

She shook her head. 'Again? You never said. But not yet surely? Not until after Christmas?'

'Maybe not immediately but very soon. I think it's best this way.'

Sitting beside him in the car she was silent. She had the distinct impression that when he had said *before it's too late* he hadn't been talking about the time. And yet he clearly didn't intend to see her again; at least not for a while. Her mind was in a spin. The devastating news he had imparted about retiring from the concert platform, their closeness. The kiss; intimate and more disturbing than anything she had ever experienced before. Finally the unsettling feeling that the fact that he was going out of her life again was somehow because of something she had unwittingly done. All of these things swirled bewilderingly in her head. She needed time and solitude in which to work them all out.

He stopped the car a few doors along the road, switched off the engine and turned in his seat to look at her.

'You're upset.'

'No. Well, yes, but . . .'

'Because of what I told you?'

'Because – yes, partly.'

'My poor Cathy. I never meant to burden you. It was only that . . .'

'You could never burden me, Gerald. It's got nothing to do with that.' She looked down at her hands. 'Will you tell me something?'

'Of course, if I can.'

'Are you going away because of me?'

'No. Whatever makes you think that?'

'Oh, nothing really. Anyway, I'm glad.' On a sudden bold impulse she reached out and drew his head down to hers, kissing him firmly on the mouth. Then, before he could speak, she jumped out of the car and ran down the road to the gate. When she got there she turned briefly and half raised her hand, then slipped out of sight behind the hedge.

Gerald sat for a long time at the wheel of the car thinking about what he had done – what he had started. She was so sweet; so uncomplicated. For a moment a sudden thought tantalised him. How good it would be to have her with him permanently. The word *sacrificial* came mockingly into his mind and he cast it out angrily. It wasn't like that. She was attracted to him, he'd always known that. She was too young and naive to know how to hide the fact. There would be no sacrifice involved if it was what she wanted. There was so much that he could give her – so much they could give each other.

Chapter Five

Una had been a little dismayed at first to learn that after the wedding Don intended them to occupy the house he had shared with his first wife. But on the Sunday afternoon when he had taken her and Rosalind along to see the house in Jay's Lane, Stanmore she had changed her mind.

Blake's Folly was a detached house, built just before the war in suburban Tudor. It occupied a corner position on a pleasant tree-lined avenue of the kind that Una had always admired and the moment they drew up at the gate Rosalind saw her expression brighten. The double oak gates flanked by two monkey puzzle trees were, to her, the epitome of respectability.

Don opened the car door with a flourish and escorted Una proudly up the curved driveway. Following them, Rosalind heard her mother's squeak of approval at the impressive entrance porch which was hung with reproduction lanterns.

But Rosalind's first impression of the house differed from her mother's. Less eager than Una to go into the house she had noted the front garden, with its clipped velvet lawn and shrubs mercilessly manicured into shape. Her heart sank. It was more like a municipal park than a garden and she thought longingly of the glorious profusion of blossom in the cottage garden at Sherwood Magna. Even the rigid and precise rows of bedding plants in the front garden at Blake's Folly looked regimented, as though they wouldn't dare to flag or drop untidy petals on the weedless soil. When she learned later that the gardener who came in twice a week to discipline the garden was an ex-sergeant major in the Royal Artillery she wasn't in the least surprised.

As the three of them stood waiting for Don to find his key and unlock the front door Rosalind peered surreptitiously through the windows. Even from the little she could see it was possible to get an idea of what was in store inside. Through the pristine net curtains she caught the glint of gilt-framed mirrors and the crystal and silver adorning mantelpiece and sideboard. But once Don had opened the door and they had crossed the threshold, vulgar opulence seemed to sneer at her from every corner. In the lounge a large squashy three-piece suite, its sides held in place by silken ropes, thick enough to moor the *Queen Mary*, squatted formidably, daring the visitor to offend its dignity by sitting on the striped plum and peacock upholstery.

In the dining room a reproduction Jacobean dining table, realistically distressed with dents and gashes, gleamed with an artificially induced patina, and everywhere one's feet sank into thick carpets in rich shades of antique red and gold.

The kitchen units were white, ranged around the walls like icebergs lying in wait for the *Titanic*. Una stood in the middle of the floor, exclaiming with pleasure as Don gleefully opened doors and demonstrated every gadget the Ideal Home Exhibition had ever dreamed of. Rosalind stood in the doorway, wistfully remembering the warm kitchen at Ivy Cottage with its pine and gingham homeliness.

But if Rosalind found the place ostentatious and unwelcoming, it was clear that Una did not share her view. As they walked round she could feel her mother growing more and more excited by the minute. Encouraged by her delighted smiles and enthusiastic remarks, Don led them proudly up the dog-leg staircase with its richly carved oak banister. At the top a square landing led to the four bedrooms and a lavish bathroom with a rose pink suite which he displayed with his characteristic flourish. He was an effusive, dapper little man with a pencil moustache and horn-rimmed glasses. Eager to encourage her approval, he looked at his intended enquiringly.

'Well, dearest, what do you think? Can you see yourself living here with me?'

Una sighed ecstatically. 'Oh, Don, of course I can. It's lovely! I'd no idea.'

He smiled with relief. 'Good. It would be such a waste to sell up and start all over again, I'm sure you agree, and anything that isn't to your taste can easily be changed.'

'Oh, I don't want to change anything,' Una said. 'Except perhaps the bedroom,' she said, peering once more into her predecessor's boudoir. 'I think I'd like to have my own choice in there – in the room you and I will share.'

'Naturally, poppet. Buy whatever you like.'

'Thank you, darling. You're so good to me.' To Rosalind's embarrassment Una gave a coy little giggle and pressed close to her future husband's side. Don slipped an arm around her waist and squeezed her affectionately.

'Our room must be just as you would want it. Just pop along to the furniture department at the shop and choose whatever takes your fancy.'

Una was just planting a grateful kiss on his cheek when she noticed Rosalind standing awkwardly by the stairhead, unsure of what she should do. 'You can choose your bedroom if you want,' she said. 'Go on, have a look round.'

Rosalind shook her head. 'It's all right. I don't mind which one I have.'

'But you haven't even looked at them yet,' Una said irritably.

Don looked round at her. 'Yes, do choose, Rosalind,' he said. 'Any one – oh, except this.' He planted himself protectively in front of the door of one of the back bedrooms. 'This one was Mother's. Have either of the other two though. And of course the same applies to you. If you want to change anything in it, please feel free.'

'I really don't mind which I have,' she said awkwardly. 'And I'm sure it'll be fine as it is.'

Later, after Don had taken them back to the flat and was parking the car, Una admonished her.

'Why do you always have to be so sullen with Don?' she said sharply.

'I wasn't.'

'Yes, you were. He's bent over backwards to please you. A lot of men wouldn't want a teenage girl cluttering the place up, you know. He's even willing to keep you while you're still getting your education, remember. You might at least try to show a bit of gratitude and interest in your new home. I just hope you realise how lucky you are.'

Rosalind muttered an apology. The truth was, she had the uncomfortable feeling that Don merely tolerated her for her mother's sake. He was pleasant enough to her it was true, but it wouldn't be easy learning to share a house with a man after so long. The next two years while she was studying for her A levels would clearly be difficult. The thought of them made her even more determined to work hard and get into business college. If nothing else had motivated her, moving away from the prophetically named Blake's Folly and the newly wed Una and Don would have been enough incentive to keep her striving for independence.

The wedding took place on the second Saturday in August. The ceremony was conducted at the register office and was followed by lunch at a local hotel, attended by a few friends and colleagues of Don's. Una had remarked more than once to Rosalind that her own colleagues in model gowns had behaved in a nasty jealous manner since her engagement to Don and that none of them deserved to be invited. Besides, she wouldn't be working at the shop any more after the wedding. There would be enough to occupy her at home, she added with satisfaction.

After lunch the happy couple left for a honeymoon in Majorca, leaving Rosalind to go home alone to the flat in Burnt Oak and prepare to pack up their belongings ready for the move to Stanmore on her mother's return. She was still alone when her O level results came through. Her only celebration was the meeting at school when she shared her success with her classmates, including Cathy Oldham who, she discovered to her disappointment, was leaving school to go to the technical college. She'd cherished a fond hope that they might become friends when they were both in the sixth form and it had been a blow to find that Cathy was leaving, whilst the sharp-tongued Carla was to stay on.

During the two weeks that Una and Don were away she received a postcard from them. It showed a picture of the hotel and, in the background an impossibly blue sea and cloudless sky. Her mother had written: *Having a wonderful time. Wish you were here*, on the reverse side, which made Rosalind smile wryly.

By the same post there was a letter from Ben. He and Freda were appearing in their summer show, *Knights and Belles*, in Brighton, and he wrote inviting her to go and spend a week of her summer holiday with them. She wrote straight back accepting. It would give her mother and Don more time to themselves. She was sure they would be pleased.

But when she told Una on her return she was anything but pleased. 'I must say I think it's very selfish of you,' she said. 'You know how much there is to do with shifting all our stuff over to Stanmore and everything. Now I'll have most of it to do on my own.'

'But I've already packed most of it up,' Rosalind said. 'And it isn't as if the place isn't already furnished. Surely all you have to do is unpack your own things. I'll see to mine when I get back.'

'If you think all I have to do is unpack you're *very* much

mistaken,' Una said with a determined look. 'I've got no intention of living with that woman's stuff in the house.' She wrinkled her nose. 'All those tassels and standard lamps and ruched cushions. Ugh! Pure thirties. No, I intend to bring the whole place up to date and that takes time.'

'But you said you didn't want to change anything but the bedroom,' Rosalind said. 'I thought you liked it.'

Una snorted. '*Like it?* You've got to be joking. I'll do it gradually, of course, bit by bit so that Don doesn't notice, but that stuff of *hers*, it's all got to go. It's too old-fashioned for words. That silver will have to be put away too. I'm not making a slave of myself cleaning that lot!' She looked at her daughter with unconcealed resentment. 'Still, if you've already said you'll go to Brighton to Ben and that floosie of his, then you'd better go, I suppose. I don't want them thinking I'm stopping you. Though I must say you might have had the consideration to ask if it was convenient first.'

Brighton was a joy. Rosalind had never been there before, even when she'd joined her parents on summer shows in the past. They'd never aspired to more than number three dates in their days together, which, Rosalind accurately guessed was the real source of her mother's present resentment.

Ben had booked her a room at the hotel where he and Freda were staying. It had an air of subdued luxury and was a far cry from the dingy back street lodgings of the past. In the daytime they took her exploring the town, showing her the little lanes with their intriguing antique and curio shops. One morning she went along with Freda to the hairdresser and had her hair cut in a short gamine style that accentuated her large expressive eyes and delicate bones. Afterwards Freda treated her to a new skirt and blouse.

'I expect you'll be allowed to wear your own clothes in the sixth form,' she said. 'I daresay you'll be glad to ditch your school uniform.'

Rosalind was grateful. She had very few clothes apart from her uniform and wild horses wouldn't have forced her to ask Don for money to spend on clothes. When she confided this to Freda she looked thoughtful.

'Don't you like him, Rossie?'

Rosalind shrugged. 'He's all right, I suppose. I just hate feeling – you know – beholden to him.'

Freda slipped her arm through hers. 'I know what you mean, love. Why don't you try to get a Saturday job? You could put the money by for your clothes then and be independent.'

Rosalind thought this a very good idea and over coffee they discussed what she might do.

In the evenings she went to the theatre with her father and Freda. Instead of the cheerless, cramped dressing rooms Ben had shared with Una when they were together, 'Ben and Benita' now occupied one of the star dressing rooms, adjacent to the stage. It boasted hot and cold running water and two comfortable chairs as well as the twin dressing table and wardrobes. Ben proudly introduced her to the backstage staff and the other artists as his 'clever grown-up daughter', and with the permission of the stage manager, Rosalind watched the show from the wings and thought Ben and Freda very good, even better than when she'd heard them rehearsing at Easter. Their voices seemed to blend together more effectively every time she heard them, and their obviously happy relationship put across a warmth and sincerity that made them popular with the audience.

It was towards the end of the week that Ben took her out on her own one morning. Freda remained behind on the pretext of having sewing to do, but it was clear to Rosalind that Ben meant to have a heart to heart talk with her. They had coffee in a small café near the hotel, then walked for a while in the late-summer sunshine, admiring the smooth green of the promenade lawns and inhaling the fresh sea breeze. Then, just when Rosalind thought she must have been wrong about the heart-to-heart, Ben bought them an ice-cream cornet each and invited her to sit down.

'Tell me, are you happy about this new marriage of your mother's?' he asked.

She paused for a moment before answering. 'It's up to her really, isn't it?' she said non-committally.

'That's not what I asked you. This chap – what's his name – Don Blake? Do you get on all right with him?'

Rosalind wondered if Freda had said something. 'He's all right,' she said. 'I suppose it's just that Una and I have been on our own a long time.'

'Exactly. It's bound to make a big difference to your life. So, how do you feel about the changes it will bring?'

'It won't be that different. Stanmore isn't far from St Margaret's. It's a nice place. And the house is better – well, *heaps* better than we've ever had before.'

'Yes, but what about *you*?' he asked impatiently. 'Look, you don't have to pretend to me, Rossie. There's something you're not happy about, isn't there? Tell me.'

She squirmed inwardly, wishing she hadn't said anything to Freda. 'No, there's nothing really. It's just that it's going to be a bit strange at first, and I don't like the idea of having him pay for things for me. But I'll get used to it. I'll have to, won't I?'

'Not necessarily.' He looked at her for a moment. 'Look Rossie, the reason I'm asking you these questions is because there's something you should know. Freda and I have had an offer – to go to Australia. As you know, we're recording a TV series when we've finished here at the end of next month. After that we're off to Oz.'

She looked at him. 'Sounds wonderful. How long for?'

There was a long pause before he replied. 'That's just it, baby. Probably for a long – a *very* long time.' He took her hand. 'Our kind of act is going out of fashion over here, you see, but in Australia it's still quite popular.' He laughed. 'And heaven knows, the country's big enough to tour for

101

yonks. TV is getting off the ground in a big way over there too. Our agent has had an offer for us from someone who caught our act here. He thinks we could make a real hit over there.'

'Oh, good. Congratulations.' Rosalind gave him her brightest smile to hide the sinking feeling inside her chest. Just when she was beginning to rebuild her relationship with her father he was about to go out of her life again. 'If it's what you want, that is.'

He looked into her eyes. 'It is, of course. It's a wonderful opportunity and we're both thrilled. The thing is, baby . . . Look, Free and I have talked this over and we both agree. We'd like you to come with us.'

She stared at him. '*Me* – come to Australia?'

'Yes. What do you say?'

Just for a moment her heart leapt with excitement. Dad and Freda actually *wanted* her with them – sharing a new life in an exciting new country. Then she thought of her own plans for the future and the snags and impracticalities came crowding in. 'I don't see how I can, Dad,' she said, shaking her head.

'Why not, love? You'd enjoy it out there.'

She sighed. 'But it wouldn't work, would it? There's my A levels for a start.'

'Oh – well, I daresay you can do them over there – or the equivalent.'

'Not if you're going to be touring. Then afterwards I want to go to business college. Study hotel management.' She looked at him. 'I really want that, Dad. It's all I've worked for.'

His face dropped. 'Yes, I know you do, love. But they must have those courses over there too. You could get into a college somewhere, surely. We'd see each other as often as we could.'

She shook her head. 'I don't think so, Dad. It wouldn't be any different than it was before, would it – when you

102

and Una were together and I was at Aunt Flora's? And I think I'd feel lonely – even lonelier on my own in a strange country. You'd feel you had to keep coming to see me too. No. Better for you and Freda to be free to concentrate on your work.'

He was silent for a moment. 'I can't see what's so special about the hotel business. Isn't there anything else you'd like to do?'

'Not really.' She shook her head. 'Anyway if I toured with you I wouldn't be able to study for anything anyway, would I?' She wanted to add: *I'd just be another piece of luggage you'd have to carry around. A dead weight*, but she knew that would hurt him so she didn't say it, even though she knew it to be true.

Almost as though he read her thoughts, Ben was silent for a moment. 'You could come over for a holiday though,' he said at length without conviction. 'You could come over every year if you wanted.'

It was so typical of Ben. Una had always said that one of his biggest faults was his inability to face up to the realities of life. 'Yes, of course I could,' Rosalind said, forcing a brightness she didn't feel into her voice. 'I'll have to start saving up right away, won't I?' She smiled at him reassuringly. 'It was lovely of you both to ask me, Dad, and I do appreciate it, but it wouldn't work, really it wouldn't. I want to study and make a career for myself. I want to be independent.' His depressed silence showed that he had reluctantly accepted the fact and Rosalind felt close to tears. Once again she was odd man out. It seemed that she didn't really fit in anywhere. She was a millstone round everyone's necks. Una's reproachful words echoed in her mind. *I hope you realise how lucky you are*. How bitter it felt to know you were a nuisance and a liability; that the best emotion you merited was guilt. She looked at Ben's anguished face and reached for his hand.

'Dad, don't feel bad about it. It's my choice. I want you

103

to go and be a big success, honestly. We'll write to each other, and as soon as I can I'll come and see you.'

He squeezed her hand. 'I want you to know that you can come any time you like, baby,' he said earnestly. 'If you change your mind and want to come out, just wire and I'll send you your fare. Promise me you'll do that?'

She smiled at him. 'Okay, if you say so.' A thought suddenly struck her. 'What will you do about Ivy Cottage?'

'We're letting it on a short lease,' he told her. 'Maybe one of these days we'll come back and retire there.'

'So you're not selling it?'

'No fear. Not after all the work we've put in. Anyway, even if we don't come back it'll be a little nest egg for Free and me in our old age.'

When Rosalind went home from Brighton it was to Blake's Folly – except that it didn't feel much like home. Una met her at the station and complained at once about the new hairstyle.

'I see you've been letting that woman influence you again,' she said scathingly.

Rosalind lifted a hand to her hair. 'Don't you like it?'

'No, I do *not*. It makes you look as if it's been cut with a knife and fork.'

'It's called the Italian cut,' Rosalind said hopefully. 'It's all the rage in Brighton.'

Una snorted derisively. 'Whoever told you that was having you on.'

Rosalind felt rebellion welling up inside her. 'No, they weren't,' she said warmly. 'I had a lot of nice compliments from the artists at the theatre.'

Una shrugged her shoulders. 'Rosalind, you really will have to learn to tell a real compliment from people just having a laugh at your expense,' she said. 'I'm sure you don't want to go around looking silly. Grow it out as quickly as you can, there's a good girl.'

She had chosen the room over the garage for Rosalind. It had two windows, one facing the front garden and another looking on to the side entrance. It was a darkish little room, shaded by the evergreen trees at the front and the wall of the next house at the side, but there was enough space for the few things Rosalind had. Una had added a desk and an armchair to the existing furniture, making it clear that she expected her daughter to spend most of her spare time here.

Rosalind saw at once that while she had been in Brighton her mother had lost no time in making changes. In spite of her decision to replace the first Mrs Blake's furniture gradually she had refurnished most of the ground floor in one fell swoop, replacing the heavy oak reproduction pieces with contemporary furniture in light woods. The heavy velvet curtains with their braided swags and tails had been replaced with plain pelmets and curtains made of brightly coloured fabrics in jazzy designs. From what Rosalind could gather it had already caused a disagreement between her mother and Don, who was of the opinion that the spindly style of furniture Una favoured did not go with the style of the house.

'I told him – we'll just have to change the style of the house then, won't we?' Una recounted to Rosalind. 'After all, I have agreed to save him money by living in the house his ex-wife chose. How many women would do that? And he did say I could change anything I liked, didn't he? You were witness to that.'

Rosalind said nothing. She hoped she wouldn't be expected to take sides in any arguments.

'Oh, yes. He said change anything you like and that's what I intend to do.' They were standing on the oak-panelled landing and Una suddenly swept her arm around impatiently. 'I hate all this dark, gloomy wood. I'm working on having it all done out in cream emulsion. And do you know, he keeps that room locked?' She pointed to one of the back bedrooms. 'It was his mother's and he keeps all her things in there, would you believe? Even her clothes! Creepy if you ask me, not to mention the waste of space. Still I had to give in on something, I suppose,' she added grudgingly. 'But I'll get that cleared out too in time, don't you worry.'

Rosalind made a non-committal reply. Her mother looked at her enquiringly.

'Well? I haven't heard anything about your holiday yet. Still climbing the ladder to success, those two, are they?'

'The show was very good,' Rosalind said as she started to unpack her case. Her back to her mother she added: 'They've had a very good offer. They're going to Australia.'

'Oh, yes? How long for?'

Rosalind could feel her mother's envy and resentment boring into her back as she put away her things. 'It's an extended tour. They might even stay there, I think. Settle down for good.'

'Huh!' Una tugged viciously at a corner of the bedspread. 'I suppose they want us to think they've hit the big time. I'll believe that when I see their names in lights.' She straightened up and looked at Rosalind, her eyes flashing like chips of ice. 'They didn't ask you to go with them though, did they? Oh, no. It only pleases Mister Bigtime to own he's got a daughter when it suits him. He won't want you hanging round his neck. Once he's left the country you won't hear from him again. Just you mark my words.'

When she'd left, slamming the door behind her, Rosalind sat down on the bed and swallowed hard at the lump in her throat. Every instinct that was in her had wanted to scream at her mother: *But he did want me. He did ask me to go too.* The only reason she had held back was that Una might have insisted on her accepting the invitation.

When the new term began she went back to St Margaret's eagerly. The sooner she could pass her A levels and move on to college, the better.

*   *   *

It was one wet afternoon in November that she met Cathy Oldham at the bus stop on her way home and heard again about the position of Saturday girl that was vacant at the Queen's Head. Her spirits rose. It was just what she was looking for. If she could only get it, it would be good experience for her as well as extra pocket money. Cathy promised to put in a word for her and two days later she telephoned to say that Rosalind could go along and see Mrs Gresham, the manageress, that afternoon after school.

The interview was a success. Mrs Gresham engaged Rosalind to work every Saturday from nine till two and then from six till ten in the evenings. The money wasn't exactly generous, but she was promised that there would be tips. It was a temporary job to last until the New Year, after which they would review the situation. Rosalind was thrilled. She had a job that would bring her extra money, get her out of the house at weekends and gain her some valuable experience too. And a bonus was that Cathy would be there too, so she wouldn't be entirely among strangers.

It was in the spring of the following year that Una had the first indication of the truth about Blake's Folly. Although she no longer worked at Hallard's with Don she had agreed to go in for a few weeks at the beginning of each new season to organise the fashion shows. Don was away for three days in March, attending a management conference in Eastbourne, and she was spending a day in the office, making out her VIP invitation list. She was deep in the list of account holders when one of the girls popped her head round the door. Una looked up irritably.

'Yes? What is it, Peggy?'

'There's someone in the showroom to see you.'

Una frowned. 'Didn't you say I was busy? Who is it anyway?'

'It's Mrs Blake.'

'What do you mean, Mrs Blake? Which Mrs Blake?'

The girl stifled a giggle. 'It's *her*,' she hissed in a stage whisper. 'You know – Mr Blake's ex.'

'Didn't you tell her that Mr Blake is out of town?'

'Yes, I did. It's you she wants to see.'

Una felt her face colouring. 'What does she . . .?' She bit off the end of the question and took a deep breath. 'I suppose you'd better send her in then, Peggy.' As the girl turned she added, 'Oh, and send down to the restaurant for a tray of tea – Earl Grey – and some chocolate biscuits.' Might as well let the woman see that she was civilised.

'Yes, Mrs Blake.' The girl withdrew, a smirk of gleeful excitement on her face. Just wait till she told the other girls about this. What she'd give to be a fly on the wall!

As soon as the girl had gone Una reached for her handbag and took out her compact, powdering her nose and tweaking at her hair. If only she'd known she would have put on something smarter. Truth to tell her knees were knocking with nervousness. Her best frock would have given her confidence. She uncapped her lipstick and applied it generously, pressing her lips together. She had just slipped it back into her bag when the door opened and Peggy ushered the first Mrs Blake in.

At first glance Una was surprised at how ordinary she was. Aged about forty-five, she had greying hair drawn back into a chignon and wore no make-up apart from a little pale pink lipstick. But there was a certain classiness about her that made Una feel over made-up and common. To compensate she smiled widely.

'Please – won't you have a chair? I've just sent down for some tea. I hope you'll join me?'

'How kind.' The other woman looked perfectly relaxed as she sat in the chair opposite and crossed one leg over the other. Una's sweeping glance of appraisal registered that she had good legs and that the char-coal grey suit she wore, although plain, was expertly cut. The white blouse was obviously pure silk and her accessories were expensive-looking. 'Actually I've come to ask a favour of you,' she said, accepting a cigarette from the box that Una pushed across the desk towards her.

Una was relieved. That meant that she was in the position of being able to grant or refuse. 'Of course,' she said sweetly. 'Anything at all that I can do, Mrs – er . . .'

'Monica.' The woman smiled. 'Call me Monica. After all, it's rather embarrassing to keep calling each other Mrs Blake, isn't it?'

Taken aback by the woman's cool composure Una nodded agreement. 'Oh – er, yes. My name is Una.'

At that point Peggy came in with the tray of tea. She searched the faces of both women for signs of battle and withdrew, disappointed.

Una poured the tea, glad to have something to do with her hands. 'So, what is this favour, Monica?'

'It's just the little desk in the dining room. It's Regency – an antique; the only genuine antique in the place as it happens. And the one piece that is actually mine. I bought it at a sale two years ago with my own money. I wondered if you and Donald would agree to my having it?'

Una was shaken. 'Did you say it was the only piece that was actually yours?'

Monica nodded. 'Yes. Everything else was Donald's mother's. We always lived with her, you know, right from the first. It was Mrs Blake senior's home. Not mine.'

Una felt as though all the breath had been knocked out of her body. 'So Don never bought the house?'

'Good heavens, no. He wouldn't leave his mother. She was widowed quite young, so I believe. And he was her only child. They were very close. Almost unhealthily so,' she added under her breath. She gave an ironic little laugh. 'Strange that she died just after I left him.'

Una crumbled a biscuit as she allowed the information to sink in. 'He still keeps her room just as it was,' she said. 'All her clothes are in the wardrobe and everything.'

Monica nodded. 'A shrine. I can well imagine.'

'What was she like?' Una asked.

Monica sighed. 'I suppose there's no harm now in saying what I think,' she said. 'And anyway, she's dead.' She looked at Una. 'She was a monster. An absolute monster. She wrecked our marriage and made my life a living hell. And she had Donald utterly under her thumb. It was always what his mother wanted. No one else mattered to him.' She smiled. 'But that's something you'll never have to put up with. The house and Donald are all yours now.'

Una had the uncomfortable impression that she would have liked to add: *And you're welcome to them*. She cleared her throat. 'Well – of course you must take the desk.' Privately she thought the thing ugly and old-fashioned. It had been next on her list for the auction room anyway. 'Just ring and let me know when you're having it collected.'

'I will. Thank you so much, Una.' Monica stood up and began to pull on her gloves, smoothing the soft kid over her fingers. 'It's been so nice to meet you. I've been trying to pluck up the courage to write, but I was passing this afternoon and, knowing that you work here, I thought I'd just pop in.'

Work here indeed! Una bridled indignantly. 'I only come in occasionally, to do a little administrative work.' She stood up and held out her hand. 'You were quite lucky to catch me actually. Goodbye. And if there's ever anything else I can do, just let me know.'

Monica looked at her curiously. 'The same goes for me, Una. I can assure you I bear no grudges. I hope you feel the same about me. And if ever you want someone to talk to . . . believe me, no one understands Donald Blake and his little idiosyncrasies like I do.'

When she'd gone Una sat for a long time deep in thought, her invitation list quite forgotten. The woman had a bloody cheek with her patronising offers of help and advice. All the same, a lot of things were clear now. Don's inhibitions in the bedroom; his strange prudish habits. The way he always undressed in the dark and refused to look at her until she'd put on her nightdress. He'd been unreasonably reluctant to dispose of that awful old furniture too and he was adamant about that room of his mother's. She felt a chill run through her veins. It was creepy – almost as though the old woman still occupied the house. As though she were still watching everything they did. Well, she'd soon put a stop to all that, Una told herself firmly. When Don got home from Eastbourne he'd find a few changes. And he'd be getting an ultimatum.

It was two days later that the row erupted. Rosalind arrived home to hear the raised voices of her mother and step-father. She stood just inside the door, her stomach quaking in the old familiar way, reminded of those far-off days when she had wakened in the night to the terrifying sound of her parents' quarrelling. In the hall tea chests were stacked ready for collection. On closer inspection she saw that they contained clothing, books and ornaments. There were several framed photographs and on top of one a rose-embellished chamber pot was precariously perched. From the landing Una's shrill voice could be heard. Rosalind could tell from experience that she was well on the way to working up one of her 'states'.

'All that stuff has got to go,' she was shouting. 'Either *it goes* or *I* do. And that's only the beginning. I want this

111

house put on the market straight away. I want a nice little bungalow on the new estate – with picture windows, central heating and a patio. And if you don't get it for me, Don Blake, you can live in this mausoleum by your bloody self!'

Chapter Six

Lying in bed in his hotel room Gerald stared at the moonlit ceiling. Although he had drunk almost half a bottle of whisky before falling into bed, sleep still eluded him and he felt depressingly sober. He turned his head and watched the curtains gently moving at the window. He hated the Swiss way of folding the shutters over the windows at night. It made the room so inky dark; made him feel so alone.

For a while he watched the floating pattern, made by the moonlight on the ceiling, then he tested his memory by picturing the scene outside the window, trying to recall every little detail. It wasn't difficult. He knew this place so well. It was here that he'd spent his ecstatic honeymoon, in those far-off, long-gone days when life was uncomplicated and love was new and exciting. In recent years this was where he always came when there was some crisis in his life, a decision to make or something to think through. It had never failed to soothe and heal him. Till now.

Far below his hotel window was the street, asleep now and grubby with the day's traffic. But it would be washed clean by morning before anyone was up. What bliss if one's life could be washed clean of cares and guilt each morning.

The pavement was bordered by shops, neat and clean, their windows tempting with artistically displayed wares. Above the little town the mountains rose in a majestic, snow-capped sweep, proud and protective. In the quiet of the night he could hear the sound of water as it flowed from the springs high in the mountains to feed the lake below. He imagined it, chuckling over smooth stones as it rippled along the channels carved out over the centuries; falling in sparkling cascades over rocky crags to run finally, tamed and subdued, gurgling under the roads through the little man-made culverts on its way to the lake. When the springs froze in winter, the lake gradually dried up and became a snow-filled hole in the ground bereft of its lifeblood until the warmth of spring released it and the little town laughed with the sound of living water once again.

Gerald felt his own lifeblood freeze as the words of Doctor Gruber echoed inside his head. Gruber was the consultant he had seen that morning at the clinic in Zurich. He had undergone all the tests and now had the initial diagnosis confirmed by two consultants, the finest in their field in the world. One in Edinburgh and one in Switzerland both recommended to him in New York by Dr Brewster. Could he really turn his back on the truth any longer? He was still comparatively young. In his prime some might say, certainly at the height of his career. Everything in him railed against the prospect of winding down, as he had been advised. To bow out now, just when he was getting rave notices; just when he knew the exhilaration of being considered the cream of his profession. It was unthinkable. But every time he rebelled against it he was pulled up sharply by the memory of that concert in New York. The terrifying night when his memory had failed him and his fingers had turned into useless lumps of dead flesh. That must never happen again. He dare not risk the shame, the humiliation. But what to do?

Still reeling from the shock in the clinic this morning he had vaguely heard Doctor Gruber telling him that with the proper drugs and treatments, a healthy diet and sensible lifestyle, he could still lead a full and useful life. He had wanted to shout, asking what a full and useful life meant when the whole purpose of one's existence had gone. Now he remembered the man's voice as he made his calm pronouncement. Soothing, placatory. His eyes all compassion as he handed out what to Gerald amounted

114

to a death sentence. Oh yes, the man had a good bedside manner, he'd give him that, Gerald told himself bitterly. No doubt he could turn it on and off at will, like a tap. Well, so he should. God knew he was paid enough for it.

He sighed. Drugs. The proper treatment. A sensible lifestyle. What did all that add up to? A regimen of pill-taking or injections that would reduce his brain to a senile pulp? A boring diet of lettuce leaves, lentil casseroles and non-alcohol wine? No parties or late nights? No cigarettes? No driving? What was the point? He might as well be dead, he decided hopelessly, blinking back the bitter tears that scalded his eyes. He pictured his friends' shocked faces. Oh, they would show compassion. Some of them might even be sincere – to begin with. They would certainly feel sorry for him, but in spite of their pity they would eventually drop him. *Poor old Gerald. He's finished, you know. Can't play any more. Can't do anything really. So sad at his age, isn't it?* It was difficult and embarrassing, being around sick people. He should know. He'd avoided them himself in the past.

There were other things in his past that he wasn't proud of. Was this illness some kind of retribution? he asked himself. His past misdeeds catching up with him? What was it the mystics called it – Karma? He thought of Daniel Oldham, the person who had been his best friend in their student days. He had treated him badly all those years ago, yet the man had come to him for help when he needed it. Perhaps this was his chance to redeem himself.

This morning after his consultation he had left the clinic like a man in a dream. All he had wanted was to get away from the bustle of the city and be alone to think. He had taken the little mountain train and come here to the only place where he could relax in familiar surroundings. Now he must make himself think about the future. Face up to what was left of his life and decide what to do with it.

Tomorrow. He smiled wryly as a hackneyed phrase leapt into his mind. *Tomorrow is the first day of the rest of your life*. Well, it would be that all right. Whatever happened, whatever he decided, he had things to do and people to see. What was the term they used? *Putting one's affairs in order*. His heart felt like lead in his chest. It wasn't exactly something to look forward to.

At last he slept. And when he wakened the sun was rising over the mountain tops. It was the way he loved to begin the day, which was why when he came here he always slept with the shutters open. Slipping out of bed, he pulled on his dressing gown and went out on to the balcony. The air was sharp and pure, clear as crystal as it hit the back of his throat. He breathed it deeply into his lungs and felt it strengthen him and lift his spirit. He watched as the sun outlined the mountain-tops in silver. The craggy peaks turned from grey through violet and rose to palest lemon, then to burning gold as the sun rose triumphantly above them into an azure sky. It was a sight he never tired of and his heart soared. He felt so well. He *couldn't* be ill. It wasn't possible.

Sitting on the balcony in the quiet of dawn he made himself think. He'd let his agent go ahead with the coming season's bookings. There were three Promenade Concerts booked; the tail end of his recording contract still to fulfil and a tour of cathedral cities with the LSO. He'd manage the recording but, as for the concerts, he would have to cancel them all. There was nothing else for it. He dared not risk another live performance. And the sooner he spoke to his agent about it, the better. This must be his priority. He took a leisurely bath and shaved, then rang down to room service for breakfast.

Over hot coffee and croissants with his favourite black cherry jam he laid his plans carefully. So far no one knew about the diagnosis except of course the three doctors he had consulted. Only Carl Kramer had witnessed his lapse at the New York concert. He would write to him and thank him for his concern and for recommending the doctor, tell

116

him it was caused by exhaustion and that he was fine now. No one need know the real reason for his retirement. No one at all apart from his doctors. He was damned if he would submit himself to the humiliation of their pity. He would find a place to live – a permanent home. That was the one thing he had never had. No more travelling. He found that the idea appealed to him. The moment he got back to England he would contact the estate agents and start searching. Somewhere in the Cotswolds perhaps – or Dorset; peaceful and serene. It would be something to look forward to.

As soon as he knew that his agent, James Kendrick, would be in the office he rang down to Reception and asked them to put through a call to London for him.

When the telephone rang James himself was at the other end. 'Hi there, Gerry. What can I do for you?'

When he made his announcement there was a silence at the other end of the line. Then James said incredulously: '*Retiring?* Are you mad? What the hell are you talking about, Gerry?'

'What I say. I'm giving up.'

'But – but for how long?'

'For *good*. I'm taking an early retirement.'

James spluttered incoherently at the other end. 'Look, what's happened to make you decide a thing like that? Has something upset you? Anyway, what the bloody hell are you doing in Switzerland? I think you'd better come home pretty damned quick and talk about this, don't you? I mean, in case you've forgotten, you've got commitments.'

'I know. I'll do the album for Zenith, but I want you to cancel the rest – the concerts.'

'*Cancel?* You're out of your tiny mind! Look, what's going on?'

'Okay, okay. I'll come home. I'll see you tomorrow, but I won't change my mind, James. So you'd better get on and cancel those concert dates right away. We don't want anyone

117

suing us, do we?' An irate James was still demanding to know what was happening when Gerald hung up. It was going to be a damned sight harder than he'd envisaged. He might even have to confide in James after all, but he'd swear him to secrecy. He began to pack. There was a train for Zurich at midday. He could catch a late-afternoon flight and be back in London this evening.

Chapter Seven

It was summer before Cathy saw Gerald again. He kept in touch, of course. From time to time she would receive a postcard, a brief message scribbled on the back. Her allowance was paid into the bank regularly on the first of every month too. But then Gerald had nothing to do with that. It was arranged at the bank on a standing order.

She thought about him a lot during the early months of the year, remembering the way he had confided in her on Christmas Day. She wondered why he didn't telephone or come to see her. Even if he was away he must come back to London occasionally. She wondered about his decision to retire too. Perhaps he had changed his mind by now. He had seemed a little depressed at Christmas. People often made hasty decisions when they were depressed. Maybe he had found a doctor who could cure this rare stiffness of the joints thing he had. By the look of the cards he sent he had been travelling again: Switzerland, Edinburgh, but she had no idea whether he was working or not. If he wasn't playing Cathy could only guess at the reason for his absence, if reason there was.

She'd said nothing to anyone about her conversation with Gerald on Christmas Day. Johnny had been surprised and slightly put out when she had discovered that he wasn't taking up her invitation to spend Boxing Day with them. She'd remarked rather tartly to Cathy that she would have thought he had better manners than to wait until the last minute and then send a message with her.

'He could have telephoned me,' she said resentfully. 'I daresay he's got a better invitation from one of his famous friends. I suppose the likes of us aren't exciting enough.'

In her chair by the window Mrs Bains gave a meaningful sniff that said more than mere words ever could.

Cathy burned to tell them that they were sadly misjudging him, but she had promised. Her lips were sealed.

Her course in Home Economics was almost through its first year. In the initial few months it had all been new and interesting, but lately Cathy had found it becoming tedious. Long warm summer days spent learning how to apply physics and chemistry to household skills seemed endless when everything outside the window hummed with the glorious promise of summer. Environmental studies were more interesting, entailing visits to housing estates, both urban and rural, but while they stood grouped around their tutor, hearing about modern drainage methods and the horrors of Victorian sanitation, Cathy longed to be by the sea or in the countryside. Back in college there were lectures on the basics of architecture and the structure of the domestic house. A lot of it was very interesting but somehow it failed to absorb Cathy. Before long she began to feel that Miss Hanley had been right and she might have chosen unwisely. The course didn't stimulate her imagination – didn't stretch her enough.

Her weekend job was pleasant enough. The Queen's Head was a small hotel and Mrs Gresham, the manageress, and the rest of her staff were kind and friendly, patiently helping Cathy over her first fumbling attempts at waitressing and her ineptitude in the kitchen. It was a far cry from helping Johnny at home, but she enjoyed the work once she'd become accustomed to the routine. She even eventually grew used to Raymond, the frighteningly volatile chef, whose explosive and unpredictable bark, she soon learned, was much worse than his bite. But she couldn't envisage herself choosing hotel work as a future career, unlike Rosalind Blair whose burning ambition seemed to be to run a hotel of her own.

She and Rosalind had become quite friendly since they had started working together at the hotel. Rosalind was grateful to Cathy for tipping her off about the weekend job at the Queen's Head and, more recently, she had been delighted when her temporary job was extended to a permanent one. She was so keen and eager to learn, which made her popular with the rest of the staff. She certainly seemed to have an aptitude for the work. She seemed a shy girl, hesitant and diffident, but her natural reserve seemed to disappear magically when she was dealing with people. It was almost as though she became a different person. Cathy grew to like her more and more as the months went by.

Gradually coming out of her shell, Rosalind confided to Cathy that she was desperately anxious to earn some money. She explained that her divorced mother had recently remarried and she didn't want to be a burden on her and the new step-father for any longer than was absolutely necessary.

Hearing about Rosalind's circumstances made Cathy wonder how she would have felt if her father had ever decided to marry again, and she decided that it would have been quite hard to accept, especially if she had resented the woman as much as Rosalind appeared to resent her new step-father. Since Daniel's death she had thought about her mother a great deal, wondering at her father's acceptance of her betrayal. She was convinced that if someone she loved let her down like that she would never get over it. She was sure she had not inherited Daniel's sweet, forgiving nature.

It had been early in the spring when Matthew had begun to invite Cathy out. Neither of them had much spare time and because of this neither of them had many friends, but they found they shared similar tastes in music and films. When *West Side Story* came to the Roxy, Matthew asked her to go with him. The beautiful, sad story made a deep impression on Cathy and the strong vibrant music of Leonard Bernstein reminded her sharply of the bitter-sweet melodies that used to echo through the house in Laburnum Close when her father was shut away on one of his creative sessions. She saved up and bought the album, playing it upstairs in her room on the record player Daniel had bought her on her fifteenth birthday. Somehow it reminded her of her father. If only he'd had more confidence in his musical abilities, she felt sure that he too could have been a famous composer.

Since seeing *West Side Story* together, Cathy and Matthew had been to the cinema several times and once or twice to dances. He was good company. Quiet and thoughtful by nature, his reactions were comfortably predictable. But although the other young people they knew began to link their names together, looking upon them as a couple, Cathy never thought of him as anything but a friend.

By the end of June she had decided that Gerald had slipped out of her life for good. She resigned herself to the fact that the novelty of having a ward had worn off for him. Sometimes she asked herself if he could have dropped her because of something she had said or done. When she remembered the brazen way she had kissed him at Christmas she went hot all over with shame. At the time it had seemed all right; a perfectly natural thing to do. Now she saw that she had revealed herself as naive and childish. It was just as well he had decided not to see her, she told herself. Remembering that occasion she would have been too embarrassed to look him in the eye.

It was just two weeks before the end of term when she swung into the house one afternoon, calling out to Johnny, as she always did, to tell her she was home. She was hanging her jacket on the hallstand when the door of the front room opened and there he stood – Gerald, a wide smile on his face.

'Cathy!'

She felt the hot blood creeping up her neck and into her face, '*Oh!* Oh, hello,' she said weakly.

He laughed. 'You look shocked.'

'I'm surprised. I didn't see the car.'

'I parked it in the next street. I wanted to surprise you. Well?' He took a step towards her. 'You don't seem very pleased to see me.'

She blushed. 'I thought I never would any more,' she said stiffly. 'I thought maybe you'd gone abroad – or forgotten about me, or something.'

'If I'd known you were missing me that much I'd have come sooner.' His eyes teased her. 'Come on, admit it. You've been much too busy enjoying college to give your poor old guardian a thought.'

She stared at him. How could he be so wrong about the way she felt? And how dare he walk in as though he had seen her only yesterday?

Seeing the flush that coloured her cheeks and the expression in her eyes his smile vanished and he reached out to take her hand and draw her towards him. 'You really *are* upset, aren't you? I'm sorry, Cathy. If I'd known . . .'

'It's all right. Of course I'm not upset,' she said, panic sharpening her voice. 'And you're right. I have been busy. Time's absolutely flown. So – what brings you here now? Were you just passing or do you have time to stay for a few minutes?'

'Mrs Johnson has very kindly invited me to tea.' He was looking at her oddly. 'But actually I've told her I can't stay.'

'No? Oh, well, it can't be helped. It was nice seeing you anyway.' Her heart beating fast, she began to push past him towards the stairs, reaching for the newel post, but he stopped her with a hand on her shoulder.

'Cathy!' He looked seriously concerned and her anger faded a little. 'Look, the reason I can't stay for tea is because I've booked a table for two – for dinner.'

'I see. Then we mustn't keep you.'

'For *us*, silly. For you and me. I want to talk to you.'

'To me? What about?'

He raised an eyebrow at her. 'Why not come along and see?' He looked into her eyes. 'I'm serious. I really do need your opinion on something. Something very important.'

He was humouring her. Just as though she were ten years old. A truculent child who had to be indulgently coaxed out of a bad mood. Tears of angry frustration pricked at her eyelids. Did he really think he could ignore her for months and then come back and expect her to behave as though he'd never been away? Avoiding his eyes she said, 'I don't think I can make it this evening, Gerald. I've got some work to do. I'm afraid it won't wait.'

He sighed. 'Oh, dear. It's worse than I thought. I really am in the dog house, aren't I?'

Johnny had come out into the hall and he turned to her. 'Mrs Johnson, will you please tell this young lady that I badly need her to come out to dinner with me?'

Johnny looked unsmilingly from one to the other. 'Off you go and change, Cathy. I'm sure you don't want to keep Mr Cavelle waiting, do you?'

Gerald looked at her, his head on one side. 'Surely your essay or whatever it is will wait for a couple of hours, won't it?'

The two of them stood looking at her. She was outnumbered. She couldn't keep up her pretence of being too busy without looking ridiculous. Without a word she turned and climbed the stairs. When she had gone Gerald turned to Johnny.

'Any idea why she's upset, Mrs Johnson?'

'She isn't a child any longer, Mr Cavelle,' Johnny told him frankly. 'She's a young woman. You can't fob her off with treats and promises. And she's still very insecure. She needs to know where she is.' And without another word she turned and went back into the kitchen.

*   *   *

124

He took her to a Chinese restaurant. Cathy had never eaten Chinese food before and she was intrigued by all the little dishes and the delicious delicate flavours. Gerald watched with an indulgent smile as she tried first one thing, then another, struggling manfully with the chopsticks. She had changed so much in the few months since he last saw her. She was taller and her slender figure had developed softly rounded curves. Her face had lost its blurred childishness. The delicate bones were more defined now, with gentle shadows that accentuated her green eyes. Mrs Johnson had been right. Since he had seen her last Cathy had grown from a schoolgirl into an attractive young woman with the tantalising promise of real beauty yet to come. Yet through it all she hadn't lost that quality of untouched innocence he found so piquant. Compared to the sophisticated women he knew she was as refreshing as a spring morning.

'Tell me what you've been doing with yourself since Christmas?' he invited.

'Nothing very much. I've been too busy working.' She went on to tell him a little about her course and about the films that she and Matthew had seen – the dances they'd been to.

He listened politely for a while, then said suddenly, 'Cathy, there's something I want you to see. I've found a house. It's in Suffolk, near the sea. Will you come and look at it with me?'

She looked up at him, the prawn she had been trying to convey to her mouth dropping back onto her plate. 'You're leaving London?'

'Yes. At least, I'm thinking seriously about it.' He dabbed at his lips with his napkin and pushed his plate away. 'That's what I wanted to talk to you about. I've been thinking of buying a house in the country. I've never had a real home, you know. I seem to have spent my entire life in transit.'

'What about when you were a child?' she asked.

'My grandfather brought me up,' he told her. 'At least he paid other people to do it. He lived alone in a large house in Manchester where he owned a cotton mill. My mother was his only daughter and he hadn't approved of her marriage to my father, apparently. They were both killed in a train crash in 1923 when I was two years old.' He smiled wryly. 'I daresay he saw it as divine retribution. I don't remember either of them at all.'

Cathy's heart was stirred at the thought of Gerald losing his parents as a baby. 'So your grandfather adopted you?'

He nodded. 'Out of a sense of duty more than anything else, I think. There was no one else to take me you see. He certainly never showed me any affection. I was raised by a series of kindly young women who had a disconcerting habit of going off and getting married just when I was beginning to depend on them.'

Cathy was silent for a moment. 'I thought I was unlucky, losing my mother when I was little,' she said. 'But at least I had Dad. But your grandfather paid for your musical education though?'

'Yes.' Gerald picked up his glass and regarded the clear red colour of his wine. 'I think he felt that as it was the only talent I had he'd better foster it,' he said with a hint of bitterness. 'Couldn't have his only grandchild turning out a total failure and disgracing him.' He grinned wryly at her. 'Besides, I daresay he was relieved to get me out of the house.'

Cathy watched thoughtfully as he took a long drink of his wine. She pictured the lonely little boy in the big old house with no one to read him a bedtime story or play with him. How sad it must have been never to have known a parent's love. It had obviously affected Gerald deeply. 'So now you're going to have a home of your own at last. Tell me about the house you've found,' she invited.

'I didn't have a very clear idea of what I wanted when I set out,' he admitted. 'Thatched roof and roses round the door, I suppose. Everyone's dream of an idyllic country home. Then I found this one. It's nothing like what I had in mind and it's far larger than I need. But it's so beautiful, Cathy. I fell in love with it the moment I set eyes on it and I just couldn't get it out of my mind. Then I had an idea. I'd already thought I might teach, so why not buy the house and turn it into a kind of music school? I could coach especially talented young pianists for the concert platform as I'd planned, but if I buy this house I could make it into a kind of musical retreat; organise weekend seminars – concerts and master classes – that kind of thing.'

'It sounds interesting, but I don't quite see where I come in.'

He looked at her thoughtfully. 'You are the closest to a family I've got. That's important to me and I'd like your opinion. Before I can even begin to think about this project there will be an enormous amount of work to be done. I thought you might be interested – have some ideas. You know, the woman's angle.' He laughed, looking at her plate of cooling food. 'And I think you'd better abandon those chopsticks and eat up your dinner. Mrs Johnson will be wanting you home. I think I'm already in her black books as it is.'

'Oh, but I want to hear more about the house. I can't wait to see it!'

'Then you'll come with me – this weekend – Sunday?'

She laughed as she obediently resorted to a fork and began to finish her food. 'I can see that if I want my curiosity satisfied I'm going to have to.'

As she finished her meal she reflected that tonight she had learned something else about Gerald. The more she was with him, the more she understood him. He was so easy to be with. She had missed him – blamed him for staying away so long. Yet now she saw that he had been busy trying to build a new life for himself. It must take courage to do that alone. To start again when your name had been famous. How selfish she had been to think only of herself. She thought excitedly of the house he planned to buy and the fact that he actually valued *her* opinion. And she couldn't wait till Sunday.

The day dawned dull and cloudy, but the low cloud thinned to a fine mist which soon melted away to reveal a clear blue sky. As the sun rose higher a fine heat haze danced on the road ahead as Gerald drove the Jaguar eastwards. As they drove he told her more about the house and the village.

'It's called Melfordleigh. Only a few houses, a church and a pub. It's the kind of place that sailors, fishermen and artists like. It's a pretty village. Two long winding streets dip down towards the sea and there are lots of little lanes running off, with surprising glimpses of little gardens and courtyards full of colour.'

'And the sea? Is there a beach?'

'Not as such. There are little creeks that run out to the sea – perfect for mooring boats. And there's a long finger of land that curves out to sea for about half a mile. It makes a wonderful walk. But the best part is that it's quite unspoilt. The tourists haven't filled it with amusement arcades and whelk stalls, thank God. Luckily it's far too quiet and tucked away for the day trippers' tastes too.'

'And your house – the one you hope to buy?' Cathy found his enthusiasm infectious.

'It stands in about two acres of grounds, at the top of the village. There's a stream running through – what used to be the millstream actually. The watermill used to be downstream and at one time Cuckoo Lodge was the miller's house.'

'Cuckoo Lodge? I like the name.'

He pulled a face. 'Do you? I thought I might change it. I'm afraid my friends might think *I'm* cuckoo, burying myself in the country.'

'But you're sure it's what you want?' Cathy asked.

'I'm sure. For me it seems the perfect answer. This way I can still be involved in music and have the peace and quiet of the country too.' He smiled at her wryly. 'I don't doubt that the very friends who'll laugh the loudest will be only too happy to come and stay once I've restored the place and moved in.'

'Weekend house parties? Sounds like fun.'

'Not unless they're willing to work,' he told her. 'This project is going to be my living, remember. If they come they'll have to be willing to take a class or give a lecture.'

'So – tell me some more about the house. How old is it?'

'The main part is Tudor, but there's an extra wing that was built on in Queen Anne's reign.'

'As old as that? And how big?'

'About six bedrooms upstairs. Downstairs it's difficult to say. Some walls may have to be taken out. There seems to have been a lot of alteration over the years. Goodness knows what might be lurking behind the hideous modern fireplaces. I'm hoping for some inglenooks.'

Cathy found herself looking forward to seeing it all for herself. She smiled at him. 'You make it all sound so exciting,' she said. 'I can't wait.'

When Gerald announced that they had arrived and drove in through broken gates that hung drunkenly on rusting hinges, Cathy felt a stab of disappointment. They stopped next to a tumbledown corrugated iron shed and Gerald switched off the engine and turned to her.

'That's what is laughingly termed the garage. At the moment it's blocking the view, but once it's down you'll be able to see the house from the gate. Come on.' He got out of the car, looking as excited as a child.

Cathy followed him hesitantly along a path of trodden grass, wondering what he could possibly see in a place as rundown as this. She'd had such high expectations and now

129

that they'd actually arrived the place was such a let down. Then, as they turned the corner of the disintegrating garage, she stopped short and caught her breath. In front of her, its brickwork glowing rose red in the summer sunshine, was Cuckoo Lodge. Long and low, its two storeys were topped by a russet-tiled roof. Two rows of windows glinted at them like welcoming eyes.

'Like it?' Gerald was studying her face carefully.

She nodded, the house's magic spell rendering her speechless. It seemed to take on an almost tangible magnetism, reaching out to her invitingly as she stood there staring. 'Oh – I see what you mean,' she breathed. 'It's lovely.'

He was fishing the keys out of an inside pocket. 'Right, come on then, let's go in and see what you think of the inside.'

The heavy front door creaked back on its hinges, opening immediately on to a long, low-ceilinged room. At first they could hardly see anything, but when Gerald folded back the shutters on the windows the sun streamed in. Their footsteps raised dust which danced in motes along the beams of golden light. Now that she could see, Cathy saw that at one end of the room a huge Victorian fireplace almost filled one wall, while at the other a door stood open on to a square hall out of which rose a staircase.

'How odd that the front door leads straight into the living room,' she remarked.

Gerald nodded. 'I mentioned that to the agent. It seems there have been many alterations over the years and at one time the place was actually used as a pub.'

Cathy looked into all the rooms. There were two others downstairs besides the large living room; both of them looking on to the back of the house. Their windows had views of the tangled garden, rank with couch grass and weeds that reached halfway up the window frames. The kitchen was a built-on lean-to affair. It was a nightmare, with only the basic facilities – a stone sink, equipped with a hand pump, a massive iron mangle and a rotting pine dresser. 'Does it have mains water and drainage?' she asked. 'And what about gas and electricity?' Dropping to her knees, she inspected a damp patch near the skirting board. 'Looks like rising damp,' she said. 'You'll be lucky if there isn't dry rot in these boards. The place has probably never had a dampcourse.'

Gerald's eyebrows rose. 'I'd no idea you were so knowledgeable,' he said. 'I'm impressed. I knew I was right to bring you.'

Standing up, Cathy dusted off her hands and gave him a long, level look. 'All this is part of my course at college. If you're going to patronise me, Gerald, I'll go and wait for you in the car.'

Suitably chastened, he reached out to touch her shoulder. 'I'm sorry.'

She stepped aside, dislodging his hand with the merest flick of her shoulder. Walking into the hall, she asked: 'Shall we look upstairs?'

There were six rooms on the floor above. Gerald remarked that two would need to be converted to bathrooms, but Cathy disagreed.

'If you want to keep all six rooms you could easily have two with en suite bathrooms,' she said. 'They're certainly big enough to be able to spare a little space. And that massive cupboard on the landing would make another for general use. You'd need to put in central heating too,' she mused. 'And the windows would probably need replacing. A house of this age is probably listed, which means you'd have to apply for permission and abide by their rules.' She looked at him, her head on one side. 'Have you checked the roof timbers for woodworm and beetle?'

Gerald began to laugh. 'Forgive me, Cathy, but I can't get over you. I shan't need a surveyor at this rate. On the other hand, I'm only just beginning to realise how much all this is going to cost me.' He pulled her to him and kissed the top of her head. 'Let's go and find some lunch. I can't face any more of this on an empty stomach.'

Cathy had quite surprised herself. She was only just realising how much information from the lectures on architecture she had actually absorbed. And putting it into practical use was much more enjoyable than she could ever have imagined. Already she was picturing Cuckoo Lodge as it could be and the prospect of having a hand in its restoration filled her with excited anticipation.

They left the car where it was and walked down through the village. Cathy adored it. Off the steep, winding main street, little alleyways led to pretty cottages, their gardens and little courtyards filled with flowers. There were surprises everywhere. When they reached the bottom of the hill the air was fresh and invigorating with the salt smell of the sea. Facing them, a forest of masts lined the quayside where dozens of boats were moored. Creeks separated by banks of glistening wet sand wound like silver threads out to the sea.

Facing the quay was the Admiral Nelson, the most amazing building that Cathy had ever seen. The first-floor frontage was a replica of a ship's fo'c'sle, its dark timber decorated with brightly painted mermaids and dolphins. And the front entrance of the hostelry was guarded by a voluptuous figurehead with flowing blonde locks and an impossibly large bosom with nipples the size of oranges.

'The landlord tells me they were all that was salvaged from a ship that was wrecked off the coast here in 1811,' Gerald told her. 'If we're lucky we might get a table in the window with a view of the quay.'

They were lucky. The landlord remembered Gerald from earlier visits. Being a classical music lover he had also recognised him as a celebrity, but, guessing that he was off-duty, tactfully kept the recognition to himself.

The food was excellent. Sitting in the fo'c'sle window was

like being at sea and Cathy enjoyed it very much as she told Gerald enthusiastically.

He enjoyed her pleasure, appreciative of the fact that she was still young enough to behave so openly. 'And the house?' He looked at her enquiringly. 'Tell me the truth. Do you think I'm a fool even to consider it?'

She looked at him carefully before deciding that he really did want her opinion. 'Well – there *is* an awful lot that needs doing,' she said guardedly. 'It's going to cost you a lot of money.'

'Yes, I'd already worked that out for myself. What I want to know is – will it be worth it?'

She smiled. 'I think so. There's a certain something about the place. It's as though it wants you to save its life. *You*, I mean. Not just anyone. Standing there, looking at it, you can almost feel it *begging* you.' She glanced up at him. 'I expect you think I'm being silly?'

'Not at all. I knew I was right to bring you. I felt that the first time I saw it.'

'Of course you'll need to get experts in to advise you,' she went on practically. 'I mean, it would be silly to run yourself into unnecessary expense. It's a sad thought, but the place might have gone beyond help.'

He nodded decisively. 'I'll get on to someone tomorrow. I've got the name of a reliable firm of architects and surveyors. I just wanted you to confirm the hunch I had about the place. You've done that. Thanks, Cathy.'

'I don't know why I'm encouraging you to buy Cuckoo Lodge,' she said. 'If you do, I don't suppose I'll see much of you.'

He looked up at her sharply. 'Why do you say that?'

She shrugged. 'You'll want to supervise the restoration to begin with. Then when you move in you'll be busy arranging your new life – your music students and weekend seminars.'

'I won't lose touch with you though.'

'Won't you?' she said wistfully. 'You did before. I've hardly seen you since last Christmas.'

He averted his eyes from her direct green gaze. 'That was different. I was out of the country for much of that time.'

'Of course. Sorry.' She spooned sugar into her coffee and stirred. It was none of her business what he did with his free time, of course. And yet he had said she was the nearest he had to family. In that respect they were both in the same boat. Suddenly she looked up and said, 'Gerald, you must have known my mother.'

He looked up in surprise. 'Yes.'

'So – what was she like?'

He shrugged. 'She was beautiful. Stunning auburn hair like yours and green eyes.'

She shook her head. 'I know all that from her photographs. I meant, what was she like – as a person?'

'Well – what can I say? It was a long time ago. She was Dan's wife – your mother.'

She twisted the spoon between her fingers. 'You know of course that she left us – Dad and me? When I was a baby. Went off with some lover.'

'I did hear something, yes.'

She bit her lip. 'Dad was so forgiving. I don't see how he could be. I know I could never forgive someone who let me down like that. He only told me what really happened a few months before he died, you know. Until then I'd always thought she died when I was little. He didn't want me to think ill of her, especially after she was killed.' She looked at Gerald. 'You did know she was killed – in a car accident?'

'Yes. And he never told you.' He smiled gently. 'That sounds like Dan.'

'I've tried not to, and I know he wouldn't want me to, but I *do* think badly of her,' she admitted. 'Dad didn't deserve to be treated like that and I don't see how anyone can leave their baby.'

134

'We none of us know what we'd do, faced with the same dilemma,' he said softly.

'I keep thinking that maybe if she'd stayed – if Dad had been happier . . .'

He reached out to touch her hand. 'Cathy, don't torture yourself, wondering what might have been. I've learned that it's no use raking over the past. What's done is done. We can never know what might have happened if things had been different. Look at me. I'm losing so much through this – this wretched ailment of mine. But it's no use wishing for something we can't have. Things happen. We have to accept, adapt, and make the best of it.'

'You said something like that once before.'

'I'm not a wise man but at least I've learned that much.'

'You've got so much courage, Gerald. I wish I had half as much.'

They walked back up through the winding street to Cuckoo Lodge to stand staring at the house again. Gerald looked at Cathy. 'You still haven't seen the rest of it,' he said. 'There's lots more.' He took her hand. 'Come on, I'll show you.'

At the back of the house was a huddle of tumbledown outbuildings: a decaying wash house, its brickwork green with moss, an unspeakable corrugated iron privy, apparently occupied by several hundred spiders, a fuel store, and a rather imposing barn built of stone and timber.

'Once these are down you'd be able to see the garden from the back windows,' Gerald said with a sweep of his arm. 'Thought the barn might make rather a good studio. It was once used as a grain store for the mill and the agent seems to think it's structurally solid.'

They skirted the buildings, wading through the waist-high grass to what had once been a beautiful garden. Cathy recognised a group of lilacs, and there were fruit trees cordoned against a sun-warmed wall of pale pink brick. Foxgloves,

135

ox-eye daisies and roses, long since gone to rampant briar, struggled for supremacy with invading nettles and rosebay willow herb. There was a huge gnarled apple tree with the remains of a swing hanging from one of its springy branches. Cathy was enthralled. 'Oh, Gerald, this could be lovely!'

A rusty iron gate at the bottom took them on to the bank of the stream where willows dipped their graceful fronds into the glassy green water. Among the reeds yellow flag iris grew in profusion, throwing their bright reflection into the stream. Looking into the dark water Cathy glimpsed a large brown speckled fish moving sluggishly among the weeds. Then suddenly she was startled as a family of mallards emerged from the curtain of willow, stirring the water into a thousand spreading ripples. The big fish vanished as the mother duck fussed noisily with her flotilla of ducklings, sending them scudding through the creamy water lilies. Cathy laughed delightedly.

'Oh, Gerald, look. Aren't they sweet? I wish I'd brought some bread so that we could feed them.'

He watched her enjoying it all. It made him ache deep inside to see her spontaneous pleasure. She was so young – so easily pleased by simple things. She reminded him so much of . . . He turned away abruptly. 'Time's getting on. I think we should make tracks for home.'

She followed him reluctantly back to the car. As he settled himself in the driving seat he said, 'I'll get that firm of architects on to it tomorrow. I wonder how long it would take them to make the place habitable? Always supposing it's possible.'

'I'll keep my fingers crossed.' Cathy sighed. 'Oh, Gerald, I do envy you. It'll be so *exciting*, watching the house come back to life again.'

He'd already started backing the car out into the lane, but now he stopped and switched off the engine, turning in his seat to look at her. 'How would you like to be part of it?' he asked. 'How would you like to come and live here with me when it's done?'

Cathy felt the warm blood creep up her neck and into her cheeks. 'What – what do you mean?'

'What I say. After all, I am your guardian – and your godfather.'

'But – I have my course to finish.'

He studied her face for a moment and then turned away. 'Of course. You have your own life – all your own friends. And then there's Matthew, isn't there?'

She frowned. 'Matthew? What does he have to do with it?'

'He's your – what do you call it? – steady boyfriend, isn't he?'

'No.'

He started the engine again. 'You talk an awful lot about him, or perhaps you hadn't realised that.' He was out on the road now and began to press his foot down on the accelerator. 'Forget that I asked you, Cathy. Silly of me to imagine that a girl of your age would want to bury herself alive in a hole like this – and with a sick old man.'

Shocked, she turned troubled eyes on him and laid a hand lightly on his wrist. 'Gerald, you're not sick. And you're not an old man. You know you're not.'

He glanced at her. 'I must seem like one, to you.'

'But you don't. And there's nothing I'd like more than to live at Cuckoo Lodge and be part of all the exciting things you're planning.'

'It's all right. You don't have to be kind or feel sorry for me, you know.'

For the next few miles they drove in silence, Cathy puzzling over what she could have done or said to upset him. She wasn't aware of having talked a lot about Matthew. And going to live at Cuckoo Lodge with Gerald would be like some kind of wonderful dream come true. But how could she make him see this without making a fool of herself again?

137

They drove for most of the way in silence, each occupied with their own thoughts. The countryside gave way to buildings. They were almost home and Cathy had begun to despair, fearing that they would part on a sour note when Gerald suddenly turned to her.

'Would you like a drink before you go home? I think perhaps we should talk.'

She nodded silently, wondering apprehensively what they would talk about.

She'd been expecting him to pull up at a coffee bar or café and when he drew the car on to the forecourt of the Dog and Feathers she was a little surprised. Apart from the Queen's Head she had never been inside a pub before, but she didn't want him to know, so she tried to look as though it was something she did everyday.

It was a typical suburban pub, with folksy decor: mock beams and chintzes, horse brasses, and a log fire that was powered by electricity. But it was comfortable enough. As it was early in the evening there were few customers and plenty of seats. Cathy settled herself at a table by the window and Gerald asked her what she would like to drink. She said the first thing that came into her head.

'A dry martini, please.' The heroines in films always drank dry martinis and it had a sophisticated, feminine sound to it.

If Gerald was surprised he didn't show it. He came back to the table with the drinks and sat down beside her. 'Cathy – first I must ask your forgiveness. I'm sorry if I embarrassed you.'

'You didn't. It's all right.' She couldn't look at him. Raising the glass to her lips she took a mouthful of the pale liquid and almost choked on the bitterness that coursed down her throat like liquid fire.

'Are you all right?' he asked, seeing her eyes water.

She nodded. 'Yes . . . it's . . .' She pulled a face. 'I've

138

never actually had one of these before. I'm sorry but I'm afraid I don't like it very much.'

Smiling gently he took the glass from her hand and put it on the table. It was the proof that he'd been pushing her too hard. She'd probably much rather have had a lemonade or Coca-Cola. She was trying so hard to please him. 'You don't have to drink it.' He leaned closer. 'You don't have to do anything you don't want to, Cathy. It was mean of me to pressure you like that. Selfish. It's just that sometimes the thought of starting again – of being alone – scares me.'

She squeezed his hand and looked earnestly into his eyes. 'But I *would* like to live at Cuckoo Lodge with you,' she said. 'When I've finished my course.' She smiled at him. 'Anyway, it's going to take ages for the place to be ready, isn't it? There's plenty of time.'

He sighed, his heart heavy. Plenty of time was something she took for granted – whereas he . . . 'Of course,' he said. 'Plenty of time.'

'And you will take me again – to see the work, won't you?' she asked. 'To see the house taking shape? I've had such a lovely day, Gerald.' She glanced at him. 'Oh, and by the way . . .'

'Yes?'

'I don't see you as an old man. And I don't feel in the least sorry for you. So there!'

He laughed, leaning across to kiss her forehead. 'I'm delighted to hear it!'

Chapter Eight

The row over Mrs Blake senior's room marked the end of the honeymoon for Una and Don. For days afterwards Rosalind had to endure mealtimes frigid with animosity when neither her mother nor Don spoke one word; embarrassingly making whatever requests were necessary through her. Once, when Una addressed a scathing remark to no one in particular about living in the past, Don looked up from his *Daily Telegraph*, his face dark with anger.

'For Christ's sake, woman! Here we are on the brink of nuclear war and all you can think of is your damned bungalow.' He pushed the newspaper under her nose. 'Here – read about it.' He jabbed a finger at the headline that read: **CUBAN CRISIS. Kennedy Calls Up 150,000 Reservists.** 'If something isn't done soon about Castro none of us will have any *need* to worry about living in the past. We won't ever see 1963!' He strode out of the room.

But even thoughts of being blown to Kingdom Come didn't prevent Una from complaining. At night, through the walls of her room, Rosalind could hear the angry hum of their voices, spiked with the odd distinguishable word or phrase – *selfish* – *obsession* – *living in the past*. Her heart sank as she buried her head among the pillows, reminded miserably of her anguished childhood. At times she almost wished she had given up her cherished career dreams and accepted Ben and Freda's invitation to go with them to Australia. Rows, even those she was not directly involved in, made her feel physically sick. Voices raised in anger made her stomach churn and her heart thump uncomfortably and all the fears and insecurities of her childhood crowded in on her till she felt suffocated and wretched.

As Una and Don quarrelled behind their closed door she would shut her eyes and force herself to picture the lovely home she would have one day. A home that would be her livelihood too. Once she had achieved that no one could ever take it away from her.

Even when Don wasn't home there was little peace. Una constantly carped about him, tacitly urging Rosalind to take her side. She began to dread coming home from school each afternoon to hear a catalogue of Don's shortcomings. The weeks went by and the Cuban crisis was resolved, but at Blake's Folly things grew worse instead of better. Don stubbornly refused to move from Jay's Lane, paying no heed to Una's threats to leave him. She began to realise that he wasn't as easygoing or as eager to please as she had been led to believe. Without referring to the fact, both of them knew that with no money of her own, no job or home, she had little choice but to stay. His calm complacency infuriated Una, who felt trapped and cheated.

'If you ask me he's some kind of pervert,' she said waspishly for the hundredth time one day in early-November as she and Rosalind were having tea. 'Keeping all his mother's things locked up in that room like some kind of holy sanctum. I couldn't put up with that, could I? I mean, it was like something out of a horror film. When he came home and found I'd turfed them all out that afternoon he went white with rage – *white!*' she repeated with lurid satisfaction. 'I tell you, Rossie, I thought he was going to hit me.' She puffed out her breath explosively. 'Not that he wouldn't be sorry if he tried anything like that, I can tell you. Even your pig of a father knew better than to lay a finger on me. Don might think he's got the upper hand, but just you wait. I'll think of something, never you fear.'

Rosalind ate up her tea quickly, wanting desperately to take herself off to her room and get on with her homework.

She hated hearing her father spoken of in those terms. And she found the atmosphere of hostility in the house oppressive and nerve-racking. She didn't really blame Don for being angry. On that awful afternoon Una had not only forced the lock on the bedroom door but thrown all Don's mother's clothes and possessions into boxes and telephoned the Salvation Army to come and collect them. All without an ounce of respect for his feelings on the matter.

Rosalind had once made the mistake of trying to make Una see his point of view. 'She was his mother, Mum,' she ventured. 'He must have been deeply hurt to see you throwing all her things out as though they were rubbish.'

Una bridled. 'They *were* rubbish,' she said unrepentantly. 'There was stuff there that must have come out of the ark. Anyway, she's dead. It's unhealthy, hoarding dead people's things.' She glared at Rosalind. 'Anyway, who asked for your opinion? It's *me* he's married to. I'm his wife and mistress of this house now. I should be able to have some say in what happens in it.'

Privately, Rosalind thought Una had got away with plenty of say so far. She had already thrown out most of the furniture without too many reproaches from Don. But she knew better than to express the opinion.

'What that poor Monica went through God only knows,' Una muttered darkly, rolling her eyes ceilingward. 'Thank heaven I wasn't here when his old cow of a mother was alive. Mind you, if I had been things would have been different.'

'Who's Monica?' Rosalind asked mildly.

'Don's first wife, of course. I told you. She came to see me when he was at that conference. Not a bit like he said she was. Really nice and ladylike. She told me a thing or two about Don and his precious mother!'

Rosalind was of the opinion that 'poor Monica' had visited Una simply to make mischief, but again, she kept

142

that thought to herself, knowing better than to antagonise Una still further.

Since the big row, Don had taken to staying out till quite late each night on the pretext of working late at the office. And with Rosalind alone in her room, busy with her homework, Una soon found time hanging heavily on her hands. As week followed week her belligerent mood changed to one of wounded martyrdom. One evening when Rosalind went downstairs to make herself a bedtime drink she found her mother poring over her photograph album. There was a glass in her hand, and beside her on the table was a half-empty bottle of gin.

'Look, Rossie,' she said, pointing to the album. 'This one was when we were in *Here We Are Again* on Clacton Pier, summer of '39, it was. Just before the war started. See, all dressed as pierrots for the opening chorus. Those were the days. I was just fifteen. It was my first job.' She shook her head and dabbed at a tear on her cheek. 'Your father was twenty-two and so handsome. I fell for him the moment I set eyes on him. They were happy days. It was before we were married of course – long before you were born.'

Trying to ignore the implication, Rosalind pushed a mug of cocoa towards her mother. 'Come on, have your cocoa, Mum. You've drunk too much of that stuff. It always makes you depressed.'

Una raised mascara-smudged eyes towards her daughter. 'Depressed? Bloody devastated more like! Oh, Rossie, I thought all our worries were going to be over when I married Don. I really thought he loved me and wanted me to be happy. But he doesn't want a wife. He wants a replacement for his damned mother. He's *useless* as a husband. He's living in the past when he was a kid and he and his mother were living here together.'

She snuffled into her handkerchief. 'He told me he admired me – said I was attractive and smart. He said he liked *strong* women. But he still wants all his own way.

143

Sometimes I get the feeling that what he really meant was that he'd like me to take a hairbrush to his backside!' She looked at Rosalind's shocked face, her eyes slightly unfocused. 'There – didn't know there were men around like him, did you? Well, you do now. Creepy, isn't it?'

She closed the photograph album with a slap and sighed despairingly. 'I tell you, Rossie, if I had any money I'd be out of this morgue tomorrow. I've been thinking lately. I've a good mind to go back to the stage. I believe my voice is as good as ever it was. I practise every morning when I've got the house to myself. I've a damned good mind to look for an agent and see what I can get.'

Rosalind's heart sank. She remembered only too vividly the tempers and depressions; the fruitless trips up and down Charing Cross Road; the dingy back street bed-sits and always being hungry. Suppose they had to move away – some place where it was too far for her to get to school? She bit her lip, ashamed at the selfishness of the thought, then reminded herself that if no one else was prepared to consider her future, she would have to take care of it herself.

'Don't be silly, Mum,' she said firmly. 'You know you don't want to start on that kind of life all over again. I'm sure Don thinks the world of you really. Why don't you say you're sorry – make up your quarrel and forget all about it?'

Although Una shrugged her shoulders dismissively, she must have taken Rosalind's advice to heart in some measure because after that evening things improved slightly. Una and Don began to speak to each other again and, to Rosalind's relief, the atmosphere in the house relaxed a little.

At Hallard's store there was to be a grand Christmas fashion show and as usual Una was organising it; travelling up to Regent Street with Don each morning and returning with him in the evenings. Rosalind was glad. At least her mother had something other than Don's intransigence over the house with which to occupy her mind. And one of the benefits was that Rosalind came home after school each day to an empty, blessedly peaceful house in which to get on with her homework.

As well as sending out the usual invitations the fashion show had been widely advertised and was to take place on 5 December. Anticipating a good attendance, it was to take place in the restaurant on the top floor of the Regent Street store. Una had been given *carte blanche* to engage any outside help she needed and had used an old contact from her theatrical days to find a professional scenic designer – a young man called Stuart Hamilton who, according to Una, had some really new and innovative ideas.

Once end of term exams were over at St Margaret's the sixth form were free to take the odd day off and Una suggested that Rosalind might like to go along and help with the show preparations. At first she was reluctant.

'I don't know the first thing about fashion shows, Mum,' she said. 'I'll only get in the way.'

'No, you won't. There's heaps to do. Holding it in the restaurant means we have just a few hours to get everything ready. Every pair of hands is needed and you're not doing anything else, are you?'

Rosalind had little choice in the matter. But when she arrived on the morning of the show she felt awkward and in the way. Everyone else seemed to know exactly what they were doing. There were florists, busy with their arrangements; hairdressers, snipping and teasing, buyers from the various fashion departments scurrying in and out of the lift pulling rails of garments behind them. Electricians balanced on top of ladders and carpenters hammered away. Even the lowliest junior assistant from the model gown department fetched and carried purposefully while Rosalind simply stood around, feeling inadequate and useless.

She was just wondering if anyone would miss her if she

crept away when a voice startled her: 'Hello. You're looking a bit lost. Anything I can do?'

She turned to see a tall young man in jeans and an open-necked shirt looking at her. He had fair hair that flopped over his forehead and his grey eyes held a hint of indulgent amusement as he looked her over appraisingly.

She blushed and lifted her shoulders in a helpless gesture. 'My mother – Mrs Blake – asked me to come along and help, but I just feel in the way.'

'Hell let loose, isn't it?' he said sympathetically. His voice was soft with the merest hint of a Scottish accent. 'It might all look chaotic but I can assure you that everyone knows what they're doing. It'll all come together beautifully by this afternoon.'

'I'm sure it will. That's why I feel in the way. It's all so organised. I'm sure if I touch anything it will fall apart in my hands and ruin everything.'

'Of course it wouldn't. But I do know how you must feel.' He smiled warmly and offered his hand. 'I'm Stuart Hamilton. I designed the set.' He pointed to the stage where sequin-scattered gauze was draped against a dark blue velvet backdrop.

'It's designed to resemble a moonlit frozen waterfall,' he explained. 'I'm just about to check and see if it works, so cross your fingers.' He cupped his hands to his mouth and shouted above the hubbub to the electrician who was waiting somewhere out of sight to turn on the lights.

As the sharp blue and white beams flooded the stage the set came instantly and magically to life, so that it shimmered and sparkled like living frost.

Rosalind gasped with delight. 'Oh! It's *lovely*!'

'I thought it was a good idea to keep it simple,' Stuart said modestly. 'Icicles and frost are so pretty aren't they? No colours to clash with the clothes.'

'No. You're very clever.'

'Not really. It's just my job.' He smiled into her eyes.

146

'You know there is something you can do. It'd save my life right at this moment.'

'Really? What's that?'

'Rustle up some coffee. I wouldn't mind betting there are a few dry throats around gasping for a cup.'

Glad to have something to do, Rosalind turned towards the kitchen. 'Of course. I should have thought. I'll get something organised.'

When she came back from the kitchen with a borrowed trolley and coffee, tea and biscuits for everyone she found herself on the receiving end of smiles of gratitude. She found Una at the back of the restaurant, in earnest conversation with Stuart. She was using the voice she reserved for people she wanted to impress.

'Rosalind, I'd like you to meet my friend, Stuart Hamilton,' she said sweetly, simpering up at the young man. 'You're not going to believe it, Stuart, but this is my daughter.'

'We've already met.' He took a cup from the trolley. 'What a thoughtful idea to lay on coffee for us all. I'm sure we're all dying for a cup.'

Rosalind blushed, grateful to him for pretending the idea had been hers.

Una looked from one to the other. 'Stuart is a freelance scenic designer,' she said.

He laughed. 'The term "freelance" is a bit of a euphemism. It's just another way of saying I'm out of work.'

Una swept his modesty aside. 'Not for long, I'm sure. Hasn't he done a wonderful job for us, Rossie?'

'Super. When the lights were on just now it looked like something out of a fairytale.'

'I know. None of those garish reds and greens usually associated with Christmas events,' Una said with satisfaction. 'I hope Stuart will be able to do this again for us. Though I'm sure some West End producer will have snapped him up by then.'

'Much as I'd like to work for you again, Mrs Blake, I hope you're right.' Stuart looked at his watch. 'Well, I think I've done about all I can for the moment. What about a spot of lunch?'

Una shook her head. 'Not for me. Lunch is out of the question, I'm afraid. As soon as I'm satisfied that everything is done here, I've got to find time to change and get my face and hair done. I shall be busy right up until we open the doors.'

He looked at Rosalind. 'What about you then? Will you join me?'

'*Me?*' Rosalind was taken aback. 'Oh, well . . .'

'Come on, I hate eating alone,' he said persuasively. 'You have to eat something and with your mother so busy . . .' He smiled. 'Nothing fancy. A glass of wine and a sandwich is what I usually have.'

Sitting in the small pub that Stuart took her to, at the back of the store in Argyle Street, Rosalind felt tongue-tied and awkward. She'd never been out with a member of the opposite sex before. At least not alone like this. At the bar, she'd tried to pay for her own lunch and been overcome with embarrassment when he'd insisted on paying. Now she sat listening to him telling her about the flat in Earls Court he shared with an old school friend called Julian Travers; his art school training and the way his career had been disrupted when he was called up for his National Service.

'Didn't you like being in the army?' she asked, feeling stupid.

He raised an eyebrow at her. 'It was a terrible waste of time, frustrating too.' He leaned towards her. 'I actually missed getting a marvellous job because of it – to do the costumes and sets for a production of *Romeo and Juliet* at Stratford.'

'Stratford on Avon?' Rosalind asked, impressed.

He cleared his throat. 'Ah – well, no. Stratford East as a matter of fact. But it would have been a marvellous shop window for me.' He put the last of his beef sandwich into his mouth and chewed thoughtfully. 'Still, maybe the big break will come eventually.'

Rosalind sipped at her glass of red wine. She found it rather acid, but would have died rather than admit it. 'What does your flat-mate – er – Julian do?' she asked. 'Is he a designer too?'

He shook his head. 'No. He's a playwright, though he works for a firm of solicitors in the daytime. He's enormously talented. As a matter of fact he's writing a musical play, with the help of a musician chum of ours. The three of us are hoping to work on it together.'

'Did you know that my mother was in the theatre before she worked at Hallard's?' she asked him.

'Una?' He looked at her over the rim of his wine glass, his eyes widening with surprise. 'No *kidding*? She never mentioned that.'

'She gave it all up some time ago.'

'Why did she do that?'

'To bring me up basically,' Rosalind said. 'She and my father had a singing act, you see. They separated – divorced. Una got custody of me. I was quite small at the time.'

'So she gave up her career? What a sacrifice. She must be a very devoted mother.'

'Mmm.' Rosalind looked into her glass and said nothing.

'And then she married Mr Blake. The general manager at Hallard's?'

'That's right.'

'And your father – do you still see him?'

'I used to. But he and his new singing partner have gone to Australia. He writes though. I had an airmail letter last week to say they've arrived safely and have their first booking.'

'You must miss him.'

'I do. He did ask me to go with him, but I decided not to.'

'I can't blame you, with a wonderful mother like yours. I'm sure she would have been devastated to lose you. Does she miss being on the stage?'

'I think so – now and again. Sometimes she talks about going back to it. That's why she loves doing these shows. It's the closest she gets to working in the theatre nowadays.'

'You know, now that you mention it, a lot of things fit about Una,' he said thoughtfully. 'She's obviously been a very beautiful woman in her time. And that voice of hers . . . so musical. It's the voice of a singer.' He leaned towards her and looked at her with eyes that seemed to melt into hers. 'But what about you, Rosalind? You haven't mentioned yourself. What do you do?'

Suddenly her mouth dried and her hands became clammy. She put down her glass, afraid that it might slip through her fingers. 'I'm still – studying,' she said, feeling her cheeks burn. Saying that she was still at school sounded so silly. Odd, she had never been ashamed of the fact before.

'Studying? You're a student then?'

'Yes. Well – no, not exactly. Not at college.' She lowered her eyes. 'I'm taking my A levels actually. I want to go on and study hotel management.'

'Hotel management. Really?' He was looking at her as though she were the most fascinating person he had ever met and she was acutely conscious of the fact that her hair needed trimming and there was a hateful spot coming on her chin. Even at this moment she could feel it shining like a beacon. 'What made you choose a career like that with your background?'

'I don't know really. It's something I've wanted ever since I can remember. When I was little and my parents were touring I used to join them in the school holidays. The hotels and boarding houses where we stayed were always so dreary.' She laughed self-consciously. 'I suppose I've always believed I could do better.' She pushed nervously at the bridge of her glasses, wishing she'd taken Freda's advice and seen the optician about having a pair of the new contact lenses fitted.

He was nodding understandingly. '*Believing*. That's the key word, isn't it? If you think positively you can make anything come true. I used to feel like you when my parents took me to the pantomime at Christmas. In the little border town where we lived, up near Berwick, we only got small touring companies and the sets were no more than tatty backdrops and curtains. I used to go home and draw designs for the sets as I'd like to have seen them: enchanted forests, castles and majestic ballrooms. I'd actually build them in miniature out of old shoe boxes, and work out how to light them to make them look real.'

'You must have had a natural talent,' Rosalind said shyly.

He smiled ruefully. 'I only wish there was some kind producer who'd share your confidence in my ability.' He looked at his watch. 'Heavens, look at the time. We'd better be getting back to Hallard's if we want to be there for the opening.'

The restaurant was almost full when they arrived. As there was nothing more for Stuart to do he sat with Rosalind at the back and watched with her as the gilt chairs gradually filled up and the assembly of elegant women filled the rows set out in a horseshoe around the catwalk. The atmosphere heightened as the excited, high-pitched chatter of the audience mingled with the soft music of the hired string quartet. On the stroke of two-thirty the curtains parted to reveal Stuart's setting and Una herself stepped out into the spotlight to open the show. She had changed out of her slacks and sweater into an elegant black velvet suit trimmed with sequins and jet beads that picked up the light glamorously as she moved. The senior stylist from the hairdressing salon on the fourth floor had swept her hair up and secured it to one side with a diamante clip. When she had made the opening introduction Stuart nudged Rosalind.

'Your mother's really terrific, isn't she? It's easy to see that this is her line of work,' he said. 'That voice of hers reaches every corner of the room effortlessly. And she looks an absolute knock-out.'

'Yes.' Rosalind felt plain and clumsy as she watched her mother step gracefully aside to make way for the first model to step on to the catwalk. Listening to her rich, resonant voice and seeing her move in that stylish and elegant way made Rosalind feel hopelessly inadequate. She'd never be as attractive as Una if she lived to be a hundred. Physically, she took after her father, whose handsome features seemed to her to sit uneasily on a feminine countenance.

Almost as though he could read her thoughts, Stuart reached for her hand and gave it a small comforting squeeze. 'I don't know when you're free, but I'd like to see you again some time, Rosalind,' he whispered.

She turned to stare at him in astonishment. Had she heard him right? Surely he hadn't said he wanted to see her again? Not *her*. 'Sorry. What – er . . .' She cleared her throat. 'What did you say?'

He laughed gently. 'I said, I'd like to see you again. You look shocked. Is it such an appalling prospect?'

She was grateful for the subdued lighting as she felt hot colour suffuse her face. '*No!* I mean, no, it isn't appalling – not at all.'

'So – you'd like to? To see me, I mean?'

'Yes.' She swallowed hard. 'When?'

He shrugged. 'What about tomorrow evening? I'm not doing anything. Are you?'

'No. That would be lov – er – very nice. Thank you.'

He slipped out of his chair and bent to whisper in her ear. 'I've got to go now. I'll come and pick you up tomorrow around seven, all right?'

'Yes – fine.' As he began to walk away she suddenly remembered that she hadn't given him her address. She half rose from her seat, then sat down again, biting her

152

lip. It would look as though she were running after him. Besides, he could always get it from the phone book if he really intended to come. She couldn't believe that he would actually turn up. She sank low in her chair, her cheeks burning and her heart beating fast. She was shaken by the way he had made her feel. What could a young man as stunningly attractive as Stuart possibly see in her?

When she told her mother that he had asked her for a date, Una stared at her incredulously. 'He asked you *out*? I do hope you didn't push yourself at him,' she said unflatteringly. 'Young men don't like girls who make the first move, you know.'

'I didn't,' Rosalind said. 'He's picking me up at home tomorrow evening.'

'Where's he taking you?'

'I don't know. He didn't say.'

'Well, if he suggests going back to his flat you say no, do you hear me?' In Una's book there was only one feasible reason for a boy like Stuart to ask a girl like Rosalind out. After all, what could possibly attract him to a plain girl with whom he had nothing in common? She looked at her daughter curiously. 'What did you talk about when he took you to lunch?'

Rosalind shrugged. 'He told me about his training and his National Service. He said that his flat-mate, Julian, is writing a musical play and he's hoping to design the sets and costumes for it.'

Una's eyes sharpened with interest. 'Did he now? Any chance of having it put on?'

'I don't think they've got that far,' Rosalind said.

Stuart arrived on time, having driven out to Stanmore in his flatmate's car, borrowed specially for the occasion. Rosalind saw him from behind the curtains of her bedroom window where she'd been watching and was inordinately relieved that he had, after all, known where she lived. She

153

had been ready for three-quarters of an hour; wearing a new dress she'd bought that morning with some of her weekend job money. She'd washed her hair and applied a little make-up. The effect was hardly dramatic, but it was the best she could do. When she saw Stuart getting out of the smart little red Mini car her heart began to drum with excitement. She'd been so afraid that even if he knew the address he might not turn up. She'd even mentioned her fear to her mother that morning. Una had laughed dismissively.

'Oh, he'll turn up all right,' she said. 'He'll be wanting to work with Hallard's again. I don't think he'd have the bare-faced cheek to come back and ask me for work if he'd stood you up.'

Rosalind reached the top of the stairs just in time to see Una already opening the front door. She too seemed to have dressed for the occasion. She wore tight-fitting black slacks and a white angora sweater. Her wrists jangled with chunky bracelets and Rosalind could see even from this distance that she was wearing her false eyelashes. As she watched, her mother embraced Stuart warmly.

'*Stuart!* Do come in, darling. How handsome you look. You know, I can't tell you how pleased I am that you've offered to take poor Rossie out. So kind of you. She doesn't have much fun, poor love. She hasn't any friends – spends most of her time tucked away upstairs with her books.' She took his coat almost forcibly from him, then smiled up at him coquettishly. 'Now, you will have a drink while you're waiting, won't you? After all, it is almost Christmas.'

Stuart smiled. 'Thank you. A drink would be very nice.'

Rosalind walked slowly down the stairs. They were in the drawing room, now furnished in a bizarre blend of peacock blue and jade which went together surprisingly well. Una stood at the new cocktail cabinet where she'd already made up a shaker full of martinis. When she caught sight of Rosalind, standing hesitantly in the doorway she said, 'Ah,

154

there you are, darling. Why don't you put some music on? That new record *Stranger on the Shore*. Or perhaps Stuart is more of a classical fan?' She looked enquiringly at him as she pressed a glass into his hand.

He shook his head. 'I like most kinds of music, thanks.' He looked at Rosalind. 'Aren't you having a drink with us?'

Una wagged an admonishing finger at him. 'Orange juice for Rossie. She's still a schoolgirl, remember. Can't have you leading my little girl into naughty ways, can we?' She sat down, crossing her legs and hitching up one velvet trouser leg to display a shapely ankle adorned with a fine gold chain. 'Now – where are you off to, you two?'

'I thought we'd go to the pictures,' he said.

'Very nice. Well, don't be late home, will you, Rossie?'

She walked with them to the front door and while Rosalind was putting on her coat, said, 'Oh, by the way, we're having a party on New Year's Eve. Would you like to come, Stuart? There'll probably be some theatrical celebrities there. You never know, you might meet someone who could be useful to you. Bring your flat-mate too if you like. Julian, isn't it? The more the merrier.'

Hot with shame and humiliation Rosalind followed Stuart silently to the car. It was the first she'd heard about a party. And as far as she was aware, Una didn't know any theatrical celebrities. If Stuart and his friend came with high expectations they were likely to be disappointed.

As he settled into the driving seat he looked at her. 'You're very quiet. Are you all right?'

She nodded. 'My mother treats me like a child. I'm eighteen.'

He laughed. 'Parents are hell, aren't they? Don't worry. My mother used to be just the same when I lived at home.' He drove in silence for a moment then he said: 'Of course, your mother is incredibly young to have a grown-up daughter.

I daresay seeing her child growing up makes her want to hang onto her youth.'

'Maybe.' Rosalind began to feel better. Stuart was so kind and understanding. She still couldn't believe that he actually wanted to take her out.

After the film they went to a coffee bar close to the cinema. During the film Stuart had held her hand. It had felt so warm and comforting in the dark, but now, as they faced each other across the small table, Rosalind found herself embarrassed and tongue-tied once again. She thought of Carla Maybridge, who was always boasting about her numerous conquests and the older men she had dated. '*You have to show them you're in control, that's the trick,*' Rosalind had heard her boasting to an eager audience. If only she could be more like her, self-assured and confident.

'Thank you for taking me out,' she said shyly. 'I enjoyed the film very much.'

'So did I.' He smiled. 'I enjoyed being with you too.'

She shook her head. 'I can't think why.'

He looked concerned. 'Why do you say that?'

Her throat constricted as she stared hopelessly into her coffee. He wasn't going to see her again so she might as well be honest. 'Because I'm not pretty. I can't think of a single interesting thing to say. And I haven't a clue when it comes to knowing how to dress.'

'I don't agree. You're much too hard on yourself.' He reached across to take her hand. 'But *if* any of those things were true I'm sure there's plenty you could do about it.'

She looked up at him. 'Such as?'

He smiled. 'Well, for a start, you have all Hallard's fashion departments at your disposal.'

'I can't afford to buy clothes from Hallard's.'

'Then there's your hair.'

'It's poker straight.'

'It's a lovely colour, like a ripe chestnut, and it's thick and shiny. Have it well cut or even permed.'

156

Her hand went automatically to her head. 'I did have it cut last summer when I went to visit my father in Brighton. Lots of people said it looked nice, but Mum didn't like it so I grew it again. I was thinking of getting some contact lenses too.'

'No need. Glasses suit you – though you could get more flattering frames. You have beautiful eyes, Rosalind. Hasn't anyone ever told you that?'

'No.' He was looking at her with such sincerity that she blushed crimson and fumbled in her handbag to hide her embarrassment.

He looked at his watch and sighed. 'Oh, dear. I suppose I'd better get you home. I don't want to get into your mother's black books.'

He stopped the car two doors away from Blake's Folly, saying that the corner wasn't a safe place to park. Turning towards her, he cupped her face in his hands and looked at her. 'You should try to have more confidence in yourself, Rosalind.' Very gently he removed her glasses and lifted the heavy fringe away from her forehead. 'You have beautiful bones. A face like something from an Egyptian frieze. You shouldn't hide it.' He drew her towards him and kissed her, his lips holding hers firmly as they trembled like a captive butterfly under his touch.

'My poor frightened little Rosalind,' he whispered, stroking her hair. 'Relax, darling. Keep telling yourself that someone thinks you're beautiful. It's true.'

When he pulled her gently into his arms she allowed herself to melt against him and when his lips sought hers again she responded as everything in her cried out to do. Closing her eyes she gave herself up to the warmth of his kiss and even when he gently parted her lips with his tongue she resisted only for a moment. It was like a miracle. Someone actually *wanted* her. Not just someone – Stuart. Handsome, talented Stuart. And because he had said she was beautiful she believed it. She actually *felt* beautiful.

157

When he released her she was trembling. He looked at her for a moment. 'Are you all right?'

'Yes. I'm fine.'

'I think you'd better go in now or your mother will be worrying.'

'Yes, of course.' She took her glasses from the dashboard where he had put them and slipped them on again. As she was getting out of the car she turned and asked him: 'When – when will I see you again?'

He laughed and she saw the gleam of his eyes and his teeth, shining white in the dimness. 'At the party of course. On New Year's Eve.'

'Oh, yes. I forgot.' She licked her lips. 'What about Christmas?'

'Off home to Berwick.'

'Of course. Well – thank you for a lovely evening, Stuart. See you on New Year's Eve then.'

'You bet.' As she got out on to the pavement he started the car. 'Happy Christmas, Rosalind,' he called out. 'Take care of yourself. And remember what I said.'

'I will. Happy Christmas.'

She stood watching until the red tail lights of the car rounded the corner and he was gone. Then she hurried indoors, hoping that Una wouldn't be waiting to quiz her about the evening. All she wanted was to snuggle down in bed, put out the light and re-live every detail of the whole magical evening, hugging his words and the warmth of his kisses to herself like some wonderful gift.

Chapter Nine

Gerald was walking across the reception hall of Zenith's offices in Marble Arch when he bumped into Kay Goolden. If he'd seen her in time he would probably have avoided her but she'd already spotted him stepping out of the lift and it was too late. As she made her way determinedly towards him, her high heels tapping on the marble floor and her face alight with determination, his heart sank.

'Gerry darling! Long time no see. What are you doing here? Have you decided to renew your contract after all?'

'No.'

'You're going to record for another company?' She shrugged. 'Well it's a shame after all these years, but I can't say I'm surprised. If it's a question of money . . .'

'It isn't. I'm retiring from music. At least from public performing.' He allowed himself a small ironic grin. 'As I'm quite sure you've heard.'

'Well, one hears so much on the grapevine,' she said with a dismissive lift of her shoulders. 'One learns to take most of it with a large pinch of salt. I must say, though, that I'd hoped it wasn't true.'

'Well, it is, so you can consider the rumour officially confirmed.'

She looked at him thoughtfully. 'That can't have been an easy decision, Gerry. I know you, remember? We go back a long way. Music has always been your whole life. What happened to bring about this change of heart?'

'Sometimes life takes a twist that makes us take stock and realise that there are other things besides work.'

She raised a cynical eyebrow. 'The road to Damascus

syndrome, eh? Very philosophical. I also heard that you'd inherited a young ward – the daughter of a deceased friend?'

'Well, you heard correctly on that count too.'

She took a step towards him and laid a hand on his arm. He caught a whiff of *Arpège*, the perfume that would always be exclusively Kay to him. She was looking marvellous; slender as ever in her dark tailored suit. She'd changed her hairstyle too. Now she wore it longer, high in front and with the ends flicked up. He was slightly dismayed at the discovery that he still found her attractive.

'Gerry . . .' She was looking almost imploringly into his eyes. 'What's the matter, love? There's something wrong, isn't there? Surely you can tell me.'

'Tell you what? Why is everyone making such a mystery of my retirement? It's just that I'm sick of concert halls – of temperamental conductors – of living out of suitcases. I want a different, a more peaceful life, that's all. Call it old age creeping on if you like.'

'Nonsense!' She laughed. 'You're in your prime and you know it.'

'Well, I don't know about that. All I know is that I want out of it. God knows I've made enough money to see me comfortably through the rest of my life. It's time I enjoyed the benefits a little.'

'And that's really all it is?' Clearly she didn't believe a word of it.

'Yes. That's all it is.'

'And you're not going to touch a piano for the rest of your days? What a diabolical waste!'

'I didn't say that.'

'No, you didn't, did you?' She paused, looking at him speculatively. 'Come and have lunch.'

He hesitated. 'If you're hoping to pump me, forget it. You won't get anything else out of me, Kay. There *is* nothing else.'

'What a hurtful suggestion. As if I would!' She laughed and slipped her arm through his. 'Come anyway – for old times' sake.'

They took a cab and Kay told the driver to go to *L'Escargot Bienvenu* in Greek Street. It had once been their special place, their favourite restaurant.

Seated at a secluded corner table upstairs, she took off her jacket. Under it was a plain white silk shirt and he noticed that she was wearing the gold chain necklace he had bought her in New York. When they'd ordered she rested her elbows on the table and leaned forward to study his face. 'You've lost weight.'

'Thanks.'

'No. It suits you, that lean, hungry look.' She smiled and reached for his hand. 'I'm sorry I was such a bitch in New York, darling.'

'It doesn't matter. Maybe it was the pressure. Our relationship had been under a strain for some time if we're honest.'

'I agree that we both needed some space. I think I've had mine. At least enough to clear my mind.' She raised an eyebrow at him. 'How about you?'

He nodded. 'Yes. Me too.'

'I'm forgiven then?'

'Nothing to forgive.'

Their food arrived and when the waiter had withdrawn she looked searchingly at him again. 'So – what have you been doing? What are your plans?'

'I've bought a beautiful old house in the country and I'm going to open it as a rather exclusive school of music.'

Her eyes widened in surprise. 'Good heavens! I don't think I quite see you as the professor type.'

'No?'

She ate in silence for a while, glancing up at him occasionally.

161

'What about this child? Is she going to be expensive – boarding schools and so on?'

'No. She's well provided for, living with the woman who brought her up. Not a problem.'

'Just as well, eh? I can't really see you as a father figure.' Kay chuckled to herself as she sipped her wine. 'So you're going to live like a recluse, out there in the sticks? Well, I give you six months at the outside. After that you'll be climbing the walls with boredom, a man like you, used to parties and masses of people around you.'

'Not a bit. I'll have my students. I'm planning to invite friends and colleagues to come at weekends and give master classes. I shall have plenty of company and a busy life.'

'And what about feminine company? Planning to live like a monk, are you?' She raised her eyebrows suggestively at him. 'I'm sorry, darling, but I'm not convinced. It doesn't sound like you at all. Not like the Gerry Cavelle I used to know and love.'

'Well, maybe I'm *not* the Gerry Cavelle you used to know and love.' Fighting down his mounting irritation, he made himself smile at her. 'Come on, that's enough about me. Tell me what you've been doing?'

'I'm leaving Zenith at the end of this month,' she told him gleefully.

'No, really?'

'Yes. I had a wonderful offer from Summit Films, almost twice what Zenith is paying me. And they approached me. I didn't even have to apply.'

'Well, why wouldn't they? You're a damned good publicist.'

'I've taken the lease on a gorgeous flat in Chelsea too.'

'Congratulations!' He raised his glass to her. 'You're obviously on the up and up. Here's to your success.'

She touched her glass to his and drank, appraising him over the rim. 'I'll be giving a flat-warming, of course. I'll see that you get an invitation. All your old chums will be there.'

162

'Ah . . .' He looked guarded. 'Thanks all the same, but I'm expecting to be away a lot after Christmas, supervising the work on the house.'

'Oh, surely you can spare one evening!' She put down her glass and regarded him speculatively for a moment. 'It really is lovely to see you again, Gerry.'

He smiled. 'Yes. Good to see you too.'

'Quite like old times, eh?' She put down her glass and leaned across the table, lowering her voice. 'Look, I don't really need to go back to the office this afternoon. Why don't we go back to your place like we used to in the old days?'

Something inside him recoiled from the predatory look in her eyes. 'I – don't think that would be a very good idea.'

'No strings.' She smiled seductively. 'Just for fun. Why not?' Her eyes narrowed as she watched his obvious discomfiture. 'What is it, Gerry? Is there someone new?'

'I haven't said that.'

'No. You're not actually *saying* much at all, are you?' She reached out to cover his hand with hers. 'We had something special, you and I, Gerry. We were damned good together. I still miss you, you know – a lot.'

He withdrew his hand uneasily from hers. 'It's over, Kay. Nothing can change that. As you say, it was good while it lasted. And there's no reason why we can't still be friends . . .'

'Oh spare me the tired old clichés, for God's sake,' she snapped, her eyes flashing fire. 'You know, there's something about you I don't quite get. Why don't you level with me, Gerry – tell me what's going on?'

'Nothing's *going on* as you put it.' He drank the last of his coffee and took out his wallet. 'I'm beginning to think this wasn't such a good idea, Kay.' He took out a note and passed it across the table. 'Perhaps you'd settle the bill for me? I have an appointment this afternoon and I think I should go now, before one of us says something we'll regret.'

'Well, don't let *me* keep you.' She picked up the note and thrust it back at him. 'Here – take this with you. I'll pay. After all, I can afford it. And it was my suggestion. Call me sometime when you're feeling more communicative.'

After he'd left she sat on for a while at the table alone. She ordered another coffee and lit a cigarette, puffing on it furiously. Why in God's name had she subjected herself to humiliation like that? And why was he behaving with such uncharacteristic stiffness? It was blatantly obvious that he had something to hide – chances were it was something he didn't want the media to get hold of if he wouldn't even tell her! She bit her lip angrily. One thing was for sure: no one brushed her off like that without living to regret it.

Chapter Ten

Cathy began her second year at college with renewed enthusiasm. Gerald kept in touch regularly. The architect's report on Cuckoo Lodge was encouraging and he found a builder who, in company with the architect, had been over the place with a fine-tooth comb. Between them, they had come up with some interesting suggestions. Gerald had made a formal offer for the house, and after some negotiations it had been accepted. It was well into the autumn before contracts were drawn up and signed, but as soon as the legal business was completed teams of workmen moved in and made a start on the marathon task of restoring the house.

'They have to install a dampcourse before they can start on anything else,' Gerald explained. 'The house has never had one apparently. You were right about that, Cathy.'

They were sitting round the fire having tea at Chestnut Grove. It was half-term and he had come to ask if Cathy would like to go down to Melfordleigh with him on Sunday to see how the work was progressing. 'It means digging down deep into the foundations and inserting a waterproof membrane. All very technical.' He laughed and Johnny, who had been watching them closely, thought he looked happier than she had ever seen him.

'Then most of the interior plaster has to come off,' he went on. 'The damp has caused it to disintegrate. But that's the exciting part. The builder rang me yesterday to say that it was covering up some very interesting earlier features.'

'So you might get your inglenook after all?' Cathy's eyes were shining. 'I can't wait to see it.'

'I warn you, it looked a terrible mess last time I was there,' Gerald said. 'But at least we're getting on. I want you to come so that you can have a chat with the builder, Cathy. I've told him about your en suite bathroom ideas and he's looking forward to meeting you.'

Neither of them saw the look old Mrs Bains exchanged with her daughter and when Cathy had gone out to the car with Gerald later, to see him off, the old lady spoke her mind with characteristic bluntness.

'That girl is getting a sight too keen on that so-called guardian of hers if you ask me,' she said, clicking her knitting needles ferociously. 'I'm not sure I trust him either. Too smart by far for my taste.'

Johnny made light of her mother's misgivings. 'At least he takes an interest in the child,' she said. 'He could just have left her here with us and acknowledged her with a card at birthdays and Christmas. He's her godfather and her guardian, Mother. He's only doing his best!'

Mrs Bains grunted. 'His best for *who*? That's what I'd like to know!' She put down her knitting and leaned forward. 'And I hardly think I have to remind you that Cathy isn't a child any more, Mary. You've seen the look in her eyes when he's here.'

Johnny had seen the look, and it worried her far more than she cared to admit, but she forced herself to laugh. 'Oh, Mother, really! It's hero worship, that's all. Mr Cavelle was her father's oldest friend. He's a musician too so she feels at home with him. He's a father figure to her. That's all.'

'Mmm.' The old lady resumed her knitting, pulling her mouth into a tight line. 'All right. You have it your way. But don't say I didn't warn you,' she added ominously. 'At her age hero worship can soon develop into something more dangerous. And that man has the look of an accomplished philanderer if I'm any judge. You heard the way he was flattering her – making out he wanted her advice about this house of his. What does a girl her age know about such things?'

'She is studying Home Economics, Mother.'

The old lady grunted. 'Huh! Home Economics my foot! Turning her head, that's what he's after. Next thing you know he'll be getting her to go there to live.' She drew her breath in through her teeth with a sharp hissing sound. 'And I don't have to tell you what road that leads to.'

'Mother, really! How can you suggest such a thing?' Johnny was concerned that Cathy might be developing a crush on her guardian but she felt sure that he would never take advantage of it. Whatever any of them might think he was a mature man; an intelligent, talented man whose name was well known. He had a reputation to uphold. Nevertheless, as she gathered the teacups together she promised herself that she would have a quiet word with Cathy sometime soon.

Sunday was bright with golden autumn sunshine and as they drove up to Suffolk Cathy's spirits were high. She looked forward so much to seeing the house again. Gerald seemed so enthusiastic. He hadn't mentioned his illness again and she hadn't asked. He had seemed so much better ever since he became involved in the restoration of Cuckoo Lodge.

When they drove in through the gates she saw at once that work had begun in earnest. The ramshackle corrugated iron garage had been removed and the house was now in full view. It was surrounded by scaffolding.

'They're re-pointing,' Gerald explained as they got out of the car. 'The old lime mortar was crumbling – letting in the weather.'

Cathy saw that all round the perimeter of the house a deep trench had been excavated. Standing looking up at Cuckoo Lodge she was slightly dismayed.

'Poor old house,' she said. 'It looks rather forlorn, doesn't it? I feel as though I shouldn't be looking.'

'Why shouldn't you be looking?' Gerald asked.

She lifted her shoulders. 'I don't know. It's the indignity of it – a bit like catching someone in their underwear.'

He laughed and threw an arm around her shoulders. 'You are a funny girl. Just you wait another few months. The "poor old house" as you call it will be positively pristine then. Restored to its former glory as they say.'

'I suppose so.' She looked up at him. 'Can we go inside?'

'Of course. It's perfectly safe. You'll just have to watch your shoes in the mud.'

They picked their way over planks to get to the front door, which Gerald opened with his key.

'This will have to be replaced,' he told her as he unlocked it. 'The wood is rotten. I'm having a replica made by a firm that specialises in them. You were right about the listing. I've had special instructions about the windows too. No knocking the walls about and installing modern "picture" windows.'

Cathy pulled a face. 'God forbid. As if you would.'

Standing in what was to be the house's main reception room Cathy drew in her breath. It looked so much larger now that the plaster was down to the original brickwork and the fireplace had been removed. 'So that's your inglenook,' she said, pointing to the cavernous chimney space.

He nodded happily. 'It will be. Can you imagine it with a massive log fire crackling away? I'm combing antique shops for some genuine fire dogs and a basket. If I can't find any I might have to have them specially made.'

At the back the outbuildings had gone, apart from the barn. And the lean-to kitchen had been demolished. As they went from room to room Cathy watched Gerald's face. His eyes were alight with pleasure as he pointed out the work that was being done. All the depression of previous months had gone. The difference it had made to him was nothing short of miraculous.

'Jack Rigby, the builder, is meeting us here after lunch,' he told her. 'It's the kitchen and bathrooms I want you to talk to him about. They're more your province than mine.'

She looked at him with surprise. 'You want *me* to advise the builder? Won't he think it a cheek?'

'Why should he? I'm employing him so I get to choose what I want. And as you are the only family I've got . . .'

'But surely he's the expert?'

'I've only asked him to listen to your ideas. If any of them are impractical I expect he'll tell you.' Gerald laughed at her doubtful expression. 'Cathy, if I still had a wife I'm sure she'd demand to have her say in the kitchen and bathroom. Builders are used to that, I assure you.'

As they walked down the hill the wind coming off the sea was sharp and salty and icy cold. The view today was different from the last time she had been here. Out to sea the waves were crested with white. The boats that were still moored by the sea wall bobbed on the swelling tide, their masts and rigging clicking and creaking in the wind. Overhead seagulls rode the wind, swooping occasionally for food, filling the air with their plaintive haunting cries.

'It's still beautiful, isn't it?' Gerald said as they stood together by the sea wall. 'In a wilder way than before. Most of the boats will be gone soon, taken into dock for the winter months. The artists and weekend fishermen will pack up their palettes and rods till spring, then the place will belong to the locals again.'

'And you'll be one of them soon.' She looked up at him. 'How long will the house take to be finished?'

'Depends on the weather. It's a race against time to get the place weatherproof before the winter sets in. If they can do that they can work on the inside till spring.' He put an arm around her shoulders. 'You look cold.' He laughed. 'Your nose is turning pink. Come on, let's get inside in the warm. I've booked a table.'

Inside the Admiral Nelson it was warm and snug and

the mouth-watering aroma of well-cooked food made Cathy realise how hungry she was. The landlord greeted them like old and valued customers and showed them to the table Gerald had insisted on: Cathy's favourite, the one by the fo'c'sle window that looked out over the sea. But after she'd made her choice from the menu he noticed that she was quiet and thoughtful.

'Is something wrong?' he asked. 'Do you want to change your order?'

'No. I'm fine.' She'd been puzzling over something he had said back at the house and was trying to summon up the courage to ask him about it.

'You're looking rather pensive. Anything worrying you?'

'No . . .' She looked up at him. 'At least . . .'

'Yes – come on.'

'It was just something you said . . .'

'Yes? What did I say?'

She bit her lip. 'You said, if I *still* had a wife . . .'

He smiled ruefully, shaking his head. 'Did I really say that?'

She blushed. 'I know it's none of my business, but it sounded almost as though . . .'

'As though I once had one? Well, it's no secret. Why shouldn't you ask, Cathy? Yes, I was married once. But it was so long ago that I hardly ever think about it now. What I said was a mere slip of the tongue. It must be this business of making a proper home for myself.' When she was silent he leaned across the table, his eyes slightly amused. 'Go on then.'

'What?'

'You want to know about her – so ask.'

She shook her head. 'It's none . . .'

'Of your business? Well, perhaps it is, Cathy,' he told her, his eyes serious. 'Perhaps it has more to do with you – with you and me – than you realise.'

She didn't know what to say. Sometimes he seemed to speak in riddles. 'If – if you want to tell me about it – about her – okay,' she said. 'If not I don't mind. Honestly.'

He reached out to cover her hand with his. 'I *do* want to. Not that there's much to tell. It didn't last very long. We were both very young, you see, very green and inexperienced. Still at college in fact. She was a musician too. We both had lofty ambitions. My grandfather was dead against it, which, as far as I was concerned, was one very good reason for going through with it. We were head over heels in love, or so we convinced ourselves. We had stars in our eyes. Nothing mattered except being together. But a few months of sharing one room and the meagre allowance my grandfather gave me, which he flatly refused to increase, soon put out the stars for us. I think being a wife was a big disillusionment for her.' He smiled wryly. 'They say that when poverty comes in at the door, love flies out of the window, don't they?'

'What happened?'

He smiled. 'The war happened. In a way that made the decision easy for us. She was from New Zealand, you see. Her parents wrote when things began to look bad, insisting that she went home. They added, a trifle half-heartedly, that I was welcome too. But they must have known that no self-respecting British male would desert his country at a time like that. We parted tearfully, vowing eternal love and making God knows what empty promises, but I think we both knew it was the face-saving escape we'd been looking for. We exchanged letters, but gradually they dwindled to the occasional line. Then, a couple of years later I heard from Sarah's solicitor that she was seeking an annulment. It wasn't a great surprise and I didn't contest it.'

'And it didn't hurt? Not at all?'

He looked thoughtful for a moment. 'I'd be lying if I said it didn't dent my ego a little. As I said, I was very young. At that age you're so sure about everything. Discovering you can make mistakes like anyone else can be pretty shattering.

But soon afterwards I went off to join ENSA and on the whole I spent the rest of the war quite enjoyably.'

'There must have been other girlfriends?' Cathy said daringly.

'True.' He smiled wryly. 'We all suffer from the rebound syndrome.'

'No one serious though?'

'No.' He paused, and for a moment his eyes clouded. 'No one serious.'

'Don't you miss your music now that you've retired?' she asked.

He shook his head. 'I haven't had time to miss it yet. I've been too busy planning for the future.' He smiled. 'There's so much to look forward to.'

The food arrived and they applied themselves to it. Cathy was learning something new about Gerald every time she saw him. As she ate she wondered if he would mention her moving here with him again. And what Johnny would say if she decided to. Deep down she had the feeling that the decision would be frowned upon. But why? After all she was almost nineteen now. By July she would be finished at college. Qualified with any luck. And Gerald was her legal guardian. Although she would prefer to do it with Johnny's blessing, she didn't really need anyone's permission.

The builder was waiting for them at the house. He was a burly man with a red face and a brusque manner. But it was clear that he knew his business well. He listened politely to Cathy's ideas, pointed out the snags and suggested modifications, while Gerald looked on. A new kitchen was to be built on at the rear of the house. Its position and specifications were decided upon. Jack Rigby made copious notes and sketches which he promised to pass on to the architect and the plumber who would soon need to begin installing the necessary pipes before plastering began.

Dusk was gathering by the time they left for home. As they headed towards London Gerald looked at her.

'I'm very proud of you, Cathy.'

She looked at him with surprise. 'I can't think why.'

'You're taking such an interest in Cuckoo Lodge. I'm grateful as well as proud.'

She glanced at him. 'Like you said, I'm your family. You're all the family *I've* got too.'

'The house won't be finished till this time next year. I expect you'll be looking for a job by then.'

'Perhaps. If I pass my exams.'

'Oh, you'll pass all right. I have every confidence in you.' She felt his eyes on her but did not turn to meet them. 'You'll probably rush off to the north of Scotland or somewhere and I shan't see you again.'

Something in his voice made her turn and say fervently, 'I'll never do that. I'll always be here, Gerald. As long as you need me.'

'You mean that?'

'Of course I mean it.'

He was slowing the car. Drawing off the road into a quiet lane, he switched off the engine and turned in his seat to look at her. 'Cathy, I think we should talk.'

Her heart was drumming fast. 'Should we?'

'You know we should. There's been a question hanging over our heads for months now. Ever since that first time we looked at Cuckoo Lodge together and I asked you if you'd come and live there with me.'

She shook her head. 'It wasn't that I didn't want to . . .'

'I know. I could have bitten my tongue out afterwards. It was too soon. I didn't mean to rush you. You wanted to finish your course, naturally.' He picked up her hand and regarded it for a moment, then he held it softly against his cheek. 'Cathy. You know what was in my mind, don't you? Maybe you've known all along. Women seem to have an instinct for these things. And you are a woman now. You're not a little girl any longer.'

She could scarcely breathe. His eyes held hers in the

dim interior of the car. They seemed almost luminous – hypnotic. Was he saying what she thought he was saying? Could she really be sure? So many times she had dreamed of a moment like this, yet she was so afraid of making a fool of herself.

When she didn't reply he turned his head and pressed his lips into the palm of her hand. 'You know what I'm trying so clumsily to say, don't you, Cathy? I'm trying to say I love you.' He smiled wryly. 'You can laugh now if you want to. If all that sounded like the foolish ramblings of a man old enough to be your father, just say so. I don't quite know how it happened. Maybe it shouldn't. So if you're going to tell me to get lost, please do it quickly and put me out of my misery, will you?'

'Gerald.' She reached out to put a finger against his lips. 'Don't. I'm not laughing,' she said softly. 'And I'm not going to tell you to get lost. I *want* to live with you at Melfordleigh. I always have. I want to be with you more than anything else in the world. Since that first time I've been so afraid you wouldn't ask me again.'

He looked into her eyes. 'Is that true? You're not just being kind?'

'Of course I'm not. I wouldn't know how to handle that kind of situation, Gerald. I mean it.'

'Would you mind saying it? Just so that I can be sure.'

She took a deep breath. 'I love you too, Gerald. It's not infatuation. It's not new either. I think I've loved you ever since that time Dad brought me to hear you play for the first time.'

When he kissed her she thought she would drown in happiness. Matthew had kissed her once or twice; clumsy embraces and awkward, embarrassed kisses under the tree by the front gate when they came home from a dance or the pictures. But nothing like this. She wasn't in love with Matthew. It made all the difference.

When Gerald released her, her head was spinning. She

felt as though her heart had swelled to fill her whole body. Every nerve tingled – every pulse throbbed. She buried her face against his neck, waiting for her heartbeat to slow and the world to stop spinning.

'Oh, Cathy, I want you so much,' he whispered against her hair. 'Will you marry me?'

She drew back her head to look at him, her eyes wide with wonder. 'Marry you?'

'Of course. What else?'

'Yes. Oh, *yes*.'

'And we'll come and set up home at Cuckoo Lodge as soon as it's ready – run the music school together?'

'I can't think of anything more perfect.'

For a while they sat in silence under the trees, her head on his shoulder. 'I promised myself I'd wait,' he confided. 'Until your course ended; until the house was finished – until you were twenty-one. Then, at the beginning of October when it looked as though a nuclear war might erupt I got to thinking. There's never enough time for the important things – the things we promise ourselves. So often we leave it till it's too late. If there's happiness to be had we should grasp it with both hands while there's still time.'

'I was frightened over the Cuba thing too,' she told him. 'But I had to pretend I wasn't because poor Johnny was so terrified. I don't think she ate or slept until it was over.'

'Understandable. She lost her husband in the war, didn't she? And she has a son of fighting age.' He drew her closer. 'Thank God for the courage of John Kennedy. I daresay the crisis made a lot of people stop and take stock of their lives.' He kissed her forehead and tipped up her chin to look into her eyes. 'Cathy, I think it might be wise to keep this to ourselves just for a while,' he said. 'Mrs Johnson may not approve.'

'Why shouldn't she approve?' Cathy said defensively.

He smiled gently. 'I think you know why. The age gap between us is bound to raise a few eyebrows.'

'What if it does?' she said defiantly. 'It's not important. If we don't mind, why should anyone else?'

'Nevertheless, I think it's something we'll have to be prepared for. Let's keep it to ourselves just for now. Say until Christmas – till your birthday.'

She looked up at him. 'We'll get engaged on my birthday?'

He kissed her. 'We're engaged now. We'll announce it on your birthday. I'll buy you a ring then and we'll do it properly.'

'Can I have the ring now?' she asked, her eyes shining eagerly. 'I could wear it on a chain round my neck till Christmas.'

He drew her into his arms and held her close. 'Oh God, Cathy. Sometimes you make me feel so damned old.'

Cathy slept hardly at all that night. Somehow the idea of keeping her engagement to Gerald secret made it all the more exciting. She decided to work extra hard at her Saturday job at the Queen's Head, saving all the money she earned for Christmas presents. This year she wanted to buy Johnny something extra special to show her appreciation for all she had done.

The following day Cathy came home from college to find Johnny alone. Matthew was still at work and Mrs Bains was at her Women's Institute meeting. Johnny was in the kitchen ironing and called out to Cathy as she was making her way upstairs.

'I've got the kettle on for a cup of tea. Do you fancy one, Cathy?'

She leaned over the banisters. 'I've got some homework I'd like to get out of the way first.'

Johnny appeared at the foot of the stairs. 'I'd like to talk to you before the others get home, Cathy,' she said. 'So could you come down now, please?'

With a feeling of foreboding Cathy took off her coat and

came back downstairs. In the kitchen two cups and saucers were laid out on the table and the big brown teapot was wearing the blue and white striped cosy Mrs Bains had knitted. Johnny pushed aside the abandoned ironing board, one of Matthew's shirts still spread on it, half-ironed, and drew out a chair.

'Sit down, love.'

It wasn't like Johnny to stop the ironing halfway through. It must be something serious. Cathy looked at her warily. 'Have I done anything wrong?'

'Of course not. I just wanted to have a quiet word while we have the house to ourselves.' Johnny poured the tea, while Cathy looked on, her stomach muscles tightening with apprehension. Deep inside she had an uncomfortable feeling that she knew what Johnny was about to say. She hoped she was wrong.

'I don't want you to think I'm interfering, Cathy,' Johnny began awkwardly. 'But I feel responsible for you and I'd hate to see you get hurt. I know that you and Mr Cavelle are good friends. He's taken his duties as guardian very seriously and that's to his credit.'

She paused and Cathy saw her swallow nervously. 'But I feel I owe it to your dear father to look after your best interests.' She looked up into Cathy's eyes. 'I somehow have the feeling that you're getting a little too fond of him, dear.' Seeing Cathy's jaw drop she hurried on: 'Oh, I know he's a very attractive man with a lot of talent and personality. He's a very romantic sort of person. But he's a great deal older than you, dear. If he knew how you felt he'd probably feel dreadfully embarrassed. So perhaps it would be wiser if you saw a little less of him until you have your feelings under control. I'm sure you know plenty of nice boys of your own age at college who'd love to take you out. And there's Matthew of course. He thinks a lot of you, I know.'

Cathy had an almost irresistible urge to blurt out the truth; that boys of her own age seemed dull and stupid after Gerald – yes, even Matthew; that she and Gerald were already engaged and planning to marry. But, remembering her promise to him, she took a deep breath and said, 'Well, if you think so . . .'

'I do.' Johnny drew a deep, relieved breath. Thank goodness the girl had taken it so well. 'I daresay he's going to be very busy with his new house in Suffolk anyway. Perhaps you could say that you're tied up with your end of term exams, or Christmas shopping – something like that. You needn't tell fibs. I'm sure he'll understand.'

'Yes, Johnny.'

'You didn't mind me saying this to you, did you, dear?'

Cathy got up from the table and replaced her chair carefully under it. 'Of course not.'

Upstairs in her room she wondered how she was going to see Gerald now that she had made this promise to Johnny. And how she would tell him about Johnny's misgivings. Odd that he had already foreseen her disapproval. The following day, during her lunch hour, she telephoned him at the flat.

'Gerald, I need to talk to you,' she said. 'Something has come up that might make it difficult to see you for a while.'

'Does it have anything to do with Mrs Johnson?' he asked perceptively.

'Well – yes.'

'I thought so. Look can you get away this afternoon?'

She felt excitement stir in the pit of her stomach. 'There isn't much on here. I suppose I could say I had a headache and duck out.'

'Right. Go to Edgware underground station. I'll pick you up there at one.'

She arrived with ten minutes to spare and was waiting by the kerb as the car drew up. He smiled reassuringly at her as he pulled out into the traffic. 'Don't look so worried, darling. We'll sort something out.'

She hadn't been to the flat for a long time. Not since the Christmas when she had cooked dinner for them both. It looked the same. And she was happy to see her father's piano still in its place. Seeing her looking wistfully at it, he said, 'We'll take it with us to Melfordleigh when we move. Then you can play it every day if you want to.' Seeing her worried expression, he crossed the room and took her hands. 'What is it, darling? Come and sit down. Tell me about it.'

'Johnny had a talk to me yesterday. She thinks I'm getting too fond of you.'

He smiled. 'Very perceptive of her.'

'She wasn't cross or nasty about it.' Cathy looked up at him. 'She said that if you knew how I felt, you'd probably be embarrassed. She suggested I stop seeing you and go out with Matthew or someone else of . . .'

'Of your own age?' He completed the sentence for her. 'Well, maybe she's right. What do you think? Maybe now that you've had time to think it over you agree with her?'

'Oh, *Gerald*!' She wound her arms around his neck and kissed him. 'I'll tell you what I think. I think anyone who expects me to stop loving you must be mad,' she said vehemently.

After a moment he put her from him with a sigh. 'Oh, Cathy – *Cathy*. Do you have any idea how much I want you?'

She pressed her head against his chest. 'What are we going to do, Gerald? It's six whole weeks till my birthday. I can't stop seeing you for all that time. I'll *die!*'

He drew her down on to the settee beside him and cradled her head against his shoulder. 'Perhaps we should go along with what Johnny wants.'

She twisted her head to look up at him in horror. 'You don't mean that? You *can't*.'

He laughed. 'No, I have to agree, it would be totally unbearable, though I will have to go away again soon,

179

just for a week or so.' For a moment he was silent, then he said, 'How do you feel about a tiny deception – just to keep things on an even keel?'

'Like what?'

'This Saturday job of yours. If you were to stop working at the hotel we could spend Saturday afternoons and evenings together.'

'Oh!' Her eyes lit up and then clouded. 'But someone might see us.'

'Not if you came straight here.'

The corners of her mouth began to lift. 'Oh, Gerald, that would be lovely.' She stopped as she remembered something. 'But I was going to save the money I earned to buy presents.'

He hugged her close. 'That's not a problem. I'll give you what you would have earned.' He looked at her. 'I know you hate being deceitful, darling, and if you don't think it's a good idea . . .'

'If it's the only way we can be together, I don't care.'

'We'll tell everyone at Christmas. Then we won't have to pretend any longer.' He felt in his pocket. 'I almost forgot. I've got something for you.' Taking out a small box he opened it to reveal a ring set with diamonds surrounding a glittering square-cut emerald. 'I chose it because it's the colour of your eyes.' Taking her left hand he slipped the ring on to her finger. She stared at it, then at him, her eyes brimming with tears.

'Oh, Gerald. It's *beautiful* and it fits perfectly. Is it really my engagement ring?'

'It is. It means that you and I have made our commitment. We are pledged to each other. We'll be married as soon as you've finished your course next summer.'

She threw her arms around his neck and hugged him close. 'Oh, I *wish* I could wear it now. I wish I could show it to everyone. Oh, Gerald, I love you so much. I wish I could stay here with you for ever.'

He reached up and took her arms from around his neck, kissing first one hand, then the other. 'But unfortunately you can't, my love. You have to go home now. Look at the time. You'll be missed.'

She sighed. 'I suppose so.'

'I'll come down with you and put you into a taxi. But remember, on Saturday we'll have all afternoon and evening together. That's something to look forward to, isn't it?'

Before she went home she took off her ring and slipped it on to a length of string Gerald found for her, hanging it round her neck under her sweater. It was so exciting to feel it there against her skin all the way home in the cab. She stopped the driver at the corner of the next street to Chestnut Grove and walked the rest of the way. Of course it would be nice to be able to tell people, she mused. But it was almost better keeping it secret.

She went along to the Queen's Head the following day on her way home from college and told them she wouldn't be working there any more. She hated letting them down just when their busy season was getting under way, and felt guilty about deceiving Johnny too. But it was for Gerald, and for him she would have done anything. Every time she thought of spending all afternoon and evening with him at the flat her heart raced with excitement. Everything else was forgotten. Saturday seemed an eternity away.

As soon as she arrived at the flat Cathy put her engagement ring on her finger. She did it in the lift and stood gazing down at its sparkle as she rose to the fourth floor. In the afternoon they listened to music and talked about Cuckoo Lodge, making plans. Later Cathy cooked a meal for which she had shopped carefully on the way there. She made a mixed grill and chips, followed by apple pie and cream, which Gerald proclaimed the best he had ever eaten. Later, as they were washing up together, she said, 'This is what it will be like when

181

we're married. Just the two of us. It's going to be wonderful.'

Gerald put down the plate he was drying. 'I wonder if you know what it means to me to hear you say that, Cathy.' He picked up a towel and carefully dried her hands. 'Leave the rest,' he said, drawing her towards him and placing her arms around his waist. Taking her face between his hands, he kissed her. He felt her trembling beneath his touch and drew her into his arms. 'My lovely Cathy,' he whispered, pulling her hard against him. 'I still can't quite believe you really want to marry me. I keep thinking I'll wake up to find I've dreamed it all.'

She looked up at him. 'How can I prove to you how much I love you?'

'You don't need to feel you have to prove anything.'

'But I want to.' She stood on tiptoe to kiss him. 'I want you to believe without any possible doubt, Gerald,' she whispered. 'We are engaged. If you . . .' She bit her lip, astonished at her own daring. 'If you want to make love . . .'

'Shhh.' He stopped her mouth with a kiss and held her so tightly she could scarcely breathe. 'I don't think you know what you're saying; what you're offering.'

'But I *do*. You said yourself – I'm not a child. And I love you, Gerald.'

For a long moment he looked into her eyes. 'You're really sure?'

'Of course.'

After a moment's hesitation he scooped her up in his arms and carried her to the bedroom. She stood impassive and motionless, shivering with a mixture of excitement and apprehension as he undressed her. Her eyes, huge and luminous, never left his, and as he joined her under the smooth sheets and felt her uncomfortable trembling, he said, 'You're shivering. Are you cold?'

She wrapped her arms around him and pressed close. 'No – just excited – and – nervous, I suppose.'

'Don't be.' He kissed her forehead. 'Cathy, don't feel you have to go through with this. It's not too late to stop if you have doubts.'

She buried her face against his shoulder. 'No – please. I haven't . . .'

'I'll try not to hurt you, darling.'

'I know. I know.'

She closed her eyes and tried to relax as he caressed her quivering body. She told herself over and over that it was going to be all right and that as long as she loved him everything would be fine. All the same when it happened she felt every muscle tensing as she bit hard on her lip to keep from crying out.

When it was over tears of disappointment trickled down her cheeks. She had fantasised about this moment – the first time Gerald would make love to her. It was going to be so special – so wonderful – but the painful and hurried coupling that had just taken place between them was so different from her dream. So devastatingly different. She could not believe that this was all there was to it.

Gerald turned to look at her. 'The first time is always difficult, darling,' he said gently touching her cheek. 'Next time it will be so much better you'll hardly believe it.' He stroked her hair and leaned across to kiss her. 'Don't cry, sweetheart.'

'But – but I must have done something wrong. It must have been my fault,' she choked. 'And you must be so disappointed with me.'

'Nonsense.' He laughed softly and drew the covers up over her. 'You'll never know how happy you've made me. And you have no idea of the wonderful life we're going to have together.'

She must have fallen asleep. When she woke she had no idea how long she'd slept or what time it was. Disorientated

183

and drowsy she stared up at the man who stood by the bed looking down at her. 'Gerald . . .?'

He wore his dressing gown and held a steaming cup. 'I've made you some coffee. It's almost time I took you home or I wouldn't have wakened you,' he said, sitting on the edge of the bed. 'You looked so peaceful lying there.'

She sat up. Then, suddenly aware of her nakedness, pulled the sheet up and tucked it around herself as she took the cup from him. 'Thanks.' As she sipped the coffee the memory of what had taken place between them slowly returned. 'I'm sorry,' she whispered, colouring unhappily. 'About what – about – you know . . .'

He took the cup from her. 'That's enough of that.' Very gently he pulled the sheet away from her. 'And please don't hide yourself from me. You're so beautiful.' He bent to kiss her breasts, then, slipping out of his robe, he slid into bed beside her once again and drew her close. At his touch and the feel of his skin against hers she felt excitement stir somewhere in the pit of her stomach, spreading its heat to every fibre of her body; shortening her breath and quickening her heartbeat – turning her blood to molten fire. Some primitive, long dormant instinct seemed suddenly to blossom, taking possession of her as she sank back against the pillows, her arms drawing him down on to her. When his mouth closed on hers the spark deep within her leapt into a white-hot, searing flame. Kisses and caresses were not enough. Her mouth opened hungrily to kiss him as she had never kissed anyone before. She arched her body towards him imploringly.

This time the pain was replaced by a breathtaking delight that was almost as unbearable in its intensity. The sheer surprise of it shocked her and she heard herself cry out, this time with sheer exultation. Together they scaled the heights of sensuous pleasure, relishing every movement, each sensation, until at last together they reached the summit. Tensing beneath him she gave one last convulsive

184

movement, gasping out his name, then lay still, her eyes staring up at him in wonder.

Side by side, their limbs still entwined, they lay staring speechlessly into each other's eyes.

'You didn't believe me, did you?' Gerald said at last, his lips against her hair.

She smiled sleepily. 'Oh, Gerald. I love you so much. I wish we were married now. I wish I could stay here with you like this for ever.'

'So do I. But we aren't married yet, my love, and you can't stay more's the pity.' He rolled off the bed and began to pull on his clothes. 'Unless you want to arouse suspicions you'd better hurry up and dress. Time I took you home.'

He drove her to the end of Chestnut Grove and then stopped the car and switched off the engine.

'Goodnight, my love.' He reached out for her. 'If you only knew what agony it is to let you go.'

She kissed him. 'I do know,' she whispered. 'It's the same for me. I can't wait for next Saturday.'

'That reminds me.' Reaching into his pocket he took out his key ring and pulled off a key. 'Take this,' he said. 'It's my spare. I have to go away for a few days next week. I'll be back on Saturday, but just in case you arrive before me.'

She put the key away carefully in her bag and got out of the car. As she walked the rest of the way she could feel him watching her and turned to wave before the privet hedge cut off her view to the car. Using her own key, she let herself quietly into the house and was already halfway up the stairs when Johnny opened the living room door and came out into the hall to look up at her.

'Cathy. Don't you want to come and have a cup of cocoa with us?'

She felt her cheeks colour as she looked over the banisters. 'Oh – not tonight, thank you,' she said awkwardly. 'I'm a bit tired.'

Johnny frowned. 'Are you all right, dear? You look a bit flushed.'

'I'm fine.'

'You're very late.'

'Yes. I'm sorry.'

'Busy night?'

'What?'

'At the Queen's Head?'

'Oh. Yes. Quite busy.'

Johnny put a foot on the bottom stair. 'Are you sure you're all right, Cathy? There's a lot of flu about and . . .'

'I'm fine, I told you. Look, I'm going to bed now. Goodnight.'

She escaped hurriedly, snapping off the landing light and closing the bedroom door behind her with relief. Leaning against it, she closed her eyes and wrapped her arms around herself, feeling her body tingle afresh as she thought of Gerald and their sensational lovemaking. She didn't want to see or speak to anyone until she'd had time to relive every moment; every single touch, word and sensation. No one, *nothing*, must be allowed to spoil the magic.

At the foot of the stairs Johnny stood looking up into the patch of darkness at the top of the stairs. Cathy's abrupt switching off of the landing light had hurt her. It seemed oddly final. And ominous too; as though instead of the light, it was the loving, trusting relationship between them that was being shut off, perhaps permanently. That hectic light in the girl's eyes, the bloom on her cheeks and the almost tangible aura of arousal she exuded had not been induced by waiting at tables at the Queen's Head. There was only one experience that brought that look to a young girl and Johnny's heart sank with despair.

'Oh, God,' she breathed. 'Oh, God, please let me be wrong.'

* * *

The following Saturday Cathy left home early, saying that she was going up to the West End to do some Christmas shopping and would go straight to the Queen's Head afterwards. The fact that Johnny accepted what she said without question filled her with guilt. She hated telling lies, specially to Johnny of all people. As she travelled up on the underground she wished there was someone in whom she could confide. It would ease her conscience if she could somehow justify what she was doing. But there was no way Johnny would ever understand or condone the intimate relationship that had developed between herself and Gerald. At least, not until they could announce their engagement. And maybe not even then.

When she arrived at the flat Gerald had not returned and she let herself in with the key he had given her. As usual everything was spic and span. A woman came in three times a week to clean and as Gerald had been away the place was meticulously tidy. She took off her coat, then, taking her ring from its hiding place around her neck, she placed it on her finger. Immediately she felt different. Now she was the future Mrs Cavelle. Going into the kitchen she prepared a beef casserole and put it into the oven, then went back into the living room and looked down into the street below. All the Christmas lights were on, giving the already darkening street a glittering magic that made her tingle with excitement. At Christmas they would be telling everyone. At Christmas it would all come true.

When the doorbell sounded it startled her. She turned, hesitating for a moment. Did anyone know she was here? Should she answer it – or what? Then she realised that Gerald must have forgotten his key. He'd guess she was already here to let him in so he wouldn't bother the caretaker. Of course. That must be it. She hurried out into the hall.

'You're a fine one – forgetting your own key. It's a good job I was here to . . .' She stopped short, the rest of the sentence unspoken. A woman stood outside; tall, blonde and very well dressed. She had her back to the door but at the sound of a female voice she turned, eyes as startled as Cathy's.

'My God, who are you?'

Piqued by the woman's abruptness, Cathy flushed. 'Excuse me, but shouldn't I be asking that?'

'Kay Goolden. Where's Gerry?' She peered past Cathy into the flat.

'I'm afraid he's not here.'

'When will he be back?'

'I've no idea.'

'Then I'll wait if you don't mind?' The woman pushed past her into the flat and began to take off her coat. Tossing it on to a chair she turned to Cathy, appraising her frankly with a sweeping look. 'Well, he must be expected or you wouldn't be here, would you? Who are you, by the way? We really should introduce ourselves.'

'I'm Cathy Oldham.'

Kay took a cigarette from a case and lit it, taking her time over the operation. She walked into the living room and sat down, giving Cathy a long appraising look. 'I'm sorry but the name means nothing to me.'

'Neither does yours – to me,' Cathy countered.

Kay smiled and tapped the ash from her cigarette. 'That's not altogether surprising. I used to work for Zenith records, Gerry's recording company. I was in PR.' She smiled. 'I suppose you could call Gerry an old colleague of mine – among other things.' She looked at Cathy, her eyes hard. 'Look, I'd rather like to talk to Gerald privately. Do you think you could make yourself scarce for a couple of hours?'

Cathy felt the hot colour staining her cheeks. Who *was* this woman and what could she possibly want with Gerald now? She said she *used* to work for Zenith. He'd certainly never mentioned her. 'No, I'm sorry but I promised to be here this afternoon. He's expecting me.'

Kay waved a dismissive hand. 'That's all right. I'll explain to him.'

'There's no need, because I'm not going anywhere.' Cathy stood her ground. 'But if you want to leave him a message, I'll pass it on.'

The woman ground out her cigarette and stood up, surveying Cathy coldly. 'Just who *are* you anyway?' she demanded. 'And how did you get in here?'

'Gerald gave me a key. And if you really want to know who I am, I'm his fiancée.' Cathy held out her hand triumphantly. 'See?'

Kay's eyes widened as she took in the ring with its obviously expensive square-cut emerald. She was clearly stunned. '*Fiancée?* For Christ's sake! He must be old enough to be your father! How old are you anyway?'

Cathy flushed. 'That's none of your business!'

Kay's eyes swept over her. 'You can't be more than seventeen – eighteen at the most.'

'Nineteen, if you must know.'

'And how did you meet?'

'Through his music.'

Kay threw back her head and gave a brittle laugh. 'My God, has he taken leave of his senses? Giving up a brilliant career for a little teenage groupie.'

'I'm *not* a groupie,' Cathy said hotly. 'I've known Gerald nearly all my life. He and my father were best friends.'

Kay's eyes narrowed as the truth suddenly dawned. So – *this* was the ward that he'd led her to believe was a child. And Gerry was stringing the kid along to believe he'd marry her. Why on earth was he doing it? It was *bizarre*.

'And it isn't because of me that he's given up his career,' Cathy went on hotly. 'It's because of his illness.'

'*Illness?*' Kay peered at her, her attention galvanised. 'What illness?'

Cathy coloured. The woman had rattled her. She'd said more than she should. She shrugged. 'It's nothing serious. A sort of arthritis. It affects his fingers and – and . . .'

Kay felt a spiral of excitement stir within her. Things were beginning to drop into place. That time in New York when he'd been so bad-tempered. He'd almost bitten her head off when she'd suggested that his playing wasn't up to standard. And the day when they'd lunched, he'd been so cagey. She'd known all along that he was hiding something. Her expression adjusted itself to one of solicitude. 'Oh, *poor* Gerry. I'd no idea. How long has this been going on?'

'I don't know. But it isn't important. He's got a new career planned.'

'That's wonderful. And you two are planning to be married?'

'Yes.' Cathy relaxed a little. 'But at the moment it's a secret. We're going to announce it on my birthday just before Christmas.'

'Your twentieth?'

'Well, no. My nineteenth.'

Kay took out another cigarette, surveying Cathy over the flame of her lighter. 'You don't think the age difference is important then?'

'Oh, no. As I said, I've known Gerald since I was a little girl. And we're very much in love.'

'Well, well, how *madly* romantic. My God, I almost forgot.' She opened her handbag and took out an envelope. 'Look, I've brought him an invitation to a flat-warming party I'm giving. I promised him I'd see he got one.'

'You promised him?'

'Yes. When we were having lunch the other day. Didn't he tell you that either? I was telling him all about my new flat. Odd that he never once mentioned you or said a word about getting married. If he had I'd have included you, naturally. You're very welcome of course.'

'Thank you.'

Kay took in Cathy's crestfallen look with satisfaction.

'I'll just pop it in the bedroom, shall I? He'll be sure to see it there.' Before Cathy could speak she was already walking across the hall, heading straight for the door. 'Don't worry,' she said over her shoulder. 'I remember where it is.'

Cathy stood waiting, her heart beating fast with resentment. She imagined those sharp eyes examining Gerald's bedroom for signs of female occupation. A moment later Kay returned, a smile still firmly glued to her lips.

'There, that's done. Now, I can see that you'd far rather be here alone for Gerry when he gets back so I'll go. It was so nice meeting you, Cathy – er – Oldham, did you say?' Cathy nodded. Kay pulled on her coat and gloves. 'Tell Gerry I'll give him a ring sometime. He'll probably be tired when he gets home and I'm sure you and he will have more important things to talk about. Good luck, my dear', she said as she reached the door. As it closed behind her she muttered under her breath, '*Believe me, you'll be needing it!*'

It was late when Gerald got home. Cathy had plenty of time to think about Kay and all that she'd said and implied. Time to wonder just how much she and Gerald had meant to each other, and how it had ended – *if* it had ended. He'd never mentioned Kay to her. Obviously she belonged to another part of his life. One that was over. If he meant to forget the past and begin anew, then it was up to her to help him. Questions and accusations would only upset him. That would be playing right into Kay's hands. Besides, it was ancient history.

After careful thought she made up her mind. She wouldn't spoil their time together by mentioning Kay's visit. She would not allow her the satisfaction. Going into the bedroom she stood looking down at the invitation in its white envelope, propped against the bedside lamp where Kay had left it. After a moment's hesitation she picked it up and tore it into small pieces, taking them back to the living room and stowing them away at the bottom of her handbag for safety.

It was barely half an hour later when she heard his key in the lock. Immediately all thoughts of Kay went out of her head. Running out into the hall she threw her arms around him and hugged him hard.

'It's so *good* to come home to a welcome like this,' he whispered holding her close. 'I'm sorry I'm so late, darling. Couldn't be helped. I missed the train I should have caught, then the next one was running late.'

'Never mind. You're here now. I made a casserole for your dinner. It's keeping hot in the oven.'

He kissed the top of her head. 'What would I do without you?'

She watched him eat, thinking how tired he looked. For the first time she noticed that he'd lost weight over the past few months and tonight there were dark circles under his eyes.

'Was it a success?' she asked.

He looked up in surprise. 'Was what a success?'

'Your meeting or whatever. You didn't say where you'd been.'

'Oh, that. Boring and tedious.' He reached out to take her hand. 'The only thing that made it bearable was the thought of coming home to you.'

She smiled. She knew now that she'd been right to ignore Kay's visit and remove the invitation.

The sight of her radiant young face tore at his heart. He couldn't tell her that he'd been to see his consultant in Edinburgh; he didn't want to dwell on the past two days when he'd been through more exhausting tests so that a satisfactory regimen of medication could be worked out. The very thought of it turned his stomach and depressed him. But for the time being at least it was over and, with her help, he could forget it for a while.

After they'd eaten they stacked the dishes into the

192

dishwasher, then Gerald put on some records and they sat down to relax together. She settled her head happily on his shoulder, telling herself that it wasn't important that they didn't make love. He was tired. It was enough that she could take care of him and love him in this different, special way. This was what it would be like to be married, she told herself contentedly.

At ten Gerald stirred and stretched out the arm that encircled her shoulders to look at his watch. 'Time I took you home, my darling.' He kissed her. 'Much as I hate to let you go.'

'You're not driving all the way to Edgware tonight,' she told him firmly. 'Come down and get me a taxi. I'll be fine.'

'It's no trouble. We only have to take the lift down to the basement carpark.'

She shook her head. 'No. You're tired. I won't hear of it.'

In the hall he helped her into her coat, buttoning it up to the neck and pulling her to him. 'I'm taking no chances with a treasure like you,' he said. 'Can't have you catching cold. Now – are you sure you're going to be all right in a cab?'

'I'll be fine, fusspot.' She slipped her arms around him and raised her face for his kiss.

They went down in the lift and crossed the entrance hall. As they stepped through the doors and out on to the pavement Gerald took her in his arms for a last kiss. Neither of them saw the man waiting in an adjacent doorway with his camera and when the flash came it startled them. Both spun round to stare in wide-eyed astonishment and as they did so the flash was repeated.

'*What the hell . . .?*' Gerald took a step towards the man with the camera but before he had a chance to reach him he had jumped into a car that drew up at the kerb and in seconds was lost among the traffic.

'Who was that?' Cathy asked in alarm.

193

Gerald shook his head. 'A newspaper photographer. I thought those days were over. He must be behind the times with his information.' He smiled as the taxi he had hailed stopped and he opened the door for her. 'He's going to be so disappointed when he finds I'm not newsworthy any more.'

But as he watched the taxi draw away, he wondered whether somehow they had got hold of the news that he was restoring Cuckoo Lodge. He hoped not. He wasn't yet ready for that particular piece of news to break. Then for a moment his blood turned cold as another thought struck him. Was it possible that the news of his illness had somehow been leaked to the press? If it had he could say goodbye to his coming marriage. What young girl would knowingly marry a man who was terminally ill?

As usual Cathy asked the taxi driver to stop at the end of Chestnut Grove. She paid him with the money Gerald had given her and set out to walk the rest of the way. She was halfway home when she was aware of footsteps behind her. She quickened her own steps, but when the following footsteps quickened too, and a hand descended on her shoulder, she gave a squeak of alarm.

'Cathy! It's all right. It's me, Matthew.'

'Oh!' She looked at him angrily. 'You gave me such a fright. What on earth do you think you're doing?'

'I've been looking for you. Mum was worried when it began to get late so I said I'd walk round to the Queen's Head to meet you.'

'Oh.' Cathy searched his face.

'They said you'd stopped working there a couple of weeks ago.'

'Yes.' She began to walk on.

'So where have you been, Cathy?'

She rounded on him. 'Mind your own business. What has it got to do with you what I do with my Saturdays?'

194

'Nothing, except when it worries the life out of Mum.' He laid a gentle hand on her arm. 'Look, wait a minute. I want to talk to you before we go in. It's for your own good, Cath.'

She sighed. The look in his eyes was making her uneasy. 'All right, get on with it then. What do you want? It's cold out here.'

'Cath, Mum is terribly worried about you and this pianist chap – Cavelle.'

'Whatever for?'

'She's afraid you're – well, that you're falling for him.'

Under the street lamp Cathy's eyes were defiant as she looked up at him. 'So? What if I am?' she challenged. 'It's my look out, isn't it?'

'She doesn't want you to be hurt, Cath. None of us do.'

'*None* of you? How many people have been discussing my life then?'

He shook his head. 'Only us, the family.' He laid his hands on her shoulders. 'The thing is, Cathy, is it true?'

'Is *what* true? I don't really know what you're talking about.'

He chewed his lip in embarrassment. 'You don't make it any easier, do you? Have you given up your Saturday job to be with him?'

'Okay – yes. What of it?'

'Nothing, if that's what you want. But why does it have to be a secret. That makes people think there's something wrong in it.'

She tossed her head angrily. 'It seems to me that these *people* you keep on about poke their noses into other people's business far too much,' she retorted. 'Now, if you don't mind, I'd like to get inside before I freeze to death.'

'You've changed, Cathy,' he said hurrying to keep up with her. 'You're just not the same girl you used to be.'

'Because I don't go out with *you* any more, you mean?' At the door she turned to him. 'If you dare say anything

195

about me leaving the Queen's Head to Johnny, I'll never speak to you again. Understand?'

'Okay, but I think you're making a mistake.'

She turned her key in the lock. 'Really? Well, who asked you, Matthew Johnson? And who cares what you think anyway?'

'I won't say anything for a little while, Cathy, but I hope you will.' He looked at her, his grey eyes serious. 'If it goes on too long I'll have to . . .'

'It won't. You'll see.' She pushed open the door and went straight upstairs. 'Everything will be clear to all of you very soon.' She looked at him over the banisters. 'Tell Johnny I'm all right and I'm going to bed.'

Her scornful demeanour had put a stop to his questions for the moment and in spite of her unkind remarks to him, she knew that she could trust him not to mention their conversation to his mother. What neither could possibly have foreseen was the bombshell that was about to explode so ferociously about their ears.

Somewhere in Fleet Street a well-known Sunday paper was about to be put to bed. Its showbiz gossip page carried the photograph taken earlier of herself and Gerald kissing outside his flat. It bore the caption:

Retired Pianist to Marry Ward

Underneath, the accompanying comment was both cryptic and cynical.

Concert pianist, Gerald Cavelle, is rumoured to be suffering from a mystery illness that has forced his retirement from the concert platform. He looked far from ill last night, however, as he kissed his fiancée passionately outside his Mayfair flat. Could the secrecy surrounding their engagement possibly have anything to do with the fact that lovely nubile Catherine Oldham is the eighteen-year-old daughter of his best friend?

Chapter Eleven

Christmas at Blake's Folly was dreary. Don, Una and Rosalind spent it alone. They ate turkey and plum pudding, listened to the Queen's speech with their tea and mince pies, and spent the rest of the day staring at the television. To Una it was simply another day – to be got through as best she could, a stepping stone towards New Year's Eve and the party she had spent so much time and trouble organising.

After she had impulsively issued the invitation to Stuart she had begun to panic. She had rashly promised theatrical celebrities. Now where was she to find any? Each night after the light was out and Don's breathing had deepened into gentle snoring, she lay awake, planning, scheming, trying to make lists in her head. Where were the guests to come from, let alone celebrities? As far as she could tell, Don had few friends and none of the acquaintances she had left behind when she married were at all suitable for the kind of gathering she had in mind. There were the models from the show of course. She could ask some of them. But girls like that must lead busy social lives. They would almost certainly be booked up months in advance. She had lost touch with all the show business people she had known during her years on the stage, and anyway, none of them came into the celebrity class. A brief vision of Saucy Stan Stacey popped into her mind. Stan, in his loud checked suit and bowler hat, had appeared at the end of every pier from Land's End to John O'Groats, billed as 'The Comic with the Rubber Face'. She shuddered at the memory of his leering innuendos and suggestive jokes. No, to be completely honest there wasn't one among them she'd wish to be associated with now.

Ben and Freda had made the big time of course. Damn them! If they had still been in England she would even have considered inviting them, such was her desperation. Then, like the answer to her prayers, salvation dropped into her hands in the shape of the *Sunday Recorder*.

That Saturday night she had gone to bed late to toss and turn until the small hours. At eight o'clock next morning she got up and went downstairs to the kitchen to make herself some tea, picking up the Sunday papers from the doormat on her way. As she sat sipping the strong brew she pushed aside Don's *Observer* and opened the *Sunday Recorder*, turning at once to the showbiz gossip page. The photograph of the couple kissing drew her attention and she began to read. Furrowing her brow, she read the piece through again. The name Catherine Oldham rang a bell. Wasn't Rossie at school with a girl of that name? Fancy someone Rossie knew marrying a well-known concert pianist! Her stomach lurched with excitement as an idea suddenly presented itself. She poured a fresh cup of tea and, tucking the paper under her arm, carried it purposefully upstairs.

Tapping on Rosalind's door she called softly, 'Rossie. Are you awake? I've brought you a cup of tea.'

Rosalind sat up, surprised at her mother's sudden thoughtfulness. 'Oh, thanks, Mum.'

'I couldn't sleep so I got up early to make a pot and I thought you might like one.' Una sat down on the edge of the bed and opened the paper. 'You might be interested in this too.' She pointed out the article. 'Isn't this the girl who was in your form at school? The one whose father died a couple of years ago?'

Rosalind reached for her glasses and slipped them on. Taking the paper from her mother, she read the piece with widening eyes. 'Yes, it looks like her. Gerald Cavelle was her father's best friend. He's her guardian. Fancy them getting engaged.' She sat back against the pillows, her face thoughtful. 'She gave up her Saturday job at the Queen's

Head a few weeks ago,' she said. 'This must have been the reason.'

Una was smiling. 'Romantic, isn't it? Just like something out of a James Mason film.' She moistened her lips. 'Rossie, I've had an idea. Why don't you invite them both to our little New Year party? You haven't asked any of your own friends. I've been worrying about that. The party is for all of us, you know. Not just Don and me.'

Rosalind looked doubtful. 'Oh, but I don't know Cathy very well. She might think it funny.'

'Why should she think it funny? You went to school together, didn't you? You worked with her at the hotel.'

'Yes, but we've never been what you'd call close friends.'

'I'm only suggesting you ask her to the party,' Una said exasperatedly. 'Everyone likes parties, don't they? Especially at New Year. And this will be a good one.'

'They might not want to come though.' Rosalind pulled a face. 'I expect people like Gerald Cavelle get invited to all the smart affairs at this time of year. They'll probably be booked.'

'If everyone thought like that no one would ever get invited anywhere!' Una argued. 'You can always ask, can't you? If they can't come they'll tell you. No harm in trying.'

Rosalind had already guessed that Una's real reason for wanting Cathy and her fiancé at the party was to show off. The thought of having to watch her mother parading them round, masquerading as their friend, made her toes curl with embarrassment. She hated the idea of subjecting Cathy to such an ordeal too.

'I don't see her any more now that she's left the Queen's Head,' she said awkwardly. 'I don't see how I'll get the chance . . .'

Una raised her eyes to the ceiling. 'For heaven's *sake*, child. Haven't you ever heard of the telephone?

200

Now – what is the name of the woman she lives with?'

Before she had time to stall Rosalind heard herself saying, 'Johnson.'

'There you are then. Just look up the number in the book.'

Rosalind was stumped for words. It seemed there was no getting out of it.

'Come on, get up and ring her now,' Una urged.

Rosalind shook her head. 'No, Mum. Not on a Sunday. The people she lives with might not like it. I'll do it tomorrow.'

Una raised her eyes to the ceiling. 'Tomorrow, tomorrow. Always tomorrow. You're just like your father. Well, just see that you do it.' She bit back the criticism that rose to her lips and forced herself to smile. 'I mean, it's only right that you should have your own friends at the party, isn't it. I want you to enjoy yourself.'

'I will have Stuart,' Rosalind ventured.

Una glared at her. 'What do you mean, you'll have Stuart?'

'He's my friend. That's what I mean.'

'But *I* asked him, didn't I? You should ask some people too. Really, Rossie, do *try* to make a contribution for once, can't you!'

It took all Rosalind's courage to telephone Cathy. Unwilling to do it with her mother listening, she did it while Una was out shopping the following afternoon. When she asked for Cathy the woman who answered the call sounded suspicious.

'Who is calling?'

'My name is Rosalind Blair.'

'Are you from a newspaper?'

'No!' Rosalind was surprised. 'No, I'm not.'

'Who are you then?'

'Cathy and I were at school together. I'm ringing to ask her to a party.'

'Oh – I see.' There was an audible sigh of relief at the other end. 'Hold on. I'll fetch her.'

'Hello.' Cathy's voice sounded strained and apprehensive.

'Hello, Cathy, it's Rosalind Blair. Congratulations on your – er – engagement.'

'Oh. Thanks.' There was a pause. 'You saw it in the *Sunday Recorder* then?' Cathy's voice was little more than a whisper. 'I wonder how many more did?'

'Yes, I saw it, and I'm very happy for you, Cathy.'

'Are you? You're the first person to say that Rosalind.' There was a pause as Rosalind struggled to pluck up enough courage to come out with the invitation, then Cathy suddenly forestalled her, 'Look, you wouldn't like to meet me somewhere for a coffee, would you?'

Taken aback, Rosalind said, 'Yes, of course I will. I'd like to. Where? And when?'

'Now – if you're free. In the Bluebell. You know, that coffee bar, near St Margaret's?'

'Okay, I know it. I'll be there. It'll take me about twenty minutes.'

'Right. I'll see you there.'

When Rosalind arrived Cathy was already there, waiting at a table by the window from which she had a view of the bus stop. The Bluebell had been a teashop, but now it was under new management and had been turned into an Italian-style coffee bar, complete with an espresso machine that hissed away irritably on the counter. Over cups of frothy coffee they sat looking at each other.

'I just had to get out of the house,' Cathy said. 'Can I tell you something in confidence, Rosalind? I feel that if I don't talk to someone soon I'll go crazy.'

'Of course you can.' Rosalind felt flattered. She would

202

have thought Carla would have been Cathy's first choice when it came to confidences.

'You said you saw my engagement blown up into a scandal in the paper?'

'Well – yes.'

'I can't tell you how awful it was yesterday morning when the papers came.' When Cathy looked up Rosalind could see the ravages of recent tears on her face. 'It was such a shock. Gerald and I were keeping it a secret you see – until my birthday on the 22nd. But someone must have leaked it to the press. I don't know whether you knew before that Gerald was a well-known concert pianist?'

'Yes, I did know.' Rosalind leaned forward. 'But does it matter all that much that the secret is out? I mean, it's the 19th now. Only a couple of days to go.'

'It's Johnny – Mrs Johnson, whom I live with. She doesn't approve, because of Gerald being a lot older than me.'

'But, is it really any of her business? I mean – she isn't a relative, is she?'

'No, but she brought me up after my – after I lost my mother. She promised Dad before he died that she'd take care of me so I suppose she feels responsible.' Cathy paused to push her hair behind her ears. 'She thinks I've been deceitful, keeping it from her – telling lies about where I was going.' She looked at Rosalind. 'I didn't tell her I'd stopped working at the Queen's Head you see. I've been seeing Gerald instead. Oh, I know it was wrong, but I didn't really have any choice.'

'Oh, I see.' Rosalind thought it was all terribly romantic and exciting, but she could hardly say so when Cathy was so obviously distressed.

'And to make matters worse we've been pestered by the newspapers ever since,' she went on. 'The phone hasn't stopped ringing since yesterday morning. I've *told* her I'm happy and that everything will be all right. Gerald came to see her yesterday too, as soon as he'd seen the paper.

He tried to explain how much in love we are and why we were keeping it quiet. It was exactly *because* he didn't want the newspapers getting hold of it, you see! He promised Johnny he'd look after me, but she's still upset. She says Gerald should have known better and that we must both have known it was wrong or we wouldn't have done it so – so underhandedly.'

Tears began to well up and trickle down her cheeks. 'I feel awful, Rosalind. I didn't want to upset Johnny. I was so happy till this happened. Gerald gave me a beautiful engagement ring. He's restoring a lovely old house in Suffolk and we were going to be married after I'd taken my exams next summer and go there to live. He's going to start a music school – with me to help. But now it's all spoilt.'

Rosalind's heart went out to her. Why should anyone want to spoil two people's happiness? Reaching out she touched Cathy's hand. 'Don't worry. She'll get over it. I'm sure you'll think of a way to put things right.'

'It's all ruined. Nothing can be the same now.' Cathy searched her handbag for a handkerchief and blew her nose.

Rosalind watched her friend's distress for a moment before she asked: 'Is the age difference Mrs Johnson's only objection?'

Cathy sighed. 'No. You probably saw in the article that Gerald isn't well. He's developed a kind of muscular complaint that makes playing difficult, which is why he's taking up teaching instead.'

'And Mrs Johnson thinks . . .'

'She keeps trying to tell me I'm still a child and that I'm taking on a sick man. It isn't true. Gerald *isn't* sick. It's just that he can't play in public any more. If some ordinary person had this thing it wouldn't affect them at all. Gerald is furious that the press somehow found out about that too.'

204

Rosalind was frowning. 'If you kept it completely secret, how do you think the paper got hold of it? Someone must have told them. Who could it have been if it was neither of you?'

Cathy sighed, her face anguished. 'That's just it, Rosalind. I've got a terrible feeling that it was my fault,' she said miserably. 'When I was alone at Gerald's flat on Saturday afternoon a woman who used to work in public relations for Zenith records came to see him.' She paused, biting her lip. 'I think I might have told her too much. She promised to keep it to herself. She said she was an old friend. I thought it would be all right.'

'Have you told him?'

Cathy stared into her cup. 'No. Do you think I should?'

'It's not for me to say, but I suppose it would be better. He might be blaming someone else. Someone innocent.'

'Oh!' Cathy looked up at her. 'I hadn't thought of that.'

Rosalind looked at her hands that lay spread on the table and saw that they were tightly clenched with tension. 'Poor Cathy. You must love him very much,' she said quietly.

'I do.' Cathy swallowed hard at the lump in her throat. 'And he loves me too. But Johnny just won't *understand*. And he'll be so cross when I tell him what I told this Kay Goolden woman.'

'Surely not,' Rosalind said soothingly. 'It'll all work out, you'll see.'

'I hope so.' Cathy looked at her. 'Thanks, Rosalind. It's good to talk to someone. I know I can trust you.'

Looking into the other girl's eyes Rosalind felt a rush of pride. She'd always admired Cathy so much and the idea of being trusted with such a personal problem, of actually being asked for advice, was almost overwhelming. 'Of course you can trust me,' she said fervently. 'Any time you need a friend, please don't hesitate.' She smiled shyly. 'You know, I've really missed you since you stopped working at the Queen's Head.'

'Me too, Rosalind.' Cathy shook her head. 'Heavens, I haven't let you get a word in, have I? I don't even know what you rang me for.'

To her own surprise Rosalind had almost forgotten about the party. 'Well, after your news it sounds a bit frivolous,' she said apologetically. 'I was ringing to ask you to a New Year's Eve party my mother is giving. But under the circumstances I don't suppose you'll want to think about parties.' Deep inside she was relieved that Una wasn't going to get the opportunity of embarrassing them all. But to her surprise Cathy's face brightened.

'New Year's Eve, did you say?'

'That's right.'

'It might be nice to get out. The atmosphere at home is awful and I've been dreading the rest of the holidays. I'll ask Gerald if he's got anything else planned. He hasn't mentioned anything. I'll let you know as soon as I can.'

Rosalind blushed. 'I think I should warn you . . . it might be embarrassing. Mum – well, she makes a fuss of people like your fiancé. You know – likes to show off and all that.'

Cathy laughed. 'Gerald is used to all that, don't worry.' She smiled. 'Thanks for listening, Rosalind. Sorry to heap all my troubles on you.'

'That's all right.'

'What about you? You take your A levels in the spring, don't you?'

'Yes, then it's off to college, I hope.'

'No boyfriend?'

Rosalind hesitated, her cheeks colouring. 'There is someone actually. You'll meet him if you come to the party. His name is Stuart Hamilton and he's a scenic designer.'

'How interesting. I'm glad. Is it serious?'

'Oh, heavens no! I haven't known him very long.'

'But you like him – a lot?'

Rosalind blushed. 'I do rather, yes.'

The moment Christmas was out of the way Una began preparing for the party in earnest. She arranged for Hallard's catering department to do the food and spent almost a whole morning on the telephone telling them exactly what she wanted. She even had the piano in the lounge tuned in the hope that Gerald Cavelle might be induced to play for them. What a coup that would be! Then she set about making the house look festive and unearthing all Mrs Blake senior's best china and glass.

Don himself was quite bemused by the frenetic whirlwind of activity. The whole house seemed to be in turmoil. He couldn't remember there being a party at Blake's Folly since he was ten years old. But Una seemed happy. She was in such a good mood in fact that she was almost as charming and affable as when they had first met. To his great relief she appeared to have overcome her violent dislike of the house. He hadn't heard a word about the modern labour-saving bungalow she'd been nagging him to buy since the idea of having a party had first occurred to her. Something for which he was deeply grateful. He was automatically in favour of anything that put that out of her mind. Another good sign was that she had invited all the executive staff from Hallard's. It seemed to indicate that she was settling down at last. Blissfully ignorant of the fact that they had only been added to the guest list to swell the numbers, Don told himself with satisfaction that at last she was beginning to appreciate her position as the wife of one of Hallard's senior executives.

On the evening of the 31st there was a fine covering of snow on the gardens of Jay's Lane. The trees that lined the road sparkled in the glow of the street lamps and lights blazed welcomingly from the windows of Blake's Folly. In the hall a huge Christmas tree, decked with tinsel, baubles and coloured lights, greeted the guests as they arrived, and in the dining room a long table was laid out with every tempting delicacy that Hallard's catering department could provide.

The sliding doors between the lounge and the sitting room behind it had been opened and the carpet covering the woodblock floor had been taken up so that the guests could dance.

Don was wearing his dinner jacket, specially dry-cleaned for the occasion, whilst Una had splashed out on a new evening dress from model gowns: a dazzling creation in scarlet and black.

Upstairs in her room, quivering with excited apprehension, Rosalind dressed and made up with as much care, skill and imagination as she could. Defying her mother, she'd had her hair cut in the short boyish style that Freda had chosen for her, and, to her surprise, in a rare fit of generosity Una had decided that she too should have a new dress from Hallard's. Rosalind had chosen one in sapphire blue watered silk with a short flared skirt and a tight fitting bodice with a stand-up collar. It was the first glamorous dress she had ever owned. She could scarcely believe the difference it made to her confidence and couldn't wait for Stuart of see her in it.

By ten o'clock most of the guests had arrived. Dancing was in full swing and the house was filled with the sound of music and people enjoying themselves. The only guests who had not put in an appearance were Stuart and his flat mate, Cathy and Gerald.

Rosalind hung around unhappily in the hall, her spirits ebbing by the minute and her heart as heavy as lead. Una, no less disappointed, kept peering surreptitiously out of the window, hoping to see a taxi draw up at the gate. It was ironic that the very people for whom the party was being given were the only ones absent. She stared resentfully at all the staff members from Hallard's, each one of them stuffed to the gills with her food and drink, making the most of her lavish hospitality. Trust that lot to turn up for a free booze-up!

On one of her forays to the hall Rosalind almost bumped into her mother on the same mission. Mother and daughter looked at each other in dismay, each of them knowing what was in the other's mind.

'I suppose you *did* ask them?' Una said accusingly.

'Of course I did. And Cathy rang to say they were coming.'

'So where the hell have they got to?' She looked suspiciously at Rosalind. 'You're sure you got the date right?'

'I could hardly get it wrong, could I? There's only one New Year's Eve in a year.'

Una clicked her tongue irritably. 'Such bad form. No apology from them – *nothing*. One would have thought that a person in his position would know better. Then there's Stuart.' Una looked first at her watch, then accusingly at Rosalind. 'It wouldn't surprise me if you'd put him off, you know!'

'Me? How could I possibly have done that?'

'Throwing yourself at him that evening when he took you out,' Una replied. 'You should play things coolly on the first date. I'd have thought you'd know that.'   .

'I do. And I *didn't*.'

'You should never show how keen you are. It puts a man right . . .' Una's words were interrupted by the sudden ringing of the bell. She gave a startled gasp, pushing Rosalind out of the way in her hurry to open the door. Outside stood Cathy and Gerald and, behind them, coming up the path and clutching a bottle of wine, Stuart, on his own.

Her complaints about their lack of etiquette quite forgotten, Una held out her hands to Cathy and Gerald.

'Catherine! And Mr Cavelle! How *lovely* to see you both. I'm *so* glad you could come.'

'I'm so sorry we're late,' Cathy said. 'Gerald had to drive over from the West End and the traffic was dreadful.'

Una waved away her apologies and reached out to pull them inside. 'Not at all. You're not all that late anyway, are you? I'm sure I never noticed the time, we've been having such fun. Now – Rossie will take your coats. Come along in. Everyone is just *dying* to meet you. You must be ready for a drink . . .' Still chattering she led them away, leaving Rosalind to greet Stuart.

Rosalind watched them go. Her mother hadn't given her time to greet her friend. Cathy was wearing a black lace dress that made her look older than her nineteen years and set off her auburn hair dramatically.

Stuart looked at her with a hang-dog expression. 'Oh, dear, am I in the dog-house?' She smiled as she took his coat. 'Not really. Mum was getting worried that her star guests weren't going to show up.'

'I'd have been here earlier but poor old Julian has flu and I had to make him as comfortable as possible before leaving. I wanted to explain to her, but . . .'

'I'd leave her if I were you,' Rosalind advised. 'She'll get round to you in a minute.'

He followed her to the cloakroom with her armful of coats. 'Wasn't that Gerald Cavelle, the concert pianist?' he asked curiously.

She nodded. 'He's engaged to a schoolfriend of mine.'

'Wow! I'm impressed.' He took one of the coats from her. 'Here, let me help you with those.' He looked at her appreciatively. 'You look terrific, Rosalind. I like the dress.'

She blushed with pleasure. 'Thanks. You look very nice yourself.' He did; tall and willowy in his dinner jacket and immaculate white shirt, his blond hair flopping artistically over his brow. 'They're dancing in the lounge,' she said. 'Shall we go in?'

For Rosalind the party began at that moment. Dancing

with Stuart to the radiogram, on the polished floor of the lounge, felt to her like wafting round some fairytale ballroom in the arms of Prince Charming. Closing her eyes she felt as though her feet hardly touched the ground. He was a superb dancer. As they danced his lips brushed her cheek and she could feel his breath, warm and gentle, tantalising her ear.

'I like the new hairstyle,' he whispered. 'You took my advice. That's a terrific compliment, you know.'

'You've got such good taste – artistic taste,' Rosalind said softly.

He drew her closer and as they swayed, Rosalind hummed dreamily to the strains of *Dancing in the Dark*. She thought it was the happiest, most romantic moment of her life.

'Now then, you two. The idea is to mingle.' Una's voice speared through her dream. 'You mustn't monopolise poor Stuart, Rossie.' She put her hand on his shoulder and Rosalind stood aside and watched helplessly as her mother danced Stuart away from her into the midst of the other guests. As they went her heart sank as she heard Una saying, 'Now, I want to hear *all* about this musical you and your friend are writing.'

As she turned away she wondered what plot her mother was hatching up this time.

Cathy looked up at Gerald. His face was drawn and pale and he'd been quiet on the drive over. 'Are you all right?' she asked.

He nodded. 'Just tired, that's all. It's been a hell of a week what with one thing and another. We needn't stay too long, need we?'

'I suppose once they've seen the New Year in we could leave,' she said. They danced in silence for a moment, then she looked up at him again. She'd been trying for days to get up the courage to tell him that the press leak had been her fault. Better do it now before her nerve failed her again,

211

then she could start 1963 with a clear conscience. She cleared her throat. 'Gerald, I've got a confession to make.'

'What can that be?' He smiled down at her.

'It's terrible, I'm afraid. I've been worried sick about it all through Christmas. When I tell you you're going to be so cross.'

'Then maybe you'd better not tell me,' he said wearily. 'At least, not tonight.'

'Oh, but I must,' she insisted. 'It won't wait any longer. That Saturday when I was alone at the flat someone came to see you.'

'Really? Who was that?'

'A woman. Her name was Kay Goolden. She said she was an old friend. She annoyed me a bit, ordering me about – behaving as though she owned the place. She even asked me to make myself scarce because she wanted to speak to you alone.'

He smiled wryly. 'That sounds like Kay. She used to handle my PR at Zenith.'

'Yes. So she said.'

'I think she sometimes felt I was her personal property.'

'Yes – well, I – I'm afraid I told her – that we were . . .'

His brow darkened as he looked down at her. 'Oh, no! You told *Kay* – of all people? Oh, well, that explains everything.'

'I'm sorry, Gerald. I'm afraid I mentioned that you hadn't been well too. I know I had no right. I . . .'

'For God's sake, Cathy! What made you tell her that?'

She felt her cheeks growing hot. 'I told you, it was the way she behaved.' She glanced up at him. 'She suggested that you'd given up your career because of *me*. She called me a groupie! I wasn't having that. It was what she implied about her relationship with you too. She hinted that you were still seeing each other.'

His eyebrows rose. 'The cheek of the woman! I ran into

212

her one day a few weeks ago and we had lunch. Apart from that I haven't seen her in months.'

Cathy searched his eyes. 'She even made sure I knew that she remembered where your bedroom was.'

'How did she do that?'

'She'd brought something for you – an invitation to a party she was giving. She insisted on putting it by your bed. She went straight to it . . .' She looked at him pleadingly. 'I *asked* her not to tell anyone about us, Gerald. She promised not to.'

'And then she went straight to the press. Well, that's Kay for you. But you weren't to know, were you?' He frowned. 'Invitation, did you say? I never found any invitation.'

'No.' She avoided his eyes. 'I tore it up after she'd gone.'

He laughed and pulled her close. 'Oh, Cathy, you're so sweet. Don't worry about Kay. She and I had something going for a time, but she was too possessive and I finished it a long time ago. This is just her way of hitting back. It's a pity Johnny had to be upset, but it's done now and there's nothing we can do about it. We'll just have to try very hard to make her see that our marriage is going to work.'

She pressed her lips against his cheek. 'Oh, Gerald, it *is* going to work, isn't it? Just think, this time next year we'll be together, spending Christmas and our first New Year at Cuckoo Lodge. It was awful without you over the holiday. And it was the worst birthday I ever had.'

He kissed her. 'I'm sorry we couldn't have spent more time together, darling. This state of affairs can't go on.' He looked thoughtful. 'As a matter of fact I've been wondering if it mightn't be a good idea to bring the wedding forward.'

'Oh, Gerald, that would be marvellous. Do you really think we could? The summer seems an awfully long way off.'

* * *

213

Una pressed herself close to Stuart as they circled the lounge floor, her cheek close to his. 'It all sounds fabulous,' she told him. 'What a wonderful plot – so original. Your friend Julian must be a very talented writer.'

'He is.' He looked down at her. 'I suppose you recognised the plot? It's really an up-dated musical version of Shakespeare's *Twelfth Night*.'

'Of course. I latched on to that at once,' she lied. 'Such a pity he couldn't come this evening. I was looking forward so much to meeting him.' She giggled. 'Julian, I mean. Not Shakespeare!'

'Yes. He was disappointed.'

'I'd love to read his script when it's finished, Stuart,' she said coyly. 'It might come as a surprise to you when I tell you that I was in the business myself before I married Don.'

'I did know actually,' he said. 'Rosalind told me.'

'Did she?' Una licked her lips carefully and treated him to a glossily seductive smile. 'As a matter of fact I've been wondering if there wasn't some way I could help you,' she said tantalisingly.

His eyes brightened. 'With contacts, you mean?' He looked around the room. 'You did say there would be some show business people here.'

She cleared her throat uneasily. 'Ah – well, New Year is a busy time for most of my showbiz friends. They're all working hard, I'm afraid. Up and down the country in panto and so on. There's dear Gerald, of course, but he's more in the classical line.'

'Yes.' He looked down at her. 'So – in what way do you feel you can help, Mrs Blake?'

She drew in her breath sharply. 'Oh Stuart – Una, *please*. Mrs Blake makes me sound like my own mother-in-law!' To her satisfaction he laughed. 'No, darling. What I wondered was whether some money might help? If you were to take a small theatre in some seaside town next summer season, and do an Out of Town première – persuade a few of the big-wigs from the West End to come and see it – it might get you off to a good start.'

He was staring at her. 'You'd really be prepared to do all that – for us?'

'If I think the play is worthy of it, of course I'd be willing to sponsor you.' She smiled dazzlingly at him. 'I mean, you have all the talent you require, Julian as writer, you on the set designs and costumes, and your other friend writing the music. It should be marvellous.'

'If you put up some money I take it you'd want to take a percentage of the box office by way of repayment?' he said thoughtfully.

Una smiled enigmatically. 'We can thrash out the conditions when I've met your friends and read the play, can't we?'

As midnight drew near Don turned off the music and switched over to the radio for the chimes of Big Ben. Una made sure that everyone's glass was full and they stood in a circle, glasses raised, poised for the birth of a new year. At the first stroke a cheer went up and there were kisses, toasts and good wishes all round. Then they all linked arms for the traditional *Auld Lang Syne*. When the music began again and they took to the floor Cathy laid her head against Gerald's chest.

'I love you so much,' she whispered. 'Can I come back to the flat with you tonight?'

He shook his head. 'Darling, you know that would only aggravate the situation. We'll set the wedding date tomorrow. We'll make it soon.'

'It can't be soon enough for me,' she told him dreamily.

Stuart held out his hand to Rosalind. 'Dance with me?'

Since the first dance with him her mother had made sure she was kept busy handing round snacks and filling glasses. She'd had to watch Stuart dancing with Una most of the evening and felt dejected and disappointed. All the confidence the new dress had brought her had faded and she felt like a dowdy wallflower again. She stared at the hand he offered, then up at him.

'You don't have to be polite. I'm sure you'd rather ask Mum.'

He looked crestfallen. 'Rosalind! Don't be like that.' He took her hand and pulled her towards him. 'I wanted to be with you, really. You're the main reason I came. But your mother has made me the most wonderful offer. I could hardly be rude to her after that, could I?'

Slightly appeased, she allowed him to slide an arm round her waist and draw her on to the dance floor. 'What offer?' she asked.

'Well, it's all very much in the air at the moment, but she just might put up some money so that we can get our musical on,' he told her with barely suppressed excitement.

She stared at him. Where would her mother get that kind of money? she wondered. Presumably from Don. But how would she persuade him to part with it? And what was behind the idea? Knowing Una there was bound to be an ulterior motive. Still, if that was Stuart's only reason for neglecting her all evening, it wasn't important.

'Have you enjoyed the party?' she asked him.

His arm tightened around her waist and he pressed his lips close to her ear. 'I'd have preferred to see more of you. Maybe we can do something about that,' he said. 'Come out with me again soon.'

She felt her heart quicken. 'All right. When?'

'I'll ring you.' He squeezed her tightly. 'I have to go now. Come out to the car with me and say goodnight.'

At the gate, under the shadow of the laurel hedge, he kissed her till she felt her spine turn to jelly. Then he climbed into Julian's Mini and waved her goodnight.

Her feet hardly touching the ground, she walked indoors. In the hall Cathy and Gerald were about to leave. Cathy reached out and put her arms round Rosalind, giving her a hug.

'Happy New Year, Rosalind,' she said, her face radiant. 'Thanks for inviting us to the party. We've had a super time.' She lowered her voice. 'And guess what? Gerald and I are bringing the wedding date forward. We're getting married very soon. I'll make sure you get an invitation.'

Rosalind said goodnight, shook hands with Gerald, then climbed the stairs. It had been a night to remember after all.

It was two-thirty when Una finally joined Don in their bedroom. From the warmth and comfort of the bed he watched her climb out of the splendid red and black evening dress and peel off her black lace bra and panties. Now that he was used to her uninhibited behaviour he had to admit that she really did have a beautiful body. Being on the plump side made her even more voluptuous in his eyes. She looked a lot like the photograph of his mother taken soon after he had been born. Soft and bounteous. He felt excitement mounting.

'You're looking very lovely tonight, Una,' he said huskily as she climbed into bed beside him. He had noticed that she was wearing the sexy black nightgown she had bought for their honeymoon.

'Am I?' Una snuggled down gratefully in the warmth. 'I think the party was a success. Don't you?'

'I do. You're the perfect hostess,' he told her. 'Harry Black, the firm's accountant, told me so more than once.'

As she switched off the bedside lamp Una grimaced. Harry Black, that common little man? What a nerve he had! When he'd danced with her he'd surreptitiously squeezed her bottom. What did he know about anything? Aloud she said, 'Really? How gratifying.' As she felt Don's hands begin to fondle her she gritted her teeth. 'Don – you know the bungalow we've been thinking about?'

217

His heart sank. 'Yes,' he said guardedly.

'Well, I've been thinking. Maybe you're right. After the space we've been used to here, it might feel claustrophobic. So I was wondering if you'd mind if I used a little of the money we would have spent on an investment instead?'

The feel of her warm soft body so close to his was arousing him so much he hardly heard or cared what she was saying.

'Investment? That sounds much more sensible, dear,' he murmured as he pushed her shoulder straps down and began to slide the nightdress over her breasts. 'But tell me about it tomorrow, eh?' His breath was rapid and moist in her ear as he moved over her and muttered urgently, 'I know it's late dear – and you must be tired – but, oh, *Una* . . .'

Resigned, she wriggled out of the nightdress and lay back, preparing herself for the passion to come, consoling herself with the knowledge that if Don was running true to form it would be mercifully short-lived. The really worthwhile things in life were sometimes almost too expensive, she reflected wryly, gazing glassily up at the ceiling.

Chapter Twelve

Gerald found the block of flats without difficulty and took the lift to the top floor. Kay took so long to answer his ring at the bell that he began to think she was out. He was just turning away when she opened the door. She wore a bathrobe and her hair was swathed, turban fashion in a towel.

'Gerald! What a surprise. Come in.' She looked taken aback. 'I'm sorry I was so long. I was in the shower.'

He stood in the spacious hallway while she closed the door. It was certainly a lavish flat. She hadn't exaggerated about that. She turned to him, her face now composed into a smile.

'So – what can I do for you?'

'Don't tell me you haven't guessed why I'm here?'

She took in his grim expression and smiled ruefully. 'You're annoyed.'

'That would be putting it mildly. Why Kay? Why did you do it?'

She shrugged. 'I'm not sure that there was a reason. Why should there be?' She walked through an open door into an exquisitely furnished sitting room. Picking up a silver cigarette box from the glass-topped coffee table she offered it to him. He ignored it.

'You came to the flat and quizzed Cathy – my fiancée. Then, after she'd naively confided in you, you ran straight to the press. Why did you do it Kay?'

She turned to him defiantly. 'Why not? You've always gone all out for publicity.' She looked at him for a moment, registering the determined set of his jaw. 'All right then, if you're set on having a reason I suppose you could say that your fiancée, as you so *quaintly* call her, was so naive that I just couldn't resist it.'

'You really are a bitch, aren't you? Have you no sense of decency at all?'

'Decency?' She lit her cigarette and blew out a cloud of smoke. 'Do you call marrying a kid less than half your age decent? I call it disgusting. It's almost like child molesting.'

'Cathy isn't a child.'

'No? You led me to believe she was though, didn't you? You gave the impression that she was in infant school.'

'I did nothing of the kind.'

'It was what you implied, Gerry. It was what you meant me to believe. Don't deny it.'

He fought to control the rage that bubbled up inside him. 'Why the hell should I want you to believe anything? It's none of your damned business. Why are you so vindictive, Kay? What is it festering away in that devious mind of yours that makes you want to hurt and destroy?'

Her eyes flashed as she viciously stubbed out her half-smoked cigarette. 'There's nothing wrong with my mind – or my body, Gerald,' she said. 'You're the one who's hurting – you're the one who's sick. I knew that in New York. Now I'm sure.'

'Once and for all, I am *not sick*!'

'Really?' Her eyebrows rose. 'Your fiancée seems to think you are. Something muscular, she said. Whatever it is must be bad to make you start behaving so irrationally.'

Suddenly he felt unutterably weary. Sinking down into one of the white leather chairs he said, 'You hurt all the wrong people – people you don't even know, who don't deserve it. You can do what you like to me, I don't matter any more, but Cathy and her family . . .'

'You *do* matter, Gerry!' She crossed the room and sank to her knees in front of him. 'You matter to me. I did it to

220

try and bring you to your senses – make you face up to the sheer stupidity of what you're doing. Why are you throwing yourself and your talent away like this? First you tell me you're about to retire and bury yourself in some frightful dump at the back of beyond, then I hear – second hand – that you're ill and that you're marrying this – this *child*. How do you think it made me feel?'

'Spiteful, apparently.'

'No!' She reached for his hands. 'I really didn't want to hurt you – or anyone else. If I did, then I'm sorry.' She looked into his eyes. 'Tell me, what's it all about? Tell me why you're doing it. Make me understand – if you can!'

He sighed. 'It's simple. I love her.'

She laughed. 'You *fancy* her, you mean. Face it, Gerry, she's every middle-aged man's fantasy with her auburn hair and great big innocent eyes; just as you are every young girl's fairytale dream. The handsome concert pianist with the romantic mystery illness! Get her out of your system, yes. But marriage!' Kay looked into his eyes. 'How long do you think it'll last? How long before the novelty wears off for you both?'

'Maybe it won't have to last.'

She frowned. 'What do you mean? What are you saying, Gerry?'

'Nothing.' He shrugged. 'Who knows how long any marriage will last?'

'I think ours would have lasted,' she said quietly.

He leaned forward and gripped the hands that lay in his. 'You believe that, do you? Well, just tell me this, Kay, would you have given up this marvellous new job of yours with Summit Films? Your fabulous salary and all your hard-won independence? Would you have given up this flat and come with me to live at the back of beyond, as you call it?' He shook his head. 'I don't think so. And as for living with a man with what you call a mystery illness . . .' He smiled wryly. 'It just isn't

221

you, Kay. You're hardly the Florence Nightingale type. Why not admit it?'

'Are you saying that you would have asked me if I had been?'

'Who knows?'

'You didn't even give me the chance, did you? Yet you believe that this girl is all of those things – unselfish, caring, ready to give up everything for you, the man she loves?'

'I happen to believe she is, yes.'

'And you think it's fair to expect it of her?'

He stopped short, his eyes suddenly hard as he stared at her. 'What would you know about fairness, Kay?'

She rose and stood looking down at him. 'I know *you*, Gerry. I know and understand you through and through; better than you know yourself probably. I spent a long time building a public image for you. You get to know a person pretty well in the process of doing that. And there's something here that just doesn't fit. What I don't get is why you have to bury yourself in the country.'

'I've changed. I want different things now. My values have altered.'

'We could have stayed here, you and I.' She swept an arm round the room. 'You could have taught here just as well as in the country. There's plenty of room for your piano and I'd be out of your way all day. She leaned towards him, looking into his eyes. 'I could have been a good wife to you without giving anything up. I'm not as selfish as you make me sound, Gerry. I'd have looked after you. And if it's money that's worrying you it needn't have been a problem. I earn enough for both of us.'

'Money is the last of my worries!' he snapped irritably, shaking off the hands that held his. 'Anyway, do you really think I'd ever allow you to keep me, Kay? God forbid! You're not the only one to need independence. At best you'd have swallowed me whole. At worst you'd have grown bored.'

222

'*That's not true!*' She swung away from him and went to the window, hiding the quick tears and the hurt his remark had inflicted. She wrapped her arms around herself protectively. 'You must have known damned well I'd come back if you'd asked me. I would even now.'

He stood up. 'No, Kay.'

'*Yes!*' She swung round to face him. 'You and I are two of a kind. We complement each other perfectly and you know it.' She went to him and put her arms around him. 'You still want me if you're honest. You want me now. Don't deny it.'

It was true. He couldn't deny that he still found her desirable, seeing her here like this, her face clean of make-up, glowing from the shower. He visualised her skin, damp and fragrant under the bathrobe, and longed for the warm, silken feel of it under his hands; the comfort of her familiar body in his arms. He felt too tired; too weak to argue. She'd always been stronger than him, always able to impose her will on his and bring him into line. It had scared him sometimes in the past. It was one of the main reasons he'd broken with her. And it still worked, even now.

Reaching up suddenly she drew his head down and kissed him hard, her lips parting invitingly, her mouth tender and passionate at the same time. For a moment he resisted, then he pulled the towel from her hair and tangled his fingers in the damp tresses. Holding her face tightly between his hands, he kissed her fiercely, almost brutally.

'Damn you, Kay,' he murmured. 'Damn you to hell!' But in spite of his outward anger he couldn't deny that giving in to what he had been fighting ever since she opened the door to him gave him a soaring sense of release.

She rubbed her cheek against his. 'Come and dry my hair for me like you used to do.' Taking his hand she began to pull him gently towards the bedroom. He went with her willingly.

*　　*　　*

When he awakened the room was dark. Raising himself on one elbow he stared down bemusedly at her. 'Have I been asleep?'

'Yes.' She sat up and switched on the bedside lamp. 'We have to talk, Gerry. What is really wrong with you?'

'Nothing's *wrong*.' He ran a hand through his tousled hair as the memory of his humiliating failure came back to him. 'I was tired, that's all. Maybe I felt a little guilty and inhibited too. I'm sorry if I disappointed you, but I did warn you, Kay. I love Cathy.'

She reached out for a cigarette. 'In my experience most men are completely amoral when it comes to sex,' she said bitterly. 'They take what's on offer. In love or out of it.'

'Don't tar us all with the same brush. I'm not like that.'

'Don't tell me you didn't want to make love to me! You'd been wanting to from the moment you walked in the door.'

Stung by her uncanny insight he hit back. 'Perhaps your technique is beginning to slip, Kay. Sex appeal doesn't last for ever, you know!'

The barb found its mark and she winced. 'Thanks!' Swinging her legs over the edge of the bed, she pulled on her bathrobe, tying the belt tightly. 'What do you think your sweet little fiancée would think if I told her what just happened – or rather *didn't* happen?' she asked, looking down at him.

'She wouldn't believe you.'

Her eyebrows shot up. 'Oh, I see. It's like that, is it? A case of try before you buy!' She frowned. 'Well, maybe you should warn her. Ask yourself seriously, are you really being fair to her – a naive young girl, with God knows what ideals and expectations? She'll be going into this marriage with stars in her eyes, expecting all sorts of things that you can't or won't want to give her. Don't you think she should be warned?'

He sprang up and grasped her by the shoulders, his eyes

224

burning as they bored into hers. 'You keep away from Cathy, do you hear? Make any more trouble for me and I'll . . .'

'You'll *what*, Gerry?' Her eyes held his with a bold challenge he couldn't meet. She pushed him away. 'Oh, relax. I won't make trouble. It might sound phoney but I really do care too much to do that. I am warning you though. Marry that girl and you'll both regret it. Hire a housekeeper, a nurse, a *whore* if you like. But if you really love the girl as much as you say, don't marry her. If you do you'll ruin her life.'

Chapter Thirteen

The first days of 1963 at Chestnut Grove were difficult for Cathy. Unable to handle the situation downstairs, she stayed in her room for much of the time, but at mealtimes when the family were gathered round the table, the air was thick with an atmosphere of disapproval. Mrs Bains wore an expression of self-righteous satisfaction. She ate in a meaningful silence broken only by the reproachful clicking of her dentures. *I told you it would all end in tears*, was etched in every line of her face. Matthew looked acutely uncomfortable and avoided Cathy's eyes, while Johnny picked at her food, looking downright miserable. Conversation was limited to hopeful comments about the weather from Matthew, and grudging requests to pass the salt.

Finally unable to tolerate the cloud of gloom that had settled over her home a moment longer, Johnny decided that something must be done to put things on a more amicable footing. It seemed that Cathy's proposed marriage to Gerald Cavelle would go ahead whether she approved or not and she could see that if she was not to lose Cathy altogether some kind of compromise must be reached.

One afternoon, just before the new college term began, she made up her mind and as soon as Mrs Bains had nodded off in the armchair for her afternoon snooze she went upstairs and tapped gently on Cathy's door.

'Cathy, can I come in?'

Cathy raised her head from the book she was reading. Johnny's voice was soft but there was a positive tone about it that she recognised of old. It meant that she had no intention of taking no for an answer. Instinctively she drew herself up straight and replied, 'Of course. The door's not locked.'

Johnny stepped inside and closed the door firmly behind her. For a moment the two surveyed each other across the room. For the first time in their long relationship, Johnny felt frighteningly helpless. Cathy was a woman now and out of her control. Was it possible to mend the rift that had opened between them? Was there anything she could do to prevent her from diving headlong into what she saw as an inevitable disaster? She must at least try. She cleared her throat. 'This can't go on, Cathy,' she said. 'I can't take any more of this terrible atmosphere. And frankly I don't see why I should.'

Cathy hung her head, feeling six years old again. 'I know. And I'm sorry. But it really isn't my fault.' She looked up, her eyes brimming with tears. 'I – Gerald and I had planned to tell you about our engagement on my birthday, but the papers got hold of the story before we had the chance.'

'It was the way you lied to me. You've never been deceitful before. I can't help thinking . . .' Johnny broke off, biting her lip. She hadn't meant to begin by reproaching the girl. It was all coming out wrong.

But Cathy was nodding. 'I know. And I hated deceiving you. But I knew you'd take it badly, and I was right, wasn't I? Look – if you'd rather I left . . .'

'*Left?*' Shocked at the idea, Johnny crossed the room and sat down beside her on the bed. 'This is your home, child. At least, for now. Anyway, where would you go?'

Cathy shrugged. 'To Gerald's flat, I suppose.'

'You'd go there and live with him?' Johnny could hardly believe she was hearing right. 'He'd let you do that?'

'No. He's already suggested that we bring the wedding forward.' Cathy turned to look Johnny in the eye. 'He isn't the kind of person you seem to think. He's good and decent and he loves me.'

'Is that why he seduced you? The man who's supposed to

227

be your guardian? The man your father put his trust in to protect and care for you? Do you really think I could ever respect a man like that?' Johnny felt the hot colour rising up from her neck to suffuse her cheeks. She hadn't meant to say it, but now that she had she was glad. It had been festering in her mind for weeks. It was better out in the open.

Cathy's eyes widened and she recoiled as though she'd been slapped. '*Seduced?* I don't know what you mean! It isn't like that.'

'No? Then what do you call it?'

'How did you know anyway?' Cathy asked, her face drained of colour.

Johnny threw up her hands. 'Oh, Cathy, *Cathy*, what do you take me for? I'm not a fool, you know. You can't keep things like that from someone who's known you as long as I have. I know you and Gerald have been lovers. It's been written all over you for weeks.' She broke off as a thought occurred to her. 'You're not expecting his child, are you? That isn't why . . .?'

'*No!*' Cathy's eyes were wide with shock. 'Is that really what you thought? Is it what everyone is thinking? That he's only asked me to marry him because . . .'

'No, of course they aren't.'

'*You* thought so.'

'Cathy, don't you see? You're like my own daughter. Please try to understand how it is for me. Ever since you were no more than a baby I've cared for you; nursed you through all those childhood illnesses; worried about you and loved you like my own child. It's only natural that when something like this happens my instincts tell me.' She spread her hands in a helpless gesture. 'If it had been some young man – some *boy* – I could have tried to talk you out of it – somehow made you see that he wasn't right for you.' Her voice thickened. 'As it is I – I've no right to tell you to do anything. I've never felt so helpless – *so useless* in my life.'

228

Cathy looked at her. 'You're wrong about one thing, Johnny,' she whispered. 'He didn't seduce me. It was the other way round. But only because I love him so much. I wish I could make you understand what it's like. I want to be with him more than anything else in the world; to belong to him. If anything happened to part us I think I'd want to die. I just wanted everyone to be as happy as I was. I never wanted to make you all miserable.' She could scarcely speak for the lump in her throat and suddenly she threw her arms round Johnny's neck and hugged her. 'Oh, Johnny, I *wish* you could be glad for me.'

Johnny's heart melted as she held the girl who was so dear to her close. Their tears mingled as she said wearily. 'I wish I could too, love. There's nothing I wish more. And I do remember how it feels to be in love, believe me. I'm not that old that I can't remember. It's just that he's so much older than you. What kind of life will you have with him?'

'A happy one. I *promise!*' Cathy pushed her hands against Johnny's shoulders so that she could look into her eyes. 'Oh, *please* say you wish us well. It means so much to me to have you on our side. Next to Gerald you're the most important person in my life. These last couple of weeks have been so awful.'

'I know they have, love.' Johnny looked at her for a long moment. 'What do you think your poor father would have said?' she asked quietly. 'Have you thought about that? The last promise I made him was to take care of you and if I thought I was letting him down . . .'

'Oh, but you're not! He would have been pleased. I know he would,' Cathy said, her eyes shining with confidence. 'Gerald was his best friend. He would have trusted him with his life. He even made him my guardian, didn't he?'

Johnny looked thoughtful. She didn't share Cathy's confidence on that particular issue but there was little point in arguing about it. She looked into the girl's eyes. 'Will you promise me one thing?'

229

'I'll try,' Cathy said guardedly.

'Will you just stay on at college and take your exams? It's only a few months after all. And that house in Suffolk won't be ready to live in for some time yet by the sound of things.'

'Well – I suppose I could.'

'It wouldn't hurt to wait another six months, would it? Just until the summer term ends. It seems a shame not to take your finals when you've got this far and worked so hard. A qualification is always a good thing to have. You never know when you might need it.' She smiled and took Cathy's hands in hers. 'You could be married from here then – a lovely white wedding with all the trimmings. I'd even make your dress for you if you wanted. And have the reception here. Matthew could give you away. I'd love that, wouldn't you?'

Cathy smiled. 'Oh, Johnny, yes, I would.'

'It's settled then?'

'I'll have to ask Gerald.'

'Of course. You do that. See what he says.' She gave Cathy a hug, then rose and went to the door. 'Come on downstairs now. I'll put the kettle on for a cup of tea.'

'Johnny . . .'

The older woman paused in the doorway. 'Yes, love?'

'Will you ask Mrs Bains to stop looking at me as though I've murdered someone?'

Johnny laughed. 'Mother just feels protective of me because she knows how worried I've been. All mothers are alike. You'll find that out for yourself someday.' She grinned. 'But she'll be fine when I've had a word with her. Just you leave her to me.'

When Matthew came home from work that afternoon and looked into the sitting room he found the three women in his life happily chatting over the teacups. The subject was clearly weddings. Dresses made of lace versus satin? Four bridesmaids or two? And the merits of a sit-down reception as opposed to a finger buffet. As he closed the door and made for the stairs he gave a sigh of relief. Even Gran was smiling. With a bit of luck the pall of gloom that had hung over the house since before Christmas had finally dispersed.

But the following day when Cathy met Gerald and put forward Johnny's suggestion he was less than enthusiastic.

'You don't really want all that fuss, do you?'

She looked at him. 'I thought you'd be pleased. Don't you see, it means that Johnny has come round to the idea?'

His eyebrows came together in a frown. 'I can't see that it's her place to "come round" as you put it. Or to dictate where and when we'll be married,' he said tetchily. 'She's not even a relative. She was only Dan's cleaning woman after all. I thought we were going to bring the wedding forward. I thought you were happy with that.'

'Johnny's always been more than just a cleaning woman,' Cathy said warmly. 'She virtually brought me up. I owe her a lot.' Dismayed, she looked at him. This was their first disagreement. 'I was happy about bringing the wedding forward. I still am in some ways. It's just that Johnny thinks I should finish my course first – take my exams and qualify. And I can see her point.'

'Why? You're never going to need to earn your living in that kind of way.'

'But I might want to get a job sometime. You never know. Johnny says a qualification is always useful.'

His eyes narrowed. 'She still doesn't trust me, does she? What does she think I'll do – run off and abandon you? Leave you penniless?'

'No, of course not. It's just a – kind of safety net – insurance.'

He looked at her for a long moment. 'So now I know what Johnny thinks. How about telling me what *you* think, Cathy?'

Her heart sank. It was so hard, trying to please everyone.

231

'I want to be with you,' she said simply. 'But I want to do what's right too, what's best – for us, for everyone.'

He shook his head and drew her close. 'You're asking for the impossible, Cathy. In the entire history of the world no one has ever yet succeeded in pleasing everyone. It's your life – your future. It's what *you* want that's important.' He held her at arm's length and looked into her eyes. 'So make up your mind. What do you want?'

'I want what you want.'

He kissed her. 'And *I* want to put my ring on your finger. The sooner the better and with as little fuss as possible.'

He held her close, drawing strength from the warmth and youthful vitality of her body. 'I'd like it to be as soon as possible. We'll have a nice long honeymoon in Switzerland, at a favourite place of mine high in the mountains. Oh, you'll love it, Cathy. I can't wait to show it to you. Meantime I'll arrange with the builders to get a couple of rooms ready for us to come back to at Cuckoo Lodge and we can live in them and supervise the rest of the work on the house.'

He kissed her again. 'Oh, just think of it, darling. Watching the house grow and blossom as the spring turns into summer; making plans. There'll be so much to do. Contacts to make; publicity and booking to organise for the school. There'll be people to see – meetings – entertaining as soon as the house is ready. That's where you'll come into your own. My perfect hostess. It's going to be a wonderful life, darling. Can't you just see it?'

'Can we let Johnny arrange the wedding? It means so much to her.'

He sighed and shook his head at her. 'You're doing it again – trying to please everyone. I'm sorry, darling, but the press are already on to us. If they got wind of a white wedding in deepest suburbia they'd have a field day. They could wreck the whole proceedings for us. No, we'll make it a very quiet affair. A register office – somewhere quiet, off the beaten track would be best. With as few people in the know about the date and location as possible. Afterwards we'll lay on lunch at a local hotel for close friends – that includes the Johnsons of course. You can leave all the arrangements to me.' He kissed the top of her head. 'All you have to do is get yourself a wedding outfit and turn up.'

Cathy tried to swallow her disappointment. 'What about witnesses – someone to give me away – your best man?'

He laughed. 'I don't think there's really any need for any of that. But if there's anyone you want to ask specially, I've no objection.'

'I thought perhaps Matthew. And Carla and Rosalind Blair.'

He shrugged. 'Fine, if that's what will make you happy.' He hugged her. 'It's your wedding, darling.'

As he drew up outside the Johnsons' house she turned to him. 'Are you coming in?'

He shook his head. 'Not today. I'll leave you to tell Johnny what we've planned.' As she made to get out of the car he reached out to draw her back. 'Cathy, wait. I meant to speak to you before – about money.'

She closed the car door and looked at him. 'What about money?'

'I think we should get a few legal loose ends tied up. Restoring the house and putting in all the things we're going to need is going to cost a bomb. I knew it would be expensive but there are some things I hadn't counted for. I take it that you agree that we pool our resources once we're married?'

She laughed. 'Of course, but you're already in charge of my money anyway.'

'Only until the end of next year when you come of age. That arrangement still stands as things are at present and of course I can only do things on *your* behalf. It would be more convenient to have it changed.'

She nodded. 'Whatever you think.'

He smiled. 'For instance, it seems rather ludicrous for me to go on making you a monthly allowance, doesn't it? We'll have a joint account at the bank of course. That means you can draw money whenever you need it, without having to ask me. And of course once the flat is sold there'll be no problem.'

'Yes, I see. All right then.'

'To make it legal and above board I'll need your signature on one or two boring old documents,' he said. 'I've made an appointment at the solicitor's for tomorrow afternoon. Is that all right?'

'Yes, fine. Mr MacAlister's?'

'No. I've had everything transferred to James Palmer, my own solicitor. It's more convenient. I'll pick you up at two o'clock.' He drew her towards him and kissed her. 'See you tomorrow then, darling. Don't worry about Johnny. She'll see it our way when you've explained.'

If Johnny was disappointed she didn't say so. And when Mrs Bains opened her mouth to express her own forthright opinion her daughter shot her a warning look that silenced her before she began.

On the day that followed, Gerald's solicitor had all the documents drawn up ready for Cathy to sign at his smart Kensington office. The transaction was over in the space of a few minutes and then they were walking out into the thin February sunshine again and making their way to the bank. Afterwards they went to Gerald's flat where he told her about the arrangements he had already begun to make for their wedding. For Cathy the day had an oddly unreal feel to it. She felt as though the whole thing was out of her control, almost as though it was happening to someone else and she was merely an observer. But then, as she told herself, she knew nothing about financial matters, or about how to arrange a wedding either. If it had been left to her she wouldn't have known where to start.

*　　*　　*

The wedding took place on a bright Monday morning in early April. The first green leaves of spring were beginning to unfurl on all the trees and Gerald told Cathy that the builders had now completed the two rooms they were to live in on the first floor of Cuckoo Lodge on their return from Switzerland.

Cathy wore a suit of cinnamon linen with a mint green blouse and hat to match. She carried a small posy of pink and cream rosebuds. Matthew, who accompanied her to the register office in the hired car, thought she looked pale, but she insisted that it was only nerves and that she would be fine the moment she saw Gerald.

The ceremony was over almost before she had time to take in her surroundings. She was dimly aware of being ushered into a small room, carpeted in blue and tastefully decked with flowers. There were two rows of chairs on which sat their few guests. The bespectacled registrar gabbled his way through the ceremony in a monotone as though he were conducting an auction sale. Finding herself finally married to Gerald, Cathy allowed herself to be hugged by a tearful Johnny and pecked on the cheek by Matthew. Rosalind squeezed her hands and wished her luck and Carla winked and told her she was lucky to have 'landed herself such a good catch'.

Gerald himself had invited one guest only. Cathy didn't notice her until after the ceremony when she came forward with congratulations. Standing on tiptoe, Kay kissed Gerald's cheek, then turned to Cathy.

'My dear, many, *many* congratulations.' She took both her hands and squeezed them gently. 'I do hope we shall be good friends. And I hope you've forgiven me for getting off on the wrong foot.' She leaned forward to brush Cathy's cheek with cool lips. 'Gerald has very generously invited me to come to Suffolk and see this wonderful house of yours when it's finished. I hope you approve of the invitation?'

Dismayed, Cathy made herself smile. 'Of course. All Gerald's friends are welcome.'

She got through the lunch, hardly tasting the food and declining all but a sip of champagne, then somehow, at last they were on the plane, bound for Switzerland. As they became airborne and safety belts were unfastened she looked at Gerald.

'I can't believe we're actually married and on our way,' she said. 'I thought it would never end.'

He slipped an arm around her and drew her head down on to his shoulder. 'If you found that an ordeal, think how much worse a big church wedding would have been.'

'Gerald – why didn't you tell me you'd invited Kay Goolden?' she asked.

He shrugged. 'It was very much a last-minute thing. She rang me last night. I thought it might be as well to have her on our side.'

'Why did she ring you?'

'Nothing specific. Just a chat.'

'What about?'

'Nothing much. Just gossip. Kay and I have a lot of mutual acquaintances. She used to handle all my publicity as you know.'

'Oh, yes. I knew that all right,' Cathy said wryly.

Gerald chuckled and took her hand. 'That's all water under the bridge now. Forgive and forget, eh? Kay is a good PR woman. When you spilled the beans like that she must have found it irresistible.'

The fact that he was laying the blame for the episode firmly at her door did not escape her. 'Obviously. So – didn't you feel it was risky, telling her we were getting married today? Weren't you afraid she might go to the press again?'

'I knew she wouldn't if she was a guest, which is why I invited her. I thought if I made her part of the conspiracy . . .' He bent to kiss her. 'How did we get into this? Why on earth are we talking about Kay when we're on our way to our honeymoon?'

She relaxed. He was right. They had a wonderful three

weeks ahead of them. Why spoil it with her silly suspicions about Kay?

Switzerland was all that Gerald had promised – and more besides. The view from their hotel window in the little ski resort of Davos enchanted Cathy so much that she couldn't stop looking at it. The mountain tops were still clothed in snow, but the brilliant sunshine turned them pink and gold like sugar frosting. She loved the hospitality of the people and the quaint buildings with their colourfully painted walls. The air was as sparkling and invigorating as champagne and Cathy felt as though she were living in a fairytale that was coming alive. They swam in the indoor heated pool at the hotel; walked the mountain paths; explored the smart little shops that were full of intriguing things; and drank rich, fragrant coffee in the cosy little cafés. Gerald hired a car and took her to Liechtenstein to see the castle, and they went for memorable drives on precipitous mountain roads to villages that looked as though they had stepped straight out of a Disney film. They dined late and danced romantically afterwards in the hotel ballroom with its glittering chandeliers.

Several times they took the ski-lift to the top of the Shatzlap and looked out over what seemed to Cathy the magical, cloud-capped roof of the world; the kind of place where, as a child, she had always imagined Santa Claus lived.

'It's a pity it's a little too late for skiing,' Gerald told her. 'I'd have loved to teach you.'

'Oh, yes. I've always wanted to learn to ski.' Cathy hugged his arm and looked up at him. 'Maybe we can come again next year and do that?'

He didn't meet her eager eyes as he replied: 'Yes – maybe.'

At night, wrapped in each other's arms under the thick duvet they would lie and look out through the open shutters at the sky that looked like black velvet studded with diamonds. And in the mornings they would wake at dawn to watch the sun come up over the mountain tops, bewitching everything it touched with a breathtaking golden beauty.

'I'll remember this for the rest of my life,' she whispered one night when they had just made love. 'I don't know how it's possible to be this happy. Sometimes I feel I shall wake up soon and find it was all a beautiful dream.'

Gerald turned his face away so that she wouldn't see the guilt that filled his eyes. She was like a child, wide-eyed with delight at every new thing. Her unselfish and unquestioning love overwhelmed and terrified him. She had taken to marriage so wholeheartedly, giving herself without reserve. To her, lovemaking was new and exciting. She approached it with an eager, uninhibited adventurousness that enchanted him. He was so lucky. *And so devious*, his conscience insisted. He battled inwardly with the accusing demons that refused to leave him alone. He would make her happy. After all, she was in love with him. It would have broken her heart if he had sent her away. *But had he encouraged her to fall in love for his own gain? And could he live up to her expectations?* He closed his heart resolutely to the answers.

Sometimes he would lie awake watching her as she slept the deep, untroubled sleep of the very young; trying to picture her as an older woman – trying to imagine what it might have been like if he had stayed married to Sarah. Or if he had married Kay. Or if the other – the only true, deep love of his life – could have been his. Until now he had refused to acknowledge to himself that this girl was the next best thing – the nearest he would ever get in this life to the one woman who had meant the world to him; the one woman he'd had no right to. Not that he hadn't been punished in the worst possible way. If there was a God he had taken a terrible revenge for what Gerald had done. But he couldn't be punished any more now. All that was over.

* * *

238

For the last two days of the honeymoon Gerald seemed a little unwell. Cathy fussed over him, but he brushed aside her concern, saying that it was merely the rich food. On the plane on the way home he slept for much of the time and Cathy had the chance to look back and reflect on their first weeks together.

She was happy; happier than she ever remembered being. She had enjoyed her honeymoon so much. Being married to Gerald was her dream come true and their three weeks in Davos had been a wonderful experience in every way. And if Gerald hadn't wanted to make love quite as often as she'd expected him to, it didn't matter, she told herself. They had all their lives in front of them. Some things puzzled her though. Some nights after kissing and caressing her passionately he would turn away abruptly, leaving her bemused and unsatisfied. Was it something she did wrong? Was she too forward? There was no one she could ask. Johnny had volunteered no information about the intimate side of married life and Cathy herself had been too shy to ask. No doubt everything would sort itself out in time, she told herself.

On their return to London they had planned to stay at the flat for a few days before going to Melfordleigh, but on the day of their return Gerald suddenly announced that he had to make a trip up to Edinburgh. Cathy begged to go with him but he was adamant.

'It's business. You'd be bored.'

'What kind of business?'

'Nothing to do with Cuckoo Lodge. Nothing that need concern you.'

'But I could look at the shops. I've never been to Edinburgh,' she told him. 'Besides, I'll miss you.' She went to him and slid her arms around his waist. 'Please take me, Gerald.' She stood on tiptoe to rub her cheek against his, but to her dismay he pushed her away impatiently.

'I said no, Cathy. We may be married but we mustn't start living in each other's pockets. I'll be back in a couple of days. If you want something to do you can start looking at furnishings for Cuckoo Lodge. Heaven knows there are enough shops here in the West End.'

He was gone three days, but to Cathy it felt like three months. The flat seemed silent and empty without him. She did as he said – shopped around for fabrics and furnishing ideas. Gerald had said they would engage the services of an interior designer when the time was right. But Cathy wanted to choose the colour schemes and some of the fabrics herself. She wanted to put her own stamp on the house.

When Gerald came home she was eager to show him the swatches of material and samples of wallpaper and carpet she had collected, but he seemed tired and preoccupied.

'I'll look at them tomorrow,' he told her wearily. 'Just now all I want is a hot bath and bed.'

He slept almost as soon as his head touched the pillow; before she had time to tell him how much she had missed him, even before she could whisper the secret suspicion she had been saving up with such excited anticipation.

'*Pregnant?*' Gerald stared at her across the breakfast table. 'For heaven's sake, Cathy. You *can't* be pregnant already!'

Swallowing her dismay, she smiled at him encouragingly. 'I can. And I think I am. Aren't you pleased?'

He shook his head bemusedly. 'But – we haven't been married a month yet. Surely it's far too soon to know?'

'Well – for sure, yes. But I'm a whole week late and I have this really magic sort of feeling deep inside.' She clasped her hands over her flat stomach. 'Oh, just think, Gerald. It'll be a Christmas baby. Won't that be lovely? It'll make up for all the misery last Christmas.'

'I think we'd better wait and see before we start making plans,' he said guardedly, his brow furrowed. 'I must confess, Cathy, I hadn't planned to start a family. Not at this stage in the proceedings. It isn't the most convenient time to choose.'

'*Convenient?*' Crestfallen, she looked at his dour expression and felt her own happiness slowly beginning to deflate. 'But – if we're going to have children – why not have them now?' She reached across the table to touch his hand. 'You do want children, don't you?'

He drew his hand away. 'Now that you mention it, Cathy, frankly, it's not the most important item on my agenda. We should have talked about it, I suppose. I just assumed . . .' He paused, looking at her face. She looked so downcast. Kay's words came unbidden into his mind. *She'll be expecting all kinds of things you either can't or won't want to give her.* How could he have been so stupid as to take it for granted that she was taking care of contraception herself when the thought of it probably hadn't even entered her head?

As she rose and began to run out of the room he got up and went to her. 'Cathy – don't get upset.' He took her by the shoulders and turned her to him. When she wouldn't look at him he tipped up her chin and saw that there were tears in her eyes. 'Darling, I didn't mean to sound unfeeling. It was just a bit of a shock, that's all. Getting the house finished and the school established is going to mean so much work and planning. You can see what I mean when I say it isn't the right time, can't you?'

She swallowed hard. 'I suppose so. It's just . . .'

He drew her close. 'But if it's happened then there's nothing we can do but make the best of it.' He kissed her forehead. 'And I daresay it will turn out fine in the end.'

She looked up at him. 'I was so pleased. I wanted you to be too.'

'I am. At least, I will be – I expect.' He took out his handkerchief and dabbed at the tears on her cheeks. 'But as I said before, let's wait a few weeks before we start thinking about furnishing a nursery, shall we?'

Her eyes shone up at him through the tears. 'I know you

241

won't mind once you get used to the idea, Gerald. Once the baby is here you'll love it. And I know you're going to make a wonderful father.'

He held her close, cursing himself for all the fools imaginable. He visualised Kay's sardonic expression when she heard the news that he was to become a father; imagined her incisive comments.

But two days later when Cathy wakened to the familiar dull ache low in her back her heart sank with sick apprehension. For a long time she lay still, willing the inevitable not to have happened. But when she rose and went into the bathroom she knew beyond a doubt that for this month at least, pregnancy had been mere wishful thinking.

Back in the bedroom Gerald did his best to hide his relief as he comforted her. 'Never mind, darling. You know as well as I do that it wasn't the best of times. Once we get the school up and running we'll go all out for a baby if that's what you really want.'

'But – what if I can't have any?' she sobbed. 'What if I lose it again?'

He hugged her close. 'You didn't *lose* it, sweetheart. There wasn't any baby to lose. It was just a little delay, that's all; probably due to your changed lifestyle. As soon as the time is right we'll have as many babies as you want. A whole football team if you like. Just you wait and see.'

Cathy laughed shakily and clung to him. 'Oh, Gerald, I do love you,' she murmured into his shoulder.

He held her close, aghast at the rash promises he had just heard himself making. What on earth was he saying? A child was the one complication he could avoid. And avoid it he would at all costs.

They moved into Cuckoo Lodge the following week. The builders had worked hard during their absence. Two rooms had been completed, a room they would be using as a living room and a bedroom with an ensuite bathroom, both

242

temporarily decorated with plain colourwashed walls and furnished basically with the furniture from the flat. In the ground-floor utility extension the builders had finished work and a firm of kitchen fitters had moved in to install units and cupboards, cooker and other appliances. Meantime, Cathy cooked meals for them on a temporary electric stove and helped Gerald with the advance publicity for the school.

A landscape gardener began work on the garden and the fashionable London interior designer, recommended to Gerald by Kay, a flamboyant little man with a beard and flowing white hair, arrived and spent a day walking round the house, making notes and suggestions for them to mull over.

Looking back later Cathy remembered those first weeks as the happiest of times. Domestically it was like playing house or camping. And acting as Gerald's secretary, planning for the school and discussing the final decor of the house and garden, was like taking part in an exciting and very grown-up adventure.

At last the builders and decorators completed their work and moved out. No more tripping over pots of paint or ladders. The house was finally theirs. Gerald's work routine and programme were arranged and advertisements appeared in the glossy magazines as well as the music journals. There were to be popular weekend seminars where young musicians could come and attend master classes with Gerald and other celebrated musicians. But during the week he planned to coach high-flying young pianists, preparing them for the concert platform. He decided that he would take no more than two resident students at a time and work with them intensively. The first of these, a grave young man called Robert Carr, sent to Gerald by a friend from the Guildhall School of Music, moved in and began work in early-July.

Cathy, in charge of domestic arrangements, engaged a daily cleaning woman and a cook-housekeeper from the village. Maggie Penrose was recommended by Ivor Morris, the Welsh chef at the Admiral Nelson. He told Cathy that he had replaced her when the hotel decided to open its new upmarket restaurant. He knew her to be a good cook and had felt guilty about her ever since, he said. He was anxious to do her a good turn.

Cathy liked Maggie on sight. Short and dumpy with a rosy complexion and fair hair scraped back into a bun, she had a no-nonsense air of reliability. Cathy learned that, like Johnny, she was a widow. She had two teenage children, a boy and a girl, who attended a secondary modern school in nearby Woodbridge. On the day that she came to be interviewed she looked round the gleaming new kitchen approvingly.

'Well now, this is some kitchen. I'd enjoy working in this and no mistake.' She ran her fingertips reverently over the smooth worktops. 'A real pleasure that'd be to keep clean.'

In her rich Suffolk accent she told Cathy frankly that she was a good plain cook, though she wasn't averse to what she called 'a bit of fiddling about' too.

'Nuthin' I like better'n tryin' out fancy new recipes when I got the time – an' the ingredients, o'course. Though I ent no good at the twiddly bits,' she warned. 'Anythin' you wants twiddly bits on you'd have to do it yourself.'

Cathy hid a smile. 'That will be fine, Mrs Penrose,' she said. 'I'm quite happy to do the twiddly bits.' She looked at the woman speculatively. 'There's just one thing. I hope you like music, because you'll be likely to hear a good deal of it if you come to work here? There's a large studio in the barn at the back and another two smaller ones in the house.'

Maggie nodded. 'Oh, the kind of music Mr Cavelle plays is all right,' she said generously. 'It's them twanging *catarrhs* I can't abide. My kids is mad about them new Beatles – 'orrible row if you asks me, with their yeah-yeah-ing! A nice bit of piano music'll make a change. I've always been very partial to that there Semprini m'self. He's classical-like too.'

There were five bedrooms on the upper floors at Cuckoo Lodge, plus the suite of rooms that Cathy and Gerald would share. These consisted of a bedroom, an adjoining dressing room and a bathroom. Gerald insisted that the dressing room must have a divan which would always be made up ready for use.

'It might be necessary for me to work on quite late into the night sometimes,' he explained to Cathy. 'Robert seems to work best late in the day and as you know he isn't an early riser. So as not to wake you I can always sleep in there if I'm late.'

But as time went by she found herself waking to an empty bed more often than not.

Now that summer was at its height Melfordleigh was once more alive with summer visitors. The quay was full of moored boats, their hulls newly painted and their sails furled. The little colony of holiday huts were full of the regular weekend artists who set up their easels daily to produce the souvenir pictures the tourists loved. The air was fresh and salty; the sun sparkled on the rippling water and at low tide the sandbanks gleamed like polished silver.

Cathy often found herself at a loose end now that everything was finished and the school was running smoothly. She spent a lot of time down by the quay, watching the boats and admiring the artists' skill. She loved to watch them capture the sea and sky with a few deft strokes of a brush. Once a week she went into Ipswich to do the week's shopping, but apart from that she had very little to do. Gerald was busy all the time; totally preoccupied with his work. He put so much of himself into his teaching, and she knew of course how important it was to him. But often she was reminded of her lonely childhood, when her father would be busy teaching all week and out playing most nights. At least then she had her schoolfriends for company, and her

Saturday music lesson with Dad to look forward to. She found herself thinking of him often and experiencing the aching loss of him afresh. Although she said nothing, it became more and more apparent with each day that passed that Gerald had hardly any time to spare for her at all.

Word had somehow circulated that Gerald Cavelle, the celebrated concert pianist, was living at Cuckoo Lodge. One afternoon Cathy walked up the hill from the quay to find a little group of spectators peering through the gates. As she passed she overheard one of them say, 'We might see him if we're lucky.' As she walked on she reflected wryly that she knew how they felt.

As the end of the summer season approached and the routine at Cuckoo Lodge became established, Cathy found herself thinking more and more of Johnny. She missed the little house in Chestnut Grove and the close family group. When she mentioned the fact to Gerald he looked at her thoughtfully.

'You're not homesick, are you?'

She shook her head. 'No, of course not. I'd like to see them all though. And hear all their news.'

For a moment he looked at her. 'Poor Cathy. It can't be much fun for you. I'll tell you what – as soon as I can see my way clear we'll take a week off and have a holiday.'

Her eyes lit up. 'Oh, Gerald, that would be lovely. When?'

'Well – not yet awhile. When there's a break between students perhaps. We'll see. Meantime, why not invite the Johnsons for a weekend? Robert is going home for a break the weekend after next. It's his birthday, so we'll have a couple of free days. The weather's still warm. I daresay they'd enjoy it.'

Cathy's eyes lit up. 'Oh, Gerald, could I? I'd love Johnny to see what we've done to the house. I'm so proud of it all.'

'Of course. You don't have to ask, darling. It's your

246

home as well as mine. Ring Johnny today and see if they can make it.'

Johnny was delighted to get Cathy's call. She said that they were all well and, yes, she would love to come for the weekend. Matthew had recently passed his driving test and had bought a second hand car. He'd probably drive them over himself. She'd ring and confirm as soon as she'd checked with him.

She rang back the same evening. She and Matthew would love to come. Mrs Bains felt that the journey would be too much for her. Her rheumatism had been playing her up lately and she really preferred to sleep in her own bed. Cathy swallowed her relief. Mrs Bains had obviously still not forgiven her for depriving Johnny of the white wedding she had planned.

On the following Friday evening Cathy waited with eager anticipation for the first sight of the car and it was just after seven o'clock that Matthew's dark green Austin A40 turned in at the gate. Cathy ran to meet them. She kissed Johnny, hugging her warmly as she got out of the car.

'Oh, it's so *good* to see you,' she said. 'I can't wait to show you everything.'

'Don't I get a kiss too?' Matthew stood grinning beside her and she turned to throw her arms around him.

'Of course. It's lovely to see you too.' She took a hand of each of them and drew them towards the house. 'Come in both of you. Maggie, our cook, has left a meal warming in the oven. It's one of her special casseroles. Almost as good as yours, Johnny.'

Johnny was impressed by the house, especially as she had seen the original photographs and knew what it had been like when they first found it. After supper Cathy took her proudly from room to room, showing her everything and finishing up in their own suite of rooms on the first floor. Johnny took in the spacious bedroom with its built-in wardrobes and tasteful furnishings. She also noted the divan

247

in the dressing room, with Gerald's pyjamas neatly folded on the pillow, and silently speculated over it. Seeing the direction of her glance, Cathy explained hurriedly: 'Gerald sometimes sleeps in here. He works very late with his student at times, you see. He doesn't like to disturb me.'

'Of course,' Johnny said.

Downstairs they sat in the small drawing room, enjoying the view of the garden in the last of the evening sunshine as they drank their coffee.

'You've obviously been busy,' Johnny said. 'It's been quite a year one way and another.'

'It certainly has. Since Gerald and I were married our feet have hardly touched the ground what with all the work on the house and the school to get . . .' Cathy broke off as she saw Matthew beginning to laugh. 'What's the matter?' she asked. 'What have I said?'

'I think Mum was talking about more national matters,' he told her. 'The Profumo scandal for instance. It's taken over the newspaper headlines for months now. And just last month, the sensational mail train robbery.' When Cathy looked blank he explained patiently, 'A gang hijacked a Royal Mail train and got away with over a million pounds. Surely you must have read about it?' His eyebrows shot up in amazement as she shook her head. 'Well – I know the Russians put a woman into space. It wasn't *you*, was it?'

'Don't tease her, Matthew,' Johnny admonished. 'I don't wonder she hasn't had time to read the papers.' She turned to Cathy and patted her hand. 'What you've achieved here is an absolute wonder, dear,' she said. 'You deserve congratulations – both of you.' She smiled at Gerald. 'Take no notice of my son,' she said. 'Teasing Cathy used to be his main hobby. He's forgetting that she's a grown-up married lady now.'

'Matthew is right,' he said. 'We really shouldn't let ourselves get so out of touch with the outside world. Maybe I should get Cathy a television. I'm sure she would enjoy it. I'm afraid she spends quite a lot of time alone in the evenings.'

When Cathy went upstairs with Johnny later to make sure she had everything she needed in her room, the older woman looked at her. The girl seemed well enough. Her skin glowed with the healthy outdoor life she seemed to be leading, and her eyes were clear and bright. When they had first arrived she had looked so radiant, but since the excitement of seeing them had worn off Johnny thought she detected a certain wistfulness about her; a vulnerability. There were tiny lines of strain about her eyes that no nineteen-year-old should have. She sat down on the bed and patted the space beside her.

'Come and talk to me. It seems ages since we had a good chinwag. So – you're happy?'

'Oh, yes.'

'Obviously it's all worked out well. I'm so glad, Cathy.'

'The school is going to be a big success,' she said. 'Gerald has a series of concerts planned for next summer. They'll be in the barn studio and open to the public. The local arts society . . .'

'I meant *you*, dear,' Johnny broke in gently. 'You personally – your marriage. It seems to me there's been very little time so far for you and Gerald to settle down and get to know each other.'

'Oh, but there has. We had a wonderful honeymoon and we work together, don't we? Not so much now that Gerald has started work in earnest, of course, but at the start we did.'

Johnny slipped an arm around her. 'So I was wrong to worry? Well, I couldn't be more glad about it.'

Cathy looked at Johnny hesitantly. 'There was one disappointment. Back in the spring I thought I was going to have a baby. But it turned out to be a false alarm.' She gave a nervous little laugh. 'Just as well, really. As Gerald said, it wasn't the right time.'

Johnny smiled wryly. 'It hardly ever is.'

'But we will have children,' Cathy went on. 'Gerald says we will. That's what I really want. It just hasn't happened yet.'

Johnny slipped an arm around her shoulder and gave her a hug. 'Well – plenty of time, eh?'

Cathy stood up. 'Yes. Plenty of time. Goodnight, Johnny. Sleep well.'

In their room Gerald was preparing for bed. He looked up as she came in. 'Everything all right?'

'Yes, fine. Isn't it good to see Johnny and Matthew again?'

'Yes.' He pulled off his tie and began to unbutton his shirt. 'Oh, by the way, I had a phone call earlier,' he said. 'We'll be having two more guests tomorrow.'

Cathy turned to him, a look of dismay on her face. 'Two more? But this was supposed to be Johnny's weekend. Who's coming?'

'Kay,' he said. 'She's bringing a young pianist she's recently come across. She seems to think he has a rare talent and wants me to hear him play. I thought that as this weekend was free it might be an ideal time.'

'But this weekend *isn't* free,' she said, feeling her colour rise. 'We have guests.'

'Only the Johnsons.'

'They're important to me,' she insisted. 'They're the only family I've got.'

He turned to look at her, his eyes cold. 'No. *I'm* the only family you've got, Cathy. And this is our business – our living. It's at a critical stage of its development. It has to come before everything at the moment. Surely you can understand that?'

'Of course I do.' She turned away. 'But I have worked hard since last spring. I think I'm entitled to one weekend at least away from school business. I haven't seen Johnny for five months. I wanted us to spend the time with her.'

'There's nothing stopping you from spending time with them,' he said sharply. 'They're your guests, not mine. And Kay isn't coming for a social visit. For God's sake, Cathy – she's trying to put some business our way.'

'*Your* way, you mean. And you're right. I'm sure it's not me she's eager to see.'

He looked at her scathingly. 'Oh, don't be so petty.'

'I'm not being petty, wanting you to be with us – with *me* for a change. I hardly ever see you, Gerald.'

'So why, when we have a free weekend, do you invite the Johnsons over?'

She stared at him. 'It was your suggestion!'

'Only because you went on about it so.' He picked up his clothes and began to walk towards the dressing room. Biting her lip, Cathy hurried after him. 'Oh, Gerald – *don't*.'

He turned. 'Don't what?'

'Don't sleep in there again tonight. Stay with me.'

He frowned. 'I'm rather tired. I thought you were too.'

'I miss you,' she said quietly. 'You hardly ever sleep in our bed with me any more.' He stood impassively as she put her arms around him and laid her head against his chest. 'What's wrong? Have I done something to upset you? Is it because I invited Johnny?'

'Of course not. Nothing's wrong. It's just – all the work and the tension of getting the school up and running. I've put everything I have into it. We both have.'

'You haven't stopped loving me, have you? You don't regret marrying me? If I've done something wrong . . .'

'You haven't done anything wrong.' He put his arms reluctantly round her. 'You're just being a silly girl. Imagining things.'

'Then come to bed.' She looked up at him, her green eyes wide and appealing.

He sighed. 'All right.'

*   *   *

251

Cathy heard the clock on the little church tower overlooking the sea strike two, and turned over for the hundredth time. All she could see of Gerald was the hump that was his back under the covers.

She had tried her best, whispering how much she loved and needed him between kisses, reminding him of his promise that they could try for a baby as soon as the school was running smoothly. But to her bewilderment he hadn't seemed interested in making love. Her body pressed close to his, even her most intimate caresses had failed to arouse him. After a few chaste kisses he had patted her as though she were a recalcitrant child and turned over, urging her to go to sleep. There must be some reason for it, she told herself. In spite of what he said. Did she irritate him? Did he find her distracting? Heaven only knew she was used to living with a musician. She tried to keep out of his way when he was working. Had she stopped being attractive to him for some reason? And, most worrying of all, what could she do about it?

She slept at last as the sky began to lighten, wakening at seven to find herself once again alone in the bed. Gerald was not in the bathroom. He had obviously risen early and gone out. Resignedly, she showered and dressed, then went downstairs to make breakfast for her guests.

Johnny and Matthew were enchanted with Melfordleigh. Cathy had booked her favourite table at the Admiral Nelson. It was to have been a surprise for Gerald too, but now he would have to stay in and wait for his own guests. She had left cold ham and a salad for the three of them in the fridge.

They all enjoyed their day enormously, arriving back at Cuckoo Lodge at six o'clock. After lunch they had gone on a boat trip with one of the old sailors who took visitors around the point by motor cruiser to see the seals basking on their remote sandbank and glimpse the many seabirds that congregated out at the very tip of the point. They had come back windblown and happily tired and as soon as they got in Johnny and Matthew went straight upstairs to change.

Cathy went into the kitchen to make sure that Maggie was happy about having six for dinner instead of four. Coming back she paused at the foot of the stairs. From the small studio came the sound of the piano – a Chopin polonaise. It was being played with a spirit and vitality that seized her attention at once, making her curious to see who the pianist was. She crossed the hall and stood at the half-open door. The studio door was ajar and from where she stood facing the open grand piano, Cathy had a view of the young man who was playing. He was fair-haired with a firm, strong jaw and cheekbones, but his eyes were on the keyboard, his head lowered in concentration, a look of rapture on his face. He was good. Brilliant even. There was little doubt that Gerald would accept him as a student. The piece came to an end and the young man slowly raised his head and looked directly at her. The suddenness of his unblinking dark blue stare startled her and she took a step backwards.

'Thank you, Simon.' Gerald rose and came into view as he moved towards the piano. He caught sight of her. 'Cathy! Come in and say hello to Kay. And meet Simon Posner, who will be joining us here.' He turned to the young man. 'Simon, this is Cathy, my wife.'

Simon rose and came towards her, his hand outstretched. He was well-built, with broad shoulders and long legs. She registered vaguely that he wore jeans and a black sweater over an open-necked shirt, and that there was a fine mist of perspiration on his brow. He was quite young – no more than twenty-two or -three – and he moved with an easy, loose-limbed grace. His handsome, strong-boned face was grave and unsmiling, but the compelling blue eyes held hers almost hypnotically. When he spoke she was surprised to hear that he had a slight foreign accent, though she could not place its origin.

'How do you do, Mrs Cavelle? It is very good of you to have us at short notice like this.'

Acutely aware of her windblown hair and grubby appearance, she put her hand into his and felt the power of the strong fingers as they gripped hers. 'You're welcome,' she said. 'I hope my husband has shown you both to your rooms. Dinner will be ready in about half an hour.' She glanced at Kay, aware that the older woman was watching her closely. She wore her own city idea of country clothes, a Jaeger suit and a long rope of pearls. Cathy forced herself to smile. 'Hello, Kay. How nice to see you again.'

'Hello, Cathy.' She took in the glowing skin and sun-streaked wind-blown hair. 'How *well* you look,' she said, biting back her resentment. 'Marriage and sea air obviously agree with you.' She stood up and came across to link her arm through Simon's. 'This young man is going to be a brilliant international concert star before he's very much older,' she announced. 'And I shall be proud to say that I discovered him. Gerald has agreed to give him the benefit of all his wonderful know-how.' She hugged Simon's arm possessively and gave Cathy a rueful look. 'I've a feeling you're not going to be seeing much of your dear husband over the next few months. In fact, I don't think your life will ever be quite the same again.'

And even Kay did not realise how prophetic or significant her words were to prove.

Chapter Fourteen

Dinner was a sociable affair. Kay went out of her way to be particularly charming to Johnny and Matthew and complimented Cathy effusively on the house and on finding such a good cook. She also encouraged Simon to tell them all a little about his background. He told them that his father, anticipating Hitler's invasion of Poland, had fled to England along with his wife and mother-in-law in 1938, shortly before Simon was born, and had immediately joined the RAF. His grandmother was Danuta Polinski, who was a well-known concert pianist in Poland during the twenties and thirties. Simon was still a baby when his father was killed and his mother took up work as a secretary and interpreter at the War Office, leaving him in the care of his grandmother for the rest of the war.

Danuta missed her musical career and the gay social whirl she had enjoyed in Warsaw before the war. Her poor grasp of the English language and her unwillingness to adapt to the British way of life made her rather isolated, but as soon as Simon was big enough to sit at the piano she found a new vocation in teaching him to play.

Simon was without inhibitions when it came to recounting his musical accomplishments and the story of his meteoric progress had everyone enthralled. By the time he was twelve he was giving concerts and when he was sixteen had already begun to teach schoolchildren, saving the money he earned to buy himself a new piano and to help pay his way at college.

In anyone else the lack of modesty would have been obnoxious, but the warmth of Simon's personality more

255

than made up for any hint of boastfulness. He charmed them all with his vivacity, his keen, blue eyes and ready smile. Even Maggie lingered as she drifted in and out to wait on the dinner table, unable to take her eyes off the charismatic young man with the fascinating accent.

After everyone else had said goodnight and gone to bed Gerald invited Kay into the smaller of the two studios, which he also used as an office. Switching on the desk lamp, he took a decanter of brandy and two glasses from a cabinet.

'Well, what do you think of him?' she asked, relaxing into one of the deep leather chairs.

Gerald filled one glass and handed it to her. He took his time over pouring his own drink, considering carefully for a moment before answering. 'Well, he's certainly talented, I'll give you that. Maybe a little on the flamboyant side for my taste, and he does seem to have picked up one or two bad technical habits, but I daresay there's nothing that can't be ironed out.'

'I like his flamboyance. It's part of his personality.'

'You would!' Gerald smiled as he sat down opposite her. 'He's full of himself, isn't he? And what about that rather pseudo accent? Is it cultivated? After all, he was born in this country.'

'He says his grandmother never spoke good English and always insisted that they conversed in Polish at home. As she brought him up, and taught him music, he obviously spoke it most of the time.' She raised an eyebrow at him. 'Anyway, you can't deny that it's terribly attractive and sexy. And it does go with the image of a concert pianist.'

'For those who still see Anton Walbrook in *Dangerous Moonlight* as the archetype!' he said with a smile. 'But then I suppose this is the professional PR view I'm hearing,' he added cynically.

Kay shrugged. 'Perhaps. I'm concerned with what sells – what the public goes for. I'm not ashamed to admit it.'

She got up and went to help herself to another brandy. 'So – will you accept him?'

'Oh yes. I'd be a fool not to, wouldn't I?'

'You can manage two students at once then?'

'Yes. While I'm working with one in the other studio, the second can be in here practising. Both rooms are fairly soundproof. These old walls are thick.' He gave her a wry grin. 'Oh, yes, he's definitely worth teaching. I just hope he hasn't become too arrogant. Doting mum and grandmama, adoring philistine audiences who love that accent and the toothpaste smile.'

'That's not fair, Gerry. And I'm sure he isn't arrogant.'

'How did you find him, by the way?'

'His mother, Anya, is a freelance researcher now. Summit Films hired her to do some Polish background research on a film. She worked with us for about two months. We got along rather well and she was telling me about her son. She's terribly ambitious for him. She took me along to a concert to hear him play. I was impressed and immediately thought of you.'

'That was very thoughtful of you.'

She held up her glass, examining the remaining drops of fiery liquid. 'As a matter of fact I'm thinking of leaving Summit and starting up my own PR agency.'

He smiled. 'And you saw Simon as a potential client! *Ah*, now we're getting to it. I was getting quite worried about you, Kay. Altruism is so uncharacteristic. I was afraid you might be going sentimental in your old age.'

'That's *not* very nice. If you're not careful I'll take him away again.' She laughed. 'Seriously, I can't see anything wrong with a little co-operation, can you?'

'Not at all. It's good business. I'm glad you thought of me.'

'I happen to think he's heading for big things. He could make a fortune for you, you know, once the word gets around that you are his mentor.' He shrugged

257

non-committally and she looked at him searchingly. 'How are you these days, Gerry?'

He gave her a quick glance. 'In what way?'

'You know damn well what way. Healthwise, of course.'

'I'm fine. Never better.'

She opened her mouth to say something, then closed it again. He looked terrible. She had been quite shocked by his appearance when they first arrived. His weight had dropped again and he looked gaunt and grey. In the old days she would have told him so bluntly, nagged him into doing something about it.

'I do hope dear little Tinkerbell isn't wearing you out, darling.' Her attempt at a joke fell flat and she added: 'How does marriage suit you, by the way? *She's* looking remarkably bright-eyed and bushy-tailed. And I must say she's done a fantastic job on the house. It's charming.' She waved a hand around the room. 'All these exposed beams and inglenooks. Very chic!'

He shrugged. 'You said all that at dinner.'

'Did you use Gideon Maidly, the interior designer I recommended, by the way?'

'Yes, partly. He was very good. Expensive though.'

She leaned forward. 'Gerry – what *is* wrong with you, darling? You're obviously ill. Are you seeing anyone about it? Are you having treatment?'

'Which one of these would you like answering?' he asked dryly.

'Any. *All* if possible.'

'Not much point in going into detail or giving you names of conditions you won't know the first thing about. Suffice to say that it's a rare muscular thing.'

'Curable?'

'No, but controllable.'

'So you're on treatment – medication?'

'Got it!'

258

She shook her head in exasperation. 'Oh, for God's sake, Gerry, do I have to *drag* it out of you?'

He banged his glass down and glared angrily at her. 'I don't know how you've got the bloody nerve to ask me personal questions after what you did last time!'

Suitably chastened she sank back in her chair. 'I wouldn't do that again, Gerry. You have my word on it. It was – I don't know – a mad sort of impulse. I suppose I was shocked and jealous, seeing Cathy and hearing that you and she were engaged. After all, you and I were close. But I know that's no excuse. It was unforgivable and I'm not proud of it.' She leaned forward to touch his hand. 'I'm only asking out of concern for you, darling, I promise. Whatever you tell me will go no further than this room.'

He leaned back in his chair, closing his eyes. 'All right, it's Parkinson's. I see a specialist in Edinburgh at regular intervals. It's a hell of a drag, having to go all that way but he's supposed to be the top man in this particular field. He's done a special research project at the university. I suppose I'm part of it – tests and so on. I have tablets and there are certain things I am advised to avoid.' He opened his eyes and looked at her. 'There are also – certain limitations – functions I find difficult, even sometimes impossible. I'm sure I don't have to spell it out for you.'

'My God, Gerry, I'm sorry.' For a moment they looked at each other, then she asked: 'Is – is there likely to be any improvement?'

He shook his head. 'Probably not.'

'Oh, Gerry. Does Cathy know the full facts – about your illness, I mean?' Again he shook his head and she stared back at him. 'But, shouldn't you tell her? I mean, she must be . . .'

'I don't think I want to discuss this any further.' He stood up abruptly and went to refill his glass. 'Can we talk about something else?'

She rose quickly. 'I'll have another one of those if you

don't mind. I feel I need it. As for discussing it, Gerry, what you're doing is madness. You're simply burying your head in the sand. She has a right to know.' She turned to him. 'If you knew about this, why on earth did you marry her? A girl of that age! It was so cruel!'

'It's none of your bloody business.'

Ignoring his indignant protest, she went on, 'Okay, tell me to mind my own business when it comes to Cathy and your marriage, but what about your work? I mean, if I'm going to be recommending more students, I have a right to know how long you're likely to be able to do this job.'

He threw back his drink in one gulp and rounded on her. 'Do you think I'd have sunk everything I've got into this place if I thought I wasn't up to working for its upkeep?'

'I don't *know*. It seems to me that you've done some pretty inexplicable things over the past year. Marrying a kid young enough to be your daughter when you knew damned well you couldn't be a proper husband to her for a start. For all I know you might have done *anything*! If you won't level with me how would I know?'

For a moment he stared at her, then he sank into his chair again. 'It's not as desperate as all that. I have good days and bad, but if I pace myself carefully I can teach on a full-time basis. My brain's all right, thank God. At least that part of it. It's what they call the motor functions that are affected.'

'And what's the prognosis?'

'What's the prognosis for any of us? What's the expression? *Life's a bitch and then you die!*'

'Oh, Gerry.' She reached out to take his hand again. 'I'm so sorry, darling.'

'Oh, for Christ's sake!' He snatched his hand away. 'There's no need to turn on the soft soap, Kay! It doesn't suit you. I think I prefer you spitting acid.'

'So work is all right. Okay, I'm glad. But you know you have to confide in Cathy, don't you?'

He turned his head away. 'She knows.'

'All of it?'

'There's no need to baffle her with a lot of frightening medical stuff.'

'It might not frighten her. Most women are amazingly strong.' She looked at him. 'Does it frighten *you*?' When he didn't reply she asked: 'Look, Gerry, have you thought? It might be hereditary. Suppose you have a child?'

'We won't.'

She stared at him. 'You mean . . .?'

'I mean – *we won't*.'

'Without telling her why? Without discussing it? Poor Cathy.'

'She's happy enough. Ask her. *Look* at her!' He avoided her accusing eyes. 'I make it up to her as much as I can. She's enjoying her life here. There's no need for you to worry about her or feel sorry for her, Kay. I'll make sure there are more than enough compensations to keep her happy.'

She shook her head. 'I hope you're right, Gerry. I hope to God you're right.'

Chapter Fifteen

Rosalind worked hard through the spring of 1963. So hard that she scarcely noticed how absorbed her mother was. As the time for exams approached she allowed herself only one evening off a week. On this she usually went out with Stuart. Ever since the New Year's Eve party she had known that she was head over heels in love, and the fact that Stuart seemed to feel the same made life complete. Having someone to love gave life a whole new dimension for her. Now she had a purpose in life. Her whole future was channelled afresh. And since her mother had been so preoccupied she had stopped being obstructive about their relationship. In fact she positively encouraged it nowadays.

Their outings were usually to the cinema or, as the weather improved, for a short drive or a walk by the river. They were both short of money and couldn't afford expensive entertainments. Occasionally when Julian was out and Stuart knew that the flat would be empty all evening, he would take her back to Earls Court. It was in Stuart's cramped little bedroom at the flat that they had first made love. For Rosalind it had been so special that every time she thought about the wonderful closeness and intimacy of the precious moments they had spent in each other's arms, her heart swelled with love and pride. At last she felt whole – a real person, who meant something special to someone.

She already knew how precarious Stuart's work was. Until he became an established designer he would be living on a knife edge, waiting for the big break. At the moment he was obliged to accept any temporary job he could find, whether it was in the artistic field or not, curtailing the time he would like to spend on his own work. She told herself that if she found a good job as a hotel manageress she would be able to support him; see him through until his outstanding talent was recognised. She would be so proud to be able to do that for him. Now it was even more important for her to do well. Each evening as soon as she had eaten she would shut herself in her room and revise till the small hours.

For her part, Una was grateful for her daughter's preoccupation with Stuart. Through him she too had a new purpose in her life. Loneliness was a thing of the past. Once more the future beckoned with a glittering promise. All she had to do was play her cards right. Her plans were taking shape and, although there were various hurdles to overcome she was confident that everything would eventually work out to her satisfaction.

Don had been sceptical at first about putting money into something as unpredictable as a play, especially by three unknown young men. But after long hours of discussion and persuasion on Una's part she had finally convinced him that with her behind it, Julian's play could not fail. She had dazzled him with visions of glamorous West End first nights at which they would be honoured guests; dangled the tempting prospect of selling the film rights for huge amounts of money; promised a future gilded with recording contracts and endless royalties. She told him he would be mad to pass up such a chance, and at last he had promised to put the money at her disposal. Now all she had to do was to set the whole thing up and reap the special reward she had in mind.

The moment she had begun to read the script she had felt in her bones that they were on to a good thing. *Sweet Violet* was a modern version of the *Twelfth Night* story, set on a mythical island in the Atlantic, the inhabitants of which were living in a time warp. The story concerned a group of Americans whose private plane made a forced landing on the island and subsequently turned the lives of the islanders upside down.

Intrigued by its originality, Una paid the boys a surprise visit at the flat to tell them how excited she was. Stuart showed her his slightly surreal designs for the costumes and sets, and Brian French, the young musician who had written the score, played some of the music to her. In spite of the condition of the rickety out-of-tune upright piano at the flat, the romantic songs and haunting, evocative themes reinforced Una's conviction that the show was a surefire winner and she promised the boys, somewhat rashly, that she would personally see to it that *Sweet Violet* would get the chance it deserved.

The weeks that followed were spent making fruitless enquiries and regretting her impulsiveness. In truth she had none of the influence she professed to have and the thought of losing face after all she'd said terrified her. They looked up to her so. If she had to climb down and admit defeat now she'd die of shame. But where could she find a theatre to rent? she asked herself. Or a cast with the talent and professional ability to do the play justice?

She'd thought at the beginning that it shouldn't be too difficult when you had the money, but she soon discovered that there were all kinds of snags. To begin with, until she began making enquiries she'd had no idea of the cost of renting a theatre, especially one close enough to London to attract the busy, influential people who mattered. Most of the popular seaside resorts within easy distance were already booked right through the summer season. And even supposing she were lucky enough to find a cheap theatre that wasn't actually falling down, how would she persuade the appropriate people to come and see the show? Who had ever heard of Una Blair? Why should any West End producer put himself out for her and a new play by a bunch of nobodies? It wasn't long before she was forced to face the reality that she couldn't do it alone. So, pocketing her pride, she went along to see Harry Montague, her old agent.

Remembering the old days of walking Charing Cross Road in down-at-heel shoes, she had her hair done and put on her most expensive outfit . . . Then, summoning up all her courage, she sailed up the stairs and into the office like a prima donna, determined to succeed in getting Monty to listen to her or die in the attempt. Luckily the girl in the outer office was new and didn't recognise her, but it still took all of Una's audacity to convince her that she was here to make Harry Montague an offer he couldn't afford to miss. At last the girl, somewhat intimidated by Una's autocratic persistence, buzzed her boss on the intercom to tell him he had an important visitor waiting with a valuable proposition for him.

As she entered the office Harry Montague looked up from his desk with unconcealed dismay. '*Una!* I didn't know it was you. Thought the girl said Blake, not Blair.'

'She did. I've remarried.'

He indicated the chair opposite. 'Well, now you're here what's this all about? I understand you're here to do me some kind of favour.'

Una made herself comfortable in the chair, making a great show of removing the fur stole that Don had bought her for Christmas. 'I certainly am, Monty. As soon as this came up I immediately thought of you.' She accepted a cigarette from the box he offered. 'In spite of the cruel remarks you made to me the last time I was here,' she added, looking at him over the flame of his lighter. Wouldn't hurt to remind him that he owed her one, she told herself.

He smiled blandly. 'Oh, not *cruel*, surely? Frank, I grant you. It's an agent's job to be frank, but never cruel.'

Una shrugged nonchalantly. 'Oh, well, whatever it was, it's water under the bridge now and I'm not one to bear grudges.' She opened her large snakeskin handbag and took out a copy of the script of *Sweet Violet*. 'Some young friends of mine have written this musical play, Monty. I happen to think it's well worth your while taking a look at it. This is only the libretto, of course, but I could let you have a score if you're interested – even arrange for you to hear some of the numbers. And I'm sure you'd be impressed by the set and costume designs.'

Monty picked up the script with a sigh and flicked through it. It was just as he thought. Most of the people who came in to do *him* a favour turned out to be looking for one themselves. He looked up at her inquiringly. 'So what do you want me to do about it when I've read it?' he asked.

'Well – I thought you might know of a theatre they could take on a short lease. Not too far away.'

'You mean they want to do a shop window? Got a cast, have they? If they're amateurs I don't hold out much hope of getting anyone to . . .'

'Exactly!' Una broke in. 'This might mean a lucky break for some of your new up-and-coming hopefuls. When you've read the play you'll see that it's not a project for amateurs. And . . .' She licked her lips. 'You're in a position to ask a few of the people who *matter* to come along and see the show.'

'Mmm. Don't want much, do you?' Harry leaned back in his chair looking thoughtfully at the three names on the script's cover sheet. 'I take it these fellers have got backing? I know I don't have to tell you that hiring a theatre, even a rundown old fleapit, isn't cheap.'

'They have the backing.'

He raised a sceptical eyebrow. 'Cash in hand or just a promise?'

'Cash in hand. No need to worry. It's all legit.'

'Yes, well, I've heard that before. Do you know who's sponsoring them, Una? I mean does their angel have the necessary wings?' He spread his hands expressively. 'Sorry to ask, but if I'm going to help – and I'm not saying I will, mind – I'll have to know what I'm

266

dealing with. I'd need to be sure there isn't a hole in the bucket.'

'The money's not a problem.' She took a deep breath and added with satisfaction, 'If you really want to know, Monty, *I'm* backing them.'

His eyes widened. '*You* are?'

'Yes.' She crossed one leg over the other, displaying the expensive snakeskin shoes that matched her bag. 'I told you I remarried last year. My husband is a very generous man. He has an executive position with a leading West End department store. Hallard's actually,' she told him with smug satisfaction. 'And he's willing to indulge me in this.'

'Oh, *very* nice.' He leaned back in his chair and clasped his hands over his ample stomach. 'So – what's in this for you, Una?' he asked shrewdly.

Una affected shocked surprise. 'For *me*?'

'Forgive my cynicism, but in my experience no one but a fool puts money into a project without some kind of incentive. It can't be profit. You know the business too well to bank on that. So . . .?'

Una sighed. 'These three young men are very talented. Personally, I think there may well *be* a profit, and a handsome one at that. But you're right. I know better than to bank on it.' She gave him a sideways glance. 'I just like being able to help young talent, that's all.'

He looked unconvinced. 'Bored with spending hubby's money?'

Una bridled. 'Look, are you interested or not, Monty? I can always approach another agent if you . . .'

'Calm down.' He waved the script at her. 'Look, I'll read the bloody thing and think about it. Can't say fairer than that, can I? *If* it's got any potential, *if* there are any parts that might interest anyone on my books, and *if* I hear of a half decent theatre that's dark at the moment, I'll maybe think a bit more. Better than that I can't promise at the moment. All right?'

Una tried not to show her relief. At least she was relieved of some of the burden and could actually tell the boys that she had an agent working on it. That would sound impressive. 'Fair enough. Thanks, Monty.' She got to her feet. 'Perhaps you'll give me a ring when you've come to a decision.' She took a card from her bag and put it on his desk. 'The number's on there. I'm home most of the time.'

He glanced at the card, noting the good address with interest. 'Okay, I'll let you know one way or the other.'

'*When*, Monty?'

He sighed impatiently. 'When I've *read* it. I'll give you a bell and tell you what I think.' He held up a warning hand. 'But if I decide it's no deal, Una, you'll have to accept my decision.'

'Of course.' At the door she turned and asked the question that had been clamouring to be asked ever since she walked through the door. 'Oh, by the way, do you still represent Ben and Freda?'

He glanced up at her. 'We're still in touch, but they have an Australian agent now. You did know they were in Australia?'

'Yes, I just wondered . . .'

'They're doing very well. Booked solid for months ahead from what I hear,' he told her. 'Plenty of TV work too. Their kind of act is very popular over there at the moment.' He paused to light a cigar, looking up at Una through the cloud of blue smoke. 'And of course Freda's a real doll. Gorgeous girl. Great voice too,' he added caustically.

Una threw her fur stole carelessly around her shoulders. 'Yes, I suppose she has, if you like that kind of thing. That syrupy stuff is old hat over here now, of course. Well, I'll have to go now. Talk to you soon, Monty.'

He waved his cigar at her. 'Sure.'

When she'd gone he picked up the script and opened it

with curiosity but little enthusiasm. Most of these amateur
efforts were a load of old crap. No reason to suppose that
this one was any different, but you never knew. No agent
worth his salt could afford to miss what might turn out to
be a bright new talent. And it took no more than a couple
of pages to tell if it had anything or not. No need to waste
too much time.

An hour later when his secretary, tired of buzzing him
on the intercom, came in to see if he'd fallen asleep, he was
still reading.

Rosalind's night off was Friday. At the end of the school
week and before her weekend job at the Queen's Head she
kept one evening for seeing Stuart. She looked forward to
it all week, promising herself that as soon as exams were
over she would see him much more often. Not long now
before all the revising and hard work were over. She was
counting the days to exam time now.

When she heard his ring at the bell downstairs she gave
her hair a final flick with the comb and hurried down the
stairs. But, as so often happened, Una was there before her.
Rosalind was halfway down the stairs when her mother
hurried out of the living room and opened the front door
with a flourish.

'Stuart darling! Come in. I've got the most marvellous
news! I can't *wait* to tell you.' With only a cursory glance
at Rosalind she chivvied him into the small breakfast room
next to the kitchen. Don was watching TV in the lounge
and anyway, this was between Stuart and her and Una
wanted to savour the moment she'd looked forward to
all day, ever since she got the telephone call. When she
saw that Rosalind intended to join them she felt a stab of
irritation, but couldn't very well exclude her.

'Come in if you're coming then. And close the door,'
she said tetchily. 'We can't hear ourselves think for Don's
wretched sports programme.'

Rosalind closed the door and sat on the chair nearest it. Stuart gave her a half-apologetic smile.

'Now,' Una began with relish, 'you'll never guess what. Harry Montague – the agent I told you about – has read the script. He likes the story and thinks it definitely has a lot going for it. He's asked me if he can hear the music next. What do you think of *that*? Isn't it exciting?'

Stuart's face lit up. 'Oh, Una, that's wonderful! We'll have to fix up a date. *Oh!*'

Seeing his face fall, Una asked anxiously, 'What? What's the matter?'

'It's our piano. You know what it's like, Una. We can't really do justice to Brian's music on that awful old thing.'

'I've already thought of that. We'll do it here,' she said triumphantly. 'There's a perfectly good piano going to waste in the lounge. I only had it tuned at Christmas.'

'Oh, that would be marvellous! I can't tell you how grateful we are to you, Una. We could never have got this far without you.'

'Not a bit of it. Talent will out,' she said. 'I just hope it all goes well and that Monty comes up trumps.'

'It won't be your fault if he doesn't. You've done wonders. We're very lucky.'

'So you agree then? I'm to tell Monty to come here?' Una was delighted. It would give her a chance to show Monty that she didn't need the likes of him to help *her* out any more. In fact she'd rub it well in that he was in her debt if *Sweet Violet* got off the ground successfully.

'Yes, please,' Stuart said. 'I'll get the other two over here just as soon as you like. Any time Mr Montague finds convenient.'

Una nodded. 'I'll get on to him first thing Monday morning and I'll let you know what he says.' She looked at Rosalind who was peering surreptitiously at her watch. 'Well, I can see that Rosalind is anxious to be off. Going to the pictures, are you?'

She stood up. 'Yes. It's *Doctor No*. Everyone says it's very good.'

'Then I mustn't keep you,' Una said magnanimously.

But the evening was already spoilt. As far as Stuart was concerned, the exciting news he had just heard already outshone James Bond's outrageous exploits. All the way to the cinema and all through the film he kept talking about the play and how wonderful Una was – how much, how *very* much, they all owed her. So much so that people seated near them began to fidget and *shush* at them angrily.

Later, over coffee in a nearby coffee bar, Stuart was still making excited plans and voicing his uncertainties.

'I wonder if he'll like my costume designs,' he said, chewing his lip. 'They're a bit way out, but then that's the point, you see. The people of St Crispin's have lived such an isolated life that they've devised their own fashions, made dyes and fabrics from plants, woven wool from their own sheep. Each character's costume is individual, you see, reflecting his own personality. And the contrasts with the modern Americans' mass produced clothes is the whole . . .'

'*Stuart!*' Rosalind looked at him. 'Do you realise that you've talked of nothing but the play ever since we left the house this evening?'

'Sorry.' He smiled ruefully at her. 'I suppose I have.'

'I bet you couldn't tell me one single thing about the film we've just seen.'

'I don't suppose I could. But it is frightfully important to us all.' He leaned across to touch her hand. 'And to you too, don't you see?'

'Me?'

'Yes. You've talked of supporting me until I can get established, and believe me, darling, I appreciate it. But if this takes off, I wouldn't need support.'

She stared at him. What exactly did he mean? She'd been looking forward to helping him – showing how much faith she had in him – proving her love. Didn't he know that? Or could he possibly mean something more significant – more exciting? That if the play were a success *he* could support *her*? That they could be married? She felt her cheeks colouring. 'Well, that would be lovely of course. But I don't think I'd want to give up the career I've been working so hard for,' she said slowly. 'At least, not until we had children.'

It was Stuart's turn to colour. '*No!* No, of course not. I just . . .' He looked desperately around. 'Look, what about another coffee? It's not too late yet.'

As he parked Julian's car outside the gate of Blake's Folly she turned to him. 'Thank you for a lovely evening, Stuart.'

'No. Thank you – for listening to me wittering on about the play.' He slid an arm along the back of the seat. 'I'm afraid it's in my mind the whole time these days. Can't seem to think of anything else.'

'I've noticed,' she told him wryly. Then, relenting: 'I don't really mind, Stuart. I just know it's going to be a success.' His preoccupied silence since she'd blurted out that awful thing about having children had made her curl up inside. If only she could turn the clock back – *unsay* it.

He drew her towards him and kissed her. 'The day I met you and Una was the luckiest day of my life.'

'Was it really?' Rosalind looked at him thoughtfully. If only he didn't always have to include her mother. 'I knew then that you had a brilliant talent, you know. Long before I fe– before we started seeing each other.'

He kissed her again, then looked pointedly at his watch. 'Good heavens! Look at the time. Your mother will murder me. She'll be wondering where you are.'

Hurt, Rosalind stared at him. 'We don't want to risk upsetting Mum, do we? Not until *after* she's introduced you to Harry Montague anyway!' She opened the door and jumped out of the car. Stuart followed, hurrying after her up the path to the front door.

'Rossie! Wait!' He caught up with her just as she was putting her key in the lock. He grasped her shoulders firmly and turned her to face him. 'What was all that about?'

She looked up at him, eyes bright with hurt tears. 'Sometimes I feel you only take me out to keep in Mum's good books,' she said. 'Well you needn't, you know. She doesn't give a damn for *my* feelings, so you're wasting your time. If you don't want to see me any more, just say so now. You needn't worry. It won't spoil your chances of getting your play put on.'

He shook her gently, then pulled her close. 'Shut up, blockhead! You know none of that is true. I go out with you because I want to.'

'Sometimes I wonder,' she mumbled into the front of his jacket.

'Well, stop wondering at once and kiss me goodnight properly.' He raised her face to his and kissed her, gently at first, then in the passionate intimate way that took her breath away and left her with trembling knees. 'Off you go now and get a good night's sleep,' he told her breezily. 'You work much too hard, you know. I worry about you, you silly little goose.'

She watched with an aching heart as he got back into the car and drove off with a wave. She loved him so much. Too much for her own peace of mind. Did he really love her too? He was so good-looking, so talented. He could surely have any girl he wanted, so why should he want her? And whatever either of them might say, he couldn't risk driving any kind of wedge between himself and the Blake household just now, could he?

It was a week later that the three young men arrived at Blake's Folly for the meeting Una had arranged with Harry Montague. They arrived in Julian's Mini, dressed in their best, neatly groomed and shaven, except for Brian who had a beard. Clutching their copies of the script – in Brian's case the fully orchestrated score, plus his own piano parts – they

273

rang the bell and then stood looking nervously at each other as they waited on the doorstep to be admitted.

Monty was already there. Una had invited him to dinner so that he could meet Don. She felt it was good policy to keep her husband advised and involved, seeing that it was his money that would make the whole project possible. The two men had been polite to each other, though it was clear that neither was completely comfortable in the other's company, and it was a relief to everyone when the meal was over.

Una opened the door and greeted the three warmly, ushering them into the lounge where Monty, Don and Rosalind were already waiting. She offered them coffee first, to break the ice, encouraging small talk. Then, when she felt the atmosphere to be sufficiently relaxed, she invited Brian to present the music of *Sweet Violet* to Monty.

Settling himself at the piano, the stocky, bearded young man played the main themes from the show, then launched into one of the songs, singing the words himself in a growling bass. Listening to his monotonous drone, Una knew that her moment had arrived. Her heart quickening, she rose from her chair and went over to the piano.

'Er – forgive me, Brian, but would it help if I were to sing it for you?' she asked with a beguiling modesty. 'I mean, your voice is . . .'

'I think "lousy" is the word you're looking for.' Brian laughed. 'Please, Mrs Blake, be my guest. I'm only too delighted. Can you follow the music or shall I play it over for you first?'

'No, I can follow,' Una said, positioning herself behind him where she could see the music. She omitted to mention that she couldn't actually *read* music, or that she'd learned the songs by heart from the tape that Stuart had given her, rehearsing the songs privately at every opportunity since with the help of the tape machine in Don's study.

She sang the song through, putting over all of the emotion and pathos the character demanded, just as she

274

had rehearsed it. Monty looked on with shrewd appraisal. He'd always known that her voice hadn't the power or the timbre of the best singers on his books, but for an impromptu rendering it wasn't at all bad, he conceded grudgingly. When the song came to an end everyone clapped and Una blushed, affecting surprise and confusion at their appreciation.

'I just thought Monty might get a better idea of the song's effectiveness with a female voice,' she said modestly.

Sitting quietly in her corner, Rosalind said nothing. Suddenly she knew what all this was about. During the singing of the song everything had dropped into place for her. All Una's altruism, the weeks of selfless striving and scheming, her apparent approval of the relationship between herself and Stuart. Now it all made sense. She looked at the faces of the men around her, all of them totally unsuspecting. Don, gazing with pride and wonder at his talented wife; the three young men, dazzled by yet another new facet of Una's appeal. Even the cynical Monty looked on benignly. It was clear that none of them saw beneath the surface to the real reason for her mother's devoted generosity.

Brian continued with the other songs and Una sang them all, Brian doing his best to join her in the duets. When at last the music came to an end and the buzz of enthusiasm died down, Rosalind was aware of her mother's eyes on her. Sidling over Una hissed in her ear, 'Make some more coffee, will you, Rossie? Really, I'd have thought you'd do it without being asked.'

When she returned from the kitchen with the tray Monty was telling them with guarded optimism that he thought they definitely had a show.

'Mind you,' he warned, 'the public is a funny animal. I've seen surefire hits close in three days flat and real turkeys run and run. There are no cast-iron certainties in this business. But I'm willing to give it a go. Now, there's a little theatre free in Stoke Newington. It's an old music hall and due for demolition. There are plans for one of those new supermarkets. It's not exactly Drury Lane, but at least it still has everything intact and working – well almost. I can get it at a knock-down rent for you from the LCC. Suppose we take it for a month and see how we go?'

The three faces looking at him were alight with enthusiastic disbelief. It was Julian who found his voice first.

'Thanks a lot, Mr Montague. That would be fantastic. Could we see the place sometime?'

'Sure.' Monty paused to light up one of his pungent cigars, drawing a disapproving glare from Don, whose mother had never allowed *anyone* to smoke in the house. Una's 'cool-as-a-mountain-stream' Consulates were bad enough, but *cigars*! She would never have trusted a man who wore a bow tie and a homburg hat either, come to that. Don fumed with resentment. Who did the man think he was – sitting there calmly dispensing *his* money as though it was some sort of largesse?

'I'll give you a bell when I've fixed it all up,' Monty was saying. 'Now, in the meantime, what do you want me to do about casting? Is there some place where you can hold auditions?'

'Have them here if you want,' Una put in.

Monty waved a dismissive hand, scattering cigar ash on the carpet. 'No, no. Too far out of town. Anyway, it looks amateurish. I'll find us a hall somewhere. Shouldn't cost much for a couple of hours or so. Let you know about that too.' He looked at the three eager young faces. 'Just one thing. What do the three of you do for a living?'

Stuart looked at the others. 'Julian works for a solicitor,' he said. 'Brian's in his last year at music college and I've been on the dole ever since I left art school. I take anything I can get.'

'Mmm.' Monty drew on his cigar. 'Well, wouldn't be a good move to give up the day job, Julian. Maybe you can fix it to take some holiday. I'll leave you to sort that out.'

276

He looked at his watch. 'Better get off, I suppose. I'll be in touch.'

They shook hands all round and Una showed Monty to the door. As she was letting him out he paused and looked at her speculatively.

'Haven't got any ideas about making a comeback, have you, Una?'

She gazed at him with wide, innocent eyes. '*Comeback!* Why on earth would I want to do that, Monty?'

'Just an idea. I thought maybe it was something you might have tucked up that scheming little sleeve of yours.'

'All I want is to help the boys.' She laughed. 'Really, Monty, what an idea! Why on earth would I want to go back to all that hard work and stress when I have a life of leisure here?' She swept an arm expressively round the spacious hallway.

Monty shrugged. 'Who knows why people do things?' As he walked down the path to his car he added under his breath, 'Especially frustrated over-the-hill singers.'

After that things moved fast. Monty was as good as his word. He hired a hall for auditions and notified a group of possibles from among his clientele for the cast. He also inserted an advertisement in *The Stage* just in case. He promised to sit in at the auditions and give the boys the benefit of his experience. The Prince Regent Theatre was hired for the month of July, but as it wasn't being used Monty had obtained permission for the boys to go in beforehand and do any necessary work. It was a good month for tourists, he told the boys. And producers weren't so busy in the summer either. It was also the silly season in the newspaper world and critics might just be tempted out of the Fleet Street pubs to look at something intriguingly fresh by a group of newcomers.

With the help of friends and relatives the three boys cleaned up the theatre and did the necessary repairs.

277

Brian found enough young musicians from among his fellow students to form a small orchestra who would play for minimum union rates. In their last year they were encouraged to get as much practical experience as they could. And all three looked forward eagerly to the date set for the auditions.

Stuart and Rosalind saw each other hardly at all during the frantic weeks of preparation. Being the only one of the three not busy in the daytime, Stuart was kept fully occupied and seemed to be enjoying every minute. For Rosalind exam time was approaching fast and she was working flat out. They spoke on the telephone regularly, exchanging all their news, and Rosalind looked forward to the time when all the work would be over and they could have some time to themselves again.

It was on the evening before the auditions that Una paid a visit to the flat in Earls Court. Stuart came down to open the door to her and he saw at once that she was upset about something.

'Oh, Stuart, can I come in?' She turned a woebegone face to him. 'I'm afraid I've got something terrible to say to you.'

Full of foreboding he led the way upstairs where Julian was busy at his typewriter, working on some revisions that Monty had suggested. 'There's a fresh pot of coffee on the go, would you like a cup?' Stuart suggested hopefully.

Una nodded and sank into a chair. She said nothing until she had taken a sip of the coffee, then, taking a deep breath, she looked at the two faces watching her anxiously. 'I don't know how to tell you this,' she said. 'I'm so dreadfully sorry.'

Stuart and Julian exchanged worried glances. Una's demeanour suggested only one thing. She was pulling out of the project – their worst nightmare. Stuart braced himself and leaned towards her. 'Please, go on,' he urged. 'Surely it can't be as bad as all that.'

'It *is*.' Una pulled out a handkerchief and snuffled into it briefly. 'It's Don. He says he doesn't see how he can possibly recoup his money and that he must – he has to – *withdraw*.' She said the last word in a hushed whisper. 'Oh God, what can I say?' She looked from one to the other helplessly.

'Not much you can say,' Julian said in a flat voice. 'Without the backing we can't even get off the ground.' He pushed the typewriter away from him in a gesture of finality. 'So – that's that. Finito! All our hard work up the Swanee, as they say.'

Stuart chewed his lip. 'The thing is, we've already hired the theatre. We're probably going to have to pay for that anyway. Then there's all the time we've put in on it. There's the hall too. Auditions tomorrow. Christ! What a mess. We'll be in hock up to our necks over this for years!'

Una sighed. 'I *know*. And I'm so *sorry*, boys, I can't tell you ...' She paused dramatically, twisting her handkerchief between her fingers. Stuart peered at her hopefully.

'What are you thinking, Una? There's something else, isn't there?'

'It's nothing. Just some mad idea Don had. It's too ridiculous even to mention. I couldn't possibly expect you to ...'

'*Tell* us! Anything to save the show,' Stuart urged her.

'Well ...' She swallowed. 'Don has this really silly notion. He started talking about it after the evening when you all came over to play the music for Monty.'

'Yes?'

She had their full attention now and went on: 'He's got the idea that he wouldn't consider the money wasted if – if *I* were in the play. You see, he didn't know me when

279

I was working in the theatre and it's always been his greatest disappointment that he's never seen me perform. That evening when I sang the songs he was . . .' she looked at them from under her lashes '. . . well, quite bowled over, and . . .'

'But that's fine. Just *great*!' Stuart almost shouted. 'It would solve everything, wouldn't it, Julian?'

His reaction was more guarded. 'What part did you have in mind, Mrs Blake?'

'Well, I think I'm mature enough to play Olive, don't you?'

Julian was relieved. If she'd had her heart set on playing the teenaged Violet they might as well have called the whole thing off here and now. Olive, she might handle reasonably well. 'I see,' he said. 'Well, if that's all right with you, Mrs Blake, I'd say that we seem to have saved the day.'

'And we've got you to thank for it, Una – again! What would we do without you?' Almost hysterical with relief, Stuart went to the cupboard. 'I'd say this calls for a little celebration, wouldn't you? Brandy, both of you? Let's drink to the success of *Sweet Violet* and the first member of our cast – Una Blake!'

'Blair,' she corrected, accepting the glass he handed her. 'Blair is my stage name. That's how my public remembers me and that's the name I'd like to see on the programme.'

'Right, Blair it is.' Stuart raised his glass. 'To the success of *Sweet Violet* and to its star, Una Blair!'

The auditions for *Sweet Violet* were held on a Friday afternoon in June. The boys arrived at the hall early, filled with excited anticipation. Monty arrived soon after and found them setting out chairs. Brian had taken the dust sheet off the piano and was running his hands experimentally over the keys.

When Stuart announced that the part of Olive had already been cast, Monty's eyebrows almost shot through the top of his head.

'Who've you got?' he asked. 'It's not really on, this, you know. I've got a really good girl lined up who's set her heart on that part.'

'Actually Una's doing it,' Stuart told him.

Monty groaned. 'Christ almighty! I should've guessed! I had an idea she had this in mind. How did she swing it on you?'

'Oh, no, it wasn't like that,' Stuart assured him. 'Her husband – you knew of course that he was putting up the backing – got slightly cold feet. But he said that he was prepared to take the risk if Una played the part.'

'That's what she said, eh?' Monty shook his head, tutting under his breath. So like Una to pass the buck. Obviously this was what she'd had in mind all along. Serve her right if she fell flat on her face on the opening night! Not that these kids deserved a flop. 'Oh, well, if that's the way it is, we'll have to put up with it,' he said resignedly. 'Though I'm not looking forward to telling my girl the part's been cast behind closed doors, I can tell you.'

By the end of the afternoon the play was successfully cast. Even Miriam Gerard, who had had her eye on the part of Olive, accepted a lesser role with good grace. The actors were briefed and a rehearsal schedule handed out by Stuart who had now assumed the position of producer. Julian would direct and Brian would be musical director. They were in business! The three went out that evening to celebrate.

Rosalind went along to the school on the first morning of the exams with a stomach full of butterflies. So much depended on getting good grades. It meant so much to her to do well. No one had wished her good luck this morning. Her mother, totally preoccupied with the play, seemed to have forgotten all about the exams. Stuart too seemed incapable of thinking of anything else. Even her father, who had been writing regularly ever since he and Freda had arrived in Australia, seemed to have dropped the habit lately. She often thought about Cathy and pictured her enjoying her new and exciting life in Suffolk with her handsome husband. She'd looked so happy on her wedding day. It must be so nice to be loved and cherished; to feel so safe and wanted.

But it doesn't matter, Rosalind told herself as she walked to the bus stop. If I do well I'll have only myself to thank. I'll have done it without any support at all. And that's the way I like it. The thought gave her a certain satisfaction, but deep inside she nursed a secret hope that once the play was under way Stuart would turn his attentions to her once more. She couldn't help comparing her mother's indifference to her with the fuss and effort she had gone to on the boys' behalf.

The exams were spread over four days and at the end of that time she felt drained. Walking home from the bus stop on Friday afternoon she felt strangely empty. The pressure was off. It was like having a burden suddenly lifted from her shoulders. She felt strangely light, as though she might blow over and float away in the first puff of wind. Nothing to do now but wait until August for the results and try not to think too much about all the questions she wished she had answered differently.

To fill in the waiting time and earn some money, she'd decided to ask at the Queen's Head if they needed any extra help. Now that she was free from all her studies she could work behind the bar – turn her hand to anything. And it was all good practice for the day when she would manage her own hotel.

She heard the row going on as soon as she put her key into the front door lock. Una and Don were going at it so hard that they didn't even hear her come in. Her heart sank as she paused anxiously halfway up the stairs to eavesdrop.

'Why didn't you ask me first?' Don was demanding. 'How do you think this makes me look? My wife on the stage in some fleapit in Stoke Newington! Sponsored by me too!'

'It makes you look a damn sight better husband than you are!' Una yelled back. 'Anyway they won't know I'm your wife because I'll be using my stage name – Blair.'

'Oh? So *my* name's only good enough for writing on the cheques, is it? That's nice to know!'

'You won't complain when the money comes rolling in, will you?' Una sneered.

'If I don't lose the lot, which is a damned sight more likely! I've been asking around and I reckon I've been taken for a ride. Everyone says that backing a play by a team of unknowns is like throwing money into a bottomless pit!'

'Rubbish! What do any of your cronies know about the theatre anyway? Most of them think that Laurence Olivier is a cigarette manufacturer!'

'You've been planning this all along, haven't you?' Don said. 'You and that common little Montague man – you've set the whole thing up. Me and those three young chaps – just to get yourself back on the bloody stage again. And all at *my* expense!'

'All I ever wanted to do was help the boys. I'm doing it for them,' Una protested. 'They *begged* me to take the part. They seem to think I'll be the making of the show. How could I let them down?'

Don gave a disbelieving grunt. 'This was the only way you could do it, wasn't it. You knew you'd never get another part unless you engineered one. I don't believe they begged you to take the part. As usual you're twisting the truth to suit yourself. And if you mess the thing up I'll stand to lose a fortune.'

'Well thank you *very much* for the vote of confidence!' Una stormed. 'They *do* want me to play the part. Ask them if you don't believe me,' she challenged, knowing that he wouldn't. 'Ever since the evening when they came here with Monty and heard me sing they've been *obsessed* with having me to play Olive. I can't disappoint them now and I'm not going to. You just want me to be shut up in this mausoleum of a house, bored out of my skull all day!'

'Don't be so stupid, Una. I just can't stand the idea of chucking away good money so that my wife can make a fool of herself, that's all.'

From where she stood on the stairs, Rosalind heard her mother striding angrily across the room in the direction of the hall. Quickly she whisked up the stairs out of sight.

From where she stood on the landing she heard Una shout, 'If you've such a poor opinion of my ability, if you think more of the money than you do of me, then perhaps I'd better move out. But don't think you can take your money out of the play now that everything's been settled.'

Don hurried after her. 'Una – listen. Come back, will you? Why do you always have to fly off the handle so?' His voice had taken on the whining conciliatory tone that always meant that she had won. 'If only you'd told me this was what you wanted,' he said. 'If you'd asked – talked to me about it. Why do you always keep things to yourself so? Can't you see, it makes me feel so – so shut out.'

Rosalind slipped into her room and closed the door. The row was all but over. As usual Don had rolled over like a whipped dog. Once more Una had got her own way, devious, though it was. She pictured the scene downstairs. Una would probably shed a few winsome tears – enough to make Don feel a brute but not enough to puff up her eyes. Then she'd allow him to kiss her and for the next few days he would give her anything she asked for. Until the next time she did something outrageous.

*   *   *

284

Rehearsals went well. Julian and Brian were pleased with the way the cast was shaping. Stuart and a group of his art school friends had made and painted the scenery and Una had found a woman to make up the costumes. Elaine Frisby, a young divorcee, was a part-time alteration hand at Hallard's. She had given up her place at art school to make an early, disastrous marriage and now she was studying in her spare time and taking what work she could to make ends meet. She had talent and imagination and jumped at this chance to work on a more creative job. The costumes for *Sweet Violet* were a challenge and a delight to her after the mundane every-day tasks she was paid for.

She and Stuart seemed to strike up an instant rapport and with his help and advice she had worked long hours every evening at the sewing machine in her bedsit in Belsize Park. The costumes must be ready in three weeks, which would be hard work, but on the day of the dress rehearsal Elaine arrived at the Prince Regent theatre in a taxi with every costume ready for fitting. Everything was now in place. Cast and production team were on their toes, incandescent with excitement and nerves.

Rosalind arrived home at Blake's Folly to find the house empty. It was ten-thirty, but with Una at the theatre so much of the time Don had taken to having his evening meal at the local pub. As she had her own meals at the Queen's Head and worked unsocial hours the three hardly ever saw each other now that the play's four-week run had started.

As she closed the door behind her and switched on the hall light she saw that there was some mail lying on the doormat. She bent and picked it up. Two bills for Don and a blue air letter, addressed to her in a handwriting she didn't recognise. She carried it through to the kitchen and opened it carefully with the aid of the bread knife. Glancing first at the signature, she

285

saw with surprise that it was from Freda and dated a week ago.

My dear Rosalind,

I am writing with the sad news that Ben was rushed into hospital yesterday morning with a heart attack. The doctors say it was brought on by overwork and strain, but that there is a good chance that he will recover with rest and care.

If you would like to come out, dear, I know he would be so pleased to have you with him. I think it would make a great difference to his recovery. He has been very depressed and dwelling a lot on the past and what he sees as his neglect of you. He is badly in need of the reassurance your presence would give him.

I'd dearly love to be able to send the air fare for you, but I'm not sure how long Ben will need to be in hospital or how much the doctor's and hospital fees will cost us. There is no NHS here and unfortunately we hadn't thought to join a private health scheme. Now that I am responsible for our finances I must take care of the money, especially as we cannot fulfil the rest of the engagements on our tour. I do hope you can understand this, Rossie. Please try to come, but don't worry. He is in good hands.

Hoping perhaps to see you soon.

My love to you,

Freda

Rosalind read the letter through twice more, her eyes blurred by tears. She had blamed her father for not writing when all the time he was ill in hospital – and worrying about her! Heart attacks were serious, weren't they? Even though Freda played it down, her father must be very ill for her to write and ask Rosalind to go over. But how could she go? How much did it cost to fly to Australia? The sea fare was probably cheaper but even that would be beyond her means. Besides, a ship would take ages. By the time she got there Ben could be . . . She bit her lip, thrusting the thought firmly out of her mind. There was only one thing for it. Much as she deplored the prospect, she would have to ask Don for the money. Or at least, ask Una to ask him. She would pay back every penny as soon as she had a job.

Backstage at the Prince Regent there was an air of excitement. Monty had come round in the interval to tell them that Louis Jacobson was in front. Jacobson was a theatrical impresario with a flair for promoting new talent. He had set several new playwrights on the road to success over the past five years and he had a string of successful shows running in the provinces and West End. Monty was very proud of the coup he had pulled off in persuading him to come and see the show.

'So far he likes what he sees,' he told a trembling, pale-faced Julian. 'Get them to give it all they've got in the second act. I'm not promising anything, but by the look on that crabby old face of his, you might just be in with a chance.'

Una arrived home bubbling over with news. Rosalind was in her room but she could hear her mother downstairs, her words tumbling over each other as she told Don about something that had happened at the performance. When she heard her mother coming upstairs Rosalind went out on to the landing to meet her.

'Mum . . .'

'Rossie. Off to bed already? Listen, you'll never guess what happened this evening . . .'

'Mum, I've had a letter.'

'Really? Louis Jacobson came to see the show. And he *liked it*! Afterwards he came back to make Julian a proposition.'

'It was about Dad. He's had a heart attack, Mum. He's very ill.'

Una stopped short to stare at her daughter. Trust Ben to spoil her big moment! 'Heart attacks are nothing nowadays,' she said dispassionately. 'They can put them right just like that.' She snapped her fingers. 'He'll be fine, you'll see. Now – Louis Jacobson has suggested that the show should be a half-hour longer. He's asked Brian to write two more numbers and he's made a few suggestions that Julian is quite excited about. He thinks he can easily incorporate them into the plot and he's going to work on them right away. If we do what LJ suggests and he approves, he's going to send us on tour with the option of going into the West End!' She threw back her head, laughing delightedly. 'Just *think*, Rossie. Una Blair in the West End. It's my dream come true! At last!'

'That's wonderful, Mum. Look, could you ask Don if he'll lend me the money to go over to Australia?'

Una frowned. 'Why on earth do you want to go to Australia?'

'To see Dad, of course. Haven't you been listening to a word I've said?' Rosalind snapped, her nerves stretched to breaking point.

'Don't speak to me like that!' Una walked across the room and twitched angrily at the curtains. 'Here I am with the chance of a lifetime within reach and all you can think about is rushing halfway round the world on some wild goose chase!'

'It isn't a wild goose chase!' Rosalind swallowed her irritation. 'Look, I'm sorry, Mum. I really do hope the show is successful, and I am pleased for you. But I can't help worrying about Dad. Freda says he wants to see me. I *have* to go.'

Una spun round. '*Why?* What has he ever done for you? I'm the one who brought you up – slaved for you – sacrificed my career. If he's ill then all I can say is, he brought it on himself. Booze and women, that's all he ever thought about when we were together!'

'He did pay my school fees. Why are you always so horrible about him? He can't have been that bad!'

When Rosalind began to cry Una crossed the room and shook her shoulder. 'Oh, for heaven's sake, Rossie, don't turn on the waterworks. Your father paid the school fees because I made it impossible for him to refuse. He's always wriggled out of his responsibilities. I'm sure there's no need for you to get in a state. At this very moment he's probably as right as rain again, sitting up in bed swilling beer, likely as not! Oh, why did that wretched woman have to write and worry you – wrecking everything like this?'

'Could you just ask Don?' Rosalind pleaded. 'I'll pay it all back just as soon as I can, I promise. And he can only say no.'

Una sighed. 'I can't ask him for any more money, can I, Rossie?' she said. 'To tell the truth there'll be a few more expenses for the show before we're finished. He's never been that keen on my doing this play anyway and I don't know what he's going to say when I tell him we're going on tour. You do see, don't you?' She looked at her dejected daughter. 'And asking for money to visit my ex-husband isn't really on, now is it?'

Rosalind's shoulders slumped despairingly. 'I suppose not,' she whispered.

All night long she lay sleepless, racking her brain to think of a way to get the money together. Maybe she could borrow it? But from whom? She didn't know anyone who could spare that much. And even if she did, how long would it take her to pay it back? There wasn't even anything she could sell.

Alone in the house next morning she wandered restlessly from room to room, wrestling with her problem. If she were ill she would want someone close to be with her. And being so far from home, in a strange country,

Ben must feel so isolated, even with Freda there. It was her duty to be there. There must be a way. It was only when she stopped pacing and found herself in front of Don's mother's china cabinet that the terrifying idea presented itself.

There had been a big row about the china cabinet when Una wanted to get rid of all the late Mrs Blake's belongings. It was the one article over which Don had stood firm, and won.

'*Mother took a great pride in her collection of Meissen porcelain. She dusted every piece of it every day of her life. Anyway, some of those pieces are very rare. They're worth a fortune.*'

His words echoed in her memory as Rosalind peered through the glass at the delicately modelled figures, painted in exquisite colours. And when the preposterous idea sprang into her head it was with the blinding force of an exploding firework. She caught her breath. *She couldn't do it*. But she must! It could even mean the difference between life and death for her father. And she wanted so much to be with him; to see him again before . . . in case . . .

With slow deliberation she tried the door of the cabinet and found in unlocked. Very carefully she selected one of the treasured pieces. It was formed like a large flower-decked shell, being pulled by four plump cherubs. She held it up to the light. The china was so delicate and translucent that you could see daylight through it; the colours so subtle and clear; the little faces and flowers so perfectly fashioned. It was an exquisite work of art. It must certainly be worth a lot of money. Once his argument had been won she didn't remember seeing Don look at the cabinet again and her mother had never taken any interest in it, dismissing the collection of Meissen as 'dust-gathering junk'. They would never notice if she rearranged the other pieces to fill the gap.

* * *

290

The little man in the antique shop in Chelsea gave her enough for the air fare and a little over. At first he had looked at her suspiciously over his *pince-nez* and asked where she had obtained the piece. The last time he had seen porcelain of such quality and perfection had been in a museum. She told him half-truthfully that it had been left to her by a relative and that she needed the money to go and visit her sick father in Australia. She even showed him Freda's letter. At last he took pity on the pale and trembling young woman. She looked so respectable and the large dark eyes behind the spectacles were so pitifully troubled that it wrenched at his heart. He'd like to think that his own daughters would make such a sacrifice if he were ill.

The money safely in her handbag, Rosalind took a taxi to Stuart's flat. She wanted to tell him about her father and her intention to go to Australia. She even meant to confide in him about the piece of Meissen. She badly needed someone she could trust on whom to unload her guilt. But when Stuart answered the door to find her standing there he looked surprised and flustered.

'Rossie!'

'I'd like to talk to you, Stuart. Is it all right?'

'Talk? Oh, well, if you want to. Come in.'

A little bewildered by his attitude she followed him upstairs, but when she walked into the small living room she saw the reason for his confusion. Stuart was not alone. A young woman sat at her ease on the settee, her shoes kicked off and her feet tucked under her. On the coffee table in front of her were two empty cups and an open portfolio of sketches.

'This is Elaine,' Stuart said. 'We've been discussing her course work. She's studying art – a correspondence course. She works part-time for Hallard's. She made all the costumes for the show.'

'Yes, I know.' Deeply disappointed and disturbed by the

girl's obvious ease, Rosalind made herself smile. She'd heard of Elaine Frisby of course, but never met her. No one had ever mentioned how attractive she was. Her complexion was clear and translucent and her blue eyes were wide and clear. She wore a loose white shirt over jeans and her long blonde hair was tied back in a soft knot on her neck. She looked confident and utterly relaxed. She even offered to make a fresh pot of coffee. Clearly she was totally at home at the flat.

Rosalind shook her head. 'No, thanks. I can't stay.' She looked at Stuart, hoping he would see how much she needed to talk to him – wishing that the girl would take the hint that she wanted to see him alone. Neither of them seemed to sense her silent plea. Or if they did, they ignored it.

Stuart stood diffidently in the doorway. 'So – what can I do for you, Rossie?' he asked in the awkward silence. 'Was there something special or is it just a social visit?'

'I – had to come up to town so I thought I'd drop in.' She looked from one to the other, then at the sketches, scattered over the table and the floor. 'You're talking shop. I won't keep you.'

'Well, if you're sure there's nothing . . . I'll come down with you.' Clearly relieved, Stuart escorted her downstairs. It was almost as though he wanted to be sure she was off the premises, she reflected unhappily. At the street door she turned to him.

'I came to tell you that I'm going to Australia,' she said. 'My father is very ill and he's asking for me.'

'Oh God, Rossie, I'm sorry to hear that.' He patted her shoulder awkwardly. 'Sorry about Elaine being here, but she's only just arrived. I said I'd give her some advice on her work, you see, and . . .'

'Don't worry. You don't have to explain,' she said stiffly.

'What you do is your own business.' She reached for the door but he put out a hand to stop her.

'Rossie! You're not annoyed?'

'Don't make out she hasn't been here before. She looks as though she owns the place!' She turned a face pink with the hurt of betrayal towards him. 'Who you entertain in your own flat is your own affair, but at least have the honesty to be open about it!'

'I never said she hadn't been here before. She made the costumes for the play, for Christ's sake!'

'Yes – well, you and she seem to have a lot in common.'

'That's right we do! Anything wrong with that?' He was clearly annoyed. 'Good God, Rossie, I'm not your personal property, you know!'

Stung, she turned to the door again. 'No, of course you're not. Why should you bother with me any more? After all, you've no further use for me now that you've got Don's money and the play's in production, have you?'

He reached out and grasped her arm. 'Look, Rosalind, why don't you admit that you've never shown the slightest interest in the show? You're even jealous of your own mother ever since we gave her a part in it. All these weeks you haven't even been to one rehearsal.'

'I've been studying. You know that!'

'And while we're on the subject, I'm getting a bit sick of having your step-father's backing thrown in my face every time you feel like it. It's a business arrangement. And none of it is down to you. It's all Una's doing!'

Without waiting to hear more she pulled the door open and ran down the street, tears streaming down her cheeks, oblivious to the curious stares of passers-by.

When Rosalind told the manageress of the Queen's Head the following day that she would have to give in her notice and the reason, her employer was sympathetic.

'There's always a job for you here at the QH, Rosalind,' she said. 'As long as there's a vacancy, of course. If you can give me an idea when you're likely to be back, I'll even keep your job open for you.'

She shook her head. 'I've no idea how long I'll be gone. And if I pass my A levels, I'll be going on to business college in the autumn anyway.' She felt sad at leaving. She'd been happy at the hotel and she liked all the staff. But all she could think about now was her father and how much he needed her. As far as she remembered no one had ever needed her before.

She'd cabled Freda that morning to say that she'd raised the money and was coming out. Now all she had to do was to book her air ticket, pack, and try to explain to her mother where the money for the trip had come from. As it happened she never got that far.

As she let herself into the house that afternoon she heard Don on the telephone in the study. He sounded agitated.

'No, there's no sign of a break in,' he said. 'And nothing else seems to be missing. But the Meissen has definitely gone. Yes, it is valuable – *very* valuable. Irreplaceable in fact. It has sentimental value as well, you see. It belonged to my late mother.'

Rosalind froze to a standstill in the hall. When the police heard they circulated all the antique shops, didn't they? The piece was so distinctive. Surely it would only be a matter of time before she was found out? Her heart began to pound in her throat and she felt as though she were suffocating. *What would they do to her?* Would she be sent to prison? But the thought of facing the police, a prison cell, Don's and her mother's fury and disgust, were all eclipsed by one thought: that of her father's disappointment when he learned that she wasn't coming after all. Maybe he would even hear of her disgrace. The shock would surely make him worse –

it might even bring on another attack and kill him! She rushed into the study where Don was just replacing the receiver.

'Please, don't let the police come. I took the porcelain shell. It wasn't a robbery. It was me!'

For a moment he stared at her ashen face, lost for words, then: '*You?* Whatever for, Rosalind? What in the world did you want with it?'

The words tumbled over one another as she poured out the reason to him. When she had finished he stared at her in amazement.

'Why does no one ever *tell* me anything in this house?' he asked. 'You only had to ask, girl. I would have given you the money if you'd asked me for it.'

'Mum said she couldn't ask you for any more,' she told him. 'Not after the play and everything. And especially as it was for Dad.'

'Are you telling me that your mother *knew* about this?'

'About Dad's illness. Not about the – about what I did.'

'She *knew*, and she did nothing to help you?' Don looked incredulous. 'And you were driven to *this* to get the money for your fare?'

'I haven't spent it – haven't bought my ticket yet,' she told him hesitantly. 'Maybe if I went back to the shop the man would let me buy the piece back.'

'Never mind all that,' Don said decisively. 'First I'll ring the police back and tell them it was all a mistake, then we'll ring the travel agents and book your air ticket.' He reached out to pat her shoulder. 'You and I have never really had a chance to get to know one another, have we?' he said gently. 'I'm not an ogre, you know. And, believe me, I do know what it means to love a parent, Rosalind. You must go to your father as soon as you can. Don't worry, we'll get you there somehow.'

'But the Meissen! The shop where I sold it is in Chelsea.

I've got a card.' She found it and gave it to him. 'The man might sell it.'

He took the card brushing her fears aside. 'He won't. It'll be all right. Leave it to me.'

Sick with relief and gratitude, she waited while he telephoned the police again to say that the piece had been found and it was all a mistake. He smiled at her as he replaced the receiver.

'There, that's done.' He rubbed his hands together. 'Now – suppose you go and put the kettle on first, eh? I think we could both do with a cup of tea. Then we'll get your flight arranged.'

Rosalind was in bed and asleep when Una burst in and snapped on the light. Squinting up through sleep-filled eyes she saw her mother standing over her with all the righteous indignation of an avenging angel.

'What the hell did you mean by it?' she demanded. 'Going to Don with your sob story, getting money out of him behind my back? You can just give it back. You're not going to Australia, Rosalind. Do you hear me?'

'I am.' Rosalind sat up in bed, groping on the bedside table for her glasses. 'The air ticket is booked now. And I didn't go to Don with a sob story,' she said. 'Dad's illness just – well, it just came out – by accident. When he heard Don offered me the money at once.'

'Came out by *accident*?' Una threw back her head and laughed mirthlessly. 'Like hell it did! What do you take me for? How could a thing like that come out accidentally? You went behind my back and asked him for the money, you devious little bitch. And after I told you not to as well! You've caused trouble between us again. I've just been accused of being a heartless, uncaring mother! That's nice, isn't it, after all I've done for you?' She folded her arms. 'Well, I'm telling you straight, here and now, that if you go on this hare-brained trip to see your father you

296

can damned well stay there. You won't be welcome in this house any more. So just sleep on *that*, my lady!' And having delivered her exit line she strode out of the room, snapping off the light as she went.

When she'd gone Rosalind lay for a long time staring at the ceiling. She'd go to Australia. And she'd stay there – make a fresh start. Maybe she could find a business college and qualify. But even if she didn't it wouldn't matter. She'd be in a new country, with someone who loved and wanted her. No one here did. Even Stuart didn't love her any more. It was strange to think that Don had been the one to show her kindness when she really needed it. He'd forgiven her for taking the Meissen, lent her the money, and perhaps the kindest of all, he had kept her desperate act from Una. When it came down to it he was the only real friend she had. She'd find work and pay him the money back, she promised herself. She'd owe nothing to anyone – stand on her own feet.

Two days later she was packed and ready. Her air ticket was safe with her passport in her handbag and she stood in the hall, surrounded by her luggage, waiting for the taxi. Una had gone off to the theatre early that morning for a rehearsal call to try out the new numbers without even saying goodbye. But Don had wished her well and pressed a crisp five-pound note into her hand as he left for the office.

'For some magazines and chocolate to pass the long flight time,' he'd said quietly. He bent to kiss her forehead briefly. 'Safe journey, my dear. I hope you find your father recovering well.'

His kind words had brought a lump to her throat. If Una would only give him the chance she'd find him a good and thoughtful husband. But she had always had a talent for bringing out the worst in everyone.

Rosalind looked at her watch and decided there was

time to make herself a cup of coffee before the taxi arrived. Slipping her coat over the banisters she went into the kitchen and put the kettle on.

She heard the front door bell as she was pouring the boiling water into the cup. The taxi was early. Going into the hall she opened the door.

'Cable for Miss Blair.' The boy handed her the envelope.

With trembling fingers she opened it and stared down at the words that danced before her shocked eyes.

Sorry to say Ben passed away ten am July 27th stop Letter following stop Freda.

She shook her head bemusedly. It wasn't true. It couldn't be! It was only a quarter past nine and the cable said ten. It was some kind of horrible sick joke. Then she remembered that Australia was ten hours ahead of English time. It was evening now over there.

The boy cleared his throat and Rosalind looked up, surprised to find him still there.

'Any reply, miss?'

'What? Oh, no. No reply – thank you.'

Slowly she closed the door and stared helplessly at the packed cases standing ready by the front door. Now she had no one. Dad had gone. She wouldn't see him again – ever. There would be no new life in Australia now. No love and no belonging. Just a greater loneliness than ever.

Oddly, the tears wouldn't come. She wanted – needed – to cry but there was a deep, hard coldness inside her that refused to thaw. Uppermost in her mind was the question of where she should go. In a little while a taxi would be here. Where should it take her now? Sitting down on the bottom stair she thought quickly, her mind suddenly crystal clear. Then she rose and went into Don's study. Lifting the telephone, she dialled the number of the Queen's Head and asked for Mrs Gresham, the manageress. When she answered Rosalind explained that she wasn't leaving the country after all – and the reason.

'I'd like to come back to work on a permanent basis if there's a job,' she said. 'I've changed my mind about going to college. There's just one thing though. Would it be possible for me to live in?'

Chapter Sixteen

Autumn at Melfordleigh was beautiful. The summer visitors began to thin out and Cathy found that she could often walk for miles along the sand without seeing a soul. She preferred the dunes. The garden at Cuckoo Lodge seemed melancholy now that summer was over and most of the flowers had gone. The roses hung sad, windblown heads and the bright petals of the dahlias were bruised with early frost. Even this year's brood of baby ducks on the mill stream, which had enchanted her all summer, had grown up and gone.

In November the shocking news of President Kennedy's assassination cast a dark shadow over the whole world. Autumn turned to winter and Christmas loomed once again. Cathy hoped it might be a chance to lift the gloom. Gerald's students, Robert and Simon, were both going home and obviously looking forward to the holiday. Cathy heard their good-natured banter and laughter as she went about her household tasks. She envied them, often wishing she could join in with their youthful camaraderie. But she kept her distance, feeling that Gerald would not approve. She had nursed a fond hope that maybe they'd invite Johnny, Mrs Bains and Matthew to Cuckoo Lodge for Christmas, but when she suggested it to Gerald he shrugged off the idea.

'Didn't you say that the old lady wouldn't travel back in the summer? It isn't likely she'll want to come here in the middle of winter, is it?' he said dismissively.

Cathy had to agree that he was probably right. Johnny wouldn't leave her mother alone at Christmas as she had in the summer. It seemed that they would be spending the holiday alone. She examined the reasons for her crushing disappointment, forced to acknowledge at last that there was something badly wrong with her marriage. All year she had seen so little of Gerald. A year ago the prospect of having him to herself for a few days would have filled her with excited anticipation, so why did she now find herself viewing the prospect with such a heavy heart?

The answer was something she would have preferred not to think about, yet as the end of their first year approached she realised that it was something she must face up to. Instead of growing closer together during the year they had been at Melfordleigh they had been drifting steadily further apart. Gerald was busy with his students. That was as it should be. It was part of their plan and she had been prepared for it. But even during his off duty hours he seemed to have little time for her; indeed, she sometimes wondered if he even noticed she was there. And the fact that she had so little to do made her all the more aware of it. The organising and administrative work she had hoped to do for the school had been taken out of her hands. Gerald had engaged a secretary, a middle-aged woman who came in twice a week to attend to his correspondence. The financial side of things was taken care of by an accountant. If they had been close to a college she might have gone back and finished her Home Economics course. But the nearest one was twenty miles away and the local bus into town ran only twice a week. It would have been impossible for her to get there and back each day.

She spent her days pottering round the house, helping Maggie prepare meals and walking – endlessly walking. By now she knew Melfordleigh as though she had been born there. She talked to the fishermen on the quay; watched the barefoot children sitting on the sea wall, hopefully dangling their bread-baited crablines; acquainted herself with the many kinds of seabirds as they foraged for food on the sandbanks at low tide.

301

Fascinated by the artists, she took up painting, buying materials from an art shop in Ipswich on one of her weekly shopping trips and taking care to work well away from the real artists. She was shy about her amateur, schoolgirlish efforts and afraid of their critical eyes. As the weeks went by she gradually improved and found satisfaction in the challenge of trying to capture the ever changing landscape of sea and sky with the aid of pigment and brushes. It was so much more satisfying than merely taking photographs, but it did not make up for her loneliness, or for the widening gulf in her marriage.

Once winter had truly set in her outdoor activities ground to a standstill. The rain and the relentless icy winds blowing off the North Sea made the dunes a wild, unfriendly place where walking was a bone-chilling ordeal. The gale-force winds were strong enough to lean on and the cold seemed to penetrate the thickest clothing. The yachtsmen and artists had all gone and even the fishermen stopped lingering on the quay to smoke a pipe, gossip and mend their nets.

Christmas was lonely. Without Robert and Simon there was no laughter or friendly chatter to brighten up the house. Cathy missed them even more than she had expected to. She had looked forward so much to this, their first Christmas together, especially after the traumas of last year. But Gerald spent most of his time in the studio, preparing work for next term and arranging next summer's concerts and seminars. He worked late into the night, retiring to his dressing room sometimes during the small hours, long after she was asleep, and sleeping late in the mornings. Cathy occupied herself between the kitchen and the drawing room, where she whiled away the long evenings watching the newly acquired television set that Gerald had bought, she guessed, to keep her amused and out of his way.

Maggie had taken two weeks off to be with her children until the new term began and Cathy missed her big breezy laugh and the village gossip she brought with her each day.

302

Bad weather kept her confined to the house and when the snow came a few days after Christmas the village was actually cut off for several days so that Robert and Simon were obliged to take a few more days' holiday.

Being shut up in the warm, comfortable house should have been cosy and romantic, especially for two people so recently married. Instead it seemed to make Gerald restless and irritable. He began to snap at her for the smallest thing. Sometimes, when he looked at her, Cathy felt it was almost as though he had difficulty in working out who she was.

The gloomy weeks merged, one into the next, like a slowly grinding treadmill until, to Cathy's relief, the days began to lengthen and the wind from the sea turned noticeably kinder. Wrapped in a thick woolly sweater and gloves, she began once more to take her daily walks down to the quay or along the dunes.

When Robert and Simon returned, Gerald worked them extra hard to make up for the holiday, but in April, just after the builders had moved in to put the finishing touches to the barn, ready for the summer seminars and concerts, Robert announced that he was breaking into his course to go off on a tour of the north of England with a youth orchestra; something of which Gerald strongly disapproved, having intended that the two students would help him with the summer seminars. He warned Robert that he would acquire bad habits and would need to begin all over again. '*If I decide that you're worth taking back,*' he added threateningly.

At the beginning of the spring term, Gerald, much against his better judgement, had agreed to take a few promising sixth-form pupils from the local grammar school at the head's request. But it was a mistake. Their comparative ineptitude stretched his patience to breaking point. Even though the students were keen and worked hard he was intolerant of their shortcomings. Cathy came to dread the days when they came for their lessons. Afterwards Gerald would crash around the house, muttering under his breath and finding fault with everything she did.

Once when he refused his dinner and flung off in a mood she followed him to the studio. Closing the door carefully behind her she stood with her back against it, watching him as he paced up and down in front of the window.

'What's the matter, Gerald?' she asked. 'Why are you so angry?'

He swung round to face her, his face dark. 'Why am I angry? *Why?*' he shouted. 'For God's sake, Cathy! Can't you use your imagination for once? What the hell am I doing? I should be at the peak of my performance – enjoying a successful career – not sitting listening to a lot of acne-covered cretins thumping the piano to a pulp. It's such a criminal waste of my time. They're never going to amount to anything if they live to be a hundred!'

'Oh, Gerald, that's unkind. They're not children. They're intelligent sixth-formers.' She didn't remind him that they were only a year or so younger than she was herself. 'They're really keen and they admire you so much. Besides, from what I can hear they sound very talented.'

'Oh, do they? Well, if you like them so much, *you* bloody well teach them!' He glared at her. 'Anyway, what would *you* know about it?' he added rudely.

'I did grow up with a musician father,' she said quietly.

'Precisely! I mean, you could hardly call what Dan did playing the piano, could you?'

Tears filled her eyes and she turned away. 'That's very cruel, Gerald.'

Instantly he was contrite. 'Oh God, Cathy, I didn't mean that.' He crossed the room and pulled her round to face him, holding her stiff body tightly. 'Dan was a good man and a fine musician.' He threw up his hands in despair. 'It's this bloody illness of mine. I get so *frustrated*, then I take it out on people who don't deserve it.'

'But I thought you wanted to be here at Cuckoo Lodge

– to teach?' she muttered. 'I thought you were tired of the concert circuit and everything to do with it?'

He ran a hand through his hair. 'I was – I *am*. But I still miss it all. I can't help it. It just takes time adjusting.'

'And you've got Simon. Surely he's rewarding? He does sound very good to me, even though my standards aren't as high as yours.'

'*Don't!*' He rubbed his cheek against hers. 'I didn't mean what I said about Dan. You know I didn't. And yes, Simon is good. That's part of the trouble if I'm honest. I see myself in him sometimes and I . . .' He sighed and turned away from her. 'I *envy* him, blast it, with his whole career in front of him. His whole *healthy* life just waiting to be lived!'

'None of us knows what's in store though,' she reminded him. 'You didn't when you were Simon's age.'

'I do now though, don't I?'

'What do you mean?' She looked at him closely, disturbed by his bitter tone, but he shrugged and drew a deep breath.

'Take no notice. I'm just feeling a bit down, that's all. It's probably the medication I'm on. The doctor said – oh, let's forget it.'

'What is this illness you've got, Gerald?' she asked.

He looked at her, his eyes guarded. 'You know what it is.'

'I don't. Not the name of it.'

'What's the difference anyway? You know how it affects me and that's all that matters.'

'Is that what makes you so cross?' she asked him. 'I mean – you would say if it was me, wouldn't you?'

He closed his eyes. 'Oh, Cathy, of course it isn't you. This – this thing I've got stops my muscles from doing what I want them to. That's what makes it so frustrating. It affects my movements as you must have noticed. Sometimes – sometimes I forget things too. It's so maddening!'

She looked at him anxiously. 'Is it painful?'

He shrugged. 'Sometimes worse than others.' He looked at her. 'That's why I sleep in the dressing room. So as not to disturb you when I'm restless.'

'You needn't worry about me. I wouldn't mind you being restless. I miss you, Gerald.'

'I know. I miss you too. But I get tired. Maybe once we've got the place up and running properly . . .'

'But once the summer starts you'll be busier than ever.' She looked at him. 'Are you sure you're not overdoing things? Gerald . . .' She touched his arm. 'Your illness – it won't get worse, will it, darling?'

He shook his head. 'No. Not if I do as I'm told and take the medication. I'll have to go up to Edinburgh to see the consultant again soon. Maybe he'll have good news for me. They're always hoping for some new breakthrough from the research they're doing up there.'

She could see that he was itching to bring the conversation to an end, but there was something else she was determined to say. 'Gerald – I've been meaning to ask you, only you seemed to have so much on your mind. Can we think about starting a baby soon? You did say we might when we were settled.'

His eyes clouded and he turned away. 'You could hardly call us settled yet, could you?'

'When then?'

'I don't know. Maybe when we've got the first summer season over. Let's wait and see, shall we?'

'Yes, but – if you were just to start sleeping in our room again . . .'

'*Leave* it for now, Cathy, there's a good girl.'

The impatient, dismissive note in his voice and the familiar lines that tightened his mouth told her all too plainly that it would be useless to press the subject further. 'At least come and have your dinner,' she said quietly. 'You should eat something. It's not good for you to go without.'

'I'm not hungry,' he said abruptly. 'Tell Maggie to keep it

for me. I might have it later.' He walked towards the door. 'I'm going to work in the other studio for a while. I don't want to be disturbed.'

She watched him turn away from her with despair. 'It's just that I get so lonely sometimes, Gerald,' she said despairingly as he was halfway through the door.

He paused, his head half-turned. 'Why don't you ask Simon to watch the television with you?' he said without looking at her. 'I think he gets lonely too sometimes. He misses Robert and it's dull for him here when he isn't working. Why don't you take him on some of those walks you like so much. I'm sure he could do with the fresh air to blow the cobwebs away.'

For a long moment she stood staring at the empty doorway, her heart heavy with hurt. Didn't he love her at all? Didn't he understand how she felt or what he was doing to her? Didn't he even care?

From that evening on Cathy spent more time in Simon's company. He enjoyed watching programmes on TV with her and when he felt in need of fresh air and some time away from the piano he would accompany her on her walks. He would just tag along without asking and at first she resented him a little. She'd grown used to walking alone and she valued her privacy and the freedom to paint if she felt like it. Besides, just at the moment it made a welcome escape from the builders' intrusion; the mess they made and their constant demands for cups of tea. The open seascape and the tangy air seemed to clear her head and calm her nerves but with Simon along she was obliged to make conversation.

But to her surprise she soon forgot her initial irritation and found herself looking forward to his company. His lively conversation and boyish sense of humour lifted her spirits and refreshed her far more than the hours of solitude. He had a youthful zest for life and looked forward to his future as a concert pianist with a confidence and certainty that made her envious.

307

Lately she had begun to be doubtful about her own future. There seemed no role for her here. Sometimes she felt that Gerald had no need of her at all. His mood swings were so frequent and unpredictable that she often felt as though she were walking on eggshells. She was barely a wife and, as the months went by, it seemed less and less likely that she would ever be a mother either.

For his part, Simon sensed the growing tension between the Cavelles. He was often a witness to Gerald's impatient sniping and cruel criticisms of his young wife. Sometimes his tutor would make oblique references to his wife's restlessness, putting it down to her inability to adjust to the change from London to village life. Simon was surprised and slightly embarrassed when he suggested that it might be beneficial to them both if Simon spent some of his free time with Cathy, indicating that she needed entertaining by someone of her own age to help her settle.

It wasn't hard to imagine how difficult Gerald Cavelle must be to live with. He was a brilliant pianist and coach – the best. Simon knew he was privileged to be taught by him. But he was brutally impatient and mercilessly critical, with his young wife no less than with his students. Simon put up with it, knowing that it was in his best interest to do so. After all, it would not be for long. But he concluded from Cathy's increasingly withdrawn manner that she found her husband's attitude intolerably hurtful.

Often when he was alone in his room he would think about her, wondering how she had come to marry a man so much older. One day, he promised himself, he would pluck up the courage to ask her outright. That day came one spring afternoon when she walked so fast that he had trouble keeping up with her. That morning he had reluctantly witnessed Gerald reducing her to tears because his breakfast egg was too hard and the toast was cold. She had clearly wanted to be alone this afternoon, but he had chosen to ignore her hints and accompany her anyway.

'Do you think you could slow down a bit?' he asked her breathlessly.

She slowed her pace. 'Sorry. I didn't realise.'

'Thanks. It felt more like rushing to catch a train than a leisurely walk.' He glanced at her sideways. 'Walking off a black mood?'

She lifted her shoulders. 'Something like that.' She'd felt so humiliated that morning, being shouted at in front of Simon. His insistence on accompanying her seemed like a further humiliation. She felt he must despise her for not standing up for herself. She despised herself too – more and more lately. In spite of the sunshine and the tangy, sea-fresh promise of summer she longed with a sudden agonising poignance for the happy uncomplicated days when her father was alive.

'Gerald's a lot older than you,' Simon said. 'I daresay that must have its drawbacks.'

His blunt remark felt like a barb, goading her into retaliation.

'Not at all,' she said defensively, quickening her pace even more. 'He's sometimes a little temperamental, but then he's a talented musician. A genius, some people say. You have to make allowances.'

'I'm afraid you'll have to make some for me too,' he said, blowing out his cheeks breathlessly. He threw himself down on the long wiry grass and lay on his back looking up at her. 'You must be fitter than me. I'm totally bushed. How about a little break?' He pulled a piece of grass and began to chew it, squinting up at her with eyes half-closed against the sunlight.

With a resigned sigh she sat down beside him. 'Sorry. And you're right,' she said. 'I was walking off a mood.' She glanced at him, but he had his eyes closed against the glare of the sun. 'I'm sure you know the reason. You heard Gerald shouting at me this morning.'

'I could hardly help it.' He opened his eyes and

glanced sideways at her. 'Why don't you yell back? I would.'

She was sitting up very straight, staring at the horizon. Her eyes were veiled with sadness. The wind blew strands of her long auburn hair across her face and she brushed them back, tucking them carelessly behind her ears. He saw that her skin was already beginning to take on a golden glow and the light sprinkling of freckles across her nose and cheekbones gave her an air of childlike vulnerability. She's *lovely*, he told himself with a small stab of surprise. Why hadn't he noticed before how beautiful she was? He tried to guess at her age. She was probably younger than him.

He missed the company of other young people at college, especially the girls. He'd always been popular with the opposite sex. He prided himself that he had a way with them. He could make them laugh, and that seemed to be the secret of success where girls were concerned. His musical brilliance helped too of course. He knew quite positively and without conceit that he was brilliant. It was a certainty that even Gerald's most scathing criticism could not waver. He still had a lot to learn, he acknowledged that. But one day he would be great and famous. He had always known it.

He chewed thoughtfully on his blade of grass. During the winter it had been easy enough to keep his mind on work. There had been little to distract him. But now spring stirred his blood and heightened his senses. In a way he had envied Robert, going off on his tour; the stimulation of meeting new people and seeing new places. He wondered how much longer he would be able to stand this isolation. He wondered how Cathy stood it too.

Feeling his eyes on her, Cathy turned to look down at him. 'Do you like it here?' she asked with a perception that took his breath away.

'Sitting here by the sea – with you, do you mean?' he asked daringly, his eyes twinkling. 'I like it very much.'

She laughed. And for a moment the bleakness in her

eyes disappeared. She looked much younger now – like a teenager.

'You know perfectly well what I mean,' she said. 'Melfordleigh – Cuckoo Lodge. Being coached by Gerald. I'm afraid he's a very hard taskmaster. A perfectionist.'

He nodded. 'I like that. I love to work hard; to be stretched. It's what I'm here for. But I do like to have fun sometimes too and, frankly, there doesn't seem too much of that around.'

'No.' She looked away. 'You must miss your friends.'

He sat up until his face was on a level with hers. 'What about you, Cathy? Do you miss your friends – going out, dances, cinema, the theatre? Having a good time? You used to live in London, didn't you? This place must be one hell of a contrast.'

'Not at all. I love Melfordleigh.' She avoided his eyes, looking out to sea again. 'Anyway, I have Gerald. I'm married.'

'Yes.' The word was loaded with meaning and for a moment neither of them spoke. 'So does all that mean giving up fun?' he asked. 'How sad! Maybe I'll pass on marriage after all.'

She got to her feet and looked down at him. 'I think we should be getting back. Maggie will need a hand with the evening meal and I daresay you should be working.'

She hurried off and he scrambled to his feet and ran after her. 'I've made you angry. I'm sorry. I didn't mean anything, you know.'

'It's perfectly all right.'

'I only thought it might be good for you to have someone to talk to. We all need a friend – someone to unburden ourselves to at times, don't we?'

'I have friends. And a husband, thank you,' she told him icily. 'Gerald is your tutor and I'm his wife. If there's anything you need please don't hesitate to ask, but don't expect me to talk about my husband behind his back.'

311

'I didn't mean you to. You've got me all wrong, Cathy. I'm sorry.' He hung back, allowing her to walk on ahead. This time he'd been too confident of his charm. She made him feel brash and callow. Maybe she was older than she looked. Maybe marriage had made her extra sensitive. Or maybe – just *maybe* – she needed help more than she cared to admit. He shrugged. Oh well, you couldn't win them all. If it was true, if she did want help, she'd come round eventually.

When they reached the quay he caught her up. 'Cathy . . .' He touched her shoulder. 'Look – friends?' He looked into her eyes and saw with dismay that there were tears in their sea-green depths.

She shook her head. 'Of course we're friends, Simon. Please, let's both forget what we said.'

'You mustn't take any notice of me, you know. I'm always putting my foot in it. I was famous for it at college.' He smiled. 'Next time just tell me to take a running jump, eh?'

She smiled ruefully. 'I'll try and remember. But I'll try not to do it when you're standing close to the edge of a cliff.'

He laughed, yet something in her voice made him wonder if her words had a deeper meaning.

In late-May Gerald was due to make another trip to Edinburgh to see the professor. He wanted to get it over with before the first of the weekend seminars, which would start in June. Simon had arranged to pay his mother a visit while he was away and Cathy quite looked forward to having the house to herself for a few days. She had given Maggie some time off so that she could be with her children for half-term. On impulse she had telephoned Johnny to ask if she would like to come and stay with her during Gerald's absence, only to learn that old Mrs Bains had been taken to hospital the previous day following a slight stroke, making it impossible for Johnny to leave London.

312

Gerald left for Scotland by the early train on Wednesday morning. Simon drove them in to Ipswich station, then drove Cathy back to Melfordleigh afterwards. He was due to leave himself later in the day.

At Cuckoo Lodge the house seemed strangely silent and peaceful. Cathy wandered through the rooms, breathing in the peace and quiet. It was strange how much more relaxed she felt with Gerald gone. Even though she saw little of him there was always a tension about the place when he was there.

In the small studio she ran her hands over the keys of her father's piano. It was ages since she'd played. Both studios were usually in use, and besides, she didn't like anyone to hear her. The standard Gerald demanded from all his students was so high that it inhibited her, especially after the cruel remark he had made about her father's playing.

After a few scales to loosen up she began to play a Brahms waltz she had learned as a child. She was very rusty but with no one to hear her she felt relaxed. It was only as the music uncoiled her taut nerves that she realised how tense she had grown over the past months.

As she came to the end the sound of clapping made her turn, startled, towards the doorway.

'What a dark horse you are. I didn't even know you could play!' Simon was leaning in the open doorway, his arms folded.

'Oh! I thought you were upstairs, finishing your packing.' She laughed self-consciously. 'I *don't* play. Not really anyway. Surely you can hear that. My father was a pianist and he used to give me lessons, but neither of us ever pretended I was another Eileen Joyce.'

He wandered into the studio in his casual way and leaned on the piano. 'You're what they call a competent player, I think.'

'Yes.' She smiled wryly. 'That about sums it up. No sparkle. No talent. If I'd lived fifty years ago I'd have

313

taught reluctant school-children to play *The Merry Peasant* and played the harmonium in chapel on Sundays.'

'No you're putting yourself down,' he said. 'Seriously, I'm surprised Gerald hasn't taken you under his wing.'

'Gerald took me *under his wing* as you call it some time ago. Now he has better things to do.' She hadn't meant it to sound bitter, but that was the way it came out. Catching the now familiar note in her voice he leaned forward to look at her for a moment. She felt his eyes searching her face and blushed crimson. Then, as he opened his mouth to say something, the telephone rang.

'Don't move. I'll get it.' He hurried into the hall, closing the studio door behind him. Cathy began to play again, but it was no use, the moment had gone. Her fingers faltered, hitting the wrong notes. She felt inhibited and self-conscious. Maybe when Simon had left and there was no one to hear she could *hammer*, as Gerald called it, to her heart's content. She closed the piano lid regretfully and stood up just as he came back into the room.

'That was my mother,' he told her. 'It seems that she has to go away on one of her research jobs. Short notice. So it looks as though my visit home is off.'

She turned to look at him. 'Oh, Simon, I'm sorry. You must be disappointed.'

He shrugged. 'A bit, I suppose, but it can't be helped.'

'It was such a good chance for you to go home though. Gerald gives you so little time to yourself.' Her face brightened. 'I know. Why don't you ask her to come here one weekend? I'm sure she'd enjoy the concerts, and you could take her out to look at the countryside.'

'You wouldn't mind?'

'Of course not.'

'That's very kind. We'll have to think about that.' He paused, looking at her. 'The immediate problem is, Cathy, what do I do with myself for the next three days?'

She frowned. 'Why – stay here, I suppose.'

He smiled. 'You don't think the locals would gossip? It's a tricky situation with Gerald away, isn't it?'

'I don't see why anyone should object. If it comes to that, how would they know? As for me, I'll be cooking for myself. Might as well cook enough for two. You could work – practise – feel free to use the studio – anything you like.' She laughed. 'Heaven knows the place is big enough.'

'Well, if you're sure . . .'

'I am, of course – unless there's something else you have in mind?'

He looked at her, wondering for one crazy moment if she could read the mad fantasy that was in his mind. She wore a faded blue cotton dress and sandals. Her arms and legs were bare and her bright hair was carelessly tied back in a ponytail. And she clearly hadn't the faintest idea of how desirable she was. For a moment he wondered how it would feel to pull the ribbon from her hair and see it cascade about her shoulders; to take her in his arms and kiss that tremulous mouth till it was bruised and tender; to see his own desire reflected in the fathomless green eyes. To . . .

'No,' he said with a casual lift of his shoulders. 'I'm completely at a loose end.'

She prepared a casserole for dinner, then went out to the mill stream with an apron full of bread and kitchen scraps with which to feed the ducks. They had recently hatched a new brood of adorable ducklings and as she watched them dive and squabble over the scraps she remembered the first time she and Gerald had come to look at Cuckoo Lodge. She had fallen in love with the place even then, in its wild, neglected state. She'd had such hopes – such dreams – about their future here. What had gone wrong with it all? What she had visualised as their home had become something close to a prison. And in so short a time. It had to be her fault. If only she knew how to put things right.

'Greedy little devils, aren't they?' She turned and found

315

Simon leaning against a nearby willow tree. Suddenly she felt annoyed with him for intruding on her thoughts. Although she refused to admit it to herself, being in close proximity to him made her feel vulnerable and defenceless.

'Every time I turn round you seem to be behind me,' she said, her cheeks pink.

'Sorry! If I'd known you wanted to be alone . . .' He began to walk away and immediately regretting her hasty words, she called out to him.

'No! Simon, come back. I didn't mean . . .'

'Look, if my being here is going to cause you any trouble I can always book into the pub,' he said. 'I thought you seemed quite happy about my staying.'

'I did. I *am*! It's just that I was deep in thought and you made me jump.'

'Deep in thought?' He looked at her. 'Anything you want to share?'

She brushed the crumbs from her hands and smoothed her apron. 'Not really. I was just thinking about – I don't know – silly girlish dreams that don't come true and – you know – things that might have been.'

'Sounds intriguing – and rather wistful.' He smiled, reaching out to take her hand. 'Look, why don't I come and help you in the kitchen? I don't see why you should wait on me. Besides, you might be surprised to find I'm really quite house trained.' He fell into step beside her as she headed back to the house. 'Then maybe you can tell me all about these broken dreams of yours over dinner.'

They ate at the kitchen table, then went to sit in the drawing room. There was a chill to the spring evening air and Cathy put a match to the fire that Maggie had left laid in the grate. Pulling a cushion from one of the chairs, she sat with her back against the settee, her arms linked about her knees as she gazed into the flames.

'When I was little my dad and I used to look for pictures in the fire,' she said.

'You miss him, don't you?'

She nodded. 'He died so young. And so unexpectedly.'

'I never knew my father,' he told her. 'But there have always been lots of photographs and letters from him. My mother and grandmother always tried to keep his memory alive for me.'

She smiled up at him. 'That's nice.'

'So – how did you come to meet Gerald?' he asked, holding his breath against another rebuff.

'He was my father's best friend. They were at college together. Before Dad died he made Gerald my legal guardian.'

So that was it? Simon gave a long, low whistle. 'And you and he fell in love? How romantic.'

'Yes. I suppose it was.'

Into the silence that followed he asked quietly, 'Was? You said *was*. Has the romance faded so soon?'

She sighed. 'You know what Gerald is like. He's very preoccupied with his work. He's finding it hard to adjust to giving up his concert work.'

'Why did he? Give it all up, I mean.'

'He developed a muscular problem. You must have noticed the stiffness in his fingers.'

'Yes. The trembling too. I thought . . .' He looked at her, busy with thoughts and speculations of his own. 'What are you going to do, Cathy?'

She looked at him, her eyes wide with surprise. 'Do?'

'Let's face it. There isn't much of a future for you here. You should at least be looking for a job; a satisfying career to make a life for yourself.'

She turned to look into the fire again. 'I thought I was going to do the administrative work for the school, but Gerald has handed all that over to Mrs French. And an agency in London is handling the bookings for the seminars.'

'Isn't there anything else you want to do?'

She shrugged. 'I was at college, studying Home Economics, but we got married before I could qualify.'

'Then why don't you go back and pick up where you left off?'

'I can't. The nearest college is twenty miles away and you know what the public transport is like here.'

'Learn to drive,' he urged. 'I'll teach you if you like.'

She looked uncertain. 'I don't know what Gerald would say.'

'Blow Gerald!' he said vehemently. 'You're entitled to a life. This place is like a morgue. I put up with it because I'll be out of it soon. Besides, I'm enjoying the work. For me it's time well spent, but if I thought I had to stay here for the rest of my life I'd go stark raving mad!'

'Well – that's you,' she said, thrusting out her chin stubbornly. 'Luckily we're not all the same.'

'Face it. You're no different from me, Cathy.' He slid on to the floor beside her. 'You're young and full of vitality. Or you should be at your age. Since I've been here I've watched all the life draining out of you. If you don't start living soon you'll be old before your time.'

She turned her head away from his intense stare. She found his eyes and his closeness even more disturbing now. When she spoke her voice trembled. 'I don't remember asking you for your opinion, Simon,' she said. 'I think you've got a cheek, telling me what I should do with my life.'

His hand reached out and closed around her arm. 'Oh, come on, Cathy. You don't really believe that. I'm only telling you what I think because I *care*. It's a damned awful waste, a lovely girl like you stuck in a Godforsaken hole with a man who doesn't give a damn about you.'

318

'Who says he doesn't give a damn?' Her cheeks flamed with hot colour, her eyes blazing with anger.

'I do! He snaps at you all the time – takes you for granted. What's more he doesn't care who knows it! He doesn't even *look* at you.' She made to pull away, but his grasp tightened on her arm. 'Running away isn't going to make it any the less true,' he said insistently. 'Be honest – with yourself if not with me. When did he last tell you you were beautiful, eh? When did he last make love to you, Cathy? Can you even remember?'

'How dare you ask questions like that?' She wrenched her arm out of his grasp. She was trembling now. Her own feelings terrifying her, making her defensive. 'Those things are private – secret things between two married people. It's none of your business. How *dare* you?' She scrambled to her feet but he quickly rose to face her, grasping her shoulders.

'Look, we've got to know each other over the past few months, Cathy. I've watched you growing more and more miserable. You're not going to deny that, are you? I don't care what you think of me, but I do care that you're throwing yourself away. Chuck me out if you like. I'll be gone from here soon anyway. Tell me to go to hell. But for God's sake *do* something about your life. Start living before you turn into a cabbage!'

For a moment she stared at him, her eyes wide and her lips trembling. He had just summed up what she'd been trying to suppress for the past months. He had dragged it ruthlessly out into the open and forced her to look at it face to face. She hated what she saw – and hated him for making her see it. But although she tried to break free from his strong grip, his hands held on to her relentlessly.

'Look at me, Cathy.' He bent to look into her eyes. 'Admit it. It's true, isn't it?'

319

Slowly she raised her face to him. It was no use trying to deny that everything he said was true. If she could just make him understand the way it had been. 'I loved him so much,' she whispered. 'I thought he loved me too. I *think* he still does – in his way. I suppose I never thought about what I needed. I never looked beyond the man – beyond Gerald himself. I just thought we'd come here, love each other and live a happy life together for the rest of our days. I saw us running the school and the seminars and concerts – as partners. To me, marriage meant belonging to each other, doing everything together, being in love – for ever.' She looked at him imploringly. 'But he does need me, Simon. He needs me – doesn't he?'

'Maybe. To look after him when he's too ill to work? To go on running things here when he's unable to carry on himself? But is that fair, Cathy? Is it what you expected – what you *want*?'

She turned away. 'I don't want to talk about it any more, Simon. It really isn't any of your business and you're making me feel disloyal. Oh, I know you mean to be kind and I appreciate . . .'

'Kind, my foot!' He grasped her arm, refusing to let her go. 'You're burying your head in the sand. You're young, with a young woman's rights and needs. Why should you . . .?'

'*Stop it!* That's enough!' She shook her head. 'Oh – I wish you'd gone home now. I wish . . .' Her sentence was cut short as he pulled her roughly to him and held her fast. His mouth came down on hers. For a moment she was stunned – unable to believe what was happening. She fought him, her fists drumming against his chest. But his arms held her as firmly as bands of steel and his lips crushed her mouth, cutting off her breath.

In spite of her struggles he refused to release her and slowly her fear and anger died, to be replaced by a traitorous excitement that erupted within her like fire. She felt the heat of it sear through her veins, dizzying her brain till her head swam and her knees buckled. Sensing her surrender, the lips that had been so hard and persistent became soft and persuasive, moving sensuously against hers, parting them gently till she heard her own small murmur of assent. Tonight she had been forced to admit so many things she had been trying to deny. Now she acknowledged that one of them was her growing attraction to Simon. For months she had felt drawn to him. He was everything that Gerald wasn't; warm and attentive – young and vitally *alive*. She hated herself for the disloyal thoughts and for the shaming desire that spread through her every nerve like an ignited fuse, but she could stop it no more than she could turn back the tide.

One hand slid down her spine to press her thighs closer to him whilst with the other he began to unbutton her dress. She shivered at the electrifying touch of his hands on her flesh. She knew that she should call a halt now – before it was too late – before things got out of hand. But the blood was pounding in her head and her heart drummed so loudly that she knew he must feel it, just as she could feel his arousal in every tensed muscle, every magnetic beat of his heart. *She wanted him.* There was no denying it. She wanted him more than she had wanted anything for a long time.

She let her head fall back as he slipped her dress from her shoulders and cupped her breasts, his voice thick with longing as he murmured, 'Oh, Cathy, Cathy, you're so lovely – so beautiful!'

In her mind she remembered the nights she had lain awake, waiting and longing for Gerald to come up to their room. The nights she had fallen asleep only to wake to a cold, empty bed next morning.

Together they sank to their knees. Simon pulled the

321

cushions from the settee and pressed her gently back on to them, then he was beside her, his passion growing as he kissed and caressed every inch of her as reverently as if she were something infinitely precious. Even on that wonderful evening when Gerald had taken her for the first time she had known nothing as headily intoxicating as this. And when at last he imprisoned her beneath him and slipped inside her, his breath warm against her ear as he whispered her name, she thought she would die of pure ecstasy.

Simon was an accomplished lover, bringing her to a feverish climax before surrendering himself. She must have fallen asleep almost instantly, and when she wakened to find her head pillowed on his chest she thought at first that she must be dreaming. Then slowly the reality of what had happened came back. She sat up. The fire was just a pile of cold grey ashes and she could see through the uncurtained window that dawn was already silvering the sky. Simon still slept, limbs spread with an almost childlike abandon over the scattered cushions. His naked body was half-covered by the rug from the settee that he had pulled over them. Very gently she drew it up over him, then gathering up the clothes that lay strewn about the floor, she padded out of the room.

In the kitchen she stood looking out across the dewy garden, shivering a little in the morning chill. But although she was cold her body still tingled with awareness. For the first time in months she felt vibrantly alive. The memory of their recklessly abandoned lovemaking stirred her, quickening her heart afresh. She closed her arms around herself as though to capture the feeling. But she could not silence the accusing word that echoed constantly in her head.

Adultery.

There was no escaping the fact. That was what she had committed. She had been married less than two years and she had slept with another man. What was even more despicable, she had done it while her husband was visiting hospital.

322

What would her father have thought of her disloyalty, her betrayal? What would Johnny say – Johnny who had tried so hard to warn her not to marry Gerald. She tried to disentangle her confused thoughts. Put some justification on her actions. but she could find none.

So – what happened now? Could she go on as though nothing had happened – live a lie with Gerald? Surely not? After last night nothing could ever be the same again. She tried to examine her feelings. Was she in love with Simon? Did he love her? If he asked her to leave Gerald and go away with him, could she do it with anything approaching a clear conscience?

She put the kettle on then went upstairs to shower and slipped into a sweater and jeans. When she came down again she found Simon in the kitchen frying bacon and eggs. He had dressed hurriedly in the crumpled clothes he had discarded last night. His hair was still tousled and his face was rough with morning stubble, but he looked cheerful and untroubled, whistling to the radio as he worked. He looked up with a smile as she came in.

'One egg or two?'

'Just coffee for me.' She sat down at the table where Simon joined her with his plate piled high. He looked at her quizzically, rubbing a hand over his jaw.

'What's the matter? Do I look that bad? I'll shave and shower when I've had this.'

'It's not that. You look fine.' She frowned at the portable radio, from which a pop group was belting forth its latest hit. *With love – from me – to you*, it blared. 'Could you switch that off, please?'

He switched off the radio and peered at her. 'What's the matter? You're not regretting last night?'

'I can't help feeling guilty, Simon. Surely you can understand that?'

He reached out to touch her hand. 'Don't regret it, Cathy. And don't feel guilty.' He looked into her

323

eyes. 'It was wonderful, wasn't it – for you as well as me?'

She tried not to meet his eyes but found it impossible. 'Yes, it was. I can't deny that.'

'Why should you want to deny it?' He stood up and pulled her to her feet. 'You *know* it was wonderful. And we have two more whole days to enjoy . . .'

'*No!*' She wrenched herself away from him and walked across to the window as if to put as much space between them as possible. 'It won't happen again, Simon. It *mustn't*. At least, not until we've decided what to do. Perhaps you'd better book yourself a room at the pub this morning after all. I need to think.'

He spread his hands, his expression innocently baffled. 'What is there to think about? What harm can it do if I stay now – after last night?' He crossed the kitchen to where she stood. 'Cathy, look at me.' He turned her to face him. 'We're not hurting anyone. Gerald needn't know if you don't want him to. What happened last night was so good – for both of us. It was no big deal. Just fun – delicious fun. Call it a little diversion.'

'Is that all it is to you?' Appalled, she pushed him away. '*A little diversion!* Is that how little you care for other people's feelings?'

He looked shocked. 'I *do* care about you, Cathy. I'd like to see you happy – enjoying the kind of marriage you deserve, but as you told me, it's none of my business. You feel Gerald needs you and you're determined to stay with him. But you and I can still be friends, can't we? Loving friends? I can give you what he can't. It could be the perfect arrangement.'

She felt her heart freeze into a solid block inside her. 'You're saying that you see me as a disappointed, neglected wife?' She said the words slowly and disbelievingly. 'Just ripe for a fling – someone to amuse yourself with until you go back to your friends and the real world.' She backed away from him, shaking her head. 'No, not me, Simon.' She pushed past him and walked to the door. In the doorway she turned. 'Ring the Admiral Nelson now and book yourself a room. I want you to be out of here before I come downstairs again.'

He hurried into the hall after her. 'Cathy . . .' She paused halfway up the stairs to look down at him. The sudden sharpness of his voice captured her attention. 'Cathy – look, Gerald knew damned well that we'd find each other irresistible before long. He's been *throwing* us together. Don't you see that? I believe he meant this to happen. He knows he can't keep you happy and he doesn't mind someone else doing it for him. So there's nothing for you to feel guilty about.'

'That's a *revolting* thing to say!' She ran up the rest of the stairs and went to her bedroom, closing the door and turning the key in the lock. She must put what had happened behind her. Try to forget it. Try to forgive herself and live with the guilt.

Gerald came home from Edinburgh in good spirits. That evening Simon asked him if he could borrow the car, saying that he had to go into Ipswich for the evening. Over dinner Gerald told Cathy about his visit to the consultant.

'There's a surgeon in New Zealand, a colleague of the Professor, who has perfected a procedure that cures this problem of mine,' he told her excitedly. 'No one here is doing it yet, but apparently this man has effected several near miracles. Some patients who were in wheelchairs have been able to walk after the operation.'

Cathy said nothing, but she remembered his claim that his condition would get no worse as long as he took his medication regularly. Obviously he had lied to her about it.

'They're sending my case notes over,' Gerald went on. 'When he's had a chance to study them he'll know whether I can benefit from the operation.'

'When would it be?'

'Probably not till the autumn, which would suit me fine,' he said. 'It will give me time to get this first important season over and assess the results.'

She noticed that he no longer made a pretence of including her when he referred to the business of the school. 'That's good news,' she said. 'Does it mean a complete cure?'

'Apparently. It's a painless operation done under a local anaesthetic, to kill off a tiny portion of the brain that has become over-active.'

She stared at him. 'It sounds horribly dangerous! Are you sure it's all right?'

He laughed. 'Of course I am. It's just a few tiny cells. They're hoping that in time it will be routine everywhere, but for now New Zealand is the place one can get it done!' He reached out to touch her hand. 'Poor Cathy. You haven't had a very nice time since we've been here, have you? I know I don't always treat you as I should, but I have been under a lot of pressure. Once this first season is over, and if this op is a complete success, things should be very different for us. I'll make it up to you, I promise.'

She smiled. 'I know. I hope it all works out, Gerald.'

He stroked her cheek with one finger. 'I might even be able to go back to the concert platform. We might be able to sell up here and go back to London. Who knows?'

'That would be wonderful – if it's what you want.'

'Just think, life could be as it was before. Parties, lots of friends dropping in all the time. You'd like that, wouldn't you?'

She simply nodded. Surely he knew that all she wanted was for things to be as they were before. And he made no mention of the baby she longed for or the close togetherness she missed so much. But if there was a chance he might be completely cured she had to be glad for his sake.

*　　　*　　　*

326

The first season of weekend seminars and concerts was a great success. In response to the advertising campaign handled by the agency, young musicians from all over the country converged on Melfordleigh by the dozen. Those that couldn't be put up at Cuckoo Lodge found rooms at the Admiral Nelson and in the smaller hotels and guesthouses. The local hoteliers were delighted with the business the school brought them. The house and the barn concert hall rang with music from morning till late at night and in between sessions Gerald 'held court' with young hopefuls who were planning concert careers.

Gerald's agent came down and, after hearing Simon play, signed him up for a concert tour to begin in the autumn. Everyone was busy, enjoying the non-stop activity, and looking round the village. They spilled out into the street and on to the quay, laughing and talking in enthusiastic groups. The only person left out of it all was Cathy. It seemed she had no part in any of it. She worked along with Maggie in the kitchen and helped the extra cleaners they had engaged, but never once did Gerald introduce her as his wife or invite her to play hostess.

In late July he received a letter from the consultant in Edinburgh. Having studied his notes and read the consultant's prognosis Professor Harbage felt that there was a very good chance of the operation being completely successful in his case. He suggested a date in late-November for Gerald's admission to his private clinic in Auckland.

Gerald read the letter to Cathy at the breakfast table.

'It's warm in New Zealand in November, isn't it?' she asked. 'I'll have to remember to pack summer clothes for us both.'

He shook his head. 'There's no need for me to drag you all that way too.'

327

She looked up at him in surprise. 'But I'd like to come. I've always wanted to see New Zealand and besides, you'll need someone – need me, won't you?'

He smiled and shook his head. 'I'll be fine. I'll need you to be here, looking after the house.'

'We could close up, couldn't we? Simon will have gone off on his tour and the concerts will have finished.'

'There's next year to think about.'

'But I never *do* anything, Gerald,' she insisted. 'You've made sure of that. Other people do all the organising and booking.'

A frown of irritation crossed his brow. 'I can't think why you're complaining. Some wives would give anything to have all the work taken off their shoulders,' he said tetchily. 'If you want the truth, Cathy, we can't really afford for both of us to go. The air fare isn't cheap, you know, let alone hotel bills and so on. The operation will be costly too. It's going to take every penny I've made this season and more besides.'

'I see.' She stood up and began to clear the table. 'Why didn't you say so? You never confide our financial situation to me, do you? So how would I know?'

But the hurt and disappointment of Gerald's apparent rejection was eclipsed by a growing anxiety that refused to go away. For some weeks now Cathy had been trying to ignore the nagging suspicion that she might be pregnant. At first she hadn't taken too much notice. Last time Gerald had assured her that it was due to a change in her lifestyle and when she missed her period she thought that the trauma of her brief affair with Simon must be responsible. But now, after ten weeks, she could ignore the situation no longer. Besides, there were other tell-tale signs. She had been feeling sick in the early mornings and the sight and odour of certain foods made her nauseous.

Whilst one part of her was filled with joyful excitement at the prospect of the baby she had longed for, she was frantic with worry. Gerald would know for sure that the child could not be his. It was months since they had made love. And she knew instinctively that Simon would want nothing to do with it. There seemed little point in telling him anyway. Ever since she had discovered that he was simply amusing himself with her she had avoided him as much as possible.

At last even Gerald began to notice that something was wrong. Looking at her across the breakfast table one morning as she picked at a slice of toast and sipped her half-cold coffee he noticed that she looked unwell. The crop of summer freckles stood out sharply against her pallid skin and her normally bright eyes were dull with anxiety.

'Why don't you go and stay with the Johnsons for a few days?' he said suddenly. Cathy looked up in surprise. 'You've been looking peaky for a couple of weeks,' he went on. 'Maybe a break will do you good.'

The thought of seeing Johnny and sleeping in her old room filled her with nostalgia. 'Oh, Gerald. That would be lovely,' she said. 'I'd love to go.'

'Ring her this morning and lay it on then,' he said. 'Stay as long as you want.'

When she heard Johnny's voice at the other end of the line Cathy's throat tightened so much that she could scarcely speak.

'Hello, Johnny. It's me – Cathy.'

'Cathy! What a lovely surprise! What can I do for you?'

'Can I come and see you, just for a few days?'

'Of course you can. Stay for as long as you like, dear. It'll be lovely to have you. Your old room is always ready for you. You know that.'

'It's not too much trouble?'

'Bless you, no. Matthew's gone up to Bradford on a six-month course and Mother is in a nursing home. I felt bad about letting her go but I couldn't manage her at home

329

any longer. I miss her though, Cathy. I miss you all. It'll be wonderful to have you back.'

Sitting in the train Cathy went over and over what she could say. She had never needed Johnny's advice as desperately as she did now, yet how could she tell her about Simon and the shameful mistake she had made? It was out of the question. Johnny had always had such high moral standards. She would feel so shocked and let down.

The little house in Chestnut Grove was just as she had left it. It seemed smaller and shabbier, but infinitely comfortable and dear. Cathy's old room was spick and span, the bed made up with Johnny's best linen sheets, and the bedspread and curtains freshly laundered. She unpacked and went downstairs to her favourite meal of roast ham with potatoes and broad beans from the garden. Johnny kept eyeing her closely as she ate, and over Cathy's favourite treacle pudding she asked, 'Are you all right? You're not looking very well, dear.'

'We've been so busy,' Cathy said, avoiding her eye. 'Run off our feet with the concerts and everything. It's been a great success. Gerald is so pleased.' She looked up. 'I didn't tell you. He is going to New Zealand in November. There's a surgeon there who has perfected an operation to cure his muscular problem.'

'That's good news. Are you going with him?'

'No.' Cathy looked down at her plate again. 'It's going to be very expensive, you see. The operation will have to be private, of course, and then there will be hotel bills and a lot more besides. We couldn't afford for both of us to go.'

'I see. Then perhaps you could come and stay here while he's away?'

'Oh, Johnny, that would be lovely!' Cathy paused. She had forgotten that by November she would be six months pregnant. There would be no hiding her condition from anyone by then. 'I'd love to come, of course. But I think Gerald wants me to stay at Melfordleigh and look after the house,' she added.

'Then maybe I could come and stay with you instead,' Johnny suggested cheerfully. 'I could spare a few days. Mother hardly recognises me when I go to the nursing home these days and Matthew will still be away. I could easily take a week or so off.'

Cathy flushed, searching her mind frantically for an excuse. 'Yes – that would be nice.' Suddenly she wished she hadn't come. Johnny was so perceptive. She'd already sensed that something was wrong. How would it be possible to keep the truth from her for two whole weeks?

Johnny had arranged to visit Mrs Bains in the nursing home the following day and Cathy was relieved when it was suggested that she take herself Up West on a shopping trip.

'Mother probably won't know you. Her memory is very erratic,' Johnny explained. 'She can sometimes be rather difficult – she gets strange ideas about people she doesn't know. Better for you to remember her as she was.'

They caught the bus together, Cathy alighting at Edgware tube station and catching a train for Oxford Circus. It was nice to be in London again. She wandered along Regent Street, stopping for a cup of coffee in a new coffee bar, then she looked round Liberty's, admiring the exotic jewellery and exquisite materials on display. She was looking at the latest autumn fashions in the window of Dickens and Jones an hour later and thinking about lunch when a voice called her name.

'Cathy! Of all the people to run into!' She turned, startled, to see Carla Maybridge standing behind her. 'I'd have known that red hair anywhere!' The other girl hugged her warmly. 'How *are* you? And how is married life?'

331

'I'm fine, thanks. How are you? You're looking wonderful.'

In actual fact if Carla hadn't seen her first Cathy would probably have walked right past her. The young woman standing before her was a very different Carla from the one she had known two years ago. She had grown her hair long and wore it straight and smooth. The red and black dress she wore was of the latest fashion; it was very short with a geometric pattern. And all her accessories were of expensive-looking cream leather: shoulder bag, gloves, and tight-fitting knee-high boots.

Carla took her arm. 'This is really wonderful. Come and have lunch with me.' She glanced around. 'You are on your own, aren't you?'

'Yes. I've come up to spend a few days with Johnny.'

'Then we must have lunch and a lovely long gossip. I can't wait to hear all about what you and that devastatingly handsome husband of yours have been up to!'

Carla took her arm and dragged her into Dickens and Jones. 'I'm working here,' she explained as she bundled Cathy on to the escalator. 'I model for an agency, modelling outfits in the restaurant. There are four of us and I'm taking my lunch break at the moment.'

'What happened to the A level course and the career in teaching?' Cathy asked as they went up in the lift.

Carla laughed. 'You've got to be joking! The sixth form was the living end. All those rotten little swots with their spotty noses to the grindstone. I couldn't stick the thought of two years of that. I threw the towel in after the first term and managed to get into the modelling school.'

In the top-floor restaurant someone was playing soft romantic music on a white grand piano. They were shown to a table by the window.

'You look as though you've done well,' Cathy said as they settled themselves.

'Not bad.' Carla grinned the old familiar grin and held

out her arms. 'Like the outfit? It's by Mary Quant. She's an absolutely great new designer. Everyone is going to be wearing her clothes soon.'

'What did your parents think of you giving up the A levels?'

Carla pulled a face. 'What do you think? You know Dad, even teaching came a poor second to the bank! But I don't live at home any more. It always was so crowded. Well, you must remember. And as we all grew older it was worse. No privacy anywhere. I got myself a little flat in Fulham – sharing with two other girls. It's no palace but we do each have our own space.' She grinned. 'We have fun too.'

Cathy felt a sharp pang of envy for the happy-go-lucky life Carla clearly led. 'And you like modelling?' she asked.

'Love it. At least there's variety to the work and you get to meet some interesting people.'

They ordered the sole, which the waitress recommended. Carla leaned back in her chair and took a long, critical look at her friend. 'If you don't mind my saying so you could do with taking in hand, my child,' she said with mock severity. 'You're looking distinctly countrified. Why don't we meet up tomorrow? That's my day off. You can get that husband of yours to treat you to some new outfits. There are super new boutiques springing up all over the place in the King's Road. I get a discount at some of them.'

Cathy shook her head. 'I don't think so, thanks, Carla.'

'Why not?' The other girl frowned and leaned towards her. 'What's up, love? You look as though you've got something on your mind.'

Cathy sighed. Carla was her oldest friend. If she didn't confide in someone soon she'd go crazy. 'As a matter of fact – I'm pregnant,' she said softly.

Carla looked at her. 'And you don't want to be, is that it?'

'I *do* want to be. I want a baby very much. But Gerald . . .'

'Doesn't?' Carla looked at her, her head on one side. 'He doesn't want anything getting in the way of this new project of his?'

'Something like that.'

'I take it he doesn't know?'

Cathy shook her head miserably. 'No.'

'Surely keeping it from him is unavoidable – unless you're planning to . . .' Carla frowned. 'Look, forgive me if I've got it wrong, Cath, but are you saying that – it isn't his?' When Cathy didn't reply she shook her head. 'God! Poor you. What a mess! How on earth did you get into it, Cath? I mean – an affair is one thing, but . . .' She bit her lip. 'I suppose there's no chance you're wrong?'

'None at all.'

'Well – is there any chance it might actually *be* Gerald's?' When Cathy shook her head again she reached out and touched her wrist. 'Oh, please don't look like that, love. It's not the end of the world.'

'It feels a lot like it,' Cathy said unhappily.

Carla bit her lip. 'Look, I think I might be able to help. How far are you?'

'I don't know. Ten or eleven weeks.'

Carla drew in her breath sharply. 'You're running it a bit fine. Why didn't you do something about it before?'

'I – thought it might be a mistake. That it might all come right. Anyway, I didn't know if there was anything I *could* do.'

Carla looked at her pityingly. 'You always were the naive one when it came to sex, weren't you?'

Their food arrived, but Cathy pushed hers round the plate disconsolately.

'Look – I know of this doctor,' Carla said quietly. 'He's been struck off as a matter of fact, but he's good. One of my flat-mates had a panic like yours a few months ago. He fixed it for her and she was fine. I can get his phone number for you if you like.'

Cathy swallowed hard. 'An *abortion* you mean?' she whispered, her eyes round. 'I *couldn't*, Carla. The idea of it makes me feel sick.'

She shrugged. 'Okay, so what's the alternative? What about this chap – the father? Would he want you to have it?'

'No! I don't want him to know either.'

'You don't love him then?'

'*No!* The whole thing was madness. It should never have happened.'

'Mmm.' Carla smiled wryly. 'Famous last words!' She sighed. 'Well if you change your mind, give me a ring and let me know.' She scribbled her number on a scrap of paper and passed it to Cathy. 'You needn't worry. I can guarantee you'd be safe enough with this doctor. It's not like having it done by some old crone in a back street with a crochet hook. Think about it.' She looked at her watch. 'God! Look at the time. I'll have to fly. Give me the bill. My treat. I'll settle it on my way out.' She patted Cathy's shoulder. 'And cheer up, love. It might never happen. It *won't* if you take my advice.'

Cathy lay awake all that night, thinking about Carla's suggestion. More than anything in the world she longed to have the baby she carried. To give it birth, love it and hold it in her arms. But she had to acknowledge that it was a vain hope. Going through with it was out of the question. She told herself she was being punished for the wrong she had done. But far worse than the fear and the pain of the ordeal she must suffer was the heartache of sacrificing her child.

She tried to comfort herself with the thought that when Gerald was cured perhaps things would be as they were before between them. Then perhaps they would have another child and she could put all this behind her. At least now she was offered a way out. It seemed like providence that she had met Carla today. Perhaps meeting her like that was a sign that she was meant to take her advice.

She rang Carla the following evening while Johnny was making the bedtime cocoa. Next morning she went out to a phone box and rang the doctor's number. A receptionist told her in a brisk, impersonal voice that she could come the day after tomorrow, at two-thirty. She was told the fee for the 'consultation and treatment' which she must pay in cash on the day of her visit. She was given an address in Islington and asked to try to arrive on time.

She arrived early. She had told Johnny she was going to visit a married school friend and might be away till late evening. She had no idea how long the 'treatment' might take. She found the house easily, a crumbling Victorian town house with peeling paintwork and an air of faded respectability. The doctor occupied rooms in the basement, reached by winding steps. A sharp-faced nurse ushered her into a room with fawn wallpaper and uncomfortable chairs upholstered in chipped brown leather. And there she sat, her heart thudding dully in her breast and her stomach churning as though awaiting execution.

When she was shown into the surgery she was reassured by the powerful smell of Dettol and the fact that everything appeared to be clinically clean. The doctor was a tired-looking man with stooped shoulders and pale blue eyes behind gold-rimmed spectacles. He enquired about her health and her circumstances – whether there was any chance she might change her mind. But his questions sounded as though they were part of a routine that he had waded wearily through a thousand times before. He reminded her of the risk she was taking and warned her that any complaint she might make would involve her in criminal proceedings too.

The procedure was done surprisingly quickly. She gritted her teeth and submitted to the discomfort and the indignity, eagerly breathing in the gas and air from the mask the nurse held for her. When the doctor had left, the woman helped her down from the table. She gave her some painkillers and a packet of extra thick pads, telling her to expect to bleed heavily for a few days. Then she took the money that Cathy had withdrawn that morning and ushered her out into the street. It was over.

She walked slowly back to the main road feeling cold and stunned as the afternoon traffic thundered by. She reminded herself that it was all over. She wasn't pregnant any more. But try as she would she could not see it as a reprieve. All she could think of was that she had just paid a stranger to kill her child.

She woke in the small hours, the pain gripping her like an iron band. Pulling her knees up to her chest she stuffed a clenched fist into her mouth to stop herself from crying out. As the pain slowly released her she felt the wetness flowing from her. Getting out of bed carefully she went into the bathroom and took two of the tablets the nurse had given her, washing them down with water from her tooth glass. She changed her nightdress and pad and was about to go back to bed when another spasm of violent pain gripped her. This time it was so agonising that she was unable to stop herself from crying out. With one hand against the wall she sank to her knees in the bathroom doorway, both hands clutching her stomach.

Johnny's bedroom door opened and the landing light snapped on. 'Cathy! My dear child!' The shocked face looked down at her. 'Whatever is the matter?'

Johnny helped her back to bed and stood looking down at the white-faced girl anxiously. 'Cathy,' she said gently, 'I believe you're having a miscarriage, dear.' Cathy nodded, her teeth clamped over her lower lip. 'I had my suspicions that you were pregnant when you first arrived,' Johnny went on. 'I think I'd better telephone for a doctor to come and see you. You seem to be losing an awful lot of blood.'

'*No!*' Cathy half rose on the bed and grasped Johnny's arm convulsively. 'I'll be all right. I don't want a doctor. *Please*, Johnny!'

The older woman frowned and looked at her doubtfully. 'It would be best, really. A doctor would give you something to help the pain and stop you from haemorrhaging. It could be dangerous, you know. and you might lose your baby – if you haven't already.'

'No – no. I'll be all right – really I will.'

Johnny stood hesitantly in the doorway. 'Shall I send for Gerald then?'

'*No!* Gerald doesn't know – he mustn't. Please do as I say, Johnny.'

'Oh, Cathy.' With a sigh, the older woman sat down on the end of the bed. 'What have you done? Have you been to someone? Have you had this miscarriage induced?'

When Cathy nodded and began to sob Johnny made up her mind. Getting to her feet she worked rapidly. Fetching an armful of Matthew's heavy encyclopaedias from his room she raised the foot of Cathy's bed on the books, then went to the airing cupboard on the landing, returning with a pile of sheets which she proceeded to tear up. As she worked she looked down at Cathy, her mouth set in a grim line.

'I wish I knew who did this to you,' she said. 'And why you felt driven to do it too, but I don't suppose you're going to answer either of those questions.' She drew up a chair and took Cathy's hand. 'Time for talking later. We're in for a long night, child. And I'm warning you now – if the bleeding hasn't eased up by daylight, you're going to hospital whether you like it or not. I'm not having this on my conscience.'

By dawn the worst seemed to be over. As the sun came up Johnny drew back the curtains and went downstairs to make tea, which Cathy drank thirstily, propped up against the pillows, her face grey against their whiteness. Johnny regarded her as she drank.

'Are you going to tell me about it now? I don't want to press you, Cathy, but I really do think you owe me an explanation.'

'I know. And I'll never be able to repay you, Johnny,' she said wearily. 'I'm really sorry to have put you in this awful situation. I wasn't prepared for what happened last night. I thought when I left the – the place where it was done that it was all over.'

'I'd like to get hold of the person who did it,' Johnny said grimly. 'Are you sure everything was properly sterilised? It could be so dangerous.'

'Yes – yes. It's all right, Johnny, I promise.'

'*Why* though?' Johnny looked at her so directly that she could hardly bear to meet the candid eyes. 'Why did you do it? You told me only last summer how much you wanted a baby. So why?'

Bit by bit it all came out; Gerald's moodiness, his refusal to include her in the running of the school, his cold indifference to her physically. Finally the relationship that had sprung up between her and Simon and the fatal night they had spent alone together last May.

'He said Gerald had *meant* it to happen, Johnny,' she said as the tears began to flow. 'He said he'd thrown us together on purpose; that it could be the perfect arrangement. It made me feel so guilty and so – so cheap. I've let you and everyone else down, haven't I?'

Overwhelmed with anger and compassion, Johnny put her arms round the girl and held her close. 'You haven't let anyone down, Cathy love. You've been the victim of two selfish men. I'd like to give Gerald Cavelle a piece of my mind. I wish I could keep you here and take care of you. But you're a grown-up married woman now. He is your husband and this is something you'll have to sort out between you, I'm afraid.' She took out her handkerchief and dried Cathy's tears, just as she had done when she was a small child. 'I do know one thing though, my girl,' she said determinedly. 'You're staying here with me until I'm satisfied you're completely well again. That's one thing I *can* do, and I'm having no arguments about that!'

Chapter Seventeen

Rosalind was eating her breakfast in the staff dining room at the Queen's Head when Bill Kendal, the night porter, came through with the mail.

'One for you, gorgeous,' he said cheekily, dropping the long envelope on to the table in front of her. 'Looks official. Brown job with a window. Don't like the looks of that. What you been up to then, eh?'

Rosalind coloured and pushed the envelope into her pocket. 'None of your business,' she said. 'Isn't it time you were off home?'

Bill assumed a wounded, indignant look. 'Well, I don't know! Try to be friendly round here and look where it gets you!' He nudged her. 'If that there's your exam results I shall expect to be treated, so don't you forget it.'

Smiling at his characteristic cheek, Rosalind finished her breakfast and went through to Reception. She didn't want to open her letter with other staff members looking on. Already the butterflies were beginning to churn her stomach. Could it possibly be her exam results? She could think of no other reason to be getting an official-looking letter.

She'd been lucky in getting the job of receptionist at the Queen's Head. When she'd applied for a job after her father's death Mary Phillips, the girl who had been there ever since Rosalind had first come to work as a Saturday girl, had just handed in her notice. To Rosalind's delight, Mrs Gresham, the manageress had offered her the job, and the room that went with it on a trial basis. After the month was out Mrs Gresham offered her the job permanently and suggested she train at the Queen's Head for management.

But she soon found that the life of a trainee-manageress meant that she was often expected to help out in other departments. As she lived on the premises she was constantly on call. She served behind the bar or in the restaurant – even in the kitchen when they were short-staffed, turning her hand to any task that needed doing. She worked long hours and she suspected that in some ways she was being exploited, but she didn't really mind. She liked being busy and the main thing was that she was learning new things all the time. Anyway, there was nothing else to do in the evenings except sit in her spartan little attic room and listen to the radio.

In the tiny office behind the reception desk she opened the envelope and saw at once with a pang of disappointment that it did not contain her exam results. It came from a firm of London solicitors at an address in Conduit Street and was written on their official-looking headed notepaper. It was short and to the point, requesting her to call into their office concerning her father's estate at her earliest convenience. It was signed by someone called Alan Knight, who she saw from the notepaper, was the firm's head clerk. Glancing at the date she noticed with dismay that the letter had been written almost a month ago. Una must have neglected to send it on until now.

Picking up the telephone she dialled the number on the letter and asked to be put through to the man who had signed it.

'Good morning, Miss Blair, Alan Knight speaking.' The voice was pleasant and not at all intimidating.

'I'm terribly sorry, Mr Knight, but I've only just received your letter,' Rosalind said anxiously. 'I've moved, you see, and it's only just been forwarded to me.'

'Don't worry about the delay, Miss Blair,' he laughed. 'Solicitors don't expect things to happen quickly. Now, when would you like to come in and see us?'

342

'Can you give me some idea of what it's all about?' she asked.

'I thought I made that clear in the letter. It's to acquaint you with the terms of your late father's will.'

Rosalind frowned. 'I know, but it says here his *estate*,' she said hesitantly. The word 'estate' puzzled her. It sounded so affluent – completely unlike Ben who, according to Una, had always done extremely well to make his money last from one pay day to the next. 'Are you sure it's me you want?' she asked. 'I wondered if there was a mistake. You see my father didn't have an estate.'

'Estate is just a legal term,' Alan Knight explained gently. 'It means his worldly goods, if you like. Money, property and so on. Shall we say tomorrow afternoon at three, Miss Blair?'

She agreed, dazedly. Her afternoons were free from two till five. 'Yes,' she said, still mystified. 'I'll be there.'

She arrived with ten minutes to spare at the offices of Turner, Turner and Braybrook the following afternoon, but Alan Knight saw her without delay. He was a tall, willowy man with thick grey hair and kindly blue eyes. Offering her a seat, he put on his glasses and opened the file containing her father's will. For Rosalind there was a strange air of unreality about the situation. Making a will seemed so out of character for Ben. She could hardly believe he had actually gone along to a solicitor and done it.

'As the only child of the late Benjamin Arthur Blair you are his sole beneficiary,' the man was saying.

'Oh.' Rosalind looked up at him blankly. 'I see.'

He turned the page. 'I expect you'll be wanting to know just what it is you have inherited?'

She shook her head. 'As far as I know my father had very little to leave,' she said.

'Not a lot of money, I'm afraid, as you've already anticipated,' said Alan Knight, peering at some accompanying documents. 'His bank account at the time of his death stood at one thousand four hundred pounds.' He glanced up at her. 'Not a fortune certainly.' He cleared his throat. 'However, as well as the money, you inherit the property known as Ivy Cottage in the village of Sherwood Magna, Northamptonshire.' He looked up at her again. 'You did know of the existence of the property, I take it?'

Rosalind had flushed a deep crimson. *The cottage!* She'd completely forgotten about the cottage. But surely Freda should have that? It was half hers. She had helped to restore it – put so much work and love into the task and looked forward to living in it with Ben one day. It wasn't fair. 'I – don't understand,' she said. 'The cottage was only half my father's. He bought it along with his – partner.'

Frowning, Alan Knight looked through the papers in front of him. 'No, there is no mistake. Your father's is the only name on the deed of ownership,' he said. 'It was his property. And now it is yours.'

'You mean it was – it was actually paid for?' Rosalind asked incredulously. 'There was no mortgage?'

'No mortgage.' The man smiled. 'Your father was sole owner of the property and now it is yours, Miss Blair. You are a woman of property, you might say.' He smiled indulgently at his little joke as he took a labelled key from the desk drawer. He handed it to her but she shook her head.

'I don't feel right about this,' she said. 'I must get in touch with my father's partner.' Seeing the man's raised eyebrows she explained, 'Dad was a singer, you see. He and his partner, her name is Freda Morton, toured with a double act: "Ben and Benita Blair".'

'Ah . . .' Light dawned on Alan Knight's face. 'This would be the Miss Morton who was with him in Australia. She is aware of the will, Miss Blair. In fact it was she who contacted us on his death. I'm surprised you haven't heard from her yourself.'

Rosalind sighed. Una would have guessed that anything with an Australian postmark would be from Freda and

344

would conveniently have 'forgotten' to forward it. 'I'm afraid not all of my mail has been reaching me,' she said. 'Have you an address for her? Is she still in Australia?'

'No, she is back in this country.' He rose from his chair. 'If you would like to wait a moment I can find her address for you.' He left the office, to return a few moments later with an address neatly written on a slip of paper.

Outside in the street again Rosalind tried hard to come to terms with the news she had just been given. Ben had left her fourteen hundred pounds – *and* the cottage. But she could feel only guilt over Freda who apparently had been left nothing. Thank goodness she was back in England and that she had her address. She must try to put things straight as soon as she could.

It was as she was coming out of Edgware Underground station an hour later that she saw Cathy Cavelle. She hadn't seen Cathy since the day she'd been married, but the girl walking towards her seemed preoccupied and Rosalind hesitated, unsure if she should intrude. They drew level and were about to pass when Cathy suddenly looked up and saw her. Her face lit up in a smile of genuine pleasure.

'Rosalind! How nice to see you. I wondered if we might run into each other while I was here.'

'How are you, Cathy? Are you staying with Mrs Johnson?'

'Yes. I've been here almost a month. I only meant to stay a fortnight, but I haven't been very well and Johnny persuaded me to take an extra couple of weeks. I'm going back tomorrow.'

'I wish I'd known before. I would have rung you. Are you better now?'

Cathy's eyes clouded for a moment. 'Oh, yes, fine now, thanks,' she said dismissively. 'What about you? You must have taken your exams by now. Any results yet?'

'Not yet. Any day. I'm trying not to think about it.' Rosalind looked round. 'Why don't you come and have tea with me? I work at the Queen's Head now. I live in. We could go up to my room. It's not very smart, but I do have a kettle.'

Cathy smiled. 'That would be lovely.'

In the tiny top-floor room with its sloping ceiling Rosalind made tea and took out a tin of biscuits while Cathy sat in her only armchair.

'You left home then?' she observed, looking round at the threadbare carpet and worn furniture.

Rosalind sighed. 'Yes. Mum and I never did get on. I know this isn't very smart, but it's better this way.'

'What will you do about going to college?'

Rosalind handed her a cup of tea and sat down on the end of the bed with her own. 'I'm working here as receptionist and trainee-manageress. If I pass my As they'll let me go to college on a day-release course.'

'Will that be as good as you wanted?'

Rosalind shrugged. 'I think so. I'm getting lots of practical experience here and I'll have the advantage of having held down a real job when I come to apply for a post.'

'Well, I'm sure Mrs Gresham will give you a good reference,' Cathy said. 'If you ask me, she's lucky to have you.'

Rosalind looked more closely at her friend. Cathy looked pale and much thinner than she remembered. She'd mentioned that she'd been ill. Maybe it was something to do with that. 'Is your husband's music school going well?' she asked. 'I expect you're enjoying life in your lovely house by the sea.'

To Rosalind's surprise Cathy's pale cheeks coloured. 'Yes. Everything is fine, thank you.' She bit into her biscuit, her eyes downcast. 'How is your mother?'

'She's well as far as I know. I don't see much of her now that I've left. She went back into the theatre, you know. She has a major part in a musical play. They're trying out for the West End at the moment. Down in Brighton.'

'That's good. And your boyfriend?' Cathy asked. 'Stuart, wasn't it? We met him at the party you gave that New Year's Eve.'

Rosalind took a drink of her tea. 'It didn't last,' she said. 'He was busy with his work and me with my studying. It fizzled out. He found someone who had more in common with him.'

'Oh, that's a shame.'

'Maybe it's just as well. I think he was more interested in Una than me. She got Don to put up the money for the show he was involved with, you see. That's how she came to get a part in it.'

'Oh, Rosalind.' Cathy reached out to touch her arm. 'That must have hurt a lot.'

She nodded. 'It hasn't been the best of years for me. My father died a couple of months ago.'

'Oh, I'm so sorry.'

'He was in Australia at the time. Freda, his partner, wrote and told me he'd had a heart attack and I was going out to see him. I was all packed and ready to leave when the cable came to say – he'd died.' She gave a helpless little shrug.

Cathy's heart went out to the other girl. She'd always seemed so lonely ever since school. Now she was all alone. From what she had seen of Una Blake she seemed a selfish, uncaring mother. Even an absent father was better than none at all. 'I know how it feels to lose your father,' she said softly. 'I still miss my own dad.'

'I never saw much of him of course,' Rosalind said. 'Unlike you I never knew my father while I was growing up. It was only much more recently that we grew closer. He wanted me to go to Australia with him, you know. I wish I had now.' She got up to refill the cups. 'As a matter of fact I've just been to see his solicitor. Dad left me all he had – a little money and a lovely cottage in Northamptonshire. I'm still trying to get over the shock.'

347

Cathy smiled. 'That's nice. It's good that he cared enough to want to provide for you.'

'Yes, but I always thought that he and his partner bought the cottage jointly. I feel guilty that she has been left out. She was much younger than him but I always thought they might get married. I know she wanted to. I'm going to write and suggest that I sell the cottage and share the proceeds with her.'

'Do you think you should? After all, your father obviously wanted you to have it.'

'I must ask her at least,' Rosalind said. 'She was always very kind to me. And I know she loved Dad very much. She might be feeling betrayed that he left her out.'

Cathy smiled. 'Not many people would be as considerate.'

'What about you?' Rosalind asked, anxious to change the subject. 'What have you been doing with your holiday?'

'Not much. I saw Carla one day. Did you know that she's a model now?'

Rosalind smiled. 'No, but it doesn't surprise me. I never did think she was cut out to teach. She opted out of her A level course in the first term.' She looked up. 'You said you'd been ill? Nothing serious, I hope?'

Cathy shook her head. 'No. I think I was a bit rundown. You know how Johnny fusses. And now that her mother is in a nursing home and Matthew is away she has no one to spoil.'

'I daresay you're longing to get back to your husband. He must be missing you too after almost a month,' Rosalind said wistfully.

'Perhaps.' Cathy hid her face in her teacup. 'He's going to New Zealand in November. I'll be on my own. Why don't you come and stay for a few days?' The invitation slipped out impulsively, startling both girls equally.

Rosalind's eyes widened as she said, 'Well – thanks, Cathy. I don't know if I can get the time off, but if I can I'd really love to come and see the house you told me about.'

Cathy stood up. 'Good. I'll be in touch nearer the time now that I know you're living here.'

Rosalind went downstairs with Cathy to see her out, then returned to her room to get ready to go on duty. As she changed she thought about their meeting. She could hardly believe the change she had seen in Cathy this afternoon. At her wedding she had looked so ecstatically happy; like a young bride should look. In love and looking forward confidently to a happy future. Now she had the appearance of a much older, careworn woman. She looked drawn and unhappy as though there were some deep sadness in her life. Rosalind wondered what could have happened to bring about such a change.

She wrote to Freda that night before she went to bed. The address that the solicitor's clerk had given her was in the Midlands. Maybe Freda's parents lived there. For the first time Rosalind realised how very little she knew about the girl who had become her father's partner.

She had expected to get a reply or a telephone call within a few days, so she was surprised to look up from her typewriter two days later and find herself looking straight into Freda's smiling eyes.

'Hello, Rossie. Do you have a room free?' she asked. 'I'd like to stay for a few nights if that's possible.'

'Certainly.' Rosalind consulted the book that lay open on the desk. 'There's a nice one vacant at the front on the first floor.' She took a key from the board behind her. 'Come on, I'll take you up myself.' She took Freda's case and they went up together in the lift.

'Thank you for your sweet letter,' Freda said, once the door was closed. 'When I read it I had to come and see you right away.' Her eyes filled with tears as she held out her arms. 'Oh, Rossie, I miss Ben so much. You're all I have left of him now.'

Deeply moved, she went into Freda's open arms and the two women clung to each other as the tears flowed.

'He talked about you all the time, you know,' Freda told her. 'He was so proud of the way you'd grown up. He was looking forward so much to your coming out to spend a holiday with us.'

'I wish I could have been in time to see him,' Rosalind whispered. 'I wish – oh, I *wish* I'd come out with you when you asked me. I'll always regret that.'

'No, you mustn't. You wanted to see your exams through. He respected that.' She held Rosalind at arm's length. 'You've taken them?'

'Yes. The results should be through any day now.'

'You'll pass with flying colours, I know you will. Ben knew it too.'

Rosalind looked at her watch apologetically. 'I'm sorry, Freda, but I'll have to get back to Reception now. But I'll be off at two. We could have a late lunch together if you like?'

Over lunch Freda told Rosalind that she would be seeing her agent while in London. 'Monty was shocked to hear about Ben,' she said. 'But I think – *hope* – he has some work lined up for me. When I got your letter I thought I could see him too while I was in town so I gave him a ring. I really need to work, Rossie.'

'I know, Freda. Look – about Dad's will . . .'

'Oh, not for the money,' Freda interrupted. 'I need to work because singing is my life. Without it, I'm nothing, especially now that Ben's gone.' She reached across to lay a hand on Rosalind's arm. 'And before you go any further about this will, Ben and I talked all that through. I know what a tough time you had after your parents parted. Ben always felt really bad about it. He wanted to make it up to you in whatever way he could and we both agreed that he should leave you everything he had, the cottage included. He went along and sorted it all out before we went to Australia.'

'But it was half yours!'

'No. Ben bought it with money he had saved after we started doing well. All I did was persuade him that it was a good investment. He got the place very cheaply.'

'Dad was hopeless with money. You must have persuaded him to save in the first place. You advised him to buy it, and you helped him restore it. You loved it.'

Freda silenced her with a shake of her head. 'No. I loved *him*, Rossie. I had my reward; the six wonderful years we shared. We both wanted the cottage to be yours. It was a good investment. Property is going up and you should get a good price for it. You deserve it, love. So let's hear no more.'

Freda went up to see Harry Montague the following morning and the moment she arrived back at the hotel late in the afternoon Rosalind could see by the look on her face that she had good news.

'I've got an audition for a part in a new musical,' she said excitedly. 'Tomorrow afternoon. I'm sick with nerves just thinking about it. It isn't a big part but I've never done anything on the West End stage before and it would be a marvellous start if only I could get it. I've always wanted to do a musical. Monty has suggested I take a new stage name so that I can make a fresh start as a solo artiste. I've decided on Benita Moore. What do you think? I wanted to keep the Benita part in memory of Ben.'

'It sounds fine to me. Very glamorous.' Rosalind smiled. 'Just like the star of a musical. Dad would have approved. I'll keep my fingers crossed for you. If you get the part and you're going to be working in London we'll be able to see more of each other.'

'I know. I thought I might find a little flat somewhere. You could come and stay – make it your home too.' Freda's cheeks were flushed with excitement. 'I mustn't count my chickens, of course, but I've got a really good feeling about this. Maybe things are looking up for us both, Rossie. Maybe we're lucky for each other.' She paused. 'Why don't you come to the audition with me tomorrow?'

Rosalind blushed with pleasure. 'Well – if you're sure I wouldn't be in the way?'

Freda shook her head. 'You know it's high time you stopped selling yourself short, Rossie. Get to know your own worth.'

The following morning the letter Rosalind had been waiting for arrived. For a long time she sat staring at it, unable to bring herself to open the envelope and read the contents. Suppose she had failed? There was no way she could go back and re-take the exams now that she had started working. And without A levels the college wouldn't take her.

Looking at her watch, she saw that she had ten minutes to spare before she went on duty, so, picking up the letter, she went up to the first floor and tapped on Freda's door.

Freda was in her dressing gown, her hair swathed in a towel, but she took one look at Rosalind's worried face and drew her inside.

'What's the matter? You look as if you've seen a ghost.'

Rosalind held out the long envelope. 'This came,' she said, her lip trembling. 'I can't open it. Will you?'

'What is it?' Freda's face cleared. 'Oh! Your exam results.' Turning away she walked across to the window, tearing the envelope open as she went. Rosalind waited, watching and hardly daring to hope as the other woman scanned the sheet of paper inside.

'You've *passed*!' Freda said, turning to her triumphantly. 'And with flying colours just as I knew you would.' She threw her arms round Rosalind and hugged her.

'Congratulations, darling! Now maybe you'll realise that you're a worthwhile person – someone who matters.' She swung Rosalind round in a sudden burst of exuberance. 'Oh, I've a feeling this is going to be a very special day for us, Rossie. A day we'll remember for years to come.'

The auditions were being held in a hall in a street at the back of St Martin's Lane. Freda and Rosalind arrived in plenty of time, but by the time they arrived at the door Freda was a bundle of nerves.

'I'm sure you've nothing to worry about,' Rosalind said, determined to sound reassuring. 'You've got a lovely voice. They'd be mad not to give you the part. What's the name of the play, by the way?'

'It's called *Sweet Violet*,' Freda said. 'Written by a new playwright, Monty says. He was telling me all about it. Apparently it was first put on in a rundown theatre in Stoke Newington, but he managed to persuade Louis Jacobson to go and see the show. He loved it and decided there and then to take it into the West End.' Freda looked at Rosalind's face, which was blank with shock. 'Louis Jacobson is an impresario,' she explained unnecessarily. 'If he has faith in the show you can bet it's a winner.' She frowned. 'Rossie – is anything wrong?'

'No! No, nothing.' She pulled herself together with an effort. 'Let's go in.' Her mind was in turmoil. What was going on? Monty must know how furious Una would be to find herself in the same show as Freda. It was a recipe for disaster. It would make for a terrible working atmosphere and could ruin the show. What could he be thinking of? Would Una be here today? She shrank from the thought of the ensuing confrontation.

But, much to her relief, her mother was nowhere to be seen. Inside the hall two rows of chairs had been set up in front of the platform. There was the usual upright piano, at which sat Brian French. Sitting in the centre of the front row of chairs sat Julian and another, older man whom Rosalind supposed must be Louis Jacobson. To her relief Stuart was not present either.

Freda joined the row of 'hopefuls' waiting to audition, while Rosalind found herself a chair in a dim corner at the back of the hall. They waited. On the stroke of two-thirty Julian stood up and announced that the auditions would begin. One by one, he called up the candidates whose names were on his list. Each in turn they handed their music to Brian, sang a song of their own choice, then read a passage from the libretto and attempted to sight-read one of the songs from the show. When Freda's name was called she walked up on to the platform without the slightest trace of nervousness. Rosalind watched admiringly, wishing she had Freda's looks and poise. Crossing the fingers of both hands, she saw her give her music to Brian and take up her position centre-stage.

The song she had chosen was one Rosalind had heard her sing before. It was *As Long As He Needs Me* from Lionel Bart's musical *Oliver* – and she sang it with a heart-felt emotion that brought a lump to Rosalind's throat. She read from the libretto with aplomb and then attacked the song she had never seen before in a strong, confident voice that Rosalind knew would have made her father proud. There was no doubt in her mind that Freda outshone the rest of the female singers auditioning that afternoon. She was so enthralled that she almost forgot the barrier that lay between Freda and a part in the show.

When she had finished there was a pause, then Julian said, 'Thank you, Miss Moore, we'll be in touch with your agent.' He glanced at his list. 'Harry Montague, isn't it?'

Outside in the street they looked at each other. 'You're sure to get it,' Rosalind said. 'You didn't look a bit nervous and your voice was wonderful. You were miles better than anyone else.'

Freda looked doubtful. 'I don't know about that. When

354

I saw that Jacobson himself was there I almost turned tail and ran. I'm going to try not to think about it.' She linked her arm through Rosalind's. 'Come on, I'm taking you out to tea. We've got your exam results to celebrate if nothing else. And I need something to steady my nerves.'

As they faced each other over the teacups Rosalind wondered whether to tell Freda that Una was playing a leading part in the show she'd just auditioned for. She hated to spoil everything for her. There was, after all, the chance she might not get the part, in which case she need say nothing. On the other hand she couldn't let her accept it first and then find out.

'Rossie – is something wrong? You're very quiet.'

'What?' She looked up with a start. 'Oh, no.'

'Only I've been speaking to you for the last ten minutes and getting no response.'

Rosalind opened her mouth to drop her bombshell – then closed it again. She couldn't do it. She couldn't spoil Freda's happy anticipation. Not today. Maybe tomorrow she'd find the courage to tell her. Who knew what might have happened by tomorrow?

But when they arrived back at the Queen's Head there was a message waiting for Freda. Monty had telephoned and left word for her to ring him as soon as possible. She rang at once from the telephone in Reception, Rosalind looking on apprehensively as she dialled the number.

Monty's secretary put her through immediately. Rosalind heard the rumble of his deep voice at the other end of the line.

'Hello, Monty. I've just got in. You wanted to speak to me?'

Rosalind watched as the other girl's face slowly took on a look of sheer disbelief. 'You're joking! My God, I can't believe it!' she said at last. 'Are you sure it's me they want? I mean, I'm virtually an unknown, apart from the work I did with Ben. This will be the first time I've done a musical play.' While Monty's voice growled on at the other end she smiled and nodded eagerly. 'The contract – you want me to come up to the office and sign it? Of course – when?' She winked gleefully at Rosalind. 'Right, I'll be there.'

At length she put the receiver back on its rest and looked at Rosalind with a stunned expression. 'Oh, Rossie, you're not going to believe this. They've offered me one of the principal roles! It seems that the actress who played Olive at the try-out wasn't really up to it. Jacobson had never really felt she was right for the part. *And they want me to play it!* Can you believe it?' She grabbed Rosalind's hands and squeezed them tightly. 'Oh, isn't it *wonderful*? I told you this would be a day we'd always remember!' She looked at Rosalind's stunned face and laughed uncertainly. 'Well, come on. Aren't you pleased for me?'

Rosalind drew her towards a chair. It was worse than she'd thought. 'Come and sit down,' she said. 'There's something you should know before you sign that contract tomorrow.'

Freda shook her head bemusedly. 'For heaven's sake – what? What's bothering you, Rossie?'

'The other actress – the one they're sacking. I'm afraid it's Una.'

The smile faded from Freda's face and she slumped in her chair. 'Oh, no! What is Monty thinking of? He should have known.' She frowned. 'He *did* know. He purposely didn't tell me, the sly old devil. He knew I wasn't auditioning for a minor role all the time.' She looked at Rosalind. 'Oh my God! What do I do now?'

'I think you should take it,' Rosalind said firmly. 'It isn't your fault they want to sack Una. She manipulated her way into the part anyway. If you don't do it they'll only find someone else – someone who won't be half as good. It's true Monty should have told you. He probably knew that you wouldn't even consider auditioning for it if he did.'

'And he'd have been right. I wouldn't!'

'But Una never considered anyone else's feelings, so why should you?'

Freda looked at Rosalind for a long anxious moment, chewing her lower lip. Then suddenly she nodded decisively. 'You're right,' she said. 'This is my big chance. Why should I lose it?'

Una closed the dressing-room door and sat down to take off her make-up. The show's pre-London run was over. This had been their last night in Brighton. They had a week out before they began fresh rehearsals for the West End opening. Brian had written another two numbers for the show, one of which was for her character. And Julian had re-written the second act curtain. Everyone agreed that the whole show had benefited enormously from the changes. Now she was really on her way to fame and success. Una could hardly wait to see her name up in lights outside the theatre.

She was wiping off the last vestiges of cold cream when there came a tap on the door.

'Come in.' She looked up through the dressing-table mirror, expecting Don. He had come down specially for the show's last night and the party that was to follow. Tomorrow they were leaving for a short holiday in Majorca. She smiled in anticipation. He'd be sure to bring her a bouquet or chocolates tonight; maybe even a piece of jewellery too.

But it was not Don who responded to her call, but Julian. He hovered in the doorway, looking uncomfortable. 'Una. Have you got a minute?' he asked tentatively.

She laughed, turning in her chair. 'All the minutes you want, darling, now that the show is over. Do come in and have a seat.' She got up and went towards the screen in one corner of the room. 'What can I do for you? Okay if we talk while I change?'

'No. I'd rather – look, sit down a moment, Una,' he said uneasily, closing the door carefully behind him. 'I have something important to say to you.'

357

Something in his tone made her pause and look at him. 'Oh, dear. Did I mess up one of your favourite lines? I haven't been upstaging someone again, have I?'

'No, nothing like that.' Julian swallowed nervously, wishing the next ten minutes could be over. The diplomatic speech he had so carefully rehearsed had completely deserted him. 'You've been absolutely wonderful in the show,' he began. 'And of course we couldn't have got off the ground without Don's support – and yours.'

Una frowned, unhappy at the turn the conversation was taking. 'Do you think you could get to the point, Julian?' she said sharply. 'At this rate we'll both be late for the party. Besides, Don will be waiting.'

'It's all right. I've seen him. I asked him to give us a minute.' Julian slipped one finger inside his collar and swallowed again. 'Right. Well you see, the thing is, we – that is, Louis Jacobson and I – feel that you aren't quite . . . What I mean is that playing the West End can be terribly demanding and . . .'

'And *what*?' Una demanded, facing him challengingly.

He tried again. 'I'm sure you'll agree that over the past few weeks the pressure has been pretty relentless.'

'I don't think I'd agree with that at all,' she said stridently. 'I'm a pro. I hope I can cope.'

'Oh, I'm sure you always do your best. But you've been looking very tired lately and your . . .' He cleared his throat. 'Your voice . . .'

'What about my voice? Are you trying to tell me that I'm not up to playing the part in the West End?' She stood in front of him, hands on hips. 'Well, come on – *are* you?'

'You've been terribly well received, Una,' he lied. 'Very popular and all that – with the cast as well as the public. It's just that Jacobson – well, no, *I* feel you deserve a rest. It isn't only you,' he added hopefully. 'There are one or two other parts that are being recast, for various reasons, and I . . .'

358

'You little *shit*!' Una's face, which had flushed darkly, suddenly drained of all colour. 'You *used* me,' she screamed. 'You were glad enough of the money I got Don to put up, weren't you? I was good enough for your tacky little show then. Now that you've got Jacobson behind you and you don't need my financial support any more you think you can just dump me! Well, you won't get away with it, I promise you!'

'Be reasonable, Una. It happens all the time. Lots of actors who do the pre-London run drop out when the show comes to Town. It's a well-known . . .'

'And what would *you* know about it?' Una spat at him scathingly. 'You're nothing more than a tuppeny-ha'penny bloody *amateur*. Don't you try to tell me what's what. I was in this business when you were still filling your nappies.'

'Well, now that you mention it, that's exactly the point,' he said boldly.

Una drew in her breath with a menacing hiss. 'You're saying I'm *too old*?' She stared at him, her eyes bulging slightly and the veins in her neck standing out. 'Well, let me tell you something, Mr Smartarse. You haven't heard the last of this. By the time I'm done with you, your name will be mud in this business. I'm going to sue you for every penny this show makes. I do have a contract, you know. You can't wriggle out of that.'

'I think you'll find that your contract is up for renewal at the moment,' he said.

She stared at him. 'Does Monty know? Is he in on this too?'

'I believe he knows that we intended not to renew your contract, that's all,' Julian told her. 'According to him you cancelled your agreement with him when you first came into the show. Our decision to recast your part in the show was nothing at all to do with him.' He paused while she took in this piece of information. 'Of course we shall see that Don receives his investment back, plus his share of the profits.'

He began to edge towards the door, but a little too late to escape Una's violent reaction. A scream of pure animal fury accompanied a flying jar of cold cream which struck him a painful and dizzying blow on the temple before falling to the floor. Without another word he fled, slamming the door behind him and leaving Una standing in the middle of the room, trembling and incandescent with rage.

Don, who had been hovering in the corridor, listening apprehensively to the ominous sounds of his wife's disquiet, appeared in the doorway, his anxious face almost hidden behind a huge bouquet of flowers.

'Oh, dear,' he said when he saw Una's scarlet face and quivering mouth. 'What on earth is the matter?'

At the sight of him she burst into floods of noisy tears. 'Take me home!' she hiccupped between sobs. 'Take me home, Don. I've been swindled – robbed! That's what's happened.'

Don looked completely nonplussed. 'But – I thought we were going to this party. Don't you want to go?'

'Go to the *party*?' she wailed. 'When I've been insulted and humiliated? I'll never be able to show my face in the theatre again.' Irritated by his bland, puzzled expression she scowled at him through her tears. 'Oh, for heaven's *sake*, Don, don't you understand? They've kicked me out of the show – dumped me. Told me I'm too old and that my voice is cracking up. Cast me aside like – like some old has-been.'

Amazed though he was, Don couldn't help admiring Julian's pluck. He'd seen him emerge from the dressing room clutching his head. Clearly he hadn't come out of the confrontation entirely unscathed. Don tried hard to keep the smile of relief off his face. He was actually going to have his wife back again. A proper wife who'd be there when he came home from the office every night, with a meal ready and maybe a smile and a kiss, like when Mother was alive. No more empty house and solitary meals. No more driving down to some seaside resort every weekend in order to spend a few hours with his wife. No more sharing her with those awful gushing stage people any more either; for ever kissing and calling each other '*dah-ling*'.

Very carefully he laid the bouquet down on the chair near the door and went to her. Putting his arms gently round her, he patted her tentatively as though she were a recalcitrant terrier.

'There, there, my love,' he said soothingly. 'If they don't appreciate you, I know I certainly do. It'll be so nice to see my little wife waiting for me in the kitchen when I come home at night; to have you all to myself.'

Una pushed him aside with an impatient snort. The very idea of being chained to the kitchen sink at Blakes Folly when she should be starring in the West End, her name in lights, was unbearable. It made her feel physically sick. 'Oh! Oh *shut up*,' she snapped, stamping her foot. 'Honestly, Don. You really do talk the most awful *crap* at times.'

Over the two weeks that followed Freda was busy. Shut away in her room all day she studied the script of the play.

'I want to be word perfect by the first day of rehearsals,' she told Rosalind excitedly. 'This is my big break and I want to make sure I do everything I can to make it a success.'

When the hotel was quiet in the afternoons Mrs Gresham let her use the piano in the bar to rehearse her songs. Secretly the manageress was quite excited herself at the idea of having a West End star staying at the Queen's Head. She planned to put up signed photographs in the bar and reception area once the show had opened.

It wasn't long before the press got to hear about Freda's potential rise to fame. *Sweet Violet*, the new musical, had received more than its share of advance publicity. Louis Jacobson had seen to that. His press office had dug out everything it could on the show's new star, from her humble beginnings in provincial variety theatres to the TV shows she and Ben had taken part in before their departure to

Australia. They had even cabled the Australian Broadcasting Commission's press office for copies of write-ups and reviews of the British singing duo's performances there.

When Freda arrived at the theatre on the first day of rehearsals she was surprised to find several journalists waiting for her at the stage door. Almost before she knew what was happening her photograph had been taken and she had been asked to say 'a few words' for the papers. By the end of the week her picture was on the front page of *The Stage* as well as on the showbiz pages of several national dailies.

'You're a star even before the opening night,' Rosalind told her as they read the reports together.

One or two of the more sensational tabloids had asked personal questions about her relationship with Ben, and she was dismayed to find that one of them reported that they had never married because Ben was still traumatised by his disastrous first marriage. Freda read the article with disbelief.

'I never said that!' she said. 'What on earth will Una say when she sees it?'

'Even if you didn't actually say it, it isn't very far from the truth,' Rosalind said.

Freda sighed. 'Which probably makes it all the more unpalatable. I'm grateful for one thing at least. They haven't dug out the vital connection between us yet.'

Rosalind shrugged. 'It's probably only a matter of time before they do.'

Freda nodded. 'I'm afraid you're right.' She looked sadly at Rosalind. 'I really don't want to make an enemy of her, Rossie,' she said. 'I know how devastated she must be at losing her part just as it was coming into the West End, but it was none of my doing. I wish these people would stop making so much of it.'

Rosalind said nothing. She knew that Una had been Freda's enemy long before this. There was nothing anyone could do to prevent the venomous feelings that would flow when she discovered that Freda had taken her coveted part in the play. For a moment her mind dwelt on kindly, well-meaning Don. He must be having a hell of a time!

'Only a few days to go now till we start rehearsals,' Freda said.

'I expect you'll be wanting to go and see your family before you start rehearsals.'

Freda shook her head. 'There's only my sister in Birmingham. I stayed with her when I first came back from Australia. We've never been close. She's ten years older than me and she has her own family.' She smiled. 'You're the nearest to a family I have now, Rossie.' She looked thoughtful. 'Actually, I've been thinking. How about you and me having a day's shopping?'

Rosalind shrugged. 'If you like. Is there something you particularly want?'

'I was thinking more of you.' Freda laid a hand on Rosalind's shoulder. 'Don't take this the wrong way, darling, but you could make so much more of yourself. If you agree I'd like to help show you how.'

Rosalind smiled. 'It's kind of you, but I'm afraid I'm a bit of a lost cause. I'm not pretty like you. I didn't inherit Una's looks and colouring. All my friends at school were pretty and I got resigned to the fact a long time ago that I'm just a plain Jane, like it or not.'

'That's not true,' Freda said firmly. 'You have good bone structure and beautiful eyes. Your hair is thick and shiny. There's so much you could do to bring out all that potential.'

'Someone else said that once,' Rosalind said wistfully. 'I had my hair cut and bought some new clothes at the time and – and I think I did look better too – for a little while.'

'Was that a boyfriend?' Freda asked gently.

Rosalind nodded. 'Stuart Hamilton. He designed all the sets and costumes for *Sweet Violet*. His friend wrote the

363

play. I met him when he designed a setting for one of Hallard's fashion shows. I think he only pretended to be interested in me so that he could get to know Una and Don better. Don put up the money for the show originally.'

'And Una played a leading part?' Freda's eyes widened. 'Ah! Now I see what you meant when you said that she manipulated her way into the play.'

'It was all a put up job,' Rosalind said unhappily. 'With me in the middle. Stuart used me to get to Don. But Una made sure she was part of the package.'

'And it took Jacobson to sort things out?' Freda nodded. 'Well, I must say that makes me feel slightly better about taking the part from her. Now . . .' She looked at Rosalind challengingly. 'Are you going to let me help transform you?'

She laughed, flattered that someone actually cared enough to want to help improve her appearance. 'I think you're on to a loser, but if you insist . . .'

'I do!'

Rosalind's next full day off was the Friday before rehearsals opened for Freda. They went up to the West End early and Freda took charge from the moment they came out of the underground at Oxford Circus. An expert haircut, a facial and make-up came first. Then they went to look for clothes. Freda picked out colours and styles that Rosalind would never even have considered buying for herself.

'Try it,' she said persuasively. 'Surely you're tired of all those dull browns and navy blues you've been wearing?' Gently but firmly she steered Rosalind towards the changing room. 'Just try some of them on and see what you think. If you don't like them we can put them back.'

But to her surprise Rosalind found that she did like the new styles and colours. She had never realised how good she looked in yellow before; how russet gold brought out the warmth of her eyes; or how surprisingly sophisticated she could look in black. By the time they came out of the shop she had bought a smart black suit and several blouses for work, a dress for evenings and two more dresses for everyday wear – all with the new short skirt length. Shoes followed. Freda scorned the sensible flat-heeled brogues that Rosalind had grown used to wearing in favour of feminine pumps with a pretty trim, and some sandals with higher heels for evenings.

'You have nice legs and feet. Why hide them in those clumpy things?' she scolded.

Over lunch Freda looked at Rosalind's shining eyes across the table. 'You know I was right now, don't you?'

Rosalind smiled. She was already wearing one of the new dresses and, on a visit to the cloakroom, she'd been unable to take her eyes off her reflection in the mirror, astounded at the new image of herself looking boldly back at her. 'Is all this really me?' she asked. 'I mean, will I be able to keep it up?'

'Of course you will,' Freda promised. 'It's just a question of getting into the habit of having your hair trimmed regularly and schooling yourself to the make-up routine. Maybe you could even think about getting some contact lenses too. Or at least some more flattering frames.' She leaned forward, her face serious. 'There's more than just glamorising to all this, Rossie,' she said. 'There's a practical side too. In a way your job is like mine; you're in the public eye most of the time. It's important that you look good. I know how dedicated you are to your work, so you must see the way you present yourself as part of it. Right or wrong, people do judge you by your appearance. And first impressions are vital.'

'I hadn't thought of it like that,' Rosalind said thoughtfully. 'You're right though. I can see that now.' She smiled. 'Thanks, Freda. You're the only person who has ever taken any interest in the way I look. I'm grateful.'

Freda squeezed her hand. 'It's been worth every minute,

love, just to see you blossom into the real you.' She paused. 'There's something else I want to say to you.'

'Yes?'

'What are you going to do with the cottage?'

Rosalind looked away. 'I don't know.'

'Why don't you put it on the market, Rossie? Realise the capital and invest it for your future.'

Rosalind looked up at her. 'I can't bring myself to do that. It meant so much to you and Dad. I'd feel as though I were selling a part of your life. Your dreams.'

'No.' Freda leaned earnestly towards her. 'That time has gone now. The cottage is yours. It's such a waste letting it stand there empty.'

'Would you like to go there again first – stay a few days, take a last look?'

'No.' Freda shook her head firmly. 'It's always a mistake, looking back. Ben and I were happy there. I'd prefer to keep my memories. I'd like to think that someone else might be as happy as we were.' She patted Rosalind's hand. 'Get in touch with an estate agent. Put it on the market, Rossie. I mean it.'

Una was sunning herself on the balcony of their hotel room when Don came back with the English newspapers. He dropped them on to the table beside her and went to find himself a cup of coffee. Idly, Una reached out and picked up the first of them, scanning the front page before turning to the inside. Fashion, gossip, horoscopes, showbiz . . . Suddenly her attention was riveted by a photograph of an attractive blonde. Immediately she sat up, pulling off her sunglasses as a familiar name halfway down the page caught her eye.

The caption over the photograph shouted at her in bold black letters:

366

Benita's Star In The Ascendant

Beneath it the piece read;

> *Lovely Benita Moore has replaced Una Blair in the role of Olive in Sweet Violet, the new musical that is taking London by storm. By a strange irony Benita also replaced Una six years ago as a singing partner and long-time close companion of Ben Blair, the recently deceased tenor. The partnership enjoyed success on British and Australian TV.*
>
> *Ben Blair began his career in time-honoured way with his wife, Una; first in end-of-pier concert party, then on the variety stage, to find considerable success at last with new partner Benita on TV and stage here and in Australia.*
>
> *It is understood that Una Blair was obliged to step down from her role following the prior to London run owing to problems with her voice. Already the critics are raving about Benita who, with her beautiful bell-like voice, stunning looks and sparkling personality is being hailed as a new Evelyn Laye.*

With a wail of anguish, Una picked up another paper – then another. In every one of them there was a write-up of the show. They ranged from a few guardedly optimistic words in *The Times* to a rave review in the *Daily Mail*. But in all of them Benita's performance was invariably praised to the skies.

When Don reappeared, smiling and refreshed from his coffee, he found his wife pacing the room in a state of near apoplexy.

'Look at *that*!' she shouted, thrusting a paper under his nose. 'And that and *that*!' She threw the other papers across the room where they spread themselves across the carpet like autumn leaves. 'This is that rat Monty's doing.'

'But why?' Don began to pick up the scattered papers. 'Why would he do a thing like that to you? He's your agent after all,' he said, perplexed, shaking his head.

367

'No, he isn't,' Una said defensively. 'He wanted to represent me again when I took the part in *Sweet Violet*, but I said no. I'd got the part on my own after all, so why should I let him take ten per cent of my earnings?'

Don frowned. 'Wasn't that a little short-sighted, dear?'

'Was it hell! I put him on to the boys and their play. I got him all that. Not that he deserved it. He said some very harsh things to me after Ben and I split up. He didn't want me then, so why should I let him take commission from me when I was on my feet again?'

'And you think this is his way of getting his own back?'

'I'm bloody sure it is!'

'But there's nothing you can do about it. You can't prove it.'

'I can try. My God, I can try. Don't you worry, I'll think of something.' Una picked up one of the papers and flicked frenziedly through it again, her heart quickening dangerously at the sight of Freda's beautiful face and the eulogies of the critics. When she thought of what that woman had taken from her . . . Ben was dead now. She would never see him again, let alone have him back. For the first time the finality of his death hit her and tears filled her eyes. She had loved him. No matter what anyone said, whatever he had done to her when they were married, she had never really stopped loving him. And they might have got back together again if it hadn't been for this Benita or Freda or whatever she called herself. Now, not content with that, she had taken Una's part in the play. Just as she was about to find the fame that had eluded her all these years, this woman had snatched it from under her nose. It was utterly intolerable.

With a sudden piercing scream that terrified the wits out of Don, she threw herself on to the bed and began to weep hysterically, drumming her feet on the quilt and hammering her fists into the pillows, until, to Don's consternation, she gave a gasp, shuddered violently and passed out cold.

*   *   *

368

Rosalind sat in her seat in the front of the dress circle and watched with pride as Freda took a final curtain call on her own. Although she wasn't, strictly speaking, the main character in the play, she received the greatest acclaim. Brian French's songs suited her voice to perfection and already she had been approached about recording an album of her songs from the show. Monty was currently negotiating the terms of a recording contract.

Rosalind had seen the show three times now. She had been there on the opening night, rigid with nerves and almost as keyed up as Freda herself. She'd enjoyed a more relaxed visit a month later. But tonight was a special occasion. She had heard that morning that Ivy Cottage had been sold for a sum that outshone all her expectations. After tonight's performance she was taking Freda out to celebrate.

Chapter Eighteen

Melfordleigh looked exactly the same as before she had left. Cathy felt a sense of surprise. Somehow she had expected changes, though she could not have said in quite what way. So much had happened in the month she'd been away. It was as though a lifetime had passed.

Johnny had accompanied her to Liverpool Street and seen her on to the train.

'You will write and let me know you got home safely, won't you?' she said, a look of concern in her eyes as the train began to draw out.

Cathy promised that she would, then watched bleakly as the train gathered speed and the homely figure waving from the platform grew smaller and further away.

Looking out of the window from her corner seat as the grimy buildings gave way to fields and trees she felt as though a whole segment of her life had been stripped away; torn from her, leaving a raw and painful scar that she was obliged to keep concealed. In four short weeks she had become a different person. Her own judge and jury, she had been found guilty and sentenced – for the crime she had committed against herself. But now that she was going home she must behave as though nothing had happened. It was going to be the hardest thing she had done in her whole life.

Gerald met her at the station. He greeted her absently, as though he had scarcely missed her. On the drive to Melfordleigh, she gathered from him that the seminars had gone extremely well. The four weekend concerts she had missed had been a great success, and Simon had been working hard in preparation for his concert debut. In fact, everything ran as well in her absence as it did when she was there.

At Cuckoo Lodge, Maggie regaled her with her own version of events. 'Should'a seen some of them music students who came to the jazz concert,' she said, rolling her eyes ceilingwards. 'Long hair and beads. Flared jeans, and some of 'em were wearing them what-ya-call-em – *caffeine* things.'

Cathy hid a smile. 'Caftans, I think.'

Maggie shrugged. 'Well, whatever they're called they look damn' silly on fellers,' she said. 'Makes 'em look a right bunch of jessies. A lot of the serious ones are getting to be as bad too. Little wire glasses some of 'em have taken to wearing.' She formed her fingers into circles, holding them in front of her eyes. 'Just like my old granny. Dunno what the world is coming to, I'll tell you. If my kids start wearing stuff like that they'll get the rough side of my tongue and no mistake.'

She also probed Cathy subtly about the illness that had obliged her to stay on at Johnny's for an extra two weeks.

'Shame, you being poorly while you was on holiday,' she said, peering closely at her. 'You're still looking peaky. Still, I daresay the sea air'll put the roses back. Always works a treat, does our bracing Suffolk air.' She glanced surreptitiously at Cathy out of the corner of her eye as she got on with peeling potatoes. 'What did you say was the matter?'

'I didn't,' Cathy said. 'It was just a touch of summer flu.'

Maggie nodded. 'Ah. Nasty, that can be at this time of year. We'll have to take care of you. Make sure you get plenty of good food and rest.'

Going upstairs later that evening Cathy found Gerald moving his things out of their room into a small one at the end of the corridor that they had deemed too small for

371

visitors or students. Standing in the doorway, she watched him for a moment.

'Why are you moving out of our room, Gerald?' she asked at last.

He glanced round at her. 'With some of the concerts and master classes going on so late I thought I might disturb you. There's a lot to do if I'm to be away for several weeks.'

'You've always slept in the dressing room anyway,' she reminded him. 'It seems a pity to move out. With so many other people around the house, sharing a room is the only chance we ever get to talk privately.'

He looked at her. 'Is there something you want to discuss?'

'No, but it's nice to talk – to be alone together sometimes.'

'I'm sure we can still find enough privacy for that,' he said dismissively. 'The summer season will be over soon. And Simon will be gone in a few weeks' time. We'll have the whole house to ourselves then.'

'But it will be almost time for you to go to New Zealand then.'

He patted her shoulder as he passed on his way out of the room. 'Not quite.'

Her heart rose as she followed him along the landing. 'Does that mean we could take a holiday, Gerald? Perhaps we could go back to Davos. I'd love to go there again.'

'Oh, I don't know about that.'

'Well perhaps somewhere in this country – somewhere we could be together, away from here.'

'I thought you liked this place so much.'

'Everyone deserves a break, surely?'

'I thought you'd just had one. Which reminds me . . .' He frowned as he deposited the armful of clothes he had been carrying on to the bed. 'You seem to have spent an awful lot of money during your stay with Mrs Johnson. I had the bank statement this morning.'

372

She felt the warm blood suffuse her face. 'I know, I meant to mention it. I bought a few new things – clothes.'

'From the amount you got through I'd say you bought enough to stage a fashion show.'

'I hadn't bought anything new since we first married, Gerald. You don't grudge me the money, do you?'

'I wouldn't if we had it. I'm still paying the builders, you know. I don't think you realise just how much the school cost to get off the ground.'

'Perhaps that's because you never discuss anything with me,' she countered.

'There's no reason why I should bother you with it – normally,' he said. 'Then there's the expense of my operation looming. It's going to be some time before we're clear of debt.'

'I see. I'm sorry.'

'Well, now that you know I'm sure you'll be careful.' He glanced at her. 'As a matter of fact I've had a bit of luck. A piece of music I wrote some time ago is about to be published.'

'I didn't know you ever wrote music.'

'As I said, it was some time ago. A rhapsody for piano and orchestra. Once royalties for that start coming in things will be easier. It will help to remind the public that I'm still around too.'

'Congratulations.' She began putting his shirts away in the drawers. 'Gerald, if we can't have a holiday, what shall we do with the two weeks we have before you leave? Perhaps we could see some of the countryside. There seems to have been no time at all for us to be together what with the school and everything.'

He sighed. 'It's a nice idea, but I may have to go up to London for some of that time. As I said, there are things I need to tie up before I leave. I'd rather like to be at Simon's first concert too.'

'I see.' Her heart sank. It was almost as though he was

373

finding every possible excuse not to spend any time alone with her. 'Maybe Johnny will come and stay with me for a few days.'

'I daresay.'

'I saw Rosalind Blair while I was home,' she went on. 'I thought it might be nice if she could visit while you're away.'

He frowned. 'Rosalind Blair?'

'Yes. She's a school friend. She was at the wedding, remember?'

'An ungainly dark girl? Glasses and frumpy clothes?' He shrugged. 'If you're desperate for company invite her by all means.'

The weeks passed drearily. Gerald was fully occupied with coaching Simon and preparing for his approaching absence. Cathy walked on the dunes. Sometimes she took her paints and tried to lose herself in the hobby, but somehow the pleasure seemed to have gone out of it. Would Gerald's operation really change anything between them? What had she done to make him fall so completely out of love with her? Would there ever really be a new start now that he had changed so much? Once he was well again would he want to go back to his old life and his friends, especially Kay?

Although she tried hard not to think of it, her mind was constantly haunted by thoughts of the baby she might have had. In the bleak small hours of her lonely wakeful nights the questions and speculations heaped one upon the other. Would her child have been a boy or a girl? Would it have looked like her? Would her father's grandchild have inherited his gentle nature and his musical talent? Now she would never know and it seemed unbearably, intolerably sad. In the dark empty hours she longed for the comfort of Gerald's arms; the closeness they had once shared which seemed now a thing of the past. Sometimes she thought she would never recover from the feeling of loss.

Before she had returned to Melfordleigh, Johnny insisted on taking her to a doctor to make sure no damage had been done. The doctor, a stranger in another part of London whom she had paid for a private consultation, had examined her thoroughly. If he had been suspicious about the reason for her miscarriage he had not shown it. To her relief he had pronounced her well, if a little anaemic. But no amount of probings or medicine – not even Johnny's wise counselling – could come anywhere near healing the deep wound in her heart. Had she made the sacrifice for nothing? Could Gerald possibly have loved her any the less if he had known of her adultery?

Late one afternoon at the beginning of October she was walking back towards the village when she saw a figure coming towards her. Too late she recognised Simon. Lately he had grown his hair longer and taken to wearing the slim-fitting shirts and flared jeans so despised by Maggie. He raised a hand to wave to her. Reluctantly she acknowledged the greeting and stood still, resigned, waiting for him to catch her up.

'Thought I might find you out here,' he said. 'I've been wanting to talk to you. I'm off next week as you know and I thought I might not get another chance.'

She kept on walking. 'I don't think you and I really have anything to talk about, Simon.'

'I think we do.' He put out a hand to stop her and she turned and looked at him. 'Sit down a moment,' he said. 'There's no hurry to get back, is there?'

'No, except . . .' She shivered. 'It gets cold in the afternoons now.' Reluctantly she sat down among the tall, wiry grass, wrapping her arms around herself.

He lowered himself beside her. 'Are you all right, Cathy?'

'Of course. Why wouldn't I be?'

'Anyone with half an eye can see you're not happy. And you don't look well either.'

'Well, that's my problem, isn't it?'

'It's not because of me, is it? You're not angry – about what happened between us?'

'No.' She glanced quickly at him. Was it possible that he had guessed? 'It's ancient history. It wasn't important anyway.'

'I know you regret it, but I want you to know that I don't. It was something special to me, Cathy. Even if I did handle it clumsily.' He looked at her. 'I meant what I said, you know. You should never have married Gerald. He isn't right for you.'

'And I meant what *I* said; that it's none of your business.' She wished with all her heart that it was time for him to leave. There would be no peace until then. Every time she was forced to look at him she was reminded of the child they had conceived.

For a moment he was silent, then he turned to her and said, 'You know she's going to New Zealand with him, don't you?'

Her head snapped round to look at him. 'Who?'

'Kay, of course. Who else? Oh, look, Cathy, I know I probably shouldn't be telling you this, but she was here while you were away. Ostensibly it was to see me and arrange the publicity for the tour, but anyone can see that there's something going on between her and Gerald. She's flying out with him on the fourth. I heard her mention it. Oh, not purposely to be with him. It's true that she does have business of her own there. But nevertheless . . .'

'Gerald is ill. He's going to New Zealand for an operation. You know all that,' she said. 'We can't afford for me to go too, so if Kay has to go to New Zealand on business it's good that she should keep him company.' She turned to glare angrily at him. 'Why are you so determined to make trouble between us?' She got up and began to walk away very fast, but he scrambled to his feet and was soon walking beside her.

376

'I'm not trying to make trouble. If it's all as innocent as you say, why didn't you know about it?'

'I *did*!' she protested unconvincingly. Tears of humiliation sprang to her eyes and Simon grasped her arm and swung her round to face him.

'Cathy! Believe it or not, I do *care* about you. I happen to think you're getting a raw deal and I don't like to see you being deceived.'

'Maybe it's no more than I deserve,' she said bitterly. 'After all, we – *I* deceived him, didn't I?'

'You think I'm being disloyal, don't you?'

'Since you ask, I think you could show more loyalty and respect to the man who has devoted more than a year of his life to your career,' she said. 'You owe him that at least.'

He walked beside her in silence for a moment. 'I meant it when I said I wanted us to be friends,' he said at last.

'*Friends?*' She stopped and turned to face him, her mind in turmoil. If he only knew! At that moment she longed to tell him of the price she had paid for a moment's vulnerability; of the heartbreaking sacrifice, the risk and pain she had put herself through. She stopped herself just in time. 'I don't want to hear any of this, Simon,' she said, her voice trembling. 'When I need help to sort out my life I'll ask someone and it won't be you. If we don't speak again I hope your concert tour – and your future career – is a success. Now will you please leave me alone?'

Simon left for his concert tour ten days later and on the following Monday Gerald began to pack. He planned to go to London first then on to Manchester where Simon was to make his debut. He would fly to New Zealand from there.

'You won't be back then?' Cathy asked as she helped him choose the clothes he would take.

'It hardly seems worth it. I can tie up a lot of loose ends while I'm in town, then fly out from Manchester the day after the concert.'

'Shall I come with you? To London, I mean.'

He turned to stare at her. 'Why?'

'I thought – you might like to have me with you,' she said quietly. 'We see so little of each other and you'll be away at least six weeks altogether.'

He fastened the case he had finished packing and turned to look at her. As their eyes met his face relaxed a little. 'I'm sorry, Cathy. All this hasn't been much fun for you, has it?' He put his arms around her awkwardly, as though she were a stranger. 'I really can't see much point in you coming to London though. You'd be bored, sitting alone for hours while I was out.'

'I daresay Johnny would put us up if I asked her,' she said hopefully.

He shook his head firmly. 'No, Cathy.'

'What is this business you have to do?' she asked.

'It's mostly to do with the school,' he told her vaguely. 'And I have to see James Kendrick, my agent, too. There is talk of a première of my rhapsody. Erhart Froebel the conductor is looking for new works to perform at a special concert he's planning for next year's Proms. James thought it might be nice if Simon could be the soloist and he's going to try to arrange a meeting between the three of us.'

'So – where will you stay?' she asked.

'With a friend.'

'Which friend?'

Gerald frowned impatiently, his moment of compassion forgotten. 'Oh, for heaven's sake, Cathy! Does it matter?'

The house seemed bleak when everyone had gone. Once again Melfordleigh seemed to be settling down for winter. Maggie had reluctantly asked for time off. Her widowed father, who lived on the other side of Ipswich, had just come out of hospital following an operation and she wanted to bring him to stay with her for a while. Cathy didn't need her anyway, so she agreed.

'Are you sure you won't mind being in this great place all on your own?' Maggie asked her anxiously.

Assuming a cheerfulness she did not feel, Cathy assured her that she would not, adding that even when the house was full she was alone.

Lying in bed in the empty house, listening to the north wind buffeting the chimneys, she thought about what Simon had told her. Was Kay really going to New Zealand with Gerald? Perhaps she was the 'friend' he was staying with in London. Next morning, obsessed with the desire to find out, she looked through the address book in the study for Kay's telephone number. For a long moment she sat staring uncertainly at the telephone. She was behaving like a suspicious wife and despised herself for it. Then, making up her mind, she reached out and dialled the number with trembling fingers. After several rings she was about to put the receiver down when it was lifted. A male voice answered by repeating the number. The voice was unmistakably Gerald's. Without speaking she dropped the receiver back on to its rest, her heart thudding dully in her chest. So it was true.

Sick with the thoughts that tormented her and desperate for company to block them out, she rang Johnny.

'Gerald left two days ago. You did say you'd come and stay.'

'Oh, Cathy.' Johnny's voice was apologetic. 'I'm sorry, love. It's impossible at the moment. Mother was rushed into hospital yesterday. It's another stroke, I'm afraid, and they aren't very optimistic this time. I have to be close at hand.'

'Of course. I understand. Poor Johnny. I'm so sorry.'

She sat for a long time in front of the telephone, then she picked up the receiver again and dialled the number of the Queen's Head. It was Rosalind who answered.

'Queen's Head. Reception. Can I help you?'

'Rosalind? It's Cathy Cavelle.'

379

'Cathy! How are you?'

'I'm fine, thanks. Look, how about coming for that visit? Can you get any time off?'

'I'd love to come, Cathy. I am due some time in lieu of overtime, and it's half term at college next week. I'm not sure how long I have off though. Can I get back to you?'

'Of course. I'll wait to hear from you.'

Rosalind rang back an hour later with the news that she could have a week off beginning the following Saturday. She sounded pleased and excited, but no less so than Cathy. Delighted at having something to do, she ran upstairs to get a room ready, choosing one that had a view of the garden and got the morning sun.

She met the train at Ipswich. Standing eagerly on the platform as it drew alongside, she watched the passengers disembark. Rosalind, to her disappointment, did not seem to be among them. She was just turning away when she felt a hand on her sleeve.

'Cathy.'

Turning, she was surprised to see her friend standing there – but a very different Rosalind from the one she had seen only a few weeks before. This tall slim girl in the smart tailored suit, with her hair cut in a sleek style, her face expertly made-up and minus the glasses she had always worn, looked totally different. The overall improvement was so overwhelming that Cathy felt it would be tactless to mention it.

'Rosalind!' she laughed. 'I didn't recognise you without your glasses.'

'Contact lenses,' she explained. 'They take a bit of getting used to, but I think the effect is worth it.'

Cathy took her case and drew her towards the barrier. 'Come on,' she said. 'We'll get a taxi. I can't wait to hear all your news.'

The taxi dropped them at the gate of Cuckoo Lodge and Rosalind stood staring in stunned amazement at the lovely old house with its mellow red brickwork glowing gently in the watery autumn sunshine.

'Oh, Cathy,' she exclaimed. 'I'd no idea it was so beautiful. You must be so proud of it.'

Cathy smiled. 'If you're interested I'll show you the photographs that were taken before the restoration work began.'

Inside Rosalind was entranced by the spacious drawing room with its inglenook fireplace and low-beamed ceiling. She was impressed by the studios, and the kitchen delighted her.

'You've managed to keep the character of the place whilst including all the up-to-date mod cons,' she said, looking round at the gleaming worktops, the cupboards and the Aga in its tiled recess.

'A bit of a cheat really,' Cathy told her. 'This part of the house is completely new. You should have seen the state of the old kitchen. I think it was added in Victorian times and it would have given you nightmares.'

Upstairs Rosalind looked into all the rooms with their pretty furnishings and bright colour schemes, expressing her approval again and again. 'Did you have a hand in the design?' she asked.

'Partly. We had the advice of a professional, but I chose most of the colour schemes and fabrics myself.'

It all seemed so long ago that she could scarcely remember the fun and excitement of it any more. The home she had helped so lovingly to restore now felt alien to her – almost like a prison sometimes. And Gerald's music school, the dream project they had planned together that had once excited her so much, now seemed like something that had nothing to do with her.

Her pensiveness did not escape Rosalind. Again she saw the sad, wistful expression that had clouded the other girl's face the last time they had met. There was something not quite right about her life. Rosalind wished they knew each other well enough for her to try and help.

Cathy suddenly smiled and took her arm. 'Come and see the barn. It's been converted into a concert hall. Then I'll show you the garden and the mill stream. Do you like ducks?'

Rosalind laughed. 'Yes.'

'Good. We'll take some scraps and you can feed them.'

Later that evening, after they had eaten and Rosalind had seen and marvelled at the photographs of Cuckoo Lodge in its original derelict state, the girls settled down before a log fire in the drawing room and Rosalind told Cathy her news – about her father's will and selling the cottage.

'I've never had any real money of my own before,' she said. 'It's a strange feeling. I've invested it for the moment, but I feel I should do something meaningful with it. Something that Dad would have approved of; that would have made him proud of me.'

'Do you have anything in mind?' Cathy asked.

'What I really want – what I've always wanted – is to buy a hotel of my own,' Rosalind said wistfully. 'If I could find a house, somewhere like this for instance, and turn it into a small hotel that would be marvellous. But the money I got for the cottage isn't nearly enough for that kind of ambitious enterprise.' She sighed. 'Isn't it funny? In some ways it seems such a lot of money, yet it isn't nearly enough to do what I really want.'

'You don't have to put down all of the money,' Cathy pointed out. 'You could get a mortgage, and probably a bank loan to start your business if you could convince the bank that it was a worthwhile venture.'

Rosalind nodded. 'I've learned a lot about management since I've been at the Queen's Head and college. Perhaps I'm not really quite adventurous enough. The idea of taking that kind of risk terrifies me. Supposing it all went wrong and I lost the money?'

'I'm sure you wouldn't.'

Rosalind shook her head. 'It would be an awfully big thing to take on by myself. I don't think I'd have the confidence.' She went on to tell Cathy about Freda's return to England and, listening to the warmth and affection in the other girl's voice, Cathy realised how much of an influence Ben Blair's singing partner was on Rosalind. A good one too by the sound of it. Clearly it was Freda who was responsible for the change in Rosalind's appearance and the new self-confidence she exuded. Cathy found herself wishing she could meet the woman who cared enough about Ben Blair's daughter to take her under her wing.

'Freda has real talent. She's been lucky enough to get a major part in a musical play in the West End,' Rosalind was saying. She went on to explain how Freda had been cast in the part her mother had lost in *Sweet Violet*.

'Oh, dear, that must have been awkward for you,' Cathy said sympathetically. 'How did your mother take it?'

'I haven't seen her. She hasn't been in touch since I left home, so I don't really know,' Rosalind said. She pulled a wry face. 'I can imagine though. She'll have been bitterly disappointed at missing playing in the West End. It was always her dream to see her name up in lights.' She sighed. 'It won't have helped when she found out that Freda was taking her part over either. I daresay poor Don is bearing the brunt of it.'

'You and your step-father got along all right in the end then?'

Rosalind blushed. 'I'm ashamed to say that I misjudged him,' she said. 'I have a lot to be grateful to him for. It wasn't his fault that I left home.' She paused, wishing she knew Cathy well enough to confide in her about the shameful stealing of the Meissen figure. It was something she had been too ashamed even to tell Freda. Maybe someday, if she was lucky, she would find a friend in whom to confide. Someone she could be sure would understand and forgive.

'So maybe it's as well you're not at home at the moment,' Cathy said with a smile.

'Yes – although . . .' Rosalind glanced wistfully round her. 'Being here in your lovely home makes me dread going back to that dingy little room of mine at the Queen's Head. It felt like a haven at first, but now it's beginning to depress me.'

Cathy could well imagine that it was. She had only been in Rosalind's room once but she knew that the lack of space, the threadbare brown carpet and porridge-coloured walls would depress her too if she was obliged to live there. 'You could use some of your legacy to buy a flat,' she suggested. But Rosalind shook her head.

'I want to save the money for the future.'

Cathy nodded. 'Well, you're always welcome here whenever you can take some time off,' she said with a smile. 'I'll be glad of the company. I get lonely sometimes when Gerald is working.'

When it was time for Rosalind to leave both girls were sorry. The week had flown so quickly and they had enjoyed each other's company so much. Cathy had enjoyed showing Rosalind the village; the quay and the dunes, the little craft shops and art galleries. Once they had lunched at the Admiral Nelson, but most evenings they had cooked together in the kitchen at Cuckoo Lodge. For Cathy it was a treat to have someone to cook for, and to have the kitchen to herself, though she did not tell Rosalind that. It would have sounded so strange that she rarely cooked a meal for her husband and did not have full access to many of the rooms in her own home.

That week Cathy had seen a side of Rosalind she never knew existed. She had always liked the quiet, slightly nervous girl, but had never realised they had so much in common or shared so many opinions. When they said goodbye at the station, promising to write and keep in touch, what had been a casual acquaintanceship had developed into a warm friendship. It was with genuine regret that Cathy waved goodbye and went back to Melfordleigh and the empty house.

Cathy had booked a call to the hospital in Auckland for early on the morning following the day scheduled for Gerald's operation. She was up bright and early on the day in question and as she made coffee in the kitchen she reflected that it would now be eight p.m. in New Zealand, whilst here it was still breakfast time. A whole world separated herself and Gerald. A whole world – and so much more. She had received two postcards from him since he left. One from Manchester, telling her of the success of Simon's first concert; the other was posted soon after his arrival in New Zealand, giving her the date of his operation.

She was just finishing her breakfast when the telephone rang. The hospital receptionist put her call straight through to the ward where a Sister told her briskly that Gerald was resting comfortably after a good night's sleep. As far as could be ascertained the operation had been a complete success and so far he was doing very well.

Cathy replaced the receiver with a sigh of relief. So – the first hurdle was over. Would this operation really turn Gerald into a different person? Would his love for her return, or would he want to turn back the clock, pick up the threads of his old life again? Only time would tell. With luck he would be home for Christmas. She must start preparing for it. Christmas had become an unlucky time for her over the past few years. Somehow something bad always seemed to happen at this time of year. But perhaps now she had reached a turning-point. Perhaps this year would be the happiest Christmas she had known since the last she had shared with Dad.

Cathy telephoned the people on the list he had left, noting with some irony that Kay's name was not included. Her first

385

call was to James Kendrick, his agent. He was delighted at the news.

'I'm glad you've called, Cathy,' he said. 'There has been quite a bit of interest in Gerald's rhapsody. You probably know that Simon is to be the soloist at its first performance next August?'

'No, I didn't know,' she said dryly.

'Yes. We finalised the details while he was here a couple of weeks ago. As you know, word soon gets around on the grapevine and enquiries have been coming in ever since. I wondered if he had any more copies?'

Cathy shook her head. 'I've no idea. I suppose I could have a look though.'

'I'd be grateful if you would. The original is with Froebel at the moment and I'm still waiting for the first batch of copies from the publisher to arrive. I don't want to let any opportunities slip.'

'I'll have a look and ring you back, James.'

When she had finished her calls Cathy looked through the music library Gerald kept stored in files in the study, but she could find no more copies of his composition. Knowing that he would almost certainly not have parted with the only copy she tried to think where it might be. He had said it was something he had written some years ago. Could there be another copy in one of the boxes stored in the attic? She pictured the boxes stacked away in the roof space and shrank from the thought of searching them. Some had come from her home, some from Gerald's flat. Most of them contained little-used things they had meant to sort out long ago. Somehow they had never got round to it, but she had very little else to do. It would be a good opportunity to deal with a long delayed chore.

On the landing she pulled down the extending ladder that led up into the attic and climbed into the void. When the house was restored Gerald had made sure the attic was wired for electric light and the floor was boarded. Finding the switch, Cathy made her way over to the corner where the boxes were stacked. Luckily they were all labelled with either her name or Gerald's. The first one she searched was full of books, which she carefully repacked and put aside. The next contained a mixture; magazines, newspaper clippings and press cuttings of Gerald's, some of them dating back more than twenty years. There was a thick manilla document wallet too. Glancing at the contents she saw that it contained some hand-written manuscripts. Perhaps the one she was looking for was among them. She put it to one side.

It was then that she noticed, right at the bottom of the packing case, an old cigar box full of letters. She took one out and looked at the envelope. It had Gerald's name and an unfamiliar address written on it in faded ink. The writing looked feminine. There were others in the box, a dozen or more of them, all with the same handwriting. After a moment's hesitation she took the letter out of the envelope in her hand. Inside was a sheet of notepaper, lilac-coloured and faintly scented. There was no address, but it was dated 20 August 1945. It read:

My darling

So the war is over at last. That terrible new atomic bomb they've dropped on Japan. It's like some frightening apocalypse. So much suffering and death makes life seem so much more precious. Fifty-five million killed in the war, so they say. What a tragic waste. But in a way it has helped to make up my mind, my love. Life is too short to resist the way fate intended us to live it. I've finally decided, my darling, to do as you say. I'll come to you. Now that peace has come your career can begin and I want more than anything else in the world to be your help and support. I want you to have the success you deserve.

387

We'll be together, just the two of us. I'll get a job and work for us both so that you can go back to college and study for the great career you must surely have.

I can't pretend that it won't be a dreadful wrench, Gerald, leaving everything behind. Leaving my darling baby will be the hardest thing I have ever done. But when we are settled perhaps I can have her to live with us. Whatever happens I can't bear to lose you. You are all I have ever wanted. I long to be close to you where I belong. To feel your arms around me and to know we need never part again. I can only pray that they will understand one day and that they will find it in their hearts to forgive me.

Please let me know as soon as you can what arrangements you have made so that we can start making plans.

My heart is always with you.

Ever your loving Jenny.

For a long moment Cathy sat staring at the signature on the bottom of the letter. *Jenny*. Gerald had said that his wife's name was Sarah and that his marriage had ended at the beginning of the war. This letter was dated 1945. She tried to ignore the vile suspicion hovering like a dark evil shadow in the corner of her mind. Surely it could not be possible . . .? The thought repelled her, churning her stomach and quickening her heart. Not wanting proof, yet unable to resist the temptation to find out, she took out another letter. It was dated a year later.

Gerald

I'm sorry we quarrelled last weekend. I hate having our precious time together spoilt, but I really can't believe that you meant to be so heartless. You promised that I could have Catherine to live with us. If Daniel agreed to a divorce I would almost certainly get custody of her, but you won't let me ask him. If I were free we could be married. Why are you so adamant about not getting a divorce – and not telling Daniel I am with you? I came to you willingly. Are you ashamed of our love?

The only way I can have Catherine with me now is to throw myself on Daniel's mercy and beg. But you even refuse to let me do this! Already I have lost more than a year of her life. I will be a stranger to her if I don't do something to get her back soon. Please try to understand what it means to me. How it breaks my heart to be parted from her. Will you please try to come home from college this weekend so that we can talk?

Yours,
Jenny

Cathy sat down on her heels. So it was true. Gerald had been her mother's lover; the man she had deserted her husband and child for. And Dad had never known. He couldn't have. And through all those years Gerald had continued to masquerade as his friend.

Bitter, angry tears scalded her eyes. Jenny, her mother, *had* loved and wanted her after all. It had been Gerald who had kept them apart. How could he have been so cruel? But what was the rest of the story? What had happened to Jenny? Maybe the rest of the letters in the box held some clues. Painful though it was she felt compelled to read them. Taking out another she saw that it was headed Trouville, France, May 1947. It read:

Oh my darling,
How I miss you! So much. So very much.
I have settled in well here. Your friends the Labeque family are very nice and the children

389

are sweet and very well behaved. You would be surprised at how well they speak English already. The little girl, Suzanne, reminds me so much of my little Catherine. She has the same green eyes and coppery hair. She is almost five, not much older than Catherine must be now. I can hardly believe that my baby will soon be going to school.

I hope your concert went well, my darling. How I would have loved to be there. It would have made me so proud to see you make your debut. But, as you said, this is best. It is not for long. Daniel would never think of trying to find me here in France and as I am living en famille, the money I earn is all mine. I will enclose as much as I can to help pay your tutor what you owe him.

I hope you will be able to come over soon. Madame Labeque says you are welcome any time. I long so much to see you, darling.

Always yours,
Jenny

At the bottom of the letter there was a postscript. It read:

Monsieur Labeque is teaching me to drive so that I can take the children to school. When I am proficient I am to have the use of Madame's car. Isn't that generous? It feels very strange to be driving on the wrong side of the road though! All my love – J

Cathy stared down at the faded writing for a long time. He had sent her to work as an au-pair in France – because, as she suggested in the letter, Daniel might try to find her? Or had it been so that she would not be tempted to try to see her little daughter and press for divorce?

There were other letters in the same vein. Slowly it became clear that Gerald had been too busy, or too occupied with his newfound success, to go over to France to see the woman who loved him. No doubt by this time he had become bored with her selfless devotion. He was afraid she would grow tired of waiting – obtain a divorce and be free for the marriage he had promised but had no intention of fulfilling. He had successfully got her out of the way.

Finally there was just one more letter at the bottom of the box. This time in a strange handwriting and penned in uncertain English. It was headed: Trouville, France, August 1948

My dear Gerald
Following the cable sent yesterday.

I cannot tell you how very sorry I was to be the bearer of such bad news. Your friend, Mrs Jenny Oldham, was taken to hospital following a crash made as she was returning from taking the children to school. Surgery was performed, but sadly she did not recover. I cabled and am writing to you as I have found no address for her husband or family among her effects. Can you please inform her relatives and make known for me the arrangements they would wish for her enterrement as soon as possible? Again, I am so sorry to write with such sad news. Madeleine and I would be happy to see you when you are next in France.

Yours in great sympathie.
Armand Labeque

With a feeling of overwhelming sadness, Cathy replaced the letters in the box and covered them with the rest of the papers from the packing case. Then she went downstairs. For a long time she sat in the kitchen, numb with shock at the discovery she had made. Gerald had been the one who had broken up her family all those years ago. He had seduced her mother and then, bored with her and irritated

391

by her constant longing for her child, had packed her off to his friends in France. But why did he not send her back to her husband? Perhaps he had been afraid that the scandal might become public and tarnish his glamorous image – threaten his promising career as a concert pianist. He had taken Jenny away from the husband and child who loved and needed her, cynically allowed her to support him through his studies, then neglected her, leaving her to die among strangers.

The sound of the telephone ringing in the study jerked her out of the daze she was in and sent her hurrying to the study to answer it. It was James Kendrick. His voice sounded so normal and ordinary that she felt as though she had just wakened from a bad dream.

'Ah, Cathy. I thought I'd better give you a call. I now have some proof copies of Gerald's rhapsody. They arrived from the publisher's just after lunch. So if you've been tearing the place to pieces you can relax. Besides, I daresay he wouldn't want to part with his own original copy.'

'Oh.' With an enormous effort Cathy pulled her scattered thoughts together. 'Oh, yes the manuscript. I have been looking but I didn't find another copy. Thank you for letting me know, James.'

'Quite all right. No more news of Gerald?'

'What? Oh, no. No more news.'

'Well, it's early days, isn't it? And the worst is over. Let me know when you hear anything. Take care, Cathy. 'Bye.'

'Goodbye.'

For a long time she sat on the edge of the chair in the study, trying to take in the full implications of the discovery she had just made – trying to make some sense of her life. But all she could think of was the baby she had sacrificed for Gerald's sake.

Cathy did not ring the hospital in New Zealand again. She could not bring herself to do it. But a week later a cheerful letter arrived from Gerald. He was recovering well, he told her. In fact he had not felt so well for a long time. The operation was nothing short of a miracle. His weakened muscles were already stronger and daily physiotherapy was helping enormously. The surgeon was delighted with his progress and would allow him out of hospital in another week's time. He would need to stay in Auckland for a further two weeks, however, to convalesce and would need to see the surgeon again for a final check before flying home. The only piece of news that did not concern his health was that he had heard from James Kendrick that the final arrangements for the première of his rhapsody at next season's Promenade Concerts had been made.

I shall look forward to next summer now with renewed enthusiasm. Who knows? Perhaps I too will be playing at next season's proms. Already my mind is buzzing with plans and ideas.

Already Cathy sensed that they did not include her. Perhaps they never had.

Maggie dropped in to see her at least twice a week.

'I don't know how you stand it, alone in this great place,' she remarked one bleak day in early-December. 'I mean, the place is usually full of people. It must be strange.' She peered into Cathy's wan face with concern. 'You know where I live if you want a bit of company, don't you? You'll have to take us as you find us, mind. Teenagers make such a muck of the place. Fast as you clean up, there they are with their clothes all over the place and their records blaring out, driving you up the pole.' She grinned good-naturedly. 'Still, the kettle's always on.'

Cathy smiled, touched by the older woman's concern. 'You must be busy, with your father there and two growing children to look after?'

Maggie laughed. 'Bless you, I'm used to that. One day they'll be gone, so better make the most of it while I've still got them. Dad's going on fine now. He's very independent – already started whittling about going home. He's quite a help to me: does a bit of shopping and washing up; pushes the Hoover round.' She patted Cathy's arm. 'Mr Cavelle be home soon now, will he?'

'In time for Christmas, I think,' she said dully. 'I haven't heard anything definite yet. It's summer over there now so he'll feel the cold when he gets back.'

'You'll have to take good care of him. Get the place well warmed up.' Maggie looked out of the window at the wintry day outside. 'Could do with a bit of sunshine myself,' she said. 'And so could you by the look of you. You'll have to get him to take you away somewhere for a nice holiday when he gets back. Before next season's rush begins.'

Before next season's rush. The words had an empty ring to Cathy. Bleakly she wondered where she would be by then.

By the second week in December Cathy was ready for Christmas. She had decided to wait until Gerald was completely well again before confronting him with her discovery. Maybe he had some explanation. Perhaps he deeply regretted what had happened all those years ago. After all, he had kept Jenny's letters. Cathy would give him the chance to put his side of the story.

The following Friday was a bleak, wintry day, the wind churning the sea into boiling fury and the sky strewn with ragged clouds. Maggie was back. She had just begun preparing Gerald's study for what she called a 'good bottoming' in preparation for his return. Cathy was on her way upstairs when she heard the crunch of car wheels on the gravel outside. Looking out of the landing window she was astonished to see Kay getting out of her car. She wore a full-length ranch mink coat, which she hugged closely round her as she made a dash for the front porch.

Maggie, who had heard her arrival too, was just coming out of the study, her hair tied up in a scarf, when Cathy ran down the stairs.

'It's all right, Maggie. I'll get it,' she called on her way. As she pulled open the door her heart was beating unevenly. What on earth could bring Kay all the way from London? Had something happened to Gerald?

The moment the door was open Kay almost fell in through it. 'God, what a place!' she gasped. 'You can hardly breathe for the wind out there. I don't know how you stand it.'

'Hello, Kay,' Cathy said dryly. 'What a surprise. Can I do something for you?'

Kay was taking off her coat and untying the scarf from her hair. 'A cup of coffee would be nice,' she said. 'A gin and tonic would be even better.' She threw the coat over a chair and looked Cathy in the eye. 'But I haven't come all this way to socialise. We have to talk, Cathy.' She looked around her. 'You are alone, I take it?'

'Apart from Maggie.' Cathy's stomach churned uneasily. 'Is it serious – bad news?'

Kay looked at her oddly. 'Perhaps we could go some-where where we won't be disturbed? I'd rather we weren't overheard.'

Without a word Cathy led the way into the drawing room and closed the door. She could hear the sound of the vacuum cleaner coming from behind the closed study door, Maggie's voice rising above it with a spirited rendering of *If You Were the Only Girl In The World*. She turned to Kay who had already made herself comfortable in a chair near the fire.

'Would you like that drink first?'

She shook her head. For the first time she looked edgy. 'I think we'd better get this over,' she said. 'Sit down, Cathy.'

In spite of the fact that she resented being told what

to do in her own home, Cathy sat in the chair opposite and looked expectantly at the other woman. Kay opened her bag and took out a cigarette. As she lit it Cathy saw that her hands trembled slightly. She drew deeply on it and blew out a thin stream of smoke before she said: 'The fact is, Gerald won't be coming home.'

Cathy's heart missed a beat. 'Something's gone wrong? His treatment . . .?'

'No, no! Nothing like that,' Kay said with an impatient shake of her head. 'Look, there's really only one way to say this, Cathy. He wants a divorce. He's leaving you.'

'I see.' She found that she was icily calm. 'And is there a reason? Am I to be allowed to hear it? I take it you know?'

Kay drew hard on her cigarette and threw back her head defiantly. 'Of course. He intends to marry me. We've been close for years, Cathy. I'm sure you know that. We should have married a long time ago. He needs me. I understand him as no one else ever could. When he married you he wasn't in his right mind. His illness clouded his judgement.'

'Really?' Cathy felt detached – unreal. It was such a bizarre situation. 'In what way?'

Kay shrugged. 'Maybe he saw it as clutching at life while there was still time. Now that he's well again and thinking rationally he knows it was a terrible mistake – for you both.'

'In other words, he's regained his sanity and turned back to you?'

Kay looked hard at Cathy. 'I must say you're taking it all very coolly.'

'Perhaps there's something you should know, Kay,' she said. 'Something I've only just discovered for myself. Gerald is a liar and a cheat. His only real consideration is himself and his career. Twenty years ago he broke up a marriage, split a family and caused a lot of suffering and heartbreak. How do you think I felt when I found out recently that the

396

family was mine? That the woman he ran away with was my mother? The wife of Gerald's best friend.'

For a long moment the two looked at each other. Then Kay said: 'I know.'

Cathy stared at her. 'You know?'

'Yes.' She ground out her cigarette. 'He told me the whole story a few days ago. I've been in New Zealand myself, Cathy. I had to go over on business, so I was able to be with him. Gerald and I have talked a lot over the past weeks. Serious illness makes people do a lot of soul searching. It was good I was there for him. He married you for a variety of reasons. You reminded him of her – Jenny. Maybe it was partly out of some wish to put right the wrong he did; partly some vague notion of regaining his lost youth. Who knows? As I said before, he wasn't himself. But all it did was give him an inflated sense of guilt and bring back memories he'd hoped were dead and buried. Now he wants to turn back the clock and return to his concert career.'

'I see. Just like that? As though I didn't exist.' Cathy looked around her. 'And what about all this? What about this house and the school, the people booked for next year's seminars and concerts? The pupils he has lined up for his return?'

Kay waved a dismissive hand. 'You can cancel them, can't you? As soon as he's back in circulation Gerald will see to it that the house is put up for sale and that you're all right financially, of course.'

'Oh, yes, that's Gerald's way isn't it? To cancel everything he's bored with. Turn over a new page in the Cavelle saga and begin a new chapter. Never mind the trail of havoc he leaves behind.'

'I tried to tell him it was wrong at the time, Cathy. He did you a grave disservice and he knows it now. He's trying to make amends, so why not let him? Oh, come now – can you honestly say he made you happy?'

'That's not the point. A marriage is between two people

397

and so is the breaking of it. Why couldn't Gerald have talked to me about this himself?'

'It's better this way. He isn't up to it yet. He knows he can rely on me to handle it tactfully.'

'He's lucky to have you. I'm beginning to see it now,' Cathy said dryly. 'What happens next then?'

'First we're going to have a holiday together. Right away from everything and everyone.'

'From me, you mean. From Melfordleigh and me.'

'Don't be bitter.' Kay reached out a tentative hand to touch Cathy's arm. 'Why not cut your losses and make a new start? You're still so young. You have your whole life in front of you. As for your mother . . . it was all so long ago. And it takes two, you know. She ran out on you and your father. Jenny had to be at least fifty per cent to blame.'

'Don't you *dare* speak my mother's name!' Cathy was on her feet, her cheeks pink and her eyes blazing. 'You know *nothing* about her or the suffering Gerald put her and my father through. She wanted to have me with her. She probably wanted to come back to us, but he wouldn't let her. He was afraid of a scandal. He thought he might be named in a divorce case. He wasn't risking that. So he sent her abroad and she died there. Convenient, wasn't it? And poor Dad never even knew that Gerald – his so-called best friend – was the cause of it all.'

'He did try to make amends, you know,' Kay said quietly. 'He even bought music from your father to pay for your school fees.'

'He did *what*?' Cathy's colour faded.

'Bought compositions of your father's. Little jingles he knew would never be published. To finance your education at some private school. He did it to try to make up for what had happened. So don't judge him too harshly, Cathy. None of us is perfect – not even you, I daresay.'

She flushed warmly, stung to silence as she wondered if

Simon had said anything to Kay about their brief affair. The other woman rose to her feet.

'I think perhaps I'd better go now.' She walked to the door, then turned. 'I wouldn't get any vindictive ideas about refusing to divorce him,' she said. 'He isn't coming back anyway, so it wouldn't make any difference, except to you.' She paused. 'I'm sure you'll see that this is best for everyone – when you've had time to calm down.'

Cathy stood perfectly still. Above the beat of her own heart she heard Kay's footsteps cross the hall. With crystal clarity she heard the slam of the front door, the clunk of the car door, then the crunch of gravel as Kay drove away.

Very slowly she sank on to the chair again and felt the tension slowly seep from her body. So – her marriage, her mockery of a marriage, was over. She was left to pick up the pieces. But there were some pieces that could never be reassembled; some shattered fragments of her life whose sharp edges would hurt her for ever.

Chapter Nineteen

When Rosalind returned to the Queen's Head she missed Cathy and Cuckoo Lodge even more than she had expected to. She had loved Melfordleigh and the natural beauty of the Suffolk coastline. The house had impressed her too. She envied Cathy in so many ways. She had so much: a lovely home and a husband she adored. Belonging to someone who loved you in return must be very special, though an underlying unease about Cathy still haunted Rosalind. There was something she couldn't quite put a finger on. Although the other girl had made her welcome and seemed genuinely glad of her company, the feeling that she was putting a brave face on some hidden unhappiness was always present. It was in the way she looked when she thought no one was observing her; in the wistful sadness lurking in the lovely green eyes. It tugged at Rosalind's heart, making her long to ask what was troubling her and try to help. If only Cathy had trusted her enough to confide it would have encouraged her to unburden herself about the shameful secret she herself was trying to forget. Telling someone was something she found she needed more and more as the months passed.

In spite of her nostalgia for the fresh sea air and Cathy's company, she continued to enjoy her work at the hotel and her days at college. Each week she learned a new facet of the hotel business and she was grateful to Mrs Gresham for allowing her the opportunity of working in so many parts of the hotel. She had tried her hand in every department now, from the kitchen, restaurant and bar to the bedrooms; from catering to housekeeping; admin to personnel. She realised that studying at college alone could never have provided her with so much practical experience.

She had seen little of Freda since the opening of *Sweet Violet*. The unsocial hours they both worked left few opportunities for meeting. The show had enjoyed rave reviews and there was even talk of taking it to Broadway some time in the coming year. How proud Ben would have been of the girl he had discovered and loved so much. Since the opening of the show Freda's photograph had appeared on the cover of *Applause*, a popular show business magazine, and there had been interviews and profiles in several glossy women's magazines too. Rosalind had cut them all out and lovingly pasted them into a scrap-book.

Although there weren't many opportunities for them to meet, Freda often telephoned and kept in touch and occasionally, on Rosalind's day off, they would lunch together. Freda had recently taken a cosy little flat in Holland Park and loved to spend her free time cooking and pottering.

Rosalind had read in the papers that Julian Travers and Brian French had completed a new musical, which would be going straight into the West End and was already in rehearsal. Freda told her that Stuart would not be doing the designs for this one. He no longer shared a flat with Julian. Both had moved to smarter flats closer to the West End and Stuart had been offered a permanent job with a television company.

As Christmas approached a party was arranged backstage for the cast and friends of *Sweet Violet*. Rosalind was invited but she told Freda she couldn't possibly go. The Queen's Head was busy now with the Christmas rush. The restaurant was booked solid, mainly with dinner dances and private firms' Christmas functions. Most of the accommodation was booked too, as many people liked to stay over after a party and she explained to Freda that she couldn't ask for time off. But a few days later when Mrs Gresham heard about the party she insisted that Rosalind must go.

'I hear it doesn't start until after the performance,' she said. 'Miss Moore rang me and explained. She says you are the only family she has and she wants you to be there very much.' As Rosalind opened her mouth to protest she held up her hand. 'No arguments. I'm going to insist that you go, Rosalind. You'll enjoy it so much, meeting all those celebrities, and you've worked so hard here. You deserve it.'

Rosalind had mixed feelings. In a way she was excited about the party, but, truth to tell, she was half-afraid of walking into a room full of such glamorous people. They were all so confident and accomplished, even the chorus girls exuded a charisma that made her feel plain and insignificant. But Mrs Gresham was adamant that she must go and Rosalind knew Freda wanted her to be there. So, swallowing her misgivings, she went out to buy a new dress, determined that at least Freda would not be ashamed of the way she looked.

It was arranged that after the party Rosalind should stay at Freda's flat for the night, and as the following day was Sunday and her day off they could spend some time together.

Rosalind arrived at the stage door at half-past ten, soon after the final curtain. Freda was in her dressing room. She had already changed into a stunning dress of white silk, embroidered with beads and sequins, and had just finished putting on fresh make-up when Rosalind arrived. She looked up at her through the dressing-table mirror, her face breaking into a smile.

'Rossie. You look lovely!' She got up and held out her hands, admiring the slim black dress with its short flared skirt and ribbon sleeves. 'And you've had your hair cut too!' She turned Rosalind round, admiring the new swinging jaw-length bob. 'Sit down and let me make up your eyes for

402

you,' she invited. 'I've got a new eye shadow that will make them look enormous.'

Very skilfully she shadowed Rosalind's dark eyes in soft shades of brown and beige, accentuating them with liner and mascara. 'There,' she said, standing back to admire her work in the mirror. 'You look fabulous.' She held out her hand. 'Now – come and meet the rest of the cast.' She laughed, giving Rosalind a quick hug. 'And don't look so terrified. Relax, darling. I want you to have a good time.'

On the stage the set had been taken down. A long table was laden with a sumptuous buffet and in one corner a bar had been set up. Whoever was in charge of music had put on a Dusty Springfield record and already several couples were dancing. Rosalind shrank as the familiar shyness engulfed her. She'd looked forward to this evening so much, convincing herself that she had conquered her old insecurities, yet now her one desire was to turn tail and run away.

Freda, feeling the reluctance in the sudden dampness of the hand she held, grasped it tightly, refusing to allow Rosalind to give way to her nervousness. At the bar she asked for two large gin and tonics and pressed one into Rosalind's trembling hand.

'Drink that,' she ordered. 'It'll make you feel relaxed in no time.' She cast her eyes around for a face that would be familiar to Rosalind. 'Look, there's Julian over there,' she said. 'You know him. And there's Brian with him. Come on. I'll take you over.'

Freda tapped Julian on the shoulder. 'Look who's here. I know you've met Rosalind before.'

He turned and looked at her. 'Of course. How nice to see you,' he said, holding out his hand and taking hers warmly. 'How is your mother?'

She gave him an apologetic smile. 'I don't really know. I left home some time ago and we don't keep in touch.'

'I can't say I blame you,' Julian said wryly. 'Though I

suppose I shouldn't say that.' He turned back towards the group he had been talking to. 'Let me introduce you. Brian you know of course. This is Paul Greirson, our musical director, and . . .' He tapped the shoulder of a man whose back was turned towards them. 'Stuart – look who's here.'

The man turned and Rosalind found herself suddenly face to face with Stuart. The shock made her heart quicken uncomfortably. Knowing that he was no longer involved with Julian and Brian, it hadn't occurred to her that he might be at the party. If it had she would probably not have come. Now there was no escape. Tentatively she offered her hand which he took, looking at her with an expression of frank astonishment.

'Hello, Rossie. How marvellous to see you again. How are you?'

'I'm fine, thank you.'

The others in the group seemed suddenly to melt away and she found herself left with Stuart. He looked very handsome. He had grown his fair hair longer in the current fashion and the dinner jacket and frilled evening shirt he wore were well cut and looked expensive. He was staring at her with open admiration. So many times she had visualised a chance meeting such as this and wondered how she would react, but now that she had recovered from the initial shock of seeing him again she found that her emotions remained surprisingly cool.

'I didn't recognise you for a moment,' he was saying. 'You look absolutely wonderful.'

She took a sip of her drink, trying to ignore the back-handed compliment. 'Thank you. I hear you've landed rather a good job. Congratulations.'

'Thanks. Yes it is going rather well. Working for TV is very exciting. What are you doing?'

'Training for hotel management, just as I always meant to,' she said. 'Boringly predictable, that's me.'

'Oh, I wouldn't say that,' he said with an appraising smile. 'I wouldn't say that at all. Will you dance?' Without waiting for her assent, he took the glass from her hand and put it on a nearby table, leading her on to the space reserved for dancing.

In his arms as they circled to a romantic tune, Rosalind was amazed at her own coolness. Just a short time ago she had thought herself deeply in love with this young man; her world had fallen apart when he had dropped her so callously in favour of someone else. Yet now when she looked at him she saw only a shallow, slightly foppish young man; self-centred and ineffectual, certainly unworthy of the tears she had shed for him. To prove it, both to him and to herself, she asked casually: 'How is Elaine?'

He looked blank.

'Elaine Frisby,' she prompted. 'The girl who made the costumes for *Sweet Violet*.'

Light dawned in the lazy blue eyes. 'Oh, *that* Elaine,' he said. 'I haven't seen her for ages.' He looked round at the other dancers. 'She might be here this evening, I suppose.' He smiled down at her. 'How is Una?'

Rosalind smiled wryly. 'I wouldn't know. I left home some time ago. Soon after my father died. We haven't made contact since.'

'Pity she never made it to the West End with the show,' he said casually. 'Jacobson always felt she was wrong for the role, you know. Between you and me, he couldn't wait to get rid of her. It sounds harsh, I know, but you can't afford sentiment with such a huge financial investment at stake. And I must say that Freda is an enormous improvement. She has a fantastic voice and brings such vibrance and vitality to the part.'

'Yes, she does, doesn't she?' Rosalind looked at him. 'I'm very proud of her. But Una and Don did get the three of you off the ground, didn't they?' she said dryly. 'I'm sure none of you will ever wish to forget that.'

To her amusement and secret satisfaction he actually blushed.

When the music stopped she made an excuse and went to find Freda, relieved that an unhappy chapter of her past had been successfully brought to its conclusion. To her relief Stuart avoided her for the rest of the evening.

After that first dance she found to her astonishment that she was in demand. She hardly sat one dance out. Even Stephen Troy, the male lead from the cast, asked her to dance, and Freda told her later that several young men had asked her who her attractive friend was. Rosalind suspected her of making it up to boost her confidence, but nevertheless she was quietly pleased with herself. The party she had dreaded turned out to be most enjoyable and she was sorry when it came to an end.

She and Freda spent a quiet Sunday relaxing until it was time for Rosalind to catch her train. Freda travelled with her as far as Tottenham Court Road underground station and waved her off, promising to ring her again before Christmas. She was going up to Birmingham to spend the two days she had off with her sister so this would be the last they would see of each other till the New Year.

As Rosalind sat in the train, her thoughts on last night's party and the coming holiday, she was suddenly aware that the glamorous blonde girl in the seat opposite was staring at her. She looked up and instantly recognised Carla Maybridge. She wore a striking black velvet coat whose huge fur collar framed her blonde head and exquisitely made-up face. Below it her long legs were encased in shiny black patent boots. She smiled in surprised recognition.

'It really *is* you, isn't it – Rosalind Blair? I couldn't make up my mind at first.'

'Hello, Carla. Haven't seen you for ages.'

'You look fabulous.' Secretly impressed by the trans-formation in Rosalind, Carla moved across to join her, engaging her in what was mainly a one-sided diatribe about her own madly gay social life and her success in modelling. 'I'm going home to see the folks,' she explained. 'I don't see them very often and when I found I was free this Sunday, I thought I'd better make the effort.'

'You won't be going home for Christmas then?'

Carla shook her head. 'God forbid! All my lot seem to have hordes of kids. You can't hear yourself *think* for the noise. Screaming babies wall to wall and sticky fingers all over your clothes! It's just not my scene. No, they're going to have to exist without their Auntie Carlie this year. I'm off to Austria instead. A whole bunch of us are going – boys and girls.' She smiled in anticipation. 'A little ski lodge high in the mountains. Log fires and après ski parties. I can't *wait*! A lot more fun than washing up endless greasy dishes and fishing the nut shells out of the loose covers.' She looked inquiringly at Rosalind. 'What are you doing these days?'

'I work at the Queen's Head. I'm a trainee manager,' Rosalind told her. 'I'll be working over Christmas. It's our busiest time.'

'God, how dreary! Poor old you.' Carla's expression transmitted her opinion of hotel management as a career. Although, she mused, it seemed to have made poor old Rosalind pull up her socks on the appearance front. Still very conservative, of course, but certainly an improvement on the plain, lumpy schoolgirl in specs and baggy cardigans. Her legs weren't bad either, now that one could actually see them.

Thinking of school reminded her of her recent meeting with Cathy. She said, 'I saw Cathy Oldham last summer, or Cathy Cavelle as she is now. Said she was up here for a couple of weeks' holiday.' She looked at Rosalind inquiringly. 'Did you happen to run into her at all?'

'Yes, I did as a matter of fact. Actually she invited me to go and stay with her in Suffolk. I went a few weeks ago. We had a lovely time.'

'*Really?*' Carla bridled. She'd received no such invitation and after the good turn she'd done her too. She raised an eyebrow at Rosalind. 'I see. So – as you've become such close friends I expect she told you about her little trauma.'

'No. What trauma?'

'She didn't tell you about her abortion? Well, I *am* surprised.'

'Cathy?' Rosalind frowned. 'Surely, you must be mistaken?'

'I don't think so, unless of course she decided not to go through with it. In that case she must be going ahead with her pregnancy.'

'She wasn't pregnant when I saw her last.'

'Oh well, in that case there's no mistake.'

Rosalind shook her head. 'Are you sure – about Cathy? I mean, it doesn't sound like her at all. It wouldn't do to go spreading stories like that if it isn't true.'

'I only know what she told me,' Carla said defensively. 'For all I know perhaps everything resolved itself without any help. And I'm not *spreading stories* as you put it. I only mentioned it because you and she have obviously become close friends.' Carla felt distinctly uncomfortable. She'd clearly said too much. As the train rumbled to a halt at Hendon Central she seized her opportunity of escape and edged towards the door. 'Look, I can't stop now. I'm getting off here. Have a call to make. Someone else I have to drop in on before going home. *Super* to see you, Rosalind. Have a good Christmas. 'Bye.' And with a waft of Chanel and a swish of fur-trimmed velvet she was gone.

The casual remark gave Rosalind plenty to think about. So much in fact that she almost went past her own station. Had Cathy really been pregnant last summer? She certainly hadn't looked at all well. If she had lost a baby it would explain a great deal. Poor Cathy. No wonder she looked sad and wistful.

When she arrived back at the Queen's Head Mrs Gresham came out of her office and met her in the hallway.

'Rosalind, you have a visitor. She's been here for over an hour. She spent a lot of that time in the bar, but I've put her in your room to wait for you. I had to use the pass key. I hope you don't mind?'

'No. Not at all.' Rosalind looked mystified. 'Who is it?'

'It's your mother, dear,' Mrs Gresham said quietly. 'And I'm afraid she seems a little – er – under the weather. I told her you might be some time but she insisted on waiting.'

Rosalind was quaking with apprehension as she pushed open the door of her room and went in. At once she could see what Mrs Gresham had meant by 'under the weather'. Una had obviously been drinking. Rosalind could smell the alcohol from here. No wonder the staff were anxious to get her out of the bar.

On closer inspection she saw that her mother had lost weight. Her skin looked sallow and her features sharp and haggard. When she saw Rosalind she stared at her accusingly.

'Where the hell have you been?' she demanded stridently. 'I've been stuck in this poky little room for hours! That snooty manageress woman made me come up here. Who does she think she is?'

'Sunday is my day off,' Rosalind said. 'And I think Mrs Gresham thought you'd be more comfortable in here.'

'I rang last night and said I'd be coming along at six. I think you might have made the effort to be here.'

'I wasn't here, so I didn't get the message. What's wrong, Mum? Why are you here?'

Una affected a wounded expression. 'Why am I here? That's a nice thing to greet me with, isn't it? I hope I have the right to visit my own daughter.' When Rosalind didn't reply she said, 'I want you to come home, Rossie. It's as simple as that. I want us to make up our differences.'

Rosalind's heart sank. Una's whining tone and maudlin expression didn't fool her. There was more to her sudden request for a reconciliation than met the eye and Rosalind knew from experience that whatever it was would not be to her advantage. She sank on to the chair opposite. 'Why, Mum? What's gone wrong?'

'Does there have to be something wrong for me to want my own daughter home with me again?'

'Why now?'

Una shrugged. 'It's Christmas. It's the time for families, isn't it?'

Rosalind sighed. 'I can't come home now, Mum. This is our busiest time. I'll be working all over the holiday.'

'Afterwards then. Say you give in your notice now and come home in January?'

'Give in my notice?' Rosalind stared at her. 'You're asking me to give up my job? I can't. I'm training for management. I go to college two days a week and I work here the rest of the time.'

'But surely if your family needs you . . .?'

'What's all this about, Mum? Why don't you just tell me? Is it Don? Have you left him?'

Una grunted. 'Huh! Chance'd be a fine thing. Look, Rossie, I've got the offer of work – up north. It's important to me. I want to take it.'

'A show?'

'No.' Una avoided her eyes. 'Just, you know, singing.'

'A tour?'

'Not exactly. Cabaret – I suppose you could say. Clubs, the northern circuit.'

'Oh, Mum, you've done clubs before. It didn't work out.'

'This is different,' Una insisted. 'Northern clubland is different now. Industry and mining are booming up there apparently. There's a lot of money around nowadays. Working men's clubs are very different places to what they were years ago. Sophisticated; glamorous even. The pay is good too. I'd get top billing. I want to do it, Rossie.'

410

'So – what's the problem?'

Una sighed and twisted her fingers in her lap. 'It's Don. He's planning to retire from Hallard's next year and he wants me to retire with him. He says he's had enough of being on his own, but I'm fairly sure I could get him to agree to a compromise. I'm going to suggest that he lets me have this one last try. If I make it, well and good. If I don't, then I'll do as he says and retire.'

'So?'

'I'm pretty sure he'd agree if I got you to come home and look after him while I'm away.'

Rosalind stared at her mother in disbelief. 'You want me to give up my training and my job so that you can go on a short tour of northern working men's clubs? Mum, why don't you face up to reality? You've got a lovely home and a good husband. You could have a life of leisure. He'd do anything for you – give you anything you wanted, you know he would. But it's *you* he wants with him, not me. I've heard about these northern clubs from some of the guests here. They might look glamorous, but the audiences are as tough as before. They'd destroy you.'

'You can't know that! You're just saying it to get out of your duty. You're as selfish as you always were, Rossie. You're your bloody father all over again.' Una stared at her daughter, for the first time taking in her new appearance. She assessed the smart, understated suit, the hairstyle and make-up. Her eyes narrowed. 'You've been seeing *her*, haven't you? That Morton bitch?'

'Freda? I've seen her, yes.'

'More than just *seen* her by the look of this!' Una sprang to her feet and revealed something hidden behind her in the chair. It was the scrapbook filled with Freda's press cuttings. She must have been looking through while she waited. She threw it at Rosalind's feet.

'The pair of you have ganged up, why not admit it?' Her eyes flashed dangerously as they swept Rosalind from head to foot. 'You always did let her influence you, didn't you? She's been trying to tart you up again too by the look of you. That cow took my big chance away from me; snatched my part just as we were going into Town with the show.' She narrowed her eyes at Rosalind. 'But of course you *know* all that, don't you? I daresay the pair of you had a bloody good laugh at my expense. I wouldn't put it past you to have put her up to it in the first place. Just to get back at me.' Her voice had risen shrilly and Rosalind stepped forward.

'Mum! Keep your voice down, please. The residents will hear and think we're having a row.'

'A row?' Una swayed unsteadily. 'Well, what if we are having a sodding row? It's none of their business. Let them think what they bloody well like. I'll shout if I want to. I'll say what I like to my selfish bitch of a daughter.' She stepped up to Rosalind and wagged a finger in her face. 'You *owe* me, Rossie. You betrayed me – you and that treacherous slut. She took the man I loved, then she stole my chance of success. Now she's poisoned my daughter's mind against me.' Her face crumpled and she choked on a sob. 'You owe me, Rossie. So are you going to come home and give me one last chance? *Are you?*'

'*No, I'm not!*' Rosalind's voice was strong and firm as she stood her ground and looked her mother in the eye. She was slightly shorter than Una but as she spoke her mother seemed to shrink visibly before her eyes. 'Face facts, Mum,' she went on. 'Freda didn't take Dad from you. They met long after you'd parted. No one stole your part either. Mr Jacobson recast it. When Freda went to the audition she didn't even know you were in the play. It was open to anyone and she got it. And as for poisoning my mind . . .' She stopped herself from saying what was in her mind. A row would get them nowhere. She reached out to touch Una's arm gently. 'Oh, Mum, why don't you give up? Let go. Don't risk making a fool of yourself. You've got so much and you're throwing it all away. I won't come home and let you do it to yourself. I wouldn't even if it *didn't* mean sacrificing all I've worked for.'

Speechless, Una stood looking at her daughter, her face working with anger. For a moment Rosalind thought she was about to collapse. Then she took a deep breath and pulled herself together. 'All right,' she said at last. 'You just think of yourself. Just stay here in your pathetic little job. You're no more than a servant if only you knew it!'

'Are you saying that what you're offering me is better?' Rosalind asked coolly.

Una snatched her handbag from the chair where she'd been sitting and headed for the door. 'Have it your way then. But don't think you've heard the last of this, my girl, because you haven't. No one tells me I'm a fool and gets away with it, especially the ungrateful child I sacrificed everything for.'

As the door closed behind her Rosalind felt all the old insecurities and inhibitions flood back. Why did Una always manage to make her feel guilty when she knew she had nothing to feel guilty about?

When Don opened the front door and saw Una standing on the doorstep his first reaction was relief. She'd been gone for hours and he was just wondering if he should go out and start looking for her.

'Una . . .' he began.

She swept past him into the hall. 'There's a taxi waiting,' she said abruptly. 'He wants paying. See to it, will you? My head's splitting.'

When he came back in he found her sitting slumped in a corner of the settee, one hand clutching her head. Kneeling, he eased the shoes from her feet. 'You're frozen, love. Where have you been? I was so worried.'

'I've been to see that daughter of mine,' she said bitterly. 'I thought we might make up our differences. I invited her to come home again – for Christmas. Maybe for good.'

'Really? Oh, I'm so glad, dear. What did she say?'

413

'You might well ask. Threw the invitation in my face. I might as well have stayed at home in the warm and saved my breath,' Una said. 'I've humiliated myself for nothing. And you should have heard some of the things she said. It's all that Morton bitch's doing. Hand in glove they are. Rosalind even keeps all her press cuttings pasted into a book.' She choked on a self-pitying sob. 'She never kept *my* press cuttings, never gave a damn about my career.'

'Never mind. Let me make you a nice cup of tea and get you an aspirin, eh?'

She nodded. 'Yes. And make it strong. In fact, don't bother. I'll have a brandy instead.'

As he put the glass into her hand, he sat down on the settee beside her. 'I know you must feel hurt and disappointed about Rosalind, dear. But she's a young woman now and she has her own life to live.' He took her free hand and held it tenderly. 'I daresay she sees Freda as more of a friend. After all, they are of an age, aren't they?'

She glared at him. 'You're saying I'm old, are you? Over the hill?'

'Of course I'm not. I'm just pointing out that we all have our own futures to think of.' He squeezed her hand and leaned closer. 'Just think of the marvellous time we'll have when I retire. We can spend a lot of our time travelling abroad, all winter if you like; follow the sun as they say. We can go to the theatre, join the golf club and socialise more – anything that takes your fancy. Just the two of us. All mothers have to let go at some stage, you know, dear.'

'You're a fine one to talk about mothers letting go,' she snapped, snatching her hand away. 'Yours still hasn't let go from the other side of the grave! I've told you, Don, I'm not as old as you. I've got no intention of retiring. I still want to *work*. I've had this offer to do the northern clubs and I really want to do it.'

He sighed. He had made his views plain, or so he thought. Heaven only knew they'd been over it enough times. He

414

couldn't face living with the person Una became after experiencing a failure. His life had been hell on earth after her exclusion from the cast of *Sweet Violet* – and since. He had come to dread those magazine articles and cover pictures of Freda Morton, or Benita Moore as she was known. Every time Una read one of those interviews it threw her into a black depression for days, especially if her ex-husband's name happened to be included. It was true that Mother had tended to dominate him when she was alive, but at least she'd had his best interests at heart. Mother was devoted to him whilst Una cared only for herself. Every instinct told him that if he gave in over this latest issue he would never know another moment's peace as long as they were together.

'*No*, Una,' he said as firmly as he knew how to. 'I'm sorry, but I'm putting my foot down. If you want to go rushing up and down the country again then you'll do it without my support.' He looked at her white face. 'It's you I'm thinking of if only you could see it. Those northern audiences are tough and demanding. They'd tear you apart. And you know what another failure would do to you.'

'Why must you take it for granted I'd fail just because that woman manipulated me out last time?' She turned to stare at him accusingly. 'You've been talking to *her*, haven't you? Rossie? She said the very same thing! You've been meeting. You've cooked this up between you.'

'No.' He shook his head. 'I haven't set eyes on Rosalind since . . .'

'Since when? Since you gave her the money to go to Australia? Is that what you were going to say?'

'No. She didn't go to Australia.'

'But she *was* going. And you did give her the money – behind my back too. That was disloyal of you, Don. It was what caused the row that split us up.' She turned in her seat to look at him. 'You could say yes to *her*, couldn't you? You gave her the money when you knew I didn't want her to go.

415

The devious little bitch went snivelling to you behind my back and you caved in and gave it to her, just like that.' She snapped her fingers.

'It wasn't like that, Una. She never asked.'

'Oh, no?' she sneered. 'It all came out by accident, didn't it? Lucky accident for *her*, wasn't it?'

'Believe it or not, it's the truth, Una.' For a long moment their eyes locked. Don held her gaze, his grey eyes unfaltering. It was Una who looked away first. But she wasn't convinced. There was something more behind this and she'd get to the bottom of it if it was the last thing she did. And if she wasn't going to be allowed her chance to make her name in the northern clubs then Don was going to have to make some concessions.

'All right,' she said at last. 'If I'm going to be kept like a bloody prisoner in this mausoleum of your mother's, I'll need to redecorate it.'

Don gave a sigh of relief. He'd dreaded putting his foot down but it seemed to have worked. 'All right, if that's what you want.'

'I do!' She looked at him. 'It hasn't been done since we were first married. And when I say redecorated I mean completely, mind. Furniture, carpets, curtains. The kitchen re-fitted, new bathroom, the lot. All done by a professional designer too. No amateurs or cowboys.'

Don tried not to wince as he did some rapid panic-stricken mental arithmetic. 'If that's what it takes to make you happy,' he said haltingly.

'It does. I'll make a start tomorrow.'

'But we're only a few days off Christmas.'

'Sod Christmas! We'll spend that in a hotel.' She got up and began to walk around the room. 'When I'm done with this house your beloved mother wouldn't know it,' she said spitefully. 'I'll see to it that there isn't one thing of hers left. I think it's high time *she* let go, don't you Don?'

Una was as good as her word. The following day she

went from room to room, notebook in hand, jotting down her ideas. Then she sat down with the telephone book and made a list of all the interior designers in the area. She was determined to transform the place, to get rid of every last vestige of the late Mrs Blake senior. On a separate piece of paper she made a note of the few pieces of Mrs Blake's furniture that Don had insisted on keeping. She would telephone a saleroom to collect the horrid antiquated monstrosities. The sooner they were out of the house, the sooner Don would know that this time she meant business.

She thought she had noted everything when she remembered the display cabinet. Don had stuck out for that, but now it would definitely have to go. But what about the contents? He had always insisted that his mother's collection of Meissen porcelain was extremely valuable. Perhaps she should contact an antique dealer about it.

Opening the glass door Una looked at the delicate figurines with dislike. She'd always hated fussy fragile things that broke if you so much as breathed on them. But nevertheless, she respected them for their value. She peered closer, frowning. If she wasn't very much mistaken there was a piece missing. Yes, there was a gap on the top shelf and the outline of its base could clearly be seen on the glass support. She took a step back and racked her brain as she tried to remember what it had been like. If she remembered correctly it had been the largest piece in the collection – a ghastly thing shaped like a shell. Yes, that was it. It had sugary flowers and four fat naked children with insipid expressions. Nauseating! But the question was, where had it gone? Don would never have sold it. He didn't need the money. Anyway, if he'd been that hard up he would surely have sold the whole collection.

Her eyes narrowed. Had he sold it so that he could give Rosalind the money for her fare to Australia? Yes, that must be it – so that Una wouldn't notice that the amount had been withdrawn from their bank account. Her suspicions well and truly aroused, she went into the study and began to rummage in his desk. There would be something – a receipt, a bill of sale, an auctioneer's invoice. When she knew the date of the sale she would know for sure she was right. But although she searched thoroughly she found nothing until, right at the back of the little stamp drawer, she found a small card. Printed on it in heavy black German text were the words:

Pegasus Antiques
Furniture, antiquarian books and objects d'art
Prop. Arnold Corbett. 125 Bently Street, Chelsea

Una found the little shop without difficulty. The old-fashioned door-bell tinkled as she went in and she wrinkled her nose at the familiar musty smell of old books and furniture. Why on earth anyone wanted to pay good money for dead people's cast-offs was beyond her. But the elderly man behind the counter seemed clean and tidy enough. He looked up at her over his half-moon glasses with a benign smile.

'Good morning, madam. Can I help you?'

'I don't know. I'm looking for a particular piece of china. An ornament. I have reason to believe that you might have bought it.'

'Well, I do often buy china and porcelain. Could you perhaps describe it for me?'

Una did her best to describe the piece, adding as an afterthought, 'I believe it was rather special. Meissen, I think.'

'Ah.' The man's face cleared. 'There was a piece recently that answered to that description. But if you were wanting to buy it, I'm afraid it was sold almost immediately. I have a client who is a keen collector of Meissen, you see. He was delighted with it and snapped it up at . . .'

'Yes, *yes*,' Una snapped impatiently. 'I didn't want

418

to buy it. All I really want to know is, who sold it to you?'

The man looked uncomfortable. 'Well, I don't normally . . .'

'It may well have been stolen for all I know,' Una put in sharply. 'It's missing, you see. But I found your card, so I think it may have been a member of my family, which would clear the mystery up and make everything all right.' She looked him in the eye. 'I don't want to have to go to the police, do I? Receiving carries a rather high penalty, I believe.'

'Ah – I see. No, indeed. Bringing in the police would be most unpleasant. Well now, let me see. I'm afraid I don't have a name for the person.'

'A description would do.' Una was beginning to lose her patience. Why couldn't the old fool just spit it out? 'Was it a man, for instance?' she prompted. 'A middle-aged man?'

'Oh, no.' For the first time the man sounded positive. 'Definitely not a man. A young woman.' He half-closed his eyes, recalling. 'Dark hair and eyes. Spectacles. A very pale face as I remember. If my memory serves me right I believe she said the piece belonged to a deceased relative. She needed the money to visit her sick father in Australia.'

Una gasped. So *that* was it! 'Did she now? Thank you, Mr Corbett,' she said on her way to the door. 'Thank you *very* much.'

'Not at all, madam. Happy to have been of help.'

'You'll never know just how *much* of a help you've been,' Una murmured under her breath.

In a nearby café she digested the shocking revelation. Rosalind had stolen the Meissen. She must have done. Don would never have given it to her. He'd rather have given her the money. Then he must have found out. *And he had let her keep the money and said nothing about it.*

She could hardly believe it, yet it all fitted now that she knew the truth. Rosalind's sudden announcement that she

419

was going to Australia, then her impulsive departure from home after Ben's death. Well, they were going to have to pay for their sly little piece of deception, Don and Rosalind. And she would be the one setting the price!

'She took it, didn't she? The lying little thief stole one of your mother's precious ornaments and you let her get away with it!'

When Don arrived home from work that evening Una was standing in the hall waiting for him. Even before he had a chance to remove his coat she had begun her accusing tirade.

'If I'd done a thing like that you'd have kicked me out, lock, stock and barrel. But not her. Oh, no! Not little miss butter-wouldn't-melt!' She stood in front of him, hands on hips, demanding an explanation. 'What's been going on, Don? I'm sick and tired of having the wool pulled over my eyes. What do you think I am – stupid or something?'

'It isn't the way you think,' he began. 'If you'll just calm down and let me explain.' He made to move towards the living room but she barred his way.

'There's only one thing I want to know,' she said. 'Did she take that ornament or didn't she?'

Don winced. 'Well, yes, but . . .'

'With or without your permission?'

'I told you, it wasn't . . .'

'*With or without, Don?*'

'Without. But as soon as she'd done it she was sorry,' he added hurriedly. 'She confessed to me and . . .'

'And you let her keep the money.' Una shook her head. 'You *fool*! You're as bad as she is. You deceived me, the pair of you. And to think I was willing to give up my career. First I made sacrifices for her, then you. And all the time you were both deceiving me rotten.'

'Una, see sense. The poor girl was desperate. She needed the money to go and see her father. She'd never have done

420

it otherwise, you must know that. If you'd only told me – if you'd let her ask, I'd have given her the plane fare happily.'

'Well, now you can *happily* make amends by letting me go and take that job,' she told him. 'I've already been in touch with my agent and said I'll go so there's nothing you can do about it now, Don.' As she spoke she was pulling her coat on. The last button fastened, she turned to him. 'And now I'm going to cook *her* goose for her. I'm going to make that little swindler wish she'd been straight with me.'

Rosalind was helping out behind the bar when Una strode into the lounge of the Queen's Head. Pushing her way to the front of the crowd she said stridently, 'I want a word with you, madam.'

The man Rosalind had been serving swung round. 'Do you *mind*? I'm being served at the moment. Wait your turn, can't you?'

'Mind your own business,' Una said, elbowing him out of the way. 'She's my daughter and I need to see her urgently on private family business, so take your drink and push off.'

The man paid for his drink and moved away with a resentful look.

Acutely embarrassed, Rosalind leaned across the bar. 'I'm on duty, Mum,' she whispered. 'Can't it wait?'

'No, it can't. I need to speak to you now.'

Afraid Una might make a scene, Rosalind asked the other girl serving to cover for her, lifted the bar flap and took her mother's arm, steering her away from the curious eyes turned in their direction. 'We can go up to my room,' she said, her heart thudding with apprehension. 'But I can only take five minutes off.'

'We'll see about that!' Una's expression smouldered unpleasantly. 'When you've heard what I have to say you might need time to take stock of the situation.' As they went up together in the lift Rosalind's heart was heavy as she wondered what was in store for her this time. She didn't have to wait long to find out. The moment the door of her room closed behind them Una came straight to the point, leaving her in no doubt about the reason for her untimely visit.

'You're a thief! You took one of Don's mother's valuable ornaments to pay for your air fare to Australia.' She held up her hand. 'Don't make things worse by trying to deny it. The man in the shop where you sold it described you to a tee, and now Don has confirmed it too.' She had the satisfaction of seeing Rosalind's face turn paper white as she sank down on the chair by the door.

'How did you find out?' she whispered.

'Never mind that. I *know*. That's all that matters to you.'

'What – are you going to do?' Rosalind asked, her stomach churning unpleasantly.

'That depends on you.'

'What do you want?'

'I want you to give in your notice here and come home. You and Don seem to be thick. Thick as *thieves*, you could say!' She laughed dryly. 'So you might as well come and keep house for him while I'm away.'

'How long would that be for?'

Una shrugged. 'I've no idea. It could be for a very long time. I hope it will!'

Rosalind sighed. It was her worst nightmare come true. But she couldn't throw away her future without some sort of fight. 'I can't do that, Mum. Frankly I don't see why I should. I asked for your help and you refused. I had to do something to get to see Dad.'

Una laughed unpleasantly. 'Oh, yes. You're your father's daughter all right.'

'And after all, the Meissen was Don's, not yours. I confessed to him what I'd done. He understood how much I needed the money and he promised me everything

422

would be all right. He said he was going to buy the piece back.'

'Well, he couldn't,' Una told her with satisfaction.

'Oh.' Rosalind bit her lip. 'I'm sorry about that.'

'Apparently the man sold it almost immediately. That's how I found out. I noticed it was missing.'

'But I know Don wouldn't go to the police,' Rosalind said. 'He wouldn't have me charged with theft.'

'Don't rely on it,' Una said grimly. 'He would if I told him to, make no mistake about that. But don't worry. Unlike you, I wouldn't stoop so low as to betray a blood relative.'

Rosalind swallowed hard. 'I can't give up my job and my training. Not indefinitely as you seem to be asking.'

'I see. In that case I'll have no alternative than to tell Mrs Gresham the real reason you had to leave home so suddenly. I didn't expect to have to resort to that, Rossie. I was sure you'd want to do the right thing and help out; put your family first.'

Rosalind stared at her, white-faced. 'You – you wouldn't,' she whispered. But even as she said it, she knew that Una would if she had to.

'I'm sure she'd feel that it would be too risky to employ a compulsive thief in a reputable hotel like this.' Una surveyed her daughter, arms folded. 'So you might as well come home while you still have a roof over your head. It's time to make your mind up, Rossie. The offer won't stay open for ever.'

Rosalind stared at her mother incredulously. 'Why are you doing this, Mum? Why are you punishing me? You know how hard I worked to get my A levels. This job is important to me.'

'You'll get another one easily enough. Hotel skivvying jobs are ten a penny,' Una sneered. 'You ask why I'm doing it? Well, if you want to know the truth, Rosalind, I'm sick and tired of your disloyalty. You and that scheming Morton

423

bitch have had a good laugh at my expense. Well, now you can laugh this off together. I wonder if she'll be there to help *you* find a job when you need it.' She turned, her hand on the door handle. 'Come to think of it, I wonder what your precious Freda would think of you if she knew you were light-fingered. Turn awkward and I might even have to let *her* know too.' She opened the door. 'You can move your things into Blake's Folly whenever you like. I'm off to Huddersfield the day after Boxing Day, thank God! I'll tell Don to expect you.'

Mrs Gresham looked at Rosalind across the desk in her office. 'Leave? But I thought you were so happy with us, Rosalind.'

'I was – I am, Mrs Gresham. It's just that there are family problems and I have to go home and help out.'

'Well, if there's anything I can do to help in any way, just say so,' Mrs Gresham said anxiously. 'It seems such a pity to leave when you've settled into your training programme so nicely.'

Rosalind swallowed hard at the lump in her throat. 'It's just that my mother has to be away from home for some time and she needs me to take care of things there.'

The manageress frowned. 'If you don't mind my saying so, Rosalind, I think that's rather inconsiderate of her. She must know how important your training is to you. Surely she could engage a housekeeper? How long will this situation last? I couldn't keep your job open indefinitely, of course, but perhaps for a month or so.'

'I – don't know.' Rosalind looked down unhappily at the hands clenched together in her lap. 'Probably for quite a long time. You'd better find someone else, I think.'

There was silence as she struggled to control her emotions. The older woman watched helplessly, waiting for further explanation. When it did not come she said gently: 'Rosalind, if there is anything wrong – anything

424

you want to talk about – I can assure you it will not go
beyond these walls. Forgive me, dear, but if there is some
problem, something personal, I'd like to think you could
trust me to help. I really hate losing you like this. It seems
such a sad waste.'

'No. I – I'm sorry, but no.' Rosalind stood up and backed
towards the door, afraid that if she didn't get out of the room
at once she might burst into tears and blurt it all out. She
couldn't risk seeing the look of incredulous shock – the
disillusionment on the face of the woman who had been
so kind to her. Much better to leave while she was still
respected. 'You can't help,' she said. 'No one can. If it's
all right with you I'll leave the day after Boxing Day.' And
she left the office hurriedly, leaving the manageress shaking
her head.

Christmas at the Queen's Head was frenetically busy, but
Rosalind was glad to be rushed off her feet. It gave her
no time to think about her ruined career prospects. When
she crept up to her room at night she was too tired to do
anything but fall into bed and sleep.

On the day after Boxing Day she packed, said a hurried
goodbye to the rest of the staff and a regretful Mrs Gresham
and took a taxi to Blake's Folly. She found Don alone
staring moodily out of the drawing-room window at the
deserted garden.

'Mum's gone then?' she said, looking round.

He nodded. 'Yes. Early this morning. I'm sorry about
this, Rosalind. I assure you, it was none of my doing.'
He turned to look at her. 'I didn't tell her voluntarily
about the Meissen. She found out; saw that it was
missing and put two and two together. Una was always
good at that,' he added bitterly. He looked at her with
genuine anxiety. 'I feel responsible for your giving up
your job. I really don't need you to keep house for
me. I told Una that, but she was adamant – said that
her conscience wouldn't allow you to stay in a position

425

of responsibility after what you'd . . .' he trailed off, looking away.

'It's all right, Don. I know,' she said.

He turned quickly. 'Look, when I said I didn't need you, I wasn't . . . I mean, you know you're perfectly welcome to stay. This is your home after all. I just didn't want you to feel obligated.'

'I know. I haven't anywhere else to go just now,' she said. 'If I could just stay here till I find another job?'

'Of course, my dear. Naturally. But couldn't you just tell your present employer that you've changed your mind and go back? Una wouldn't know. And once she's engrossed in this new job of hers she'll probably forget all about it.'

Rosalind sighed. Don obviously didn't know of Una's threat to tell Mrs Gresham everything. 'No, I can't do that,' she said. 'It doesn't matter. I didn't really want to work there any more anyway.'

'Oh, I see.' He looked relieved. 'Well, I suppose we may as well make the best of it. Shall we start by having a cup of coffee? Then we can work out some kind of routine.'

As they sat together over coffee at the kitchen table Don told her dejectedly that he doubted whether Una would return. 'I think our marriage is probably over, Rosalind,' he said. 'I've tried my hardest to please her, but I've come to the conclusion that my way of life isn't hers and never will be.'

'It's since she went back into the theatre,' Rosalind said. 'Before that she'd settled down; resigned herself to other work. She quite enjoyed her job at Hallard's – until Stuart and Julian came on the scene.'

'Now she's driven by this manic ambition to make the big time,' he said with a sigh. 'The trouble is, I'm afraid she's fooling herself. I'm terribly afraid that history will repeat itself. And what will become of her then, I dread to think.' He looked up at her bleakly. 'The trouble is that in spite of everything I still love her.'

426

'If she fails this time maybe she'll come home and settle down again,' Rosalind said without conviction.

Don sighed. 'Well – maybe. But I've decided. I'll be here for her one more time, Rosalind. If she still wants me, that is. After that . . .' He lifted his shoulders helplessly. 'After that, I'm going to have to admit defeat.'

Upstairs in her old room Rosalind unpacked her clothes and put them away. Then she went downstairs and began to prepare a meal for Don and herself. When they had eaten he asked hesitantly if she would like to watch television with him for a while.

'I don't want you to feel you have to spend your free time with me,' he said. 'You must live your own life – do as you please. Maybe we could turn one of the other bedrooms into a sitting room for you so that you can entertain your friends. I don't want you to feel that you're shut up with only an old man for company. It's not right.'

Rosalind was too touched by his kindness and concern to tell him that she didn't have any friends. She'd been too busy at the Queen's Head to have any social life.

'I can't think why Una insisted that you should come and keep house for me,' he went on earnestly. 'But at least it's good to know that she cared enough to want to see me looked after.' He smiled at her. 'And I have an idea that she thought I could keep an eye on you too; that we'd look after each other. It proves to me that she does still care for me – for us both. I'm sure that underneath that brittle exterior she's as soft and caring as any other wife and mother.'

Rosalind said nothing. She had no intention of disillusioning Don any further by telling him the bitter truth.

By the time the nine o'clock news began she was already yawning. Over Christmas she had worked long and hard and she was tired. She was about to make her excuses and say goodnight when a news item suddenly caught her attention. She leaned forward in her chair, concentrating

427

on the screen. The newsreader was talking about an air crash that had occurred the previous day – somewhere in the Swiss Alps.

'It is now thought that the crash was caused by severe weather causing ice to form on the plane's wings,' he announced. 'There were no survivors of the crash and it has now been confirmed that among the casualties was Gerald Cavelle, the internationally renowned concert pianist who was to have spent a holiday in Switzerland following a stay in a New Zealand hospital. A tribute to the pianist follows this news bulletin.'

Shocked, Rosalind turned to stare at Don. 'That's Cathy's husband,' she said. 'Cathy, my school friend. Don't you remember? She brought him to a party here just before they were married.'

'Of course. I remember them both,' Don told her. 'Poor child. What a terrible thing to happen.'

'They spent their honeymoon in Switzerland.' Rosalind froze, her hand flying to her mouth as a thought occurred to her. Suppose Cathy was with him? Suppose she had been killed too?

'Do you know her family?' Don asked.

Rosalind shook her head. 'She has no family. Just the people she lived with after her father died. I'll telephone Mrs Johnson first thing tomorrow. I must find out whether Cathy was with him.'

428

Chapter Twenty

It was late afternoon when Matthew drove into the centre of the little market town and pulled over to the side of the road.

'Better have a look at the map,' he said, looking anxiously out at the darkening winter sky. 'The weather seems to be getting worse and it's almost dark too.' He leaned forward, peering through the windscreen. 'I seem to remember we have to turn off just after Wickham Market and I don't want to miss the turning. We could be wandering around in the dark all night on these country roads.'

Rosalind spread out the map on the dashboard and pointed. 'We're here. I think that's the turning you're after, about three miles along the road.' She looked at him. 'Last time I came it was by train, so I'm not much help, I'm afraid.'

He smiled at her. 'You've done wonders. I wouldn't like to have made the trip alone. I have driven to Melfordleigh before, but that was a year last September. It all looked very different on a fine summer afternoon with the sun shining.'

Rosalind had met Matthew only once before, at Cathy's wedding. When they first set out on the drive to Suffolk they had been slightly shy of one another but the shared journey with its attendant difficulties had soon broken the ice. By the time they got as far as Wickham Market they were talking easily and felt as though they had known each other all their lives.

*   *   *

After hearing about the air crash on television the previous night Rosalind had decided to go over to the Johnsons' house first thing the next morning. Mary Johnson answered the door looking pale and haggard from worry and lack of sleep. She invited Rosalind into the living room.

'When I heard the news about Gerald Cavelle on television last night I was so worried in case Cathy was with him,' she explained. 'I had to come over and find out.'

'No, thank God, she wasn't,' Johnny told her. 'I spoke to her just a few days ago when I rang to wish her a happy birthday. I had thought that Gerald would try to get home for that. But she said she was alone and that she'd be spending Christmas alone at Melfordleigh too.' She shook her head. 'Heaven knows what Gerald came to be doing on a plane to Switzerland. I just knew at the time that something was wrong. I could hear it in her voice. But she kept insisting that everything was all right.' Johnny sighed. 'I tried to get her to come here to us for Christmas, but she wouldn't. As it happens, with Mother so ill in hospital it wouldn't have been a very happy occasion. I've been ringing her number ever since I heard the dreadful news,' she went on. 'But I can't get any reply.'

'I'll go to Melfordleigh,' Rosalind said decisively. 'Cathy's going to need someone. I know I'm not as close as you are, but as you say, someone should be with her.'

Johnny looked at her with relief. 'Oh, I'd be so grateful if you would, dear. Mother is so ill. I have to stay here in case she takes a sudden turn for the worse. But are you sure you can get the time off?'

'That's not a problem. I've given up my job,' Rosalind told her. 'I've come home to keep house for my step-father while my mother is away, but he can manage without me for a few days. In fact he suggested it himself. I'll get on the first train I can.'

'No need,' Johnny said quickly. 'Matthew is home and he has some leave due. He'll take you. He was going anyway, to bring Cathy back here to stay with us, but he was reluctant to go alone.' She smiled ruefully. 'You know how awkward men are on occasions like this.' She shook her head. 'My poor Cathy. Heaven knows what this will have done to her.'

'I could go right away if that's all right?' Rosalind said.

Johnny looked doubtful. 'I think we should make sure she's actually there first. I don't want you to have a wasted journey. Matthew thinks she's probably taken the telephone off the hook to avoid being pestered by the press. If I can't get any reply from the house today I might contact the local police and ask them to make tactful enquiries for me.' She smiled at Rosalind. 'I can't tell you what a relief it is that someone is going to her. If you'd like to go home and prepare I'll telephone you as soon as I have any news.'

Rosalind did as Johnny suggested. Back at Blake's Folly she packed a bag and set about making sure Don had plenty of food prepared, though he assured her that he could always eat at the local pub if he ran out.

Johnny's call came late that afternoon.

'I had to get in touch with the police in the end,' she said. 'It was as Matthew thought – the phone was off the hook. Cathy is there, but apart from the daily woman no one has seen her. Matthew will come and pick you up at ten tomorrow morning if that's all right?'

'I'll be waiting.'

'I've told him to bring her back with him, if she'll come.' Rosalind heard her sigh at the other end of the line. 'Oh dear, troubles never come singly, do they?'

It was already dark by the time they reached Melfordleigh; the dense inky darkness of the countryside that neither of them was used to. As they travelled along the country lanes the twin beams of the headlights picked up the slanting shafts of rain and the wet glisten of the road. On either side tall hedges obscured their view and Rosalind saw only too well

431

what Matthew had meant about getting lost. But as they crested the hill and dipped down into Melfordleigh they saw with relief the lighted windows of the village houses winking a warm welcome.

As Matthew nosed the car into the gateway of Cuckoo Lodge Rosalind hopped out, a newspaper held over her head against the driving rain, and ran to open the gate. The house was in darkness and they looked apprehensively at each other as they stood under the porch.

'I hope she's in,' Matthew said. He rang the bell and together they listened to it echoing emptily through the house. After a few moments the porch lantern went on and the front door opened an inch or two. A round-faced woman peered out.

'Who is it?' she asked warily.

'Matthew Johnson and Rosalind Blair,' he said. 'We're friends of Mrs Cavelle and we've come to see her. Is she at home?'

Maggie held the door open and beckoned them in with a sigh of relief. 'Sorry about that,' she said. 'But you wouldn't believe the nosy parkers we've had sniffing round here. Reporters mostly.' She shook her head. 'Like vultures, they are, taking advantage of folks's grief to fill their papers.' She looked at their rain-spotted coats. 'Take off them wet things and give them to me. I'll hang them up by the Aga to dry. And you must be spittin' feathers for a nice cup of tea. I'll get the kettle on this minute.'

'Where is Cathy?' Rosalind asked as they followed Maggie to the kitchen. 'How is she?'

Maggie closed the door carefully. 'Won't come out of her room. Soon as I heard the news on telly I got on my bike and came straight round. She seemed – I don't know, numb, I suppose you'd call it. Made one or two phone calls, cool as you please. Took a few more yesterday. Mr Cavelle's agent and people like that I think they were.

432

Then the papers started pestering. After that she took to her room and stayed there.'

Matthew looked concerned. 'She is – all right, isn't she?'

'Oh, bless you, yes. I mean, she hasn't locked the door or nothing. I've been taking her meals up and she's even eaten a little bit. As my dad was at home to stay with the kids I moved in here with her – didn't seem right, her being left all alone at a time like this.'

'That was very kind of you,' Matthew said. 'My mother has suggested that we take Cathy back with us to London.'

Maggie nodded. 'Good idea. She needs her friends round her.' The kettle began to whistle and she made the tea. 'I'll get a couple of rooms ready for you,' she said as she poured three cups. 'Then I'll get off home, seein' as you're here. Leave you to it like.'

They sat drinking their tea while Maggie went up to tell Cathy they were here. 'I suppose you've known Cathy a long time?' Rosalind said, looking at Matthew across the kitchen table.

He looked up. 'Only since she came to live with us after her father died. She was sixteen then and I resented her like mad to begin with. Mother seemed to be making such a fuss of her. I suppose I felt a bit pushed out.' He grinned sheepishly. 'Well, I was only a teenager myself at the time. But pretty soon we grew to be like brother and sister.' He sipped his tea thoughtfully. 'Between you and me, Rosalind, she never should have married Cavelle. Mother was worried to death at the time. She always knew it would end in tears.'

Rosalind looked up, shocked to hear him voicing such an opinion at a time like this. 'But they loved each other,' she protested. 'They were so happy. No one could have foreseen a tragedy like this. It must be devastating for her.'

'I don't think they were all that happy actually,' Matthew said. 'Cathy was so much younger than him. I think she was dazzled by his fame and all that success.'

433

Rosalind shook her head. 'Surely not? Cathy was far too sensible for that.'

'I don't know. Mother felt she was looking for a father figure. Maybe she was right. I had a feeling something wasn't quite right the last time I saw her.' He sipped his tea. 'Between you and me, I have a feeling that something happened during Cathy's visit last summer. I wasn't at home at the time and Mother hasn't actually said anything but I've had the distinct impression that she was disturbed about Cathy's well-being.'

Rosalind frowned, reminded of Carla's hints about a pregnancy. 'Well, whatever happened it's over now,' she said. 'And in the worst possible way. She's going to need our support in any . . .' She broke off as the door opened and Cathy came in. She wore a dark skirt and sweater which accentuated her pallor and the hollows under her eyes and cheekbones. Her bright hair was tied back and looped at the nape of her neck. She looked very young and very vulnerable. But in spite of her gaunt appearance she seemed composed and greeted them warmly.

'Rosalind and Matthew! How good to see you both.'

'Mother was worried,' he said, going to her. 'You know how she is. She's been trying to ring you ever since we heard the news on TV. She wanted to come down herself only Gran is very poorly.' He reached out a hand and patted her awkwardly on the shoulder. 'We're all – you know, really sorry about what's happened.'

'Thank you, Matthew.' Cathy frowned. 'I should have realised that you would have heard about the crash. I should have rung Johnny. It's just that the last couple of days have been a nightmare what with the press and everyone. Can you imagine people jostling each other for interviews at a time like this?'

'They're so insensitive,' Matthew agreed. He slipped a finger inside his collar. Cathy looked so cool and normal that it unnerved him. Tears would have been embarrassing and hard to cope with, but this icy calm was worse if anything. 'Well, I'll – er – go and bring in the bags,' he said, eager to escape. 'Shall I take them straight upstairs?'

'Yes. You'll find Maggie up there. She'll show you where to put them.'

When he had gone Rosalind got up and crossed the room to Cathy. 'Mrs Johnson wants us to take you home,' she said. 'Cathy – we're here now. If there's anything either of us can do . . . If you want to talk about it . . .'

'I don't!' Cathy turned away. 'My marriage is over, Rosalind. I've got to get used to it. Gerald has gone. I'm on my own now.'

Rosalind felt her blood chill at Cathy's unnatural calm. 'But – there must be things to see to; things we can help you with? What – what about the – arrangements – the . . .'

'The funeral? That's all being taken care of by James Kendrick, Gerald's agent. He and Kay Goolden are organising it all. It will be very quiet, next week in London. But there is to be a memorial service later, probably in the Savoy Chapel.' She looked up at Rosalind with eyes like the winter sea. 'They've taken it out of my hands.'

Rosalind swallowed, trying to see through this hard, icy barrier Cathy had put up to the real feelings beneath. 'Oh. I see. That's good of them. It must be a – relief.'

'Oh, yes. They've organised it all down to the last detail, like some kind of glossy PR exercise. Kay used to do all Gerald's PR, you know.'

'Yes, I remember.' Rosalind felt uneasy. She also seemed to remember that it was the Goolden woman who had leaked Cathy and Gerald's engagement to the press and caused untold trouble for her. 'In that case why don't you close up the house and come back to London with us tomorrow? Mrs Johnson is longing to look after you and there's nothing to stay here for, is there?'

'No. Maybe there never was.' Cathy looked at Rosalind as though she were seeing her for the first time and her expression relaxed a little. 'Thank you for coming, Rosalind. It was kind of you to think of me. I'll have to be in London for the funeral, so yes, maybe I will come back with you and Matthew.' She gave herself a little shake as though coming out of a dream. 'I'm forgetting myself. Have you eaten? You and Matthew have had a long drive. What must you be thinking? I'll make you something.'

'No, don't bother. We'll go to the pub. The Admiral Nelson, isn't it? All three of us? It will do you good to get out of the house for a while.'

Cathy shook her head. 'I'd rather not. I'm not hungry and I don't feel up to facing people – not yet. But don't let me stop you.' She turned towards the door. 'I'd better go and put a match to the fire in the drawing room. It hasn't been lit since Gerald left.'

As she went out she passed Maggie in the doorway with hardly a glance.

'Well, your rooms are ready,' the housekeeper said. 'I'll get off home now that she's got some company.' As she buttoned her coat she looked at Rosalind and lowered her voice. 'I don't like the look of her,' she whispered. 'It takes people in funny ways sometimes. She's heading for some kind of reaction if you ask me. Simmering away like a little pressure cooker. I've put you in the room next to hers – just in case.' She tied a plastic rainhood firmly over her hair. 'Well, I'll be off and brave the elephants as my son used to say when he was a little 'un. My address is on the phone pad if you want me.' She paused in the doorway. 'Oh, by the way, there's a casserole in the fridge. It just wants warming up. I made it for dinner but all she wanted was an omelette. Shame to let it go to waste. G'night, then.'

'Goodnight. And thank you.'

Rosalind went to the fridge and took out the covered dish, putting it into the Aga's oven gratefully. She and Matthew hadn't eaten since the sandwich lunch Johnny had packed for them and they were both hungry. She found plates

436

and cutlery easily enough and was laying the table as he came in.

'That smells good. I could eat the proverbial horse.' He rubbed his chilled fingers and held them out over the heat of the Aga. 'What did you make of Cathy?'

'I don't know. Maggie says she's heading for some kind of reaction.'

'Sooner we get her home the better if you ask me,' Matthew said. 'Mother will know what to do, she always does.' He nodded towards the table. 'Have you persuaded her to eat with us?'

'I thought I'd try,' Rosalind told him. 'Though maybe we should just leave her for tonight.'

Cathy did not appear again, and after they had eaten Rosalind and Matthew decided to call it a day and retired to their respective rooms. It had been a long cold day and they were both weary. Rosalind was pleasantly surprised to find that Maggie had thoughtfully put an electric blanket in her bed, and, snuggling down in the warm, lavender-scented softness, she soon found her eyes closing in sleep.

She had no idea what wakened her. For a moment as she lay there in the unfamiliar bed she could not make out where she was. The rain had stopped and the night sky had cleared. The moon was shining in at the window, flooding the room with its milky light. Then she heard it – the sound that must have wakened her; the sound of sobbing. And it was coming from next door. From Cathy's room.

Getting out of bed, she pulled on her dressing gown and tiptoed out on to the landing. For a moment she stood outside Cathy's door, wondering what to do. Should she go in and try to comfort her, or would she rather be left alone? Then she heard the sound again; muffled as though it came from under the bedclothes. It sounded so heartbroken; so lonely and forlorn, almost childlike. Rosalind didn't stop to think again. Opening

437

the door quietly she went in and crossed the room to the bed.

'Cathy,' she whispered. 'Cathy – please let me help. I can't bear to hear you crying all alone like this.'

She sat up at once, brushing at her wet cheeks with her knuckles and struggling to control her emotions. 'I'm sorry. I didn't mean to wake you,' she said fumbling under the pillow for a handkerchief. 'Please go back to bed, Rosalind. I'm all right – really.'

'No, you're not.' Rosalind laid a hand on her arm. 'It's right that you should grieve,' she said. 'But not alone like this. Not when I'm here to share it. I know it must be terrible for you, losing your husband . . .'

'But it isn't!' Cathy burst out. 'He wasn't my husband, you see. We didn't have a marriage. Not a real one.' She blew her nose. 'And – and just before Christmas, after he was sure that his operation was successful, he sent word to me that he wanted a divorce. He didn't come and ask himself. He sent word with Kay Goolden – the woman he intended to marry.'

Rosalind was stunned. Just for a moment she wondered if Cathy was in her right mind. Surely what she was saying could not be true? Surely no one could be so cruel and heartless? Then she remembered what Johnny had said about her strangeness on the telephone – about spending Christmas alone. Lost for adequate words, she reached out and took both of Cathy's hands in hers. 'Oh my God, Cathy. How awful for you.'

'He and Kay were going to meet in Switzerland – to have a holiday there together. In Davos, the place where he and I spent our honeymoon.'

Rosalind drew in her breath sharply. 'Oh, Cathy, you must have been so hurt. Oh, if only you'd got in touch. You really should have talked to someone about it.'

'I couldn't.' Cathy was shivering violently now. She looked at Rosalind with dark, hollowed eyes. 'His asking me for a divorce wasn't the worst thing, you see. If he'd come home I was going to have to leave him anyway – because of something I'd found out.'

She told Rosalind of the discovery she had made in the attic that fateful afternoon. About what happened between Gerald and her mother all those years ago; about the break-up of her parents' marriage and the disillusionment and failure of her own, ending with the brief affair that had led to the pregnancy she had been forced to terminate. The words came haltingly at first, then gained momentum as though a flood of emotion had been released. And as she poured it all out, the bitterness, guilt and regret that had tangled together into a brutal snare over the past weeks, gradually loosened its stranglehold on her.

'And the worst – the *terrible* – part that hurts so badly is that it was all for nothing, Rosalind,' she said, choking on the words. 'I gave up the baby I wanted so much for *nothing*. Gerald never really cared for me at all. I believe he wanted me off his hands almost as soon as he married me. And as soon as he was healthy again he decided to dump me. Why he married me in the first place I can't understand. I've gone over and over it, trying to make some sense of it. Trying to find a reason. Perhaps I reminded him a little of my mother and he thought marrying me was a way of making amends; in the same way as he must have thought buying Daddy's music to help pay my school fees was making amends.'

She shook her head angrily. 'I don't really know what was in Gerald's head. I've given up trying to work it out. All I do know is that it was all a mistake. A disastrous mistake. And now I'm left to pay the price for the rest of my life.' She laid her head on Rosalind's shoulder as fresh tears coursed down her cheeks. 'And now – I know this sounds awful – now he's dead and – and I'm not even allowed to hate him!'

'Of course it isn't awful.' Rosalind held her close, letting her weep out all the bitterness and grief against her shoulder.

Through the other girl's thin nightdress she felt her birdlike thinness and was consumed by pity for the friend she had always admired and envied so much. Cathy, who had seemed to have the best of everything life had to offer, had secretly suffered this terrible hurt and double betrayal. Suffered it all alone. Rosalind had a sudden vivid memory of the New Year party she and Gerald had attended at Blake's Folly; the starry, almost incandescent happiness in Cathy's eyes that night as she looked forward so eagerly to marrying the man she loved. The memory made her own eyes fill with tears of pity.

At last Cathy stopped crying. Her breathing returned to normal and she composed herself. 'You won't mention any of this to Johnny, will you?' she said. 'Or breathe a word of it to Matthew?'

'Of course I won't.'

Cathy took a long shuddering breath as she dried her eyes. 'Johnny knows about the baby, of course, but not the rest. I'll tell her in my own good time. For now I'd rather it was just between you and me.'

'Of course.' Rosalind looked at her. There was a little colour in her cheeks now and her eyes looked less haunted. 'Do you feel better now?'

Cathy nodded. 'Much better, thanks to you.'

Rosalind smiled. 'There's nothing to thank me for. I'm glad I was here – that I could be a friend to you.'

Next morning Cathy appeared at the breakfast table looking much more like her old self. While Matthew took the car to the local garage for petrol she and Rosalind walked round the house together, making sure that everywhere was secured.

'I'll drop a note in at Maggie's house on the way,' Cathy said. 'She has a key and she'll look in each day and make sure everything is all right.'

'What will you do?' Rosalind asked. 'Afterwards, I mean. Will you live here, or sell the place?'

Cathy shrugged. 'It's the only home I've got. It's much too big of course. I suppose the sensible thing would be to sell it. I haven't really thought about it. I'll have to think about getting a job too. Most of our money was tied up in this place and we still owe some of the money for the building work.'

Rosalind looked thoughtful. 'I wouldn't imagine there are many jobs to be had down here, except in the holiday season.'

'You're right. I don't suppose it's practical to think of staying here.' Cathy looked around her and sighed. 'I do love this place though. It was such fun, seeing it rise from its derelict state. I hate the thought of abandoning it again – going back to London.'

'It would make a marvellous hotel,' Rosalind said. 'Or a conference centre. That barn conversion would make a fantastic conference hall.'

Matthew arrived back and whistled from the hall below. Cathy took a last look round and smiled wistfully at Rosalind. 'Maybe someone will buy it with that in mind,' she said. 'I'll have to remember your idea when I advertise it. Come on, we'd better go or Matthew will be cross. He's always hated being kept waiting.'

Cathy settled into her old room at Johnny's, happy to get away from the scene of so much trauma; to give in and let motherly Johnny fuss over her for a while. Gerald's interment took place a week later at a quiet little church in Hampstead. There were few people present and it was a private affair, kept out of the public eye, unlike the planned memorial service which was scheduled for three weeks later, to be followed by a reception at the Savoy. Cathy dreaded the theatrically staged affair with its invited galaxy of celebrities and show business razzmatazz. It hung over her head like the Sword of Damocles during the three intervening weeks. She knew it would be impossible to put the past behind her until it was over.

On the day she dressed carefully, knowing that the press and TV would be out in force. Whatever had happened she would not let herself down. She had chosen a charcoal grey suit and dressed her hair in a smooth chignon topped by a black velvet pillbox hat. Johnny and Rosalind would be going along with her and Matthew had taken the day off and would arrive in time to drive them.

When they arrived the host of glamorous guests had already begun to assemble. Almost at once Cathy spotted Simon with an older woman whom she took to be his mother. He had written to her after the crash and she had replied briefly and politely. She had no wish to see him today and to her relief he made no attempt to speak to her. Kay arrived with James Kendrick and his wife. She looked elegant in black and white, but her face, half hidden by the wide brim of her hat, still bore the traces of recent tears. Cathy found to her own surprise that she felt nothing but a detached pity for the older woman. She had wanted Gerald for so long and to have him taken from her a second time must have been a cruel blow. She moved impulsively towards her, but Johnny, who now knew of Gerald's betrayal and the proposed divorce, steered her tactfully in the opposite direction, away from Kay and from the threatened attention of the press, gathering in packs around the main entrance to the chapel.

Leaving the front pews to the celebrities, the four of them sat quietly and anonymously in a pew near the back. They sang the hymns and listened to the florid eulogy that traced Gerald's career and triumphs – the courage with which he faced his illness and the subsequent collapse of this brilliant musical career – to the cruel irony of his accidental death. A well-known violinist who had been one of Gerald's college friends spoke of him in glowing terms after which Simon

442

moved to the grand piano which had been placed below the pulpit and played an arrangement of the theme of the emotive last movement from Rachmaninov's Second Piano Concerto.

Cathy sat and listened to it all, trying not to notice the whirring of the TV cameras at the back of the chapel; trying not to think about the darker side of Gerald that no one would ever guess at. Rosalind sat on one side of her, Johnny on the other. From time to time they glanced at her, but neither touched her, sensing the carefully controlled emotions, wound as tightly as a coiled spring, admiring her strength and dignity. For her part Cathy was infinitely grateful for their tacit support.

But it was as they came out of the chapel that the real ordeal began. The reporters and TV cameras were there in force. They crowded eagerly round the doors as they opened, snapping frenziedly at the many celebrities as they emerged. Somehow Rosalind and Johnny were borne ahead by the rest of the crowd, but Cathy found herself trapped by a group of reporters. As Matthew grasped her arm firmly in an attempt to steer her out of the way, she was almost blinded by the flash of a camera. One hand went up instinctively to protect her eyes and when she removed it she found herself surrounded by reporters firing a volley of bewildering questions at her.

'How long had you been married, Mrs Cavelle?'

'Are there any children of the marriage?'

'Have you any plans to continue with the music centre in Suffolk?'

'How did you feel when you heard about the air crash?'

Then a steely-eyed woman reporter pushed forward till she was standing directly in front of Cathy.

'Tell me, Mrs Cavelle. Is there any truth in the rumour that your husband was planning to divorce you?'

Seeing her look of shock and distress, the panic in her eyes, Matthew took her arm. 'Leave her alone,' he shouted angrily. 'Can't you see you're upsetting her?'

Cathy felt as though her feet hardly touched the ground as he pushed her along in front of him, heading for the hotel. The sea of faces that parted for them seemed to melt and merge one into the other, and everything around her began to swim out of focus. From somewhere a long way off she heard a man's voice call out, 'Careful! She's going to faint!' There was a roaring in her ears and she felt arms catch her as everything went black.

When she came round she thought at first she must be dreaming. She seemed to be in a small room – an office of some kind. She was lying back in a chair and a strange young man was sitting beside her, gently chafing her hands. He had dark brown hair and concerned brown eyes. When he saw that she was coming round he smiled.

'Hi there. Welcome back.' As she tried to get up he put out a hand to stop her. 'It's all right, don't get up yet. You passed out for a moment, that's all. Luckily I happened to be there at the time. Your brother has gone to get you a glass of water.'

'How silly of me.' She struggled into a sitting position. 'I don't think I've ever fainted before.' She wondered uneasily if the man was someone she should remember. 'Please don't feel you have to stay,' she said, embarrassed at the furore she seemed to be causing. 'I'm quite all right now, really.'

'It's okay. All in the day's work.' He smiled. 'I'm a doctor. I told your brother I'd stay till he got back.'

'Matthew's not my brother. Thank you for staying with me, but I don't need a doctor – really.' She racked her brain feverishly to remember who he was. Could he have attended one of the master classes at Melfordleigh – stayed at Cuckoo Lodge? He had an accent she couldn't quite place. 'I promise you I'll be fine now,' she assured him.

'There's no way I'm going to leave you alone,' he

444

said firmly. 'I mean, that'd look pretty ungallant now, wouldn't it?'

'Have we met?' she asked. 'I'm sorry but I don't remember . . .'

'No reason why you should.' He shook his head. 'I'm forgetting my manners. I should have introduced myself. I'm Paul Franklin. Doctor Paul Franklin.'

Relieved, she took the large firm hand he offered. 'How do you do? I'm Catherine Cavelle,' she returned.

His smile was replaced by a puzzled frown as he stared at her intently.

'Did you know Gerald?' she asked. Suddenly she placed the accent. 'Ah – you must be from New Zealand. Are you from the hospital?'

'I qualified in a New Zealand hospital,' he told her. 'Which is hardly surprising, seeing that I was born and grew up there.'

'So you . . .' Whatever Cathy had been about to say was cut short by the arrival of Johnny, closely followed by Matthew and Rosalind.

'Cathy! Are you all right?' Johnny asked, bustling in and putting a glass of water into her hand. 'Those dreadful reporters. Like jackals with their horrible questions. It really shouldn't be allowed. Now – Matthew's brought the car round so if you're feeling up to it I suggest we all get off home.'

'I'm fine now, Johnny. There's no need to fuss.' She got to her feet. 'This is Doctor Franklin. He very kindly kept me company while Matthew went to find you.'

Johnny turned to the young man. 'Oh, dear, do forgive me, Doctor Franklin. How rude you must think me. Matthew told me how kind you'd been. It was so lucky you happened to be passing when Cathy fainted.'

'Not at all. I did nothing.' He smiled at Cathy. 'I can see you're in good hands now so I'll go. I hope you feel better soon.' As Matthew and Johnny escorted her out of

445

the room he turned to Rosalind. 'Excuse me. Am I right in thinking that's Gerald Cavelle's daughter?'

Rosalind looked surprised. 'Heavens, no! She's his widow.'

'His *widow*?' Paul Franklin's jaw dropped in surprise and just for a moment he seemed lost for words. But as Rosalind made to follow the others he stopped her.

'Look, I have to see her again. I wonder if you could tell me where I can get in touch with her?'

Rosalind looked doubtful. 'Well – I don't know if I should give that kind of information to a comparative stranger.'

'Oh, I'm not a stranger,' he said. 'I promise you I'm not. And it really is very important that I speak to her.' He spread his hands. 'I'd talk to her now but I'm sure you'll agree this is neither the time nor the place.'

'No.' Rosalind looked at the tall young man in the dark suit. He looked so sincere, so earnest. What should she do? 'Suppose I gave you a telephone number where you can contact her? Would that do?'

His dark eyes smiled their relief. 'Oh, that would be marvellous.'

Rosalind tore a page from the back of her diary and scribbled the Johnson's phone number on it. 'You'll be able to reach her here for the next week or so. It will be up to her, of course. I can't guarantee that she'll see you.'

'Of course. I understand that. Thanks a lot, Miss . . .'

'Just call me Rosalind.'

'Thanks, Rosalind.' He paused. 'Oh – another thing. I'd be grateful if you were to prepare her, tell her that I'll be calling her in a couple of days' time. I think I can safely say that she and I will have a great deal to talk about.'

Rosalind bit her lip anxiously as she watched him walk away. What interest could this young Doctor Franklin have in Cathy? Had she done the right thing?

*　　*　　*

446

Cathy wakened on the morning following the memorial service feeling stronger than she had for months. Over breakfast she told Johnny that she would be going up to Kensington to see James Palmer, Gerald's solicitor, as he had written requesting she should. It was time she set about sorting out her financial affairs.

When Johnny knew what she planned she asked if Cathy would like her to go along too, but she refused.

'I'm going to have to start doing things by myself,' she said. 'So I may as well begin now.'

Johnny watched her go from the window of the front room, her heart going out to the slender figure in the dark grey coat, walking bravely up the street with her head held high. She was so young to have been through such trauma. She longed to help and support her but knew that Cathy was right to tackle it by herself. There would be many things to face alone in the years to come. Johnny knew very well that however much she wished, she would not always be around to help her. Briefly she wondered what the future held for the girl who was a beloved daughter to her in all but name. Surely Gerald Cavelle would have left her well provided for? At least she would not have to worry about money.

But Johnny was soon to be proved wrong.

When Cathy learned that she was Gerald's sole beneficiary and that he had left her the house she was relieved. But her relief was to be short-lived. The solicitor quickly followed the statement by telling her that there was still a large mortgage on the house and more money owed to the builders for the restoration work, plus other amounts outstanding for furnishings, advertising and other sundries.

'All Gerald's business documents including unpaid bills were placed by him in a safety deposit box at the bank,' he told her. 'Before he left for New Zealand he sent me a key, along with instructions to deal with things if anything were to happen.'

Cathy felt the colour leave her face. So she couldn't even

be trusted with that? 'Will my own money meet the debts?' she asked in a small voice.

The solicitor looked puzzled. 'Your money? But you had a joint bank account. Everything was transferred to that at the time of the marriage.'

'But there was the money my father left me – from the sale of our house,' she said. 'Gerald said he had invested that for me.'

Clearly uncomfortable, the man cleared his throat. 'Invested it, yes, Mrs Cavelle – in Cuckoo Lodge and the establishing of the music school at Melfordleigh.'

She stared at him. 'You mean it's – all been spent – used up? It's gone?'

'I'm very much afraid so, yes.'

A feeling of panic quickened her heartbeat. 'But – I didn't know. I wasn't asked – never gave my permission.' She shook her head. 'Surely . . .'

The man took a document from the file in front of him and passed it across the desk to her. 'This is your signature, isn't it?'

She stared down at the name signed on the bottom line and remembered the day Gerald had brought her here to this office to sign it. He had said it was for joint ownership of the house. But he hadn't mentioned that her own money was to be tied up in it.

James Palmer was looking at her with some concern. 'Surely your husband explained it to you?' he said. 'You must have been aware . . .'

'*Yes!*' Suddenly she felt foolish and naive. How stupid the solicitor must think her. She made herself laugh. 'Of course, I remember now. How silly of me.'

The man looked at her sympathetically. She was so young to be widowed, let alone burdened with a massive debt like this. 'I assume you'll sell the house and effects?' he asked. 'It is what I would strongly advise.'

448

'Yes.' She nodded dazedly. 'It seems the only thing I can do.'

'Do you wish me to write to all the creditors and explain the situation?' he asked. 'I'll ask them to give you time to sell the property, though I must warn you that if they press for immediate payment we shall have to go for voluntary bankruptcy?' He saw the look of wide-eyed fear and distress on Cathy's face and added quickly, 'I'm sure they will all agree to wait a while. It will be to their advantage to do so. I'll make sure they know that.'

Outside in the street the sun was shining; thin lemon-coloured winter sunshine that somehow made the cold wind blowing down Kensington High Street feel even keener. Cathy shivered and pulled her coat collar up. What was she to do? She was penniless. The owner of a great house, yet no home. An overwhelming number of debts and no money with which to pay them. She had thought when Gerald died that he could hurt her no more. How wrong she had been.

As she pulled on her glove the emerald in her engagement ring flashed in the sunlight. At least she still had that, she comforted herself. It had ceased to be a symbol of Gerald's love a long time ago. Now at least it would provide enough money for her to live on for a while.

Chapter Twenty-One

It was the day after her interview with the solicitor that Paul Franklin telephoned and asked to meet Cathy. Still numb with shock about her financial situation her first impulse had been to refuse. She had hesitated, racking her brain for a polite excuse, but Paul was so persuasive that in the end she had promised to ring him back. When she asked Johnny's advice on the matter the older woman had suggested that she invite him to the house.

'I don't know who he is or what he can possibly want to see you about,' she said. 'But I think you'd be well advised to meet him on your own territory. Ask him to come here to tea.'

Cathy rang Paul back the next day with the invitation which he accepted delightedly.

Although there had been a fall of snow during the night, the sun was shining and Johnny's comfortable sitting room was warm and homely with a bright fire burning in the grate and its window looking on to the sparkling white garden outside. Johnny welcomed Paul and showed him into the sitting room where Cathy was waiting, then she left the two of them to talk.

'It was very good of you to invite me,' he said as he took the chair Cathy offered, close to the fire. 'I can't get over the snow out there. You know, this is the first time I've seen it.' He laughed a little self-consciously. 'It must sound crazy to you, but I haven't been able to stop looking at it ever since I first drew the curtains this morning.'

'I'm afraid the novelty will soon wear off once it gets to the slushy stage,' Cathy warned him. There was a pause as

450

she watched him rub his chilled fingers and hold them to the blaze. She cleared her throat.

'So – what was it you wanted to speak to me about, Doctor Franklin?'

'Oh, please call me Paul.' He looked up and their eyes met. 'I guess I should get to the point,' he said uneasily. 'I don't want to take up too much of your time. I don't want to intrude either.' He looked at her uncertainly. 'I don't know how much you know about Gerald's life? I mean – the part before you were married; before you met.'

'Quite a lot as it happens,' Cathy said. 'He and my father had been close friends since they were students. When my father died he made Gerald my legal guardian.'

'And you fell in love and married?' He smiled. 'How romantic.' Cathy gave a small non-committal shrug and he went on. 'So you must have known that he was married once before? A long time before.'

'Of course I knew.' Cathy tried to hide the unease she felt. Why all these questions? Could Gerald somehow have been in this young doctor's debt? Was there even more to uncover about his past? Was she going to spend her entire life discovering things about that other, darker side of Gerald he had so successfully hidden?

'I don't quite understand where this is leading,' she said. 'Do you know something I don't know about Gerald? Have you come to drop some kind of bombshell?'

'No – well . . .' He smiled ruefully. 'It rather depends on how you see it.' He paused, looking at her apprehensively. 'I guess there's no way to break a thing like this gently,' he said. 'Gerald Cavelle is – was – my father.'

For a long moment Cathy stared disbelievingly into the grave brown eyes. There had to be some mistake. Gerald had no son – no children at all. 'You say you're his *son*?' She shook her head. 'But your name – Paul Franklin?'

'Franklin is my mother's maiden name. She reverted to it after they divorced. It isn't surprising you didn't know

451

about me. Gerald himself didn't know I existed until just a few weeks ago. He and my mother parted in 1939, just before the war began. When she went home to Auckland she didn't know that she was already expecting me.'

'And she never told him?'

'No. I think she was afraid he might make demands if he knew about me. Seems she wanted him out of her life. It was never a good marriage. For years she let me believe my dad had died in the war. I was eighteen before she told me the truth.'

'How strange that must have felt.' Cathy was looking at him, searching his features for some resemblance to Gerald. Apart from his build and colouring, she found none.

He smiled wryly. 'You can say that again! By then he was a well-known concert pianist. A big name in the world of classical music. Once I knew who he was he started to be something of an obsession with me – an idol if you like. I began to collect all his records – magazine articles – pictures. Once, when I heard that he was touring Australia, I saved up and bought a plane ticket to go and hear him play.' He shook his head. 'I was so damned *proud*. I wanted to turn around and tell everyone he was my dad. For weeks before I went I fantasised about how I'd go round and surprise him afterwards and we'd be reunited. But when it actually came to the crunch I just couldn't get up the nerve, I chickened out – just came home without seeing him.' He smiled ruefully. 'Much to Ma's relief, I might add. I think she was scared I might bring him back with me.'

'So – did you ever meet him?'

Paul nodded. 'Oh, yes – finally. When I heard on the hospital grapevine that he was in Auckland, having surgery in Professor Harbage's clinic, I had to go and see him. Even Ma couldn't help but agree when she knew he was ill.'

'He must have been very surprised,' Cathy whispered.

'Oh, he was.' Paul smiled. 'We only met that one time,

452

but I think he liked me. I like to think he was pleased to know about me.'

'Did he tell you he was married?'

'No. And I certainly never expected him to have a wife as young as you. When you told me your name the other day I thought you must be his daughter. I thought I was discovering a half-sister!'

Cathy smiled. 'Sorry to disappoint you.'

'Oh, no!' Paul coloured. 'Not at all! I'm *glad* really. I mean – oh, God, I'm sorry.' He shook his head. 'I've put my big foot in it again. I'm always doing that.'

'No, you haven't. Did you come all the way over here just for the memorial service?' Cathy asked.

'Oh, no. I'm here to complete my studies. I'm hoping to specialise in cardiology, you see. As soon as I knew there was a chance to come over and work at one of your great teaching hospitals, I applied. It's so exciting all the pioneering work they're doing now with transplants. I wanted to be in on all of it.' He looked up shyly. 'It was a kind of scholarship. I got it for qualifying with highish marks.'

'Congratulations.'

'But I didn't hear I'd won it till after the air crash.'

'So Gerald never knew?'

'No, more's the pity. It seemed such a marvellous chance in every way. To study and to see more of him too. Hear him play again, maybe. He'd told me about the fine old house by the sea where he was holding master classes and teaching. I hoped I might get a chance to see that too.' He sighed. 'Sadly I only got here in time to attend his memorial service.'

Cathy felt her heart contract for this young man who had wanted so badly to know his father. 'And your mother?' she asked.

He shrugged. 'She was thrilled about the scholarship of course. Not so keen for me to spend time with Gerald though,' he admitted. 'They parted on bitter terms. When

453

I was born she didn't even give me his name, so you can guess how strongly she felt.' He sighed. 'When she saw that I was determined to get to know him while I was in England she was pretty upset. I regret that now, specially under the circumstances.'

'But you had a right to find out who your father was,' Cathy said. 'And you must have been proud of his brilliant talent. Have you inherited it?'

'*No!*' He laughed and shook his head. 'Oh, I play a bit, but Ma is the musician. She teaches music at the local college.'

He glanced at her hesitantly. 'Is there a chance I could maybe visit Suffolk and see Cuckoo Lodge?'

Cathy sighed. It was the request she'd been dreading. 'I don't know Paul. The truth is, I'm going to have to sell the house. I don't know what my future plans will be at the moment.'

He nodded. 'I understand. But I'd really like to see it before you sell. If that's at all possible. See the place where he lived and worked. It'd mean a lot to me.'

'Well – I'll think about it and let you know,' she said non-committally.

Johnny came in with the tea trolley and Paul jumped to his feet to help her, his eyes lighting up like a small boy's when they lighted on the plates loaded with sandwiches and three kinds of home-made cake.

'Hey, you really shouldn't have gone to so much trouble, Mrs Johnson, but I must say it looks wonderful!'

When he had gone Johnny glanced at Cathy as they washed up together. Ever since Paul Franklin left she'd been quiet and pensive.

'He's nice,' she said. 'You haven't told me what he wanted. Did you find out who he is?'

Cathy picked up a plate and dried it thoughtfully. 'He's Gerald's son.'

Johnny stopped to stare at her. 'Did you say his *son*?'

'From his first marriage,' Cathy explained. 'It was before the war and it only lasted a short time. Paul's mother went home to New Zealand when the war broke out. She didn't realise that she was pregnant until after they parted. She never told Gerald. He didn't know about Paul till he went over there to have his operation.'

Johnny shook her head. 'How many more secrets in that man's past? I wonder. So, what did Paul want? Will you be seeing him again?'

'He wants to see Cuckoo Lodge. He wants to find out as much as he can about the father he never knew and I think he sees me as some kind of link.'

'Will you take him to Suffolk?'

Cathy looked at Johnny with clouded eyes. 'How can I? Gerald was some kind of idol to him. How can I smash that? I wouldn't have the heart to tell him what kind of man his father really was, and I was never any good at pretending. Better to leave things as they are.'

Johnny looked doubtful. 'Surely it wouldn't hurt to let him see the house where his father lived?'

Cathy sighed. 'That would mean I'd have to go back myself and I don't want to do that.'

Johnny looked shocked. 'But you have to Cathy. You know that, even if it's only to pack up and put the place on the market.'

She sighed. 'I know. I've imposed on your hospitality for far too long.'

'Imposed on my hospitality!' Johnny looked shocked. 'You know very well that you're family to me, Cathy. I think of you as a daughter, so don't let me hear you saying things like that.' She dried her hands and hung up the tea towel. 'You must know that you're welcome to stay here for as long as you want,' she said. 'Having you here has been a treat for me. I've been at such a loose end with Mother in hospital and Matthew away so much.'

455

'I know, Johnny.' Cathy bit her lip, feeling ashamed of the thoughtless remark. 'I'm sorry. Nevertheless, you're right. It is time I started thinking about the future.'

Johnny was peering at her. 'You don't hate Melfordleigh that much, do you?'

'I don't hate it at all. I love it. It's just the memories. The pain and disillusionment I went through there; the mistakes I made. The – the loss. I can't help thinking that there must have been some way I could have done things better, differently – made it all work.'

'You couldn't,' Johnny said putting a hand on her arm. 'Forgive me for reminding you, love, but you know now why Gerald married you. He was your guardian – obliged to care for you until you were twenty-one. And marrying you was just a legal way to get his hands on the money your father left you so that he could buy Cuckoo Lodge and set up the school. But what's done can't be undone. It's over now and you have to try to put it behind you and start making plans. You won't do that by running away and I think you know it.'

She looked at the doubt and anxiety etched on Cathy's face. 'Look, I tell you what – why don't you take Rosalind with you? She's a sensible girl and you seem to get along together. Then you could invite Paul to go and stay for a weekend. Kill two birds with one stone as it were. No need to shatter his dream of the father he never knew. You can put on a bit of an act just for a couple of days for his sake, can't you? You'll probably never have to see him again once you've done it.'

Cathy went round to see Rosalind next morning with her proposition. Rosalind's face broke into a smile when she answered the door. Over coffee Cathy told her about Paul Franklin's visit and his revelation about who he was, explaining that he wanted to visit Melfordleigh.

'It's all going to be rather difficult,' she said. 'And I

456

wondered if you'd be free to come down too? I know you like it there and it would help me out.'

Rosalind smiled. 'Oh, Cathy, I'd love to come. Keeping house for Don is okay. He's so kind and considerate, but it gets lonely and boring by myself in the house all day. I miss the life and the bustle of the Queen's Head and all the people I used to work with even more than I expected to.'

'There's one thing I don't understand,' Cathy said. 'Why did you let your mother browbeat you into giving up your job and your training course just so that she could go and take this job?'

Rosalind looked at her for a long moment. This was something she'd been dreading, but she knew she owed it to Cathy to confess. 'She – found out about something I did,' she said haltingly. 'She threatened to go to Mrs Gresham and tell her. I had no choice.'

Cathy looked puzzled. 'But what could you possibly have done that was so terrible?'

Rosalind couldn't look at her. 'I – stole something. One of Don's mother's antique porcelain figures. I needed the money to go to Australia when Dad was ill. Mum wouldn't help. She wouldn't even ask Don to lend me the money. I was desperate, Cathy! I'd have done almost anything.' She looked up fearfully but saw only compassion in the other girl's eyes. 'Don found out almost at once of course. He missed the piece and notified the police so I had to tell him. He was marvellous about it and gave me the money anyway. But he wasn't able to buy the figure back and eventually Mum found out.'

Cathy reached out and took both her hands. 'Oh, poor Rossie.'

'So now you know the worst about me,' she said. 'You know what sort of person I am.'

'I know that you were desperate to see your father, and that you put yourself into a dangerous situation because of it. And I know that your mother used it against you. I'd say you'd been punished more than enough.' She reached out to take both Rosalind's hands. 'We all make mistakes. Sometimes we're pushed into doing desperate things that are completely against our characters. I know that all too well.'

Rosalind looked relieved. 'I'm so glad I've told you. Maybe now I can start to forgive myself.' She paused. 'There's something else I have to tell you – if you don't already know. I've been seeing – someone since Christmas.'

Cathy smiled. 'Matthew, you mean?' She knew that since Rosalind and Matthew had made the trip to Melfordleigh they had been out together a few times. Matthew had confided as much to her on his weekend visits home.

Rosalind coloured. 'That's right. He's taken me to the theatre once and out to dinner twice.' She looked at Cathy. 'You know that he's looking for another job now that he's qualified? Well, he rang me yesterday and said that he's being interviewed for one in a practice in Ipswich next Friday.'

Cathy's eyes widened with surprise. 'Ipswich? I don't think even Johnny knows about that. He must feel you're rather special to confide in you.'

'Oh, no! I daresay he just wanted to keep it to himself until there was something positive to tell,' she said.

Cathy was looking closely at her. 'You like him, don't you, Rossie?'

'Yes, I do.' Rosalind's colour deepened. 'He's the first man I've ever felt I could trust. I can relax with him. He's so easy to talk to. He seems to understand. I've even told him about the porcelain figure. I thought he might not want to see me again after that, but I had to be honest with him.'

'And it made no difference? I'm really pleased,' Cathy said sincerely. 'You and he are ideally suited. You're both quiet and deep-thinking. You both . . .'

'Hey, stop it!' Rosalind stopped her with an embarrassed

458

laugh. 'We're just friends, that's all. You'll be choosing the bridesmaids' dresses in a minute!'

Cathy joined in the laughter, noticing how pretty Rosalind was with her eyes shining and her cheeks pink. This was the first time Cathy had seen her looking really happy. 'I'll tell you what,' she said. 'We'll go down to Melfordleigh next Friday and take Paul along. Then, as Matthew will already be in the area, why don't we ask him to come and join us there for the weekend?' She sighed. 'It may be the last time any of us has a chance to stay there. I'll be putting the house on the market next week.'

'Oh.' Rosalind's face dropped. 'That's a shame. Don't you want to live there any more?'

'It just wouldn't be practical,' Cathy told her. 'It's much too big. I couldn't keep it going as a music school, and anyway, I'll have to get a job of some kind. Gerald left me nothing but a pile of debts, you see. Everything we both had went into the house and the school.'

'Oh, no. I didn't realise. Poor Cathy.'

'I can't blame him for that,' she said quickly. 'After all, he never expected that plane to crash, did he? If we'd been divorced as he planned, Cuckoo Lodge would have been sold anyway, so it seems it was on the cards all along.' She looked at Rosalind. 'By the way – what I told you about Gerald and our marriage, the divorce and everything from the past ... I don't want Paul to know any of it. He's built up such an ideal image of his father, I don't want to disillusion him. There isn't any point. Now that Gerald is dead there's no reason he need ever know.'

'Of course. Just as you say,' Rosalind promised.

'This weekend will be for Paul's benefit,' Cathy went on. 'I was lucky. I had a wonderful father and I was close to him for sixteen years. Paul had only newspaper clippings and records, so I think I owe him that.'

* * *

When she telephoned Paul and invited him to Melfordleigh for the weekend he was overjoyed.

'I can't tell you how much it means to me, Cathy,' he said excitedly. 'To see the place where he lived; the house he loved. To be able to touch his things – play his piano. Thanks, Cathy. I can't tell you how much I'll look forward to it.'

Cathy had intended that they should travel to Suffolk by train, but Paul had telephoned to say that he'd hired a car for the weekend. 'I thought that way I'd be able to see more of the countryside,' he explained. 'While I'm here I intend to see as much of Britain as I can.'

He picked her and Rosalind up the following Friday evening. Cathy had written to Maggie and asked her to open up the house and when they arrived they found fires lit and the rooms ready for them. Matthew was already there, sitting in the drawing room with his feet up on the brass fender.

'Hi!' he said when they walked in. 'Your housekeeper let me in, Cath. She told me to tell you that there's a meal waiting in the oven if you're hungry.'

Rosalind stood in front of him, trying to assess his mood. 'Well,' she said. 'Are you going to tell us how the interview went? Is there any news?'

'Not really.' Matthew stood up and stretched his arms above his head with exaggerated nonchalance. 'Unless you want to say hello to the new junior solicitor in the firm of Hawkins, Hawkins and Mather.'

Rosalind gave a whoop of delight and threw her arms around him. 'Oh, *Matthew*! That's wonderful.'

Cathy echoed Rosalind's congratulations and Paul shook his hand. Then, sensing that they wanted to be alone, Cathy took Paul's arm and steered him towards the kitchen.

'Come and help me dish up this meal,' she invited. 'It's too dark to see much now but tomorrow I'll show you round the house and the village.'

* * *

Saturday morning dawned bright and clear. Although it was still only late-February the weather was mild and springlike and as soon as they had breakfasted Matthew and Rosalind wrapped up in their warmest clothes and went for a walk down to the quay. Sitting on the wall and looking out across the calm water Rosalind said suddenly: 'Matthew. About two o'clock this morning I woke up with this crazy idea.'

He laughed. 'How crazy?'

'I don't know. Impossibly crazy perhaps. That's what I want you to tell me.'

He smiled and slipped an arm around her shoulders. 'Then you'd better explain it to me, hadn't you?'

'Cathy says she has to sell Cuckoo Lodge.'

'That's right. Gerald died owing quite a lot of money.' He looked at her, one eyebrow raised. 'Don't tell me you're thinking of buying it?'

Rosalind bit her lip. 'There – I knew you'd think it was crazy. Oh, well, it *was* two in the morning when I thought of it.'

'No, wait.' He was frowning. 'I mean, what would you do with it?'

'I've always wanted a hotel,' she told him simply. 'It's been my ambition ever since I was a little girl. Cuckoo Lodge would be perfect. Even the name is just right. But you're right. It's a mad idea.'

'Hang on, I didn't say that. It was a surprise, that's all.' He looked at her thoughtfully. 'Do you think you could do it? You must think there's a possibility.'

'I feel fairly confident that I could run it. What I don't know is whether I'd have enough money. I told you my dad left me a cottage? Dad and Freda had done a lot of work on it – made it really nice. I sold it for a good price as a weekend retreat.'

'Well, Cuckoo Lodge is equipped for guests,' he said. 'There'd be nothing for you to buy and no alterations to be

461

made. But . . .' He looked at her. 'Even if you had enough money for the deposit and could get a mortgage, it would be hard work, you know. You'd have staff to pay. You couldn't run it alone. It could be years before you saw any profit.'

'I realise that. But if I just made enough to live on I'd be happy. It would be *my* business, you see – and my home too. I'd be working for myself; answerable to no one. Doing what I've always dreamed of doing.' She turned her face up to his, eyes shining with excited enthusiasm. 'I want it, Matthew. What would I have to do to get it?'

Catching some of her excitement, he hugged her closer. 'Well – first you'd have to find out what sort of price Cathy is hoping to get for the place. You'd probably need a bank loan to start the business. For that you'd have to work out a business plan – present a set of figures so that the bank could see you know what you're doing. Then there'd be a mortgage to fix up.'

'I'm sure I could do the business plan. I lay awake for hours last night working all that out in my head . . .' Suddenly the light went out of Rosalind's eyes and her face dropped.

'What? What's the matter?'

'No bank would give me a loan though, would they, Matthew? I wouldn't get a mortgage either. Not after – after what I did.'

'You've got to put that behind you, Rossie,' he said sternly. 'It was something you did out of desperation – a private matter, between you and your step-father. He accepted your explanation and understood. You gave the money back to him and he forgave you. As it was never reported to the police there's no record. No one even knows about it apart from you and your parents.'

She sighed. 'That's right, I suppose.'

'Of course it is. Your mother was simply playing on your conscience when she bullied you into giving up your job.' He drew her close. 'You've got to try to forget it, darling.'

She looked up at him. 'I don't think I ever will.'

'But you *must*. You can't let one incident like that ruin your life.' He bent and kissed her. 'If that is the worst mistake you ever make you'll be doing well.' He jumped down from the wall and held out his hands to her. 'Come on, I'll treat you to lunch at the Admiral Nelson, then we'll go back and ask Cathy what she thinks of your plan.'

Paul wanted to see everything, each room in the house, the grounds and garden, ending with the converted barn where the concerts and master classes had been held. He stood in the auditorium, looking at the shallow stage and the rows of seats, enthralled by everything he saw.

'And you helped with it all?' he said, looking round him in admiration. 'All the restoration, the decor and everything? I can't imagine why anyone would want to give it all up.'

'I've no choice, Paul,' she told him. 'Gerald died still owing a lot of money. It has to be paid back.'

Back in the house she left him running his fingers experimentally over the keyboard of Gerald's piano in the larger of the two studios while she went to make coffee. When she came back he turned to her, his eyes bright with an idea.

'Why don't you keep the place on, Cathy – open it up as a kind of shrine to Gerald?' he said. 'All the people who were his fans could come to pay homage; to see his home and all the things he lived and worked with. Like Elgar's birthplace in Worcestershire. I've been there. Hundreds of visitors go to see that every year. You could still run concerts in the barn to help finance the place. You said you were going to have to get a job, so why not right here?'

Cathy's heart sank. How could she tell him why the idea appalled her so? 'It would be too much of a gamble, Paul,' she said gently. 'Elgar was a great composer. His music will

463

live on. Gerald was a concert pianist. Oh, a brilliant one, I grant you, but others will follow him. People soon forget. Maybe there would be a few visitors the first summer. After that it would run at a loss.' She looked at his crestfallen face. 'I'm sorry, Paul, but I couldn't afford it. Gerald's creditors are pressing for their money. They need to be paid now, otherwise I'll have to settle for bankruptcy and I don't want that.'

'I never meant for you to do it alone.' He reached for her hands. 'Look, Cathy. I have some money. My grandfather left me some. I'd willingly put it into a project like this. Gerald was a composer too. There's his rhapsody and maybe there are more compositions that he never showed to anyone.' He pressed her hands. 'Please – at least think about it.'

She pulled her hands away and walked to the window. 'I don't have to think about it, Paul. I need to sell. If you want to buy Cuckoo Lodge and do it yourself, I can't stop you. But I couldn't take on a project like the one you suggest.'

There was a long pause as she stared unseeingly out of the window, but she could still feel his eyes on her back. 'And if I were to ask you why you're so against it?' he said at last.

She turned to face him. 'I've told you why. I'm not against it as such. It's just that I don't think it would work.' She looked down at her hands. 'And I don't want to be a part of anything like that.'

He got up from the piano and went towards her, his eyes searching hers uneasily. 'Were you unhappy with him? Is that it?'

She shook her head. 'I was much too young – too immature for marriage. Oh, it was my fault. I was warned but I ignored the warnings, refused to see the difficulties.' She sighed. 'You needn't concern yourself with that.' She looked at him. 'Paul – please don't put your money into Cuckoo Lodge. You'd lose it all and I'd hate to feel responsible for that.'

But he wasn't listening. 'You say I shouldn't be concerned that your marriage was unhappy, Cathy,' he said quietly, 'but I am. Ever since the day I first saw you I've known there was something about you – some deep unhappiness. I wish I knew what it was. I wish there was something I could do . . .'

'There isn't. And I'm fine.' She forced a smile. 'How morbid we're getting. Come on, let's go down and look at the village before it decides to rain.'

But already the sky was overcast and by the time they reached the quay the rain had begun. The water in the harbour that had been so smooth and calm was choppy now, the rising wind whipping it into angry little wavelets that slapped against the harbour wall. They ran to the Admiral Nelson for cover and found Matthew and Rosalind sitting in the lounge overlooking the quay.

'We were just going to have lunch, why don't you join us?' Matthew suggested. He looked at Cathy. 'Rossie has an idea she wants to put to you anyway.'

Paul, who was utterly enchanted by the quaint old pub, went off to the bar to buy drinks and Rosalind leaned across the table. 'Cathy – what would you say if I told you I want to buy Cuckoo Lodge?' she asked, trying in vain to suppress the excitement in her voice.

Cathy's eyebrows rose. 'I'd say that at this rate I shan't have to advertise. Yours is the second offer I've had this morning.'

'The second?' Rosalind's face dropped. 'Whose was the other?'

'Paul's. But he was only half serious and I think I've talked him out of it,' Cathy told her. 'He wanted to turn the place into some kind of living memorial to Gerald.' Rosalind and Matthew stared at her in silence. 'I know,' she said. 'It would never work. He'd be pouring money into a bottomless pit and I told him so. But you, Rossie – what would you do with it?'

'I'd open it as a hotel,' Rosalind told her. 'We've just been talking to the landlord here. Apparently this is the only residential place in the village apart from the bed and breakfast places and the holiday cottages. He turns people away all the time, so I wouldn't be short of business.' She leaned forward, her eyes shining. 'And as for the off-season, remember what I said about letting the place out for conferences – using the barn as a conference hall?'

'I do indeed,' Cathy said guardedly. 'It's a lovely idea but . . .'

'There's the money I've been saving,' Rosalind went on, anticipating the next question, 'that I got from the sale of the cottage, remember? Matthew thinks it might be enough for the deposit. He's going to help me apply for a bank loan and a mortgage.'

'You should get the place valued first, Cath,' he put in cautiously.

'Yes, I know. Well, if you're serious I'll start doing something about it first thing on Monday morning.'

By the time Paul came back to the table with the tray of drinks he found the other three in good spirits. He took the news that Rosalind meant to make an offer for Cuckoo Lodge resignedly, but later that afternoon, as he and Cathy were walking on the dunes after the rain had stopped, he said: 'I'd like to take something of Gerald's home with me when I go.' He sighed. 'I suppose I have to admit that buying the house was kind of a stupid idea when I live on the other side of the world – just a pipe dream really. All the same . . .'

Cathy turned to him. 'I'd like you to have his piano.'

'His *piano*?' He stopped in his tracks and turned to her. 'You mean you wouldn't *mind*?'

'Not at all. It should be yours by right.'

'Oh, Cathy. I don't know what to say. That's so generous.'

'Of course transporting it might be a problem.'

466

'Never mind that. I'll get it home somehow.' He looked at her. 'I'd like you to come over and see Auckland sometime, Cathy. I think you'd like it there. Of course we don't have olde worlde pubs or wild, windswept coastlines like this, but it is beautiful and I have to say that our weather has yours licked.' He grinned disarmingly. 'The natives are friendly too. What do you say?'

She smiled. 'It sounds nice, but I've got an awful lot of planning to do, Paul. A whole new life to sort out for myself.'

He stopped walking and reached out to take her hand. 'Look, you're not saying that this weekend – I mean – it won't be the last we'll see of each other, will it?'

She shook her head, acutely aware of the hand that held hers. 'I don't know, Paul. You have your studies at the hospital. I have so much to attend to. Maybe it would be best.'

'I don't agree.' He was looking at her with earnest brown eyes. 'I'm going to be here for a whole year. Surely we could see something of each other during that time? I'd really like us to get to know one another better.'

'Well – maybe.'

'And don't forget that Gerald's rhapsody gets its first performance in August at the Promenade Concerts. We just have to go and hear that together.'

'Well . . .' She couldn't meet the compelling eyes that looked into hers. 'I – just don't know,' she hedged. 'It's a long time ahead. Six whole months. Let's leave it for now, shall we?'

She made to move away but he held on to her hand. 'Look – maybe this is the wrong time to be saying this and I'll be putting my foot in it all over again, but we only have these two days so I want you to know how I feel. It's as though I've known you for years, Cathy, not just days. We have so much in common. We can't just say goodbye and leave it at that.'

She'd sensed this coming and now she felt something very close to panic tightening her throat. 'Paul, we don't really know each other at all. You know nothing about me. You think that because I was married to your father we automatically have things in common . . .'

'No, you've got it all wrong.' He was shaking his head. 'It isn't just that. I . . .'

'I'm probably nothing like you think.' She pulled her hand forcibly from his grasp. 'I don't want to talk about it any more, Paul. Let's go back. It's beginning to get dark and I'm cold.'

Sleep did not come easily to Cathy that night. The weekend was proving so much more traumatic than she'd imagined. Paul clearly saw his father as some kind of saintly genius and her as his adjunct – the closest link he could form – which was why he wanted to cling to her. Keeping up the charade of Gerald's honour and integrity was becoming more of a strain with each passing hour. As she tossed and turned she wished fervently that the weekend could be at an end so that they could leave for London again. As for Paul's suggestion that they see each other again during his stay in England, that was the hardest thing to cope with. She liked him so much. She found his warm personality, his sense of humour and his dark good looks attractive and infinitely appealing. In any other circumstances, if he had been anyone other than Gerald's son, she would happily have agreed to see him again. As it was, how could she allow him to get any closer without revealing the unpalatable truth about his father?

It was early next morning when she was wakened by someone tapping on her bedroom door.

'Can I come in?' Rosalind put her head round the door. 'I know it's early but there's something I need to talk to you about.'

Cathy sat up, rubbing the sleep from her eyes and

yawning. It had been four o'clock by the time sleep had finally claimed her. Her head felt heavy and her eyes ached. 'Come in and sit down,' she invited. 'Don't tell me you've had another brilliant idea.'

'I have as a matter of fact.' Rosalind perched on the end of the bed drawing up her knees and hugging them. 'I don't know what it is about this place but I feel a different person here – so alive and full of vitality. It must be the air.'

Cathy smiled. Privately she felt that Rosalind's good humour had more to do with Matthew than Melfordleigh. 'Okay, are you going to tell me about it then?' she said through another yawn.

'Right. I can't imagine why I didn't think of this before. It's been staring us in the face all the time.'

'Mmm? What has?'

'You've been saying that you need to look for a job, right?'

'Right. I do – and soon.'

'Well, the answer is obvious. Why don't we go into partnership – run Cuckoo Lodge together? After all we get along together, don't we? I've had experience and training in hotel work and you did your Home Economics course.'

'Well, yes, I suppose you're right.' Cathy was suddenly wide awake and staring at her friend. The idea was so simple and so obvious that there must surely be some snag. 'But – but would it really work?' she stammered.

'It could. I'm sure it could. We'd have to work out the details, of course, but if the money I've got would pay off what Gerald owed we could count that as my share of the business, then we could start with a clean sheet; run the place as a hotel, each draw a salary and pay the existing mortgage off out of our profits. We might not even need a bank loan. It's perfect, Cathy!'

She felt her heart leap with excitement, and had to force herself to be cautious. 'On the face of it, yes, but it all sounds a bit too good to be true. 'Have you spoken to Matthew about it?'

'Yes, last night. I kept him up till the small hours. He says that if my money is enough to settle the debts, and if you agree of course, he doesn't see why it shouldn't work out fine. He's even offered to draw up a proper partnership agreement for us so that everything is fair. He says he'll do all the legal work for us as a gift.'

Cathy was smiling now, her weariness forgotten. 'Oh, Rossie, wouldn't it be fun? I hardly dare think about it. Do you *really* think we could make a go of it?'

'I've told you, I'm sure we could. I've worked it all out. If we got a move on and advertised we could have a good first season *this* year. The landlord of the Admiral Nelson will send us his overflow if we ask him. I sounded him out yesterday – without giving anything away, of course. And while we're doing that we could be advertising and booking conferences for the winter months. And the beauty of it is that as the place already belongs to you, there'll be no waiting for contracts to be finalised. We could start right away! As soon as you like.'

Cathy jumped out of bed and pulled on her dressing gown. 'Let's go and get Matthew up this minute and start working out the details,' she said excitedly.

Rosalind laid a hand on her arm. 'Cathy – what about Paul?'

'What about him?'

'He's going to feel rather left out of all this, isn't he? Especially when he wanted the place himself. Do you think we should wait and talk about it later, when we're alone?'

Cathy sank back on to the bed again with a sigh. 'I suppose you're right.' She looked at Rosalind. 'I don't know what to do about him, Rossie. He wants us to go on seeing each other. He's going to be over here for a whole year. It's going to be so difficult to avoid him.'

'Why should you want to?' she asked. 'He's so nice and he's obviously very taken with you.'

'But he's Gerald's son.'

'Biologically, maybe, but that's all. They never knew each other, did they?'

'But he thinks of him as some kind of hero. I couldn't keep up that kind of pretence.'

'Then don't. Tell him the truth.'

Cathy stared at her. 'How could I?'

'Why not? We all have to cope with the truth at some time, Cathy. It's part of growing up, isn't it?' She leaned forward. 'If you can't bear to hurt him then you must care about him a little. If that's the case you'll want to go on seeing him. I don't see why you should let a thing like that stand in your way.'

Cathy shook her head, her eyes troubled. 'I keep thinking of Dad and how much he meant to me,' she said. 'I was so lucky to have had him all the time I was growing up. All Paul has is this image he's built. How can I shatter that?'

'What about *your* images, Cathy? You believed in Gerald, didn't you? He was a hero to you too once. You gave your life to him, and you had to find out the hard way. And what about me? My mother did her best to poison my memories of my father. I knew he wasn't perfect but it didn't make any difference. I loved him the way he was.' She touched Cathy's arm. 'Even with all Gerald's faults he was a musical genius. Paul can still be proud of that.'

'I know that what you're saying is right,' Cathy said. 'I just don't want to be the one to tell him.'

'Because you think he'll hate you for pulling down his dream? And having him hate you is the last thing you want?'

For a long moment they stared at each other. Rosalind had interpreted Cathy's thoughts with uncanny accuracy, but she wasn't sure she was ready to face them. 'You're right,' she said at last. 'It would be better to wait until

471

the three of us are alone. Today we'll just relax and enjoy ourselves.'

'Okay, only don't bury your head in the sand,' Rosalind warned. 'Don't spend the rest of your life throwing away chances of happiness. They don't come along so often that we can afford to waste them.'

The four of them spent the day pleasantly enough. The weather was fine again and over breakfast Paul suggested a drive inland.

'Might as well make the most of the car while I've got it,' he said. 'See a bit of Suffolk. I'm really keen to take a look at these ancient Brecklands I've heard so much about.'

Although he asked Rosalind and Matthew to go too, they declined. Matthew had telephoned some married friends in nearby Woodbridge to tell them about his new job and they had invited him to take Rosalind along to lunch. They left soon after eleven and Cathy and Paul set out soon after. As they drove along the lanes in the winter sunshine Cathy was quiet. She felt stupid and tongue-tied and the more she searched her mind for some intelligent topic, the blanker it became. For a while Paul struggled to make conversation.

'I think I might buy myself a car to use while I'm here,' he said. 'It'd be cheaper than hiring and it would certainly help me to see more of the countryside in my spare time.' He glanced at her. 'I could always sell it when it's time to head for home again.'

'Yes. That sounds like a good idea.'

'If I do that will you come out in it with me?' he asked, glancing at her.

She looked at him. 'If you do what?'

'Buy a car. I'll need someone to show me the way around.'

She sighed. 'Look Paul, there's something I should tell you. I'm planning to go into partnership with Rosalind and run Cuckoo Lodge as a small hotel.'

472

'That's a great idea.' He looked slightly puzzled. 'You're not still worried about my crazy idea for the place, are you?'

'No. What I mean is that I won't be living in London any more. We – you and I will be a long way apart.'

'So what's new?' He drew the car into the side of the quiet country road and turned in his seat to look at her. 'We've been a long way apart ever since we met, Cathy. And it seems to me that's the way you want it to be.'

'You're wrong. I don't, not really. It's just with you being Gerald's son. It makes things – difficult.'

'I don't see why. I know you and he weren't happy together, but that has nothing to do with you and me. There's no reason why we shouldn't get along.' When she didn't reply he reached out to cup her chin, turning her head towards him so that she was forced to look at him. 'Well, is there?'

'No. No, of course not.'

'Then why do you hold me at arm's length like this?'

'I think you've already made up your mind about what kind of person I am,' she said.

He shook his head. 'Okay, so maybe I'm wrong about you. I don't happen to think I am, but I'd like the chance to find out. Can't you at least give me that?'

She opened her mouth to start to tell him, then closed it again. If she were to tell him the truth – the whole truth – not only must she indict Gerald but herself as well. She had been far from blameless, and suddenly she knew that Rosalind was right: she could not bear Paul to be disillusioned about her. She sighed and shook her head.

'It's no use. I'm sorry but I don't want to have this conversation with you, Paul,' she said. 'Perhaps we'd better go home now.'

His face was dark with angry frustration as he started up the engine again. 'Okay, if that's the way you want it,' he said tightly. 'I think I finally got the message.'

473

For a while they drove in silence, then in a vain attempt to put things on to a friendly footing, she said, 'When we get back to London I'll arrange for the piano to be moved and put into storage. Is that all right?'

'Do what you like with it. It's not important,' he said raggedly. 'I don't give a damn any more.'

For the rest of the way back to Melfordleigh Cathy was rigid with misery. Paul sat silent and stony-faced beside her, clearly hurt and bewildered by her attitude. Sending him away like this, giving him all the wrong ideas, was the last thing she wanted to do. But what other course was there?

After tea they locked up the house and set off on the journey home. Cathy announced that as Matthew was going to spend a few days with his mother she would travel with him.

Rosalind drew her aside. 'Have you and Paul had a row?' she asked.

'No, but I just can't face being alone with him any more this weekend.'

'Well, you can't let him drive back on his own. It looks so rude,' Rosalind admonished, clearly shocked at her behaviour. 'I'd better go with him if you won't.'

They said their farewells at the gate and Cathy climbed into Matthew's car, acutely aware that she was upsetting everyone's arrangements. Noticing her pensive silence Matthew kept glancing at her and after a few miles asked if she was all right.

'Not regretting your decision to go in with Rossie, are you?'

She shook her head. 'No. I'm looking forward to it.'

'Then why are you so fed up?' He glanced at her. 'Come on, Cath, we've known each other too long for play-acting. Does it have something to do with Paul?'

She nodded, swallowing hard at the lump in her throat.

'He seems like a good bloke.'

'Yes, he is.'

'Are you going to see him again?'

'No.'

Matthew glanced sideways at Cathy's pale stricken face. She obviously didn't want to talk about it. He gave up trying to work out what had gone wrong and concentrated all his attention on the road ahead. Although he had grown up in a house of women he'd never been very good at understanding them. Cathy especially had always been hard for him to puzzle out. He congratulated himself that Rosalind seemed less complicated.

Rosalind was suffering a silent travelling companion too. Paul's face was grim as he gripped the steering wheel with white-knuckled hands, staring at the empty road with unnecessary concentration.

'Did you enjoy seeing your father's house?' she asked.

'Yes, thanks.'

'We were lucky with the weather.'

'Yes.'

'Apart from the shower yesterday.' She looked at him. 'Did you know that East Anglia has the lowest rainfall in the country?'

'No. Really?'

'Look, Paul – about Cathy . . .'

He turned to stare at her. 'If you're going to tell me to lay off, I already got the message,' he said bitterly. 'She thinks I'm a creep.'

'That's not true!'

'Well, whatever, she doesn't want to know.'

'You're wrong there too. She likes you very much.'

'Oh, really? You could have fooled me! What's she like with folks she doesn't like?'

'It's just that she's had a bad time. Maybe it's all a bit too soon for her.'

'I only wanted to see her again, damn it . . . for us to get to know one another,' he said bleakly.

475

'I know. And I'm sorry.' Rosalind sat in silence, struggling with her conscience. What had happened between these two people was nothing to do with her. Or was it? Cathy was her best friend – soon to be her business partner. She was unhappy and so was Paul. If she were to tell him the truth about what held Cathy back, would she be interfering in what didn't concern her? He might take it badly in which case she would make matters worse. On the other hand . . . Should she keep her mouth firmly closed and mind her own business? Yes, she should. She *really* should mind her own business.

'Paul – would you pull over and stop, please?' She glanced at him, her heart thudding dully in her chest.

He looked surprised. 'Is something wrong?'

'Something is very wrong,' she told him. 'But with Cathy, not with me. I've decided that I'm going to try and put it right – even if it's none of my business. Someone has to.' She looked at him apprehensively. 'And, Paul, I'd better warn you – you may not like what I'm going to tell you, so be prepared.'

When Paul dropped Rosalind off at Blake's Folly she was surprised to see most of the lights blazing. It was unusual. Normally when Don was alone, he ate in the kitchen and sat in the little breakfast room which was easy to heat. Taking her weekend case from the back seat, she thanked Paul and ran up the path, opening the door with her own key. Inside the front door she stopped short. At the bottom of the stairs various pieces of luggage were strewn carelessly around, and as Rosalind closed the front door she heard Una's voice. She sounded upset.

'Why don't you just go ahead and say it? *I told you so. Serves you right.* You'd have every right to.'

'I shan't say anything of the kind,' Don replied mildly. 'I'm just grateful you've come home.'

The voices came from the sitting room and through the

476

half-open door Rosalind could see her mother, her hair awry and her mascara running unheeded down her cheeks as she stood facing her husband.

'Oh, Don. I don't deserve a husband like you,' she sobbed, fumbling for a handkerchief in her handbag. 'I've made such a mess of everything. I can't tell you how awful it was. Those horrible coarse audiences! They talked and laughed all through my act, then complained that they couldn't *hear* me! In one place they actually *threw* things!'

Don pulled out a large white handkerchief and put it into her trembling hands. 'Poor love,' he said, taking her tenderly in his arms. 'What things? Were you hurt?'

'Well, no. Not hurt. It was mostly bread rolls, but it was so *humiliating*. Imagine – me, Una Blair – a West End star being pelted with bread rolls!'

'Never mind. It's all over now,' he said soothingly. 'You're home where you belong and I'm glad.'

Una nestled her head against his chest. 'Oh, Don, so am I. I've been such a silly vain fool.' She looked up at him with brimming eyes. 'Where is Rossie?'

'She's gone away for the weekend with her friend Cathy,' he told her. 'I thought the break would do her good. She's a good girl, Una. One of the best. She's worked really hard since you've been away.'

'Oh, well, I'm glad she made herself useful.' She looked up at him with appealing brown eyes. 'You won't tell her my tour was a failure, will you?' she begged.

'Of course I won't. Not if you don't want me to.'

'And, Don – do you think we could still go on that cruise you were planning? I'm so tired.'

Rosalind tiptoed back to the front door, opened it and closed it again with a bang.

'Hello!' she called. 'I'm home, Don!'

He and Una came out into the hall together, smiling and hand in hand. Rosalind put down her case and affected surprise.

'Mum! How are you?'

'I'm fine. Exhausted of course after the tour. Had a nice weekend have you? Don told me you'd gone away with Cathy.'

'It was very nice. Well, you'll be wanting to talk. I'll go up now then.'

She was almost ready for bed when there was a tap on the door and Una slipped into the room. 'Just thought I'd come and have a chat,' she said, sitting down. 'Don and I have been making plans. As soon as he retires next month we're off on a long cruise. Don says you've been a great help to him while I've been away. As you've nowhere else to go you can stay on here and mind the house for us while we're away.'

'That won't be possible, Mum. I'm going into business with Cathy. We're planning to start almost immediately.'

Una sat up very straight and stared at her daughter. 'Business? What business?'

'You must have heard that Gerald Cavelle was killed in a plane crash.'

'Yes, I heard. Dreadful of course, but I don't see . . .'

'She and I are going to run her house in Melfordleigh as a hotel.'

Una smirked. 'Oh, is *that* what you mean by business? You're going to work for her – as a domestic.'

'No. We're going into partnership.'

Una sighed patiently. 'Correct me if I'm wrong, but I've always understood that to go into partnership you have to put up some money?'

'That's right.'

'So where will you get that money, may I ask?'

'Dad left me his cottage. The one he bought in Northamptonshire. I sold it for quite a good price.'

Una's face turned bright pink. 'Ben left – left *you* that cottage?' she spluttered. 'But – but what about me? I was his wife!'

478

'No, Mum. You're Don's wife.'

Una sprang to her feet. 'Don't be so insolent, you devious little bitch! You've had all that money ever since Ben died and you said nothing to me about it. How could you?'

'I was working at the Queen's Head when I found out. We hadn't been in touch. I didn't think you'd be interested.'

Una paused, her eyes narrowing. 'I'd have thought that a celebrity like Gerald Cavelle would have left his wife well provided for,' she said. 'Why does she have to take in lodgers?'

'She's not taking in *lodgers*, she's turning Cuckoo Lodge into an hotel,' Rosalind said patiently.

Una laughed. 'What's the difference? It could hardly have a better name, could it?' she said scathingly. 'You're the cuckoo if you ask me. You're getting taken for a ride if you could only see it. Know what they say – a fool and his money . . .'

'The partnership is all being drawn up legally,' Rosalind said, swallowing down the anger slowly mounting inside her. 'It's being done tomorrow. It's all going ahead, Mum, whatever you say. And it's going to be a success.'

'I see. So you're walking out now that you don't need free board and lodgings any more?'

'I had a good job, Mum. You forced me to give it up because it suited you. And I think I've worked quite hard for my board and lodging, as you put it.'

'It was a tuppeny-ha'penny job and you know it,' Una said unrepentantly. 'Which reminds me – what would Cathy Cavelle say, I wonder, if she knew that her prospective business partner was a common thief?'

'She knows I took the Meissen. She also knows that I took it out of sheer desperation – when no one else would help me when Dad was ill.'

Rosalind saw the door open quietly and Don appeared in the doorway. Una, who had her back to the door, went on, 'I can see now why you were so keen to be at your father's bedside. Still, he left you the cottage anyway, so it hardly matters any more, does it? I suppose I should be thankful that scheming Morton cow didn't get her hot greedy little hands on it. That must have been a blow for her.'

'Will you come downstairs now, Una?'

She sprang up, scarlet-faced, and turned to him. 'Don! How long have you been there? I didn't hear . . .'

'That is painfully obvious.' His face was dark as thunder. 'Come downstairs, I want to talk to you. I think it's high time you and I had a little chat. If you're really planning to stay this time, I'm going to need to lay down a few rules. And if when you've heard them you don't agree, I suggest that you take the luggage that's still down in the hall and leave again before you create any more trouble.'

The colour drained from Una's face as she stared first at Rosalind and then at Don. Her eyes bulged and her mouth worked as though she was about to let loose a stream of invective. Rosalind braced herself, but the tirade never came. Instead Una walked meekly to the door and through it on to the landing.

Before he closed the door behind him Don turned to Rosalind and, to her surprise, closed one eye in a triumphant, conspiratorial wink.

Rosalind unpacked her weekend case and put her things away. Would Don really succeed in taming Una? Somehow she thought he would. Una must know by now the elusive stardom she had longed for would never be hers and Rosalind thought she was wise enough to settle for what Don had to offer.

It wasn't until she was in bed with the light out that Rosalind allowed herself to think back over the journey home and the revelations she had made to Paul about his father. When she first began to speak his reaction had been distinctly cool. He had refused to look at her and as she stumbled on her blood had chilled with misgivings.

'He should never have married Cathy,' she told him. 'I

480

don't suppose you know that when he was killed he was on his way to meet another woman – the woman he intended to marry? He had already left Cathy. He'd sent this other woman to ask for a divorce. And that wasn't the only way he had betrayed Cathy. He – wasn't a real husband. He shut her out in every possible way. He made her very unhappy.' She paused. She had already said too much. Far too much. Yet there was so much more she could have told him about Gerald's coldness and his betrayal – its disastrous consequences. When she looked up again she saw that Paul was looking at her.

'What you're saying isn't entirely new,' he said quietly. 'I've heard it all before – from my mother. Years ago he treated her in much the same way. She always said that he put all his emotional energy into his music. There was never anything left over for relationships. When they were first married they were very poor. They lived on her money – the allowance she got from her parents. Once he didn't need it any more ...' He lifted his shoulders helplessly. 'She never really got over the way he treated her. Because of it she never married again.' He sighed wistfully. 'All the same, I'd still like to have known him. You only have one father.'

'I know.' Rosalind sighed. 'I'm sorry. I shouldn't have said anything. It's none of my business really. It's just that Cathy is my friend and I know it hurt her to have to pretend to you. She's a very honest person.'

He sighed. 'Do you think that was the reason she brushed me off?'

'I'm sure it was. She didn't want to disillusion you.'

'So ...' He looked at her with new hope in his eyes. 'So you're saying that if I ...'

'I'm not saying anything, Paul. I've absolutely no right to. I just wanted to put right the misunderstanding

between you, that's all. What you do about it now is
up to you.'

She turned over and punched her pillow. She hoped to
heaven she'd done the right thing. But even if she hadn't
it was too late to change anything now.

Chapter Twenty-Two

'We could do gourmet dinners in the winter months,' Rosalind said. 'I learned some very good recipes from the chef at the Queen's Head when I was there. That reminds me, do you think we could afford to keep Maggie on to help us? Oh, and I thought we might make a special arrangement with the boatmen on the quay to run trips out to the point to see the seal colony. You know, a reduced rate for parties. Now . . .' She placed a piece of paper on the table between them. 'I've made a list of the best magazines and papers to advertise in. Look.' She pointed. 'These at the bottom are the ones that specialise in conference venues.'

'Hang on!' Matthew raised a hand to stop her flow of excited chatter. 'There are a few other things to sort out before we get to that stage!' he told her with a rueful smile. 'Boring little legal details for instance.'

The three of them were seated around Johnny's dining table, making plans for the future of Cuckoo Lodge. Rosalind's excitement was infectious. Her cheeks were pink and her eyes shone with enthusiasm as she looked from one to the other.

'Oh, I know all that,' she said impatiently. 'But I don't think either of you realises that this is my dream that is coming true. I've got a perfect right to be excited!'

Matthew reached for her hand and gave it a squeeze. 'Of course you have. It's just that there are a few hurdles to be got over first.'

They had already established that the money Rosalind had received from the sale of the cottage, plus what Cathy had got from the sale of her emerald engagement ring, would be enough to pay off Gerald's creditors. Matthew had made an appointment to see Gerald's solicitor and arrange for the settlement of outstanding debts. But he had yet to draw up a satisfactory legal partnership for them both to sign.

'The one disadvantage of not needing a bank loan,' Matthew said thoughtfully, 'is that a bank manager would vet your business proposal and know whether it covered everything. I'm not sufficiently experienced in business matters, especially the hotel trade, to say. Is there anyone who's experienced in the trade who'd have a look at your figures and give you advice?'

The girls were silent for a moment, then Cathy looked up. 'What about Mrs Gresham at the Queen's Head?'

Rosalind's eyes brightened. 'Of course! Why didn't I think of her? Shall we go along this afternoon and see her, Cathy?'

'Of course.' She got up from the table. 'I'll go and give her a ring now and make an appointment.'

Mrs Gresham turned out to be just what they needed. She brought up several items the girls hadn't thought of, but applauded them on their enterprise and seemed optimistic for its success. Rosalind's business plan impressed her too.

'I'm glad to see that you learned something useful while you were with us,' she said with a smile. 'I only wish you could have stayed on to take over from me when I retire in a couple of years' time.'

On the way home Rosalind decided that at least one of them should learn to drive. 'We'll get a ticket for one of those cash and carry places and get our supplies cheaper than we could at the shops,' she said. 'But the nearest one is bound to be miles away so we'll be missing out if we don't drive.'

Cathy smiled to herself. The change in Rosalind since they'd begun to plan their new partnership was incredible.

For the first time in her life she found herself required to act as a steadying influence, constantly pulling Rosalind up and making her take things one step at a time. Sometimes it was a bit like riding a runaway horse. 'Can we afford to buy a car though?' she asked cautiously.

'We can't afford not to!' Rosalind retorted. 'And for that we *will* need a bank loan, but that shouldn't be a problem. Oh, it's all so exciting. I can't wait to get started.'

'Me neither,' Cathy agreed. 'I thought we might put the first advertisement in next week and if we ask Matthew very nicely perhaps he'll give us some driving lessons?'

They parted when they got to Rosalind's bus stop and Cathy walked the rest of the way home to Chestnut Grove, her mind busy with plans. The small front gardens in the Grove were bursting with promise. Daffodil bulbs were thrusting their spears above the ground and here and there yellow and purple crocuses flaunted their brightness. They seemed to Cathy to symbolise a new beginning.

As she turned in at the gate her thoughts were of Rosalind's idea that they should buy a car. She remembered how much she had longed to learn to drive at Melfordleigh and wondered how long it would take to learn. She let herself into the house and hung up her coat in the hall. From the living room came the muted buzz of voices. Johnny hadn't mentioned that she was expecting a visitor and she wondered vaguely who it could be. So when she opened the door and saw Paul sitting in the chair by the fireplace her heart gave a lurch. He stood up when she came in.

'Hello, Cathy.'

'Paul! Hello.' Her heart had begun to beat unevenly and she felt the colour warm her cheeks. She'd thought when they left Melfordleigh that she wouldn't see him again. Part of her had ached with sadness at the thought while another part had told her firmly that it was best to forget him.

Acutely aware of the tense atmosphere, Johnny got up from her chair. 'Ah, there you are then. Doctor Franklin has been waiting for almost an hour, Cathy.' She looked uncertainly from one to the other. 'Well – I'll leave you to talk.' She moved to the door. 'If you'll excuse me, I should be getting the meal started.'

'Of course. Thank you for letting me wait, Mrs Johnson,' Paul said politely.

As the door closed Cathy looked at him. 'Is there something I can do for you, Paul?' she asked coolly. She was annoyed – with herself for showing her vulnerability and with him for coming here uninvited.

'I had to come – whether you wanted me to or not.' His voice was low and harsh as he looked into her eyes. 'Rosalind told me the way it was between you and Gerald. On the drive home from Melfordleigh.'

'She told you? I don't . . .'

'Cathy – why didn't *you* tell me? I always knew he wasn't good at relationships. I never had any illusions about what he was like. God knows my mother went on enough about the way he used people. But I always secretly thought it might have been partly her fault. I thought in your case he might have been different.'

Cathy was shaking her head incredulously. 'Rosalind *told* you? I can't believe it!'

'Yes. Look, don't be angry with her. She did it for you. She knew you'd never tell me yourself.'

'She had no right.' Cathy turned away. 'I didn't tell you because it was none of your business. Besides, I didn't want to spoil your image of the ideal father.'

'I didn't have one. Not in that sense.'

Cathy turned back to look at him, wondering just how much he really knew. 'Rosalind shouldn't have said anything.'

'I'm very glad she did. I understand now why you were so cool. The important thing is that it's all cleared up. We can be friends now, without any misunderstandings.' He cleared his throat. 'Cathy, now that all that is out in the

486

open, can we see each other again? After all, there's no reason why not.'

'I'm going to be very busy with organising the new business,' she hedged. 'I really don't know. Besides, you will be busy too and . . .'

'*Cathy!*' He took a step towards her. 'Listen. I'm not taking no for an answer any more.'

'Just – just how much did Rosalind tell you?'

'That you and Gerald weren't happy. That he shut you out of his life and was planning to divorce you. She told me about the letters you found too; about the affair Gerald had with your mother all those years ago.' He took a step towards her, his arms outstretched. 'What a terrible shock that must have been for you. I'm so sorry, Cathy.'

It was no use. Now that he knew half the truth she would have to tell him everything. There was no other way. She stepped back from his outstretched arms. 'Yes, it was, but there's more than that, Paul, much more, and you'd better know all of it.' She turned away, afraid to see the look on his face when she told him the whole truth.

'She told you that Gerald shut me out of his life – rejected me. Did she tell you how his rejection destroyed me?' she asked quietly. 'Did she tell you that I turned to someone else – another man – because of it? That I would have had his child if I hadn't – hadn't . . .'

'Cathy! What are you saying?'

'I was so *lonely*,' she told him, struggling to control her voice. 'So lonely and so unloved – unwanted. I felt it had to be my fault – that there must be something terribly wrong with me to make him so indifferent. So – when someone came along and – treated me like a woman it was like coming alive again. I . . .' She shook her head. 'I gave in. I was so weak and feeble that I allowed myself to be taken in by insincere flattery and lies. When I found I was pregnant I didn't know what to do. I wanted the baby more than anything in the world, yet I knew I couldn't have it.'

Her voice choked on the words. She was crying now, tears coursing down her cheeks to drip unheeded from her chin. 'I had to abort my child, Paul, to keep my infidelity from Gerald. Can you imagine what that did to me? Especially when I found that he had actually encouraged the affair to keep me quiet and occupied – as though I were some bothersome, fractious child in need of amusement. Since he died I've discovered that I made the sacrifice for nothing. Gerald only married me to gain control of the money my father left me. He never cared anything for me at all.'

For a long moment there was silence. She longed to escape from the room without having to see his reaction, but it was as though she was rooted to the floor. She stood staring out of the window, noticing small insignificant things like the tiny buds on the lilac tree; a bird pecking at some unseen insects on the lawn; a solitary dry brown leaf, a relic from last summer – a dead past. Then she felt his hands on her shoulders as he gently turned her towards him.

'Cathy, what can I say? I had no idea you'd gone through this – this terrible trauma.'

She couldn't look at him but kept her head down. 'Well, now you know all about me and why I tried to save you the disillusionment of finding out. People are seldom what they seem are they? If you want to go now and forget we ever met, I'll understand.'

'*Go?* What are you saying? What do you take me for, Cathy? Now that you've trusted me with this confidence, leaving you is the last thing I want to do. Do you think I don't know what it must have cost you to tell me all that? To relive it?'

For the first time she looked up and searched his eyes. She saw compassion and understanding there. No trace of blame or reproach.

'Now I'm going to tell *you* something,' he said with a smile. 'When I first saw you at the memorial service I was completely stunned. I couldn't take my eyes off you.

488

I thought you were the most beautiful girl I'd ever seen and I spent most of the time trying to work out some way I could find out who you were – how I could get to speak to you. I'd just decided it was hopeless when you fainted in all that crush and I saw an opportunity to help, I just couldn't believe my luck. It was as though fate had stepped in. Don't you see, Cathy? The way I felt then had absolutely nothing to do with the fact that you were Gerald's wife. Nothing to do with the fact that he was my father. And nothing has changed. Anything that happened in the past to either of us is totally irrelevant. All I care about is that we're here, you and me. Together. I want to try and make up for what you've been through, Cathy. Will you let me?'

'Why should you want to?'

'*Why?* Do I really have to tell you why?' Reaching out he took her face very firmly in both hands and raised it towards him, kissing her gently. 'Does that tell you anything about why?'

The kiss told Cathy a lot of things. It told her that she was fighting a losing battle; that his touch and the feel of his lips on hers meant more than she could ever have imagined it would. When Gerald died she had told herself she would never trust enough to give her love to another man but she hadn't bargained for the tumult that Paul aroused in her. The pounding of her heart and the clamour of her senses.

'You know I'm going away,' she said breathlessly. 'To live and work in Melfordleigh with Rosalind.'

He laughed. 'It's hardly a million miles away. I'll come down – at every possible opportunity – even if it's only for a couple of hours. I want to spend time with you, Cathy. I want us to have time to discover each other. And I'm warning you, I won't be turned away. I won't take no for an answer, because I know deep down that we can have something good together.' He drew her closer and kissed her again, this time with all the depth and passion he had held at bay. She felt the tension seep out of her as she relaxed in his arms. She allowed herself the luxury of response, her lips parting for him, her arms holding him close, her fingers in his hair. It was like coming home; like a long cool drink after the heat of the day. His arms were warm and safe. In that moment nothing else seemed to matter. Yet even in her response a warning voice somewhere deep inside told her to take care. Hearts were so easy to break and so hard to mend and hers seemed especially fragile.

'I'll come to Melfordleigh as often as I can,' he whispered. 'Will you like that? Will you look forward to seeing me?'

'Yes. Of course I will.'

'Cathy . . .' He looked into her eyes. 'Cathy, I . . .'

'*No*.' She stopped him from completing the sentence, her fingers against his lips. 'Don't say it. We have a long way to go yet before either of us can say that.'

'Why?' He took her fingers from his lips and held them against his cheek. 'When can I say it?'

'I don't know. One day perhaps. When we're both sure beyond a shadow of a doubt.'

'I am now.'

'No. Not yet. It's just a word, Paul, too easy to say and too hard to live up to. It's important to me to wait.'

By April Cuckoo Lodge had had its first Bank Holiday weekend, for which, thanks to a brief spell of beautiful weather and a sudden rush of visitors, all their rooms had been full. It had been slightly nerve-racking. Would anything go wrong? Would their visitors be comfortable and satisfied that they were getting good value? They needn't have worried. With Maggie's placid good sense and capability in the kitchen, they pulled through. Everyone went home happily and after that it was plain sailing. The landlord of the Admiral Nelson sent along any customers who enquired about good accommodation and by the beginning of June they had fallen into a comfortable and happy working routine.

Matthew, now settled in the new legal practice in Ipswich, was a regular weekend guest, sleeping good-naturedly on any camp bed or settee that happened to be available. Paul too made regular, sometimes unheralded, appearances whenever he could snatch some time off, driving down in the middle-aged Ford Consul he had bought.

Rosalind's enthusiasm knew no bounds. She was full of plans for the future. She suggested that when they'd saved enough they might build an annexe so that they could take more visitors.

'The reception rooms are big enough to take more,' she pointed out. 'The dining room could take at least three more tables. And it's just as easy to cook for twenty as ten so why not?'

'Before we think of building annexes we could probably convert the attics into a couple more rooms,' Cathy said practically. 'It might be worth getting a builder in to look at them.'

Rosalind's plans for expansion included turning the larger of the two studios, now vacated by Gerald's grand piano, into a restaurant for non-residents with a carvery and salad bar. She was arranging to apply for a licence to serve alcohol too. Her energy often left Cathy breathless. She had never seen her friend happier or more fulfilled. And she guessed that Cuckoo Lodge was only partly responsible for the transformation. She felt sure it was only a matter of time before Rosalind and Matthew would announce their engagement.

One weekend in late June Paul managed three whole days off. The weather was glorious and after dinner on his first evening he and Cathy walked down to the quay together. The sea was smooth and glassy with only the merest swell to sway the boats moored in the harbour. Above them the cloudless sky was a serene, milky blue and the air was clear and tangy.

Paul took a deep breath. 'Ah – that's so good after

London,' he said. 'I take back all I said about your weather. Nothing to touch a perfect English summer evening.' He looked at Cathy. 'It's great to be here like this. I miss you,' he said softly, taking her hand. 'A whole lot more than you realise. I miss your amazing hair and those green eyes; your laugh and the way your mouth curves. Sometimes I think I must be mad to stay up there away from you.'

'Your work is important. You know it is,' she told him practically.

'I only wish I could give my mind to it,' he said wryly. 'At the moment I can't think of much else but you.' He bent to kiss her, then pulled her arm through his as they walked. 'Cathy, the Promenade Concerts start next month. I've been looking forward to going to the Albert Hall and hearing the première performance of Gerald's rhapsody.' He looked down at her. 'You will come with me, won't you?'

She sighed. 'I know I said I might come, but we're fully booked at Cuckoo Lodge. I don't see how I can leave Rossie with all the work.'

'I've already thought of that,' he told her. 'I've spoken to Matthew and he's promised to come and help that weekend. As a matter of fact he had an idea. It seems that Rossie's friend Freda will be off to America with the cast of her play in a few weeks' time. Apparently she's invited Rossie and Matthew up to a farewell performance and a party, but Rossie has the same doubts you've just expressed – about leaving you to cope alone. This way you could repay the favour.' He looked at her doubtful face and squeezed her hand. 'Oh, please say yes, Cathy. I'm sure Maggie would put in a few extra hours too, if you asked her.' He bent to look into her eyes persuasively. 'You must agree that it's kind of a special occasion. You might think that's a strange way to look at it, but if it wasn't for Gerald we wouldn't be here now.'

'You're still very proud of him, aren't you?'

'Do you mind? Does that hurt?'

492

'No, of course not.' She squeezed his hand. 'It's as it should be. He was your father – and a musical genius. It will be a very special occasion as you say.'

'So you'll come?'

She smiled. 'Yes, I'll come with you, Paul.'

To the amusement of two fishermen who were unloading their boat close by, he lifted her off her feet and swung her round. '*Great!* You're wonderful, Cathy! The most wonderful girl in the world and I . . .'

She shook her head. 'Shhh. Remember what we said?'

He shook his head in frustration and they walked on for a while in silence. 'You still don't really know how you feel about me, do you?' he asked at length. 'I wonder if you know how that makes me feel?'

'I know that I look forward to seeing you and I love being with you,' she told him. 'You're the nicest, kindest and most sincere man I've ever known.'

He pulled a face. 'God! That sounds so damned tame. Don't you know that a man likes to be thought exciting and irresistible; wild and fiery and passionate and . . .' He stopped as she began to giggle. 'Don't *laugh*,' he said woundedly. 'I'm not joking, Cathy. Nice, kind and sincere sounds more like an agony aunt or a cocker spaniel than a lover.' He stopped walking and pulled her round to face him. 'I want to be your lover, Cathy,' he said angrily. 'Don't you realise that I want to sweep you off your feet? I want to pick you up and carry you off to bed and make love to you until you beg for mercy.' He looked into her eyes and she saw the deep hurt and frustration there. 'I'm just like any other man. *I want you.* And if you won't let me say what I really mean – what's in my heart – that will just have to do.'

'Oh, Paul, I'm sorry.' She drew his head down to hers and kissed him. 'I know how you feel and I know I'm being unfair to you. If only I could make you understand. I – I *think* I feel as you do. It's just that I'm afraid to trust

493

those feelings, desperately afraid of being hurt. And afraid of hurting you too.'

'So . . .' He lifted his shoulders helplessly. 'What do I have to do to prove that you can trust me – and trust what you feel yourself?' he asked exasperatedly.

She sighed. 'That's just it. I don't know.' She shook her head. 'It really isn't fair. I realise that. Maybe you should give up on me. I wouldn't blame you if you wanted to.'

For a long moment he looked down at her. 'You know, sometimes I almost wish I could,' he said. 'Most of the time I'm afraid you're going to tell me to get lost – that I'll lose you. Sometimes I even wish you would. At least I'd know where I was. If you are going to do that, Cathy, I'd rather you did it now.'

'I can't blame you for feeling that way.' She slipped her arm through his and hugged it close. 'Let's not spoil the time we have by arguing. I've planned so much for us to do.'

But Paul's obvious discontentment with their relationship had set the mood for the weekend. For the rest of the time he was quiet and by the time he left on Monday morning Cathy was uneasily aware that she was about to lose him. Later that afternoon she confided her fear to Rosalind as they worked together in the kitchen.

'I can't see the problem,' she said. 'You do love him, don't you? It's obvious to me by the way you look at him.'

'Yes, I do. And then again, I don't know. I'm not sure I know what love is any more. I know that he makes me happy; that I want to be with him; that each time we part is harder than the last. But is that enough?'

Rosalind shook her head. 'What else is there?'

'I felt all that for Gerald. I was so *sure*, Rossie. I wouldn't listen to anyone. I thought he loved me too, but in the end all the promises were empty. The people who warned me were right. Our marriage just – disintegrated, like dust.' She sighed. 'Now I'm completely confused. Did I ever

494

really love him at all? If I had, how could I have turned to anyone else?'

'Because he neglected you.'

But Cathy shook her head helplessly. 'If only there was some way of knowing for sure.'

The local builder Rosalind had asked to give them an estimate for converting the attic telephoned two days later to ask if it would be convenient for him to come and assess the job the following day.

'There's still a lot of junk up there,' Cathy said. 'Things of Gerald's and mine that have been packed away ever since we first came here. I've been putting off sorting through it for ages. I'd better go up and do it before he comes.'

'Shall I give you a hand?' Rosalind asked. But Cathy shook her head.

'I'd rather do it alone.' She was remembering the last time she'd looked through the boxes in the attic. The letters from her mother were still there. Now she would be forced to make a decision about what to do with them.

Seeing her pensive look, Rosalind touched her hand. 'I forgot about those boxes,' she said. 'Shall I ring and put the builder off? After all, there's no hurry, is there?'

'No. It's time it was all cleared up,' Cathy said decisively. 'Time I stopped putting it off. Besides, there's nothing to be gained from hanging on to a lot of rubbish.'

'But you won't throw everything away, will you?' Rosalind was looking at her. 'You might regret it if you decide too quickly. Would you like me to help you go through it?'

But on her own insistence Cathy was alone when she climbed the loft ladder that afternoon. Now that she had made up her mind she was determined to lay the ghosts from the past once and for all.

There were fewer boxes than she remembered. Her own things were fairly impersonal. Most of the odds and ends from the house in Laburnum Close had been destroyed before she and Gerald married. The contents of Gerald's boxes on the other hand were more difficult to sort. She began by putting the box of letters to one side. She would take them downstairs and read them just once more before burning them. There were some old clothes which she put aside for the Salvation Army. Then the box of books; she would have to look through them – perhaps donate them to the local library. Then she came to the manilla folder that contained the hand-written music manuscripts which she now knew to be her father's. On the afternoon when she had found her mother's letters she had abandoned these. Now Kay's cold words came back to her: *Gerald tried to make amends, you know. He even bought some of your father's compositions to pay for your school fees. Little jingles that would never have been published.*

Slowly she opened the folder and looked at the manuscripts. Seeing her father's neat, sloping handwriting again brought quick tears that stung her eyes and blurred her vision. If only he had said that he couldn't afford to send her to St Margaret's, she wouldn't have minded. All those hours spent teaching and composing these so-called jingles. They had been for her – to give her what she had set her heart on. And she hadn't even known.

Downstairs the house was quiet. It was a warm, sunny day and all their visitors were out. Maggie, having prepared the vegetables for the evening meal, had gone home for the afternoon and Rosalind had gone into Woodbridge on the bus. Cathy went into the small studio, now used as a sitting room, where her father's baby grand piano still stood under the window and sat down on the stool. Through the open window came the scents of summer, honeysuckle and roses and the clove pinks that grew in clumps at the edge of the drive. The curtains moved gently in the breeze and a solitary bee buzzed against the window pane.

She hadn't played for months and her fingers felt stiff as

496

she ran them over the keys. The piano could do with tuning, she told herself. Dad would have been horrified. He was always so particular about the instrument's maintenance. Opening the folder she drew out the first of the manuscripts and, to her surprise, saw her own name written on the title page. 'Cathy's Theme' was written in capitals at the top. Then, in brackets (For my darling daughter). Her throat tightened. Why had he never told her he had written something specially for her? Why had he never played it for her?

She raised the music stand and rested the manuscript against it. Her fingers faltered a little over the first notes, then gradually, to her delight, she found that the music was familiar. As the tune slowly came back to her, her fingers relaxed and slipped easily into the nostalgic melody. She had heard it so many times before, when Dad was alone, working away at the piano in his studio back in the childhood days that seemed so far away. Kay had been wrong to describe his work as unpublishable jingles. This one was good – very good. It was heartachingly evocative; wistful and haunting. Maybe he could have made money with it if he had submitted it to a publisher – made his name even. But that was so typical of Dad. He had never had any real confidence in himself. She came to the end, paused, then played it through once more, savouring the unforgettable theme and brilliantly simple harmonies. She would cherish it always, she told herself. Whenever she wanted to feel close to him she could always get it out and play it. When she heard the front door slam and Rosalind's voice call out to her she rose and put the manuscript away carefully inside the piano stool. Just for now she would say nothing, she decided. 'Cathy's Theme' would be her secret.

The builder announced that he could make three rooms out of the roof space. And as the floor was already boarded and the electricity supply connected it would not be too difficult.

He left, promising to send in his estimate as soon as he could. Rosalind was excited.

'I thought we could make those rooms into our own summer quarters,' she said. 'A room each and a bathroom. Because, you see, we could hardly expect visitors to use a loft ladder, could we? Then we'd have two more rooms to let.'

Cathy laughed. 'I have an idea that you and Matthew will be married before those attic rooms are ready,' she said, privately wondering just how much their marriage would alter the position. But Rosalind was shaking her head.

'Whatever happened I'd never want to give up Cuckoo Lodge,' she said. 'The first time I saw this place I loved it, and on the day we moved in it was like coming home. This is my dream, Cathy. Matthew knows that. This is the first real home I've ever had, and it's my career too. It's all I've ever wanted.'

Paul telephoned to say that he had bought the tickets for the Promenade Concert and booked Cathy a room at a nearby hotel. But on the morning she was to leave for London she found herself feeling nervous and apprehensive.

'I wish I didn't have to go,' she told Rosalind over breakfast. 'It's going to bring back so many unwanted memories.'

'Just go to the concert and enjoy being with Paul,' Rosalind advised. 'Try and think of it as any other concert.'

But in spite of her misgivings, Cathy felt a little thrill of excitement as the afternoon train drew in to Liverpool Street Station. One slight disappointment was that Paul was working at the hospital until later so he wasn't able to meet her. He had arranged to pick her up later and take her out to dinner before the concert.

She took a taxi to the hotel and found she had plenty of time to shower and change into the new dress she had bought specially for the occasion. It was made of a beautifully soft silky material in a silvery green that matched her eyes. The skirt was of the new mid-calf length, swirling around her legs and setting off her black patent sandals. She dressed her hair in a French pleat and clipped on a pair of diamante earrings which were her only jewellery.

Paul arrived on time, looking handsome in black tie and dinner jacket. Apart from the suit he had worn for the memorial service it was the only formal clothing she had ever seen him wear. It suited him and she told him so. He looked pleased.

'Not as much as that dress suits you,' he told her. 'You look like some kind of wood nymph, all russet and green.'

It was a warm evening and they ate at a little bistro at a table in the open air. The food was good and the atmosphere relaxed. Cathy couldn't help wishing they could stay there all evening instead of going to the concert. But she said nothing. This evening was so important for Paul and she would do nothing to spoil the occasion for him.

It was a long time since she had been in the Albert Hall and she was awed anew by its vastness and Victorian splendour. Paul was impressed too as he gazed up at tier upon tier of crimson draped boxes and gilt ornamentation. They settled in their seats and Cathy opened her programme. Rhapsody for Piano and Orchestra by Gerald Cavelle was the third item on the programme and would not be played until after the interval. She breathed a sigh of relief when she read that the soloist was not Simon after all, but another well-known pianist who, the programme told her, was also responsible for arranging the piece for piano and orchestra. The brief programme notes outlined Gerald's career and mentioned his tragic death in an air crash. As she read them, Cathy wondered at her strange feeling of detachment. It was as though she were reading about a total stranger.

The familiar frisson of excitement rippled through the audience as the musicians began to take up their positions on

499

the platform and tune their instruments. The leader arrived, acknowledging the flutter of applause with a discreet little bow before taking his place. Finally the conductor, Erhart Froebel strode on to the platform, immaculately attired in white tie and tails.

As she applauded, Cathy was reminded poignantly of the concert her father had taken her to when she was twelve; the first time she had seen her childhood idol, Gerald Cavelle and heard him play. Instinctively she reached for Paul's hand. He returned the pressure of her fingers, smiled reassuringly as the lights were lowered and the conductor raised his baton.

When the first half of the concert ended and the lights went up for the interval they made their way to the bar. Standing amidst the crush waiting for Paul to get her a drink, Cathy heard a familiar voice at her side.

'*Cathy!* How nice to see you!' Carla looked at her most glamorous in an exquisite creation of white and silver. At her elbow stood a tall distinguished looking man of about fifty. 'It's good to see you back in circulation, darling,' she gushed. 'I was so sad about your loss.' She turned to the man at her side. 'May I introduce you to Adam Meynard? Adam, this is Cathy Cavelle, one of my oldest friends.' The man nodded polite acknowledgement. When he'd gone to join the queue at the bar, Carla leaned toward Cathy confidentially. 'Isn't he *gorgeous*? One of the best photographers in the business. Met him on an assignment in Paris and he was *completely* bowled over! He's taking me to New York next month. You wouldn't *believe* what he has planned for me and . . .' She broke off as Paul rejoined them.

'This is Doctor Paul Franklin, Carla.' Cathy turned to Paul. 'Carla, an old schoolfriend of Rosalind's and mine.'

As Paul offered his hand Carla's face was a study. Her eyes flicked over him with unconcealed admiration as she flashed him her most dazzling smile. 'Well, *hello*. How lovely to meet you!' Rejoined by her escort she took a sip of her drink and leaned towards Cathy. 'Well, *well*! Didn't waste much time, did you darling?' She gave them a little wave as they moved away. 'Watch for me in all the glossies,' she called. 'Adam says he's going to make me a star!'

Paul and Cathy looked at each other in stunned silence as the couple were swallowed up by the press of people, then simultaneously they burst out laughing.

As they resumed their seats Cathy felt her nerves begin to jangle once again. Seeing Carla had provided a welcome little diversion but now she was reminded that the music they had come to hear, Gerald's rhapsody, was about to be played.

The conductor led the soloist on to the platform and the applause died down as he settled himself at the piano. She stole a look at Paul's face. It was eager with anticipation and she felt her heart contract for him. He looked so young, so vulnerable and suddenly she felt a closeness, a sweet affinity with him. Reaching out as the lights dimmed she took his hand and smiled at him. He smiled back, his dark eyes holding hers for a second before the conductor's baton came down and the music began.

As the first few bars of exquisite melody flowed from soloist and orchestra Cathy's heart almost lurched to a stop. Even with the skilful and elaborate orchestration she could not fail to recognise the piece being played – not as 'Rhapsody' by Gerald Cavelle, but as 'Cathy's Theme' by Daniel Oldham. Gerald had stolen it – passed it off as his own. How *dared* he? It was the ultimate infidelity – the final act of betrayal. The bitterness of bile filled her throat and mouth. She wanted to leap to her feet and scream that it was all a terrible deception. That Gerald Cavelle was a thief, a liar, a *cheat*! That the man who should be receiving the acclaim was her father. Inside the pain of it tore her apart as she silently cried his name over and over. *Daddy – Oh, Daddy – Daddy. I'm sorry. So sorry.* Hot tears streamed down her cheeks at the injustice as the music swelled and

501

pulsed through her, its sweetness melting her bones while its bitterness broke her heart into a million pieces.

Then she turned and saw the look on Paul's face. It was radiant with pride and delight. Catching her look, seeing the glimmer of tears in her eyes, he smiled and reached for her hand.

'Isn't it just – *wonderful?*' he whispered, shaking his head as adequate words escaped him.

As she watched him she felt her anger slowly evaporate. Gerald may not have written this music, but he hadn't stolen it either. Daniel had sold it to him; sold it so that he could give Cathy the things he wanted her to have. He would never have published the music himself; probably never even have played it to anyone. This way at least it would live on to be enjoyed. And Gerald couldn't possibly have imagined the pleasure it would bring to Paul, the son he had never known. Gerald Cavelle was dead and so was Daniel Oldham. Things like credit, success and acclaim meant nothing to them any more. But Paul was alive and so was she. Between them, the two fathers had left them a legacy of love and life to share. Things that were infinitely more precious than riches.

The music came to an end and the audience roared its approval in a storm of applause. The soloist and conductor acknowledged their appreciation with smiles and bows; the applause continued, refusing to let the soloist leave the platform. Gerald Cavelle's rhapsody was an outstanding success. Tomorrow the record companies would be clamouring to buy the recording rights. The royalties would pour in and the dishonoured debts and broken promises that Gerald Cavelle had left behind would be no more than an insignificant memory, eclipsed by this newfound fame. It was strangely ironic, Cathy told herself, that fate often had a roundabout way of settling scores.

As the applause began to die Paul was pulling at her hand. 'Shall we slip out?' he said urgently. In the corridor he looked at her. His eyes were still shining and his cheeks flushed. 'I couldn't have sat through another piece of music,' he said, 'however good. I'm far too excited.' He grasped both her hands. 'Oh, Cathy – *Cathy*! Wasn't it marvellous? I had no idea he was as brilliant as that. Why on earth didn't he take up composing before? He could have been even more famous as a composer.' He pulled her close and kissed her. 'God! I think this must be the proudest moment of my life.'

She smiled and said nothing. She'd already made up her mind to let him go on believing the music was Gerald's. It was to be her gift to him. But a gift he must never know about. A sacrifice she could make from the depths of her heart only for the man she loved.

Paul said he wanted to end the evening by the river, so they took a taxi to the Embankment and stood looking out over the black satin water in the mellow warmth of the summer night. The sky was clear, bright with a thousand stars; the river shimmering with reflected lights. A magic night. The kind of night that gave rise to memories.

Cathy touched his hand as it lay on the parapet. 'Paul. There's something I have to tell you.'

He turned to look at her, his dark eyes slightly apprehensive. 'What is it?'

'Just that I love you, that's all.'

For a long moment he stared at her. Then, 'Just? Did you say *just*?' He let out his breath on a shaky, tremulous laugh. 'I thought you were about to shatter my evening by telling me you didn't want to see me again. All evening I've had this awful feeling that you only came to the concert with me as a final gesture because you were about to send me packing.' He took her shoulders and turned her towards him. 'Would you mind saying it again for me?' he asked. 'Just in case I didn't hear it right the first time.'

'I love you, Paul Franklin,' she said softly. 'I think – no, I'm *sure* now that I always have.'

'Again,' he demanded.

503

She was laughing now, though tears were not very far away. 'You haven't told me yet.'

'Only because you refused to let me. You know I love you, Cathy. With all my heart. For ever. I've loved you since the first moment I set eyes on you. And, I believe, even before that. Somehow I think you've always been there, waiting for me in the shadowy corners of my dreams.' He kissed her and for a long moment they clung to each other. 'But what made you so sure, tonight of all nights?' he asked at last.

She smiled gently as she hid her tear-dewed face against his shoulder. 'I think it might have had something to do with the music,' she said. 'Though don't ask me how.' She looked up at him with shining eyes. 'And now do you think you could walk me back to the hotel, please? I think we have some catching up to do.'

He drew her close and kissed her long and deeply. 'I said this was the proudest night of my life,' he said huskily. 'I never expected it to be the happiest too.'

Pressed close to each other, their arms entwined, they walked all the way back to the hotel. And beneath their feet the pavement sparkled with stardust.

ORANGES & LEMONS

Jeanne Whitmee

Evacuated from the turmoil of war-torn London, young Shirley Rayner finds herself billeted at the home of Tony and Leonie Darrent, stars of the West End stage and screen – a far cry from her humble background as the illegitimate daughter of an East End cinema usherette.

At first the transition is a difficult one, as Shirley clashes with the daughter of her adoptive family. Imogen Darrent is unhappy and insecure, despite her privileged upbringing, and feels threatened by the chirpy Cockney thrust into her life. But gradually the two manage to reconcile their differences and become the best of friends. Shirley shows promise as an actress, and, coaxed out of her painful self-consciousness, Imogen slowly blossoms too. Throughout the long, hot summer days of the war years she and Imogen dream of one day finding fame and fortune in the theatre.

When peace is declared their paths divide; Imogen's to drama school in London, Shirley's back to work in her grandparents' East End greengrocer's shop. But the link remains in the form of the unlikely relationship between matinée idol Tony Darrent and Shirley's usherette mum, Gloria. As a result Shirley's dreams of stardom seem to crash around her feet, as she remains her grandparents' only support . . . but her determination gives her the courage to win through, finding not only her true self, but also a lasting love.

FICTION
0 7515 0930 2

THIS YEAR, NEXT YEAR

Jeanne Whitmee

Realising the hopelessness of her love for her employers'
only son, Maryan Brown decides to secure her unborn
child's future by marrying her childhood sweetheart.

After the birth of her daughter, Maryan is determined that
the child will never know her true parentage. She is to
have the life she deserves, and Maryan pledges herself to
that end.

Then comes the Second World War. Maryan and Amy are
parted by the evacuation, and when the two are reunited
they are strangers. Amy's ambition to become an actress is
not what Maryan envisaged for her. Events estrange the
two even further and the split that follows heralds
heartache for them both.

But from despair and tragedy comes a new understanding
between them . . . and for Amy, true love where she least
expected it in this compelling and heart-warming saga.

FICTION
0 7515 1410 1

| ☐ | Oranges and Lemons | Jeanne Whitmee | £5.99 |
| ☐ | This Year, Next Year | Jeanne Whitmee | £5.99 |

Warner Books now offers an exciting range of quality titles by both established and new authors. All of the books in this series are available from:

Little, Brown and Company (UK),
P.O. Box 11,
Falmouth,
Cornwall TR10 9EN.

Telephone No: 01326 317200
Fax No: 01326 317444
E-mail: books@barni.avel.co.uk

Payments can be made as follows: cheque, postal order (payable to Little, Brown and Company) or by credit cards, Visa/Access. Do not send cash or currency. UK customers and B.F.P.O. please allow £1.00 for postage and packing for the first book, plus 50p for the second book, plus 30p for each additional book up to a maximum charge of £3.00 (7 books plus).

Overseas customers including Ireland, please allow £2.00 for the first book plus £1.00 for the second book, plus 50p for each additional book.

NAME (Block Letters) ....

....

ADDRESS ....

....

....

☐ I enclose my remittance for ....
☐ I wish to pay by Access/Visa Card

Number ☐☐☐☐☐☐☐☐☐☐☐☐☐☐☐☐

Card Expiry Date ☐☐☐☐